THE ALTERRAN LEGACY SERIES
Book 1: Colony Earth

By
Regina M. Joseph

ISBN: 0615659969
ISBN 13: 9780615659961
Library of Congress Control Number: 2012911347
CreateSpace, North Charleston, SC

The Alterran Legacy Series

Colony Earth
Khamlok

CHAPTER 1
THE HUNTING PARTY

"**L**and in the clearing directly below," Lil commanded his ship as he grimaced at the unpacked campsite beneath him. At times like this, he regretted that he'd softened Alterran discipline, but conditions on Earth had left him no choice. Only a tensing of his clean-shaven jaw betrayed his revulsion for the task that lay ahead. Fearful for their survival because their advanced weaponry and food supply might soon be exhausted, he'd ordered his most trusted guardsmen to prepare for this hunting experiment. Three transport craft followed his sleek, silver, triangular *tri-terran*, none of them disturbing the clear blue sky with their invisibility. Descending, he admired the magnificent northern glacier distantly gleaming in the morning sun. Immersion in pristine nature is the only redeeming feature of this planet, he sighed. After landing, he paused a moment, bent his head reverently, stroked his imperial insignia, and whispered, "And so it begins…" Memories flooded his mind of his proud, ancient heritage; he was a direct descendant of the venerable Zeya, who'd ushered in their glorious Age of Wisdom. Now, all that noble achievement might well be lost. He cherished the memories a moment, felt rage rising at the unfairness of his people's senseless loss, and then cast them aside to focus on the hunt. The survivors' lives, even the preservation of a glimmer of their civilization's existence in the restless evolution of this universe, rested on his shoulders.

Standing at the hatch, he straightened his stance and embraced his calm, inner certitude learned from his ages-old training before announcing, "En.Lil." Recognizing his self-assured voice, the ship's controls caused the hatch to swing silently upward. A crisp breeze swept through the cabin, rippling his form-fitting silver uniform. He sniffed the pleasant smell of lavender. Squinting into the blinding light of the rising sun, Lil quickly donned his eyewear, fleetingly annoyed at the necessity of physical exertion. On Alterra, the electronic system known as the Net that blanketed their physical world would have instantly implemented his desire for eyewear. Stranded in this primitive prison, he'd made many unpleasant adjustments, never complaining about fulfilling his command duties, even though they required personal interaction with the guardsmen. So different from the life for which he'd been trained. In one lone respect, he was grateful—at least his people had a chance at life.

Although the lower peninsula was warming after being released from the glaciers' icy grip, the early morning temperature remained frigid. Shivering, Lil felt the nanobytes convert his clothing into the same tightly woven green-and-brown tunic and leggings worn by his troops. For this experiment, he'd had the replicator create knee-high black riding boots like those pictured in ancient histories, only simulated to appear as leather—a material forbidden on Alterra, but one that they'd need to learn to refine in the unpleasant days that lay ahead. He found it sadly ironic that an advanced society had reverted to scouring its ancient legends for survival guides. Near his shoulder glowed his cherished insignia of the purple sacred triangle, which evinced his imperial rank as second named successor to the supreme leader of Alterra. His destiny was to rule after the reign of Anu, his father. Disembarking, he became visible outside the colony for the first time during his centuries on Earth.

His guardsmen, having spent two days in the meadow preparing, were ordered to prepare to hunt with a wolf pack, horses, hawks, and ravens. He had no guide for reverting to primitive living; it might not be their fate, but it fell on his shoulders to plan for contingencies. Mimicking Earth hunters, the men had created a deep trench toward which they would stampede their mastodon prey. Not yet completely abandoning their weaponry, they'd cut the trench with a laser and carried their soundguns programmed to stun. Lil forbade them to rely on soundguns alone; in the future, if his people couldn't produce power to regenerate the fuel cells, the guns would become useless.

On the perimeter, the hunters' saddled horses stood ready, obeying the newly learned *mencomm* command for discipline. The gray wolves watched in the tall grass, with pointed ears alertly waiting to be summoned, while the hawks circled high overhead and ravens blackened the trees nearby. Twenty guardsmen, lounging around a flickering reddish globe that simulated campfire, ate their breakfast rations. Their unpacked tents and equipment lay strewn about. Normally rigidly disciplined, the men felt exhilaration from their days in the meadow, outside the shield of the Net. A few even succumbed to merriment, using the only objects at hand. Entertaining them was Erjat, a mine guardsman half as tall as the others, who wagered that he'd throw a glowglobe farther than his companion, Mika, would. Mika grabbed the orb from Erjat's hand and balanced it atop his finger, causing it to twirl as rapidly as a twister that he'd seen in his scouting. Drawing back his arm, he threw it in a high arc. Rainbows spewing like colored lightning lit up the expanse of the meadow. The globe danced in the brisk wind along with the leaves of autumn, slowly losing its spin and eventually floating to the ground about fifty yards away. Azazel, the tallest guardsman, laughed and shouted, "I bet one night duty on Erjat."

Beside him, Tamiel grinned, slapping his hand. "You're on!" He looked forward to besting Azazel for once. Erjat ceremoniously bowed with his globe to his jeering audience, but seeing the captain materialize in the meadow, abruptly jerked upright.

Cutting a path through the chest-high foliage with a laser embedded in his dark glove, leaving a charred black streak in his wake, Lil strode toward the unpacked camp. The bushes rustled with scurrying small animals, and escaping multi-hued birds angrily squawked as they darted away. Nearing his guardsmen, his piercing, cobalt-blue eyes flashed disapproval; he caused his eyewear to become temporarily transparent to deliver his message. *So on Earth as on Alterra, discipline must always be maintained.* The white-haired guardsmen, their normally clean-shaven faces now stubbly, grew silent and fell into line, reflexively cringing with remembrance of the searing punishment they would have received at home. Standing at attention, they gave their captain the sacred triangle salute of respect. Returning their salutes, Lil inspected the line, trusting that, with his recent experiments at building personal rapport, his displeased stare would serve as a sufficient reprimand. Stopping before the tall, hawk-nosed man whose distinctive features, taller height, and muscular physique distinguished him from the others, he asked, "Azazel, how did the tunic program perform? Are these garments functional?"

"Excellent, sir. They insulate well and provide camouflage." His dark eyes focusing straight ahead, Azazel replied formally, yet with a hint of surprise and more inflection than the usual monotone. The past few days had produced many surprises. At first, detachment from the Net had caused them disorientation. Although on Alterra the Net permeated the entire planet, the Alterrans hadn't yet felt a need to expand beyond their colony, ships, and mines on Earth. Here in the meadow, a few men couldn't stifle the anxiety of isolation until Jared activated the mental connection, or *mencomm*, which permitted telepathic communication. For Azazel and most others who'd adjusted, their increasingly independent mood matched the vibrancy of their verdant surroundings. Azazel, more than any other, was absorbed by the fantasy of stepping into his beloved ancient legends, every one of which he had saved on his recorder.

Since embarking on his experiments, Lil had pondered the men's newfound enthusiasm and wondered if he welcomed it. The structure of their society had been carefully controlled by his family for so long that he couldn't remember a time of spontaneity. Theirs was a time of change, however unwanted, and he decided to be tolerant; to see, for once, what would unfold without his detailed direction. "Resume your duties. Break camp and be ready to go in five minutes." Tamiel exchanged a grateful glance with Rameel that their commander made his own rules, feeling an odd emotion—trust.

Climbing a hillock covered in autumn wildflowers gently swaying in the breeze, Lil saluted his first officer, who stood near the forest path at the head of the double-breasted line of saddled horses. The animals stood with the discipline of trained battle horses, even ignoring the menacing ravens silently lining the branches of nearby trees. "Good morning, Jared," he said amiably, removing his gloves. "It *is* beautiful here, is it not? Much better when not blurred by cloaking."

"Absolutely, sir," replied Jared with a salute, one of the few men permitted to address him. "And this forest is thick with songbirds, sir. You'll enjoy them."

"Why so many ravens?" Lil asked, gazing at the numbers of chillingly alert birds staring at him. He instructed his tunic to transform into a protective shield if one so much as flapped a wing at him. "We only had implants for a few."

"Sir, we implanted only six. The others follow their lead. We don't know why." Unnerving, Jared thought, as if they were a controlled army. He patted the neck of a saddled, chestnut mare, which the day before he had taught to obey at his mental command. All the horses caught in this meadow had been spotted mares, except for one black stallion that ruled like a king. "These horses are fully prepared for the hunt, sir."

"Good." Lil took a deep breath of the fresh air and admired a dense flock of pigeons passing overhead. "It's amazing what's developing on this planet after the glacier's long reign. But we're here to work. Discipline *is* a little lax, isn't it?" Lil asked, raising his eyebrows and tilting head toward the glowglobe incident.

"They're excited, sir," Jared replied with a bit of his old fear of the House of En. "After we overcame withdrawal, they diligently applied themselves as you'd expect. Their game this morning was a trifle, sir." Regretting the too-assertive response, he diverted attention by ordering a hawk to perch on his outstretched glove. Being linked with the birds, he much preferred the hawk, which killed for food, to the ravens, which gave him the uneasy feeling that they'd kill for amusement.

Lil scowled. "A trifle? *Nothing* is a trifle." In his own mind swelled his grandfather's derisive laughter at the foolishness of permitting the slightest leniency. *All things are connected, En.Lil. Do not be swayed into inaction because the infraction is seemingly small. An ocean is comprised of individual droplets of water. Let nothing go unchecked.* He felt his stomach muscles tighten, and he fought down the unwanted voice in his head. Grandfather, your methods won't work here. Lil wouldn't extinguish Jared, he needed him. Lil's course was set. He had to move forward, no matter what the cost, no matter what he had to endure. Glancing at the animals, he said with a hint of sarcasm, "Everything *other* than the camp is ready?"

Jared straightened into formal military stance, relieved not to be punished. "Yes, sir. Horses and wolves have accepted the implants and are in position awaiting our thoughts. We can observe through their eyes. The hawks have located the herd exactly where you predicted." He momentarily closed his eyes. Feeling men and animals becoming linked as one through *mencomm*, he gazed through a hawk's eyes as it coasted toward the sparkling river that gushed with late summer glacier melt. He felt the hawk's eyes sharpen as it floated over a grove of tall oaks to a small meadow and spied a small mastodon herd, which casually grazed during a pause on its southward winter migration. Jared opened his eyes. "Perfect timing, sir. I'll have the camp packed in a few minutes."

"Don't keep me waiting," Lil snapped impatiently, although he actually welcomed having a few moments to admire the clarity of the landscape. He'd long observed the lands of Earth but always through the hazy glaze of his invisibility shield. He studied the awakening meadow filled with colorful autumn wildflowers, where the early morning mist still lingered in patches. Craggy hills spotty with crimson and yellow-leaved bushes rose opposite them. "Alterra used to be beautiful like this," he whispered softly with nostalgia as he plucked a wildflower and twirled it. In the forest, ribbons of light streamed through the thick limbs of the fir trees, illuminating the animal trail they would take. Startled, he blinked hard. Did he see shadows moving among the trees? Activating extra sensors embedded in his eyes at birth, he amplified his view. The shadows had vanished, and scans using the sensors in his clothing found no sentient life. "Jared," he demanded through *mencomm*, "have you thoroughly searched this area for Earth people?"

Pulling the lead horses into position, Jared replied, "Yes, sir. All precautions have been taken. Our instruments found nothing, and Azazel led a team that searched with the wolves and hawks." Jared omitted the eerie feelings the men had experienced since the sensors had provided no explanation. Mika had rubbed his neck, exclaiming that something cold had tickled him, but then Mika was always joking. He'd come from guarding the mines, where discipline among the few, isolated guards had been relaxed.

Lil, having been trained in his original youth to observe the slightest nuances, didn't doubt his senses. He swept with sensors while peering through the foliage. Detecting nothing further, he reluctantly ceased; perhaps he wasn't accustomed to the clarity of being uncloaked. Impatient to conclude his distasteful task, he turned away from the forest and asked, "Yamin is recording everything, per protocol?" Lil had considered abandoning protocol to hide their actions, but his ingrained duty saw the importance of an accurate historical record. Would historians perceive him as traitor or savior? It depended on whether any historians lived to tell the tale. At the moment, history was his to mold.

"Yes, sir," replied Jared, hoping that the captain would appreciate the disciplined horses, which were captured only two days ago running wild in this meadow. Seeking the captain's approval was a new motivation, even though all the men remained wary. The House of En was feared, and under successive generations of supreme leaders leading to Ama, Lil's grandfather, they'd deployed technology to become increasingly oppressive. "Yamin found a way to record *mencomm* so that we preserve the animals' visuals, as well as our own. He brought aerial recorders to capture a three-dimensional view with full sound."

"Good," Lil said evenly, although pleasantly surprised that his tolerance enhanced the performance of a few. He commanded aloud so all could hear, "We move out in ten minutes."

The guardsmen packed the remaining camping equipment, using their tunic controls to float their tents above their heads and fold them into small squares. Mika caused the wolves to catch the floating squares in great leaps and then race one another to the uncloaked hovercraft to deposit them in his hand. "Everything's a game with you, Mika," scolded Azazel. "You've spent too much time at the mines."

"It's good practice," he said, laughing. "All in the line of duty, my friend. Just like Yamin." Mika pointed to Lil's adjutant, who was levitating the remaining glowglobes and camping equipment into the ship as if he were conducting an orchestra.

Closing the hatch after the last equipment was stowed away, Yamin reported, "We're done, Captain. Permission to send the ship to the trench?"

"Granted," Lil replied, thinking his own departure order to his *tri-terran.*

Picking up swords and knives that glinted in the morning sun, the men tucked them into pouches on their horses. Azazel grabbed the gleaming sword from the scabbard slung across his back and performed a flowing series of lunges and jabs leading to a pose in an ancient fighting stance as the others pointed at him, laughing.

"Now who is fooling around?" jabbed Mika, strapping his own hardware around his waist. "What legend are you fantasizing this time?" He donned a helmet that fit tightly over his elongated forehead.

"Enough!" snapped Jared, his angry order ringing in the men's minds. Not yet accustomed to the mental communication sounding in their minds as loudly as a shout in the ear, with wide eyes they jumped to stand at attention. Jared angrily strode past them, trying to emulate the captain's icy stare through suddenly transparent eyewear. "The captain has been indulgent. Far more indulgent than he'd be on Alterra. Mount your horses." Using *mencomm*, Jared summoned the wolves, who leaped from the tall grass to sprint to his side, startling the horses as the men were attempting to mount. Rameel was thrown to the ground, and he got up shaking dirt from his clothing, a petulant look on his face until the nanobytes cleaned them. Only a few days before, these wild horses had been stalked by the wolf pack. Now, with the implants controlling their minds, they were partners. Jared closed his eyes, concentrating to calm the horses. Use of the forbidden *mencomm* was new to him as well, but he'd learned to control the horses better than the others had. Approaching the horses hesitantly, the men mounted, having learned to ride only the day before.

"Finally," Lil muttered to himself; at least Ama would never learn of this incident. It would be bad enough if his father or the Council knew. *Grandfather, I perform my duty*, he thought defiantly. If the House of Kan discovered his action, they'd use it to rekindle their claims to the Alterran leadership, a risk he discounted because surely no Kans would long survive. Jared handed him the reins to the black stallion; it tossed its head and defiantly snorted that it was the leader. Unfazed, Lil pulled the reins tight, stared into the stallion's eyes, his eyewear again becoming transparent, and asserted his control over the animal's stubborn mind. Still proud, the stallion calmed, standing straight and perfectly still, awaiting Lil's command. He donned his helmet, stuck his booted foot into the stirrup, and swung into the saddle; he'd absorbed riding instruction from the Teacher. Like his men's clothing, his boots and tunic had been programmed to grip the animal's side and cushion his ride. Looking at his men's faces, he saw their mixed emotions. Tales of ancient legends had always been popular on Alterra, and now they were living one. Azazel and Kamean openly enjoyed it, while Rameel went along only out of distasteful necessity.

"Communicate only by *mencomm*," he ordered. They galloped closely through heavy forest, the hawks and the racing wolves guiding them. Lil felt his horse's muscles through his legs. Jared, riding beside him, zapped low-lying branches with his laser to clear the path. After traveling several miles, a sharp squawk from the leader hawk signaled Lil to focus through its eyes. Seeing the steep downward slope leading to the forest's end, he ordered the group to slow its pace. As they slowed to stop, they failed to notice the crude shelter covered with foliage, in which two Earth women were awakened by the noise.

Keeping their mental connection, the hunters silently dismounted. Following the path to the forest's edge, they stealthily emerged to scamper soundlessly down the steep hillside, taking up covered positions behind rocks or heavy brush. Lil slid on his belly behind a boulder, flanked by Jared and Azazel. They peered over the top using their eye magnification to study the mastodon herd watering by a small pool near the swollen river. Lil saw the terrain through the hawk's eyes as it floated lower in the breeze and circled above the herd. A suspicious sentry bull lifted its nose, sniffing for predators. Smelling nothing in the wind blowing the tall grasses, the bull indulged in a bite of juicy tree leaves. Calves playfully chased one another within their mothers' circle. The migration trail that had once thundered with huge herds was becoming more sparsely traveled as the mastodon numbers dwindled. These wary survivors stayed close together, the males guarding the perimeter.

Jared ordered the wolves to creep through the tall grass downwind of the herd. When the wolves were in position, the hunters observed through their eyes. "Look at the tusks on that big bull," Jared said through *mencomm*. "He's so big he couldn't have fought during the mating seasons." The bull weighed about five tons, with pointed ivory tusks that extended five meters. From their observations of Earth people, the Alterrans knew that the tusks and heavy hide were valuable prizes.

"He's the leader," Lil observed, scrutinizing the animal through alternately wolf and hawk eyes. "When we make him bolt, the others will follow." Finding a wolf distracted by a squirrel, he said irritably, "Jared, get the mottled gray one nearest the river in line."

Jared gently nudged the mind of the youngest wolf, Gor, while being careful to avoid over-stimulation. *Mencomm* worked better with the more intelligent birds. Gor, his favorite, obeyed. Through his eyes, they now saw a coughing calf, hidden under its mother's belly, being gently stroked by her trunk. With all in position, Lil closed his thoughts to others, desiring to observe in private a moment longer. The guardsmen had extensively gathered data about Earth and its creatures, which their scientists studied at their nearby colony. Glaciers had once covered this entire area, leaving the rapidly rebounding Earth rich in nutrients that fueled the burgeoning life. In this area, they'd recorded diminishing herds of mastodon, while the numbers of other mammals were exploding. The herbivorous mastodons migrated north in the spring for the lush summer vegetation. With their massive size and fearsome tusks, their only predators were hominids; from observing them, he'd had the idea for the trench. After a kill, the hominids' women quickly took over, leaving nothing on the carcass behind. Their teamwork and efficiency had impressed him.

Lil flipped around. From behind, he had heard crackling twigs. Studying the tree line, he detected no motion. Reengaging *mencomm*, through the horses' eyes he spotted two young

Earth women crouching low in the bushes. In recent missions when flying in his cloaked *tri-terran*, he'd seen these two gathering plants close to a village north of his colony; he hadn't known that they foraged so far. The pair had caught his attention because their appearance differed dramatically. One was tall, nearly to his shoulder, with light complexion and light, straight hair, while her short companion, resembling what he'd observed of the local tribes, had a dark complexion and black, curly hair.

"They must have heard the horses and followed us," Lil said with an irritation that pierced every guardsman's mind like a sword prick. "Search for others." Closing his thoughts, he clenched his teeth and wondered, *What else will go wrong today?* "One bad deed leads to another," his old teacher Jahkbar had preached during his true youth. He'd been groomed to rule a technologically advanced, cultured civilization, not to personally command small Guard units roaming a primitive planet. This post was Ama's cruel trick. He scanned the brush, switching to the hawks' eyes as they dashed through the trees. He found no one else lurking in the dense brush, although he noticed unnatural shadows again.

"Sir, revealing ourselves to Earth people violates the Non-Interference Directive," Azazel warned, wondering why they hadn't adapted their individual bubble transporters for the hunt; they could then have remained cloaked until the need arose to fire a weapon or to touch a surface outside the bubble. Lil, like all the House of En, never explained his actions. Although he might be a named successor, his father, Anu, was the ultimate authority on Earth; if they made it back to Alterra, Ama would be merciless toward their actions, whatever the merits of their motives. "I recommend that we abandon this experiment and return to Hawan."

Lil snapped, his cobalt-blue eyes blazing in such fury at Azazel's boldness that Azazel felt them burning into him. "You should have discovered them before we began. Be glad that I'm forgoing punishment! They've already seen us, and this experiment is too important to abandon so quickly. Proceed according to plan."

"Sir, respectfully reconsider," Azazel protested, knowing that none of his companions would dare to express a contrary thought. "When they tell their people, they'll search for us. If Anu finds out, we'll receive more than a pain lesson. I recommend we deal with this problem now. Since we have no way of keeping prisoners, we must eliminate them."

"I'll answer to my father and the Council, not you," Lil rebuked him, tempted in his indignation to apply discipline there on the spot. He caught himself, realizing uncomfortably how ingrained the instinct to inflict corporal punishment had been inculcated in him through the millennia of his training. He would find other methods to end disciplinary laxness; to his last breath, adapting to Earth would *not* mean abandoning harmony and stability. On Alterra, no guardsman would have dared to question his orders; no one would on Earth. "They've done nothing wrong. Causing unnecessary harm is forbidden by our law. Move on."

Azazel, carefully controlling his thoughts from the cold fury that he recognized as Lil's probe, dutifully resumed viewing the herd. In prior Earth missions, he had never expressed his thoughts, even though he'd felt that the House of En could use his advice. *Mencomm* must unleash suppressed thoughts, he realized cautiously. He was a fool to believe Lil's promises; his House planned eternal rule.

Controlling his anger, Lil ordered evenly, "Jared, prepare the wolves to attack." After Lil focused on the leader hawk and assured himself that the herd's activity hadn't changed, he ordered, "Men, return to the horses."

Passing the hiding women, the hunters mounted the horses. Following the captain, they descended the steep hillside, navigating around bushes rather than cutting a swath by laser. Metallic recording spheres floated alongside. The hunters regrouped in a clearing at the hill's base, which was hidden from the herd by small boulders, remnants of mountains broken by the glacier. Ahead, down the jagged path veering through the rock bed, lay their trench and waiting ships. The hunters spread out and hid behind foliage while Lil and Jared rode to a higher vantage point. Lil planned to see if the animals could organize themselves to carry out general attack orders. Lil commanded, "Begin."

Chilling howls came from the wolves scampering to encircle the herd. Straining to see into the tall grass, the bellowing mastodons became nervously entangled as they jostled one another to form a tight defense pack. The hawks and ravens swarmed over the lead bull's head, viciously tearing into his ears, now dripping blood. They teasingly zoomed to safety, circling back to attack the eyes of one and the exposed skin of another. Rearing on his massive hind legs, the furious bull swatted his trunk into the swirling cloud, only to see its amorphous black shape part and reform into a deadly triangle ripping a hole into the hide of the screaming, pawing female beside him. She staggered and fell. The fiendish ravens soared high into the air as if they were molecules of a single organism covered by a shadowy blackness, blocking Jared's commands, coalescing into a taught, undulating vertical shaft with a fine downward point. The dark, pillow-like cloud swirled above the herd, its target the unlucky female. Swooping down, they bored into her wound, entering her body and flying out through her terrified mouth until her tattered body tore apart. Having tasted death, the ravens triumphantly squawked and ominously hovered above the bull, which bellowed at them and thrust his trunk through the air.

"Jared, control those blasted ravens!" Lil demanded, appalled at the carnage; they were doing this for survival, not to become savages.

"Captain, when that black shadow appears, I lose contact," Jared explained as levelly as possible, his voice not betraying that his stomach was churning with shame at the thought of being responsible for the raven killing machine. After a moment, he added, "I'm feeling contact again. I'll stop this right now, sir."

"Disperse them and disable the receptors," Lil snapped. "Yamin, be sure that the recorders capture those black shadows."

"Yes, sir," came Yamin's voice through *mencomm*. "The sensors aren't providing any data to explain them."

The swarm ceased the attack, fluttering at eye level to brazenly taunt the bull while moving slowly toward the hunters. Slipping away from the herd, the enraged bull pursued. The hidden wolf pack sprang from the tall grass, growling and nipping at his heels. He spun in circles, lashing out with his tusks. Goring a wolf with his tusks, he tossed it through the air. The wolves reformed at the bull's rear, snarling and nipping at him. Shaking his injured head, the bull galloped to rejoin his herd. Agitated, the mastodons jerkily paced their tight circle, raising their trunks to angrily trumpet at their attackers. Mothers closely guarded their calves.

Watching through wolf eyes, Jared instructed the wolf pack to avoid the bulls, not wanting to lose another; the implants were in short supply, and they might depend on these animals in the future. The wolves again circled the herd, gradually coming closer until they could nip the heels of undefended females while the swarming hawks distracted the males. In disarray, the mastodons loosened their circle, and the sickly calf separated from its mother. Frightened and coughing blood, it bolted down the river trail with the wolves racing in pursuit. Unable to find her calf, the mother repeatedly bellowed until she glimpsed it in the distance. Clouds of dust rose as she gave chase, catching the lead bull's attention. With the ravens no longer attacking him, he pursued the female, swiftly overtaking her with his powerful stride. Alarmed at their leader's disappearance, the remaining mastodons stampeded in a panic. The wolves skillfully guided the sickly calf toward the waiting hunters. The two Earth women ran along the crown of the hill, carefully navigating low boulders while carrying their spears and bags of plants, keeping the escaping herd in sight as it rounded the bend. They slipped down a dried streambed and slid behind a copse of bushes to watch more closely.

The calf passed Erjat and Mika, who were hidden behind dense foliage and low-lying rocks sharing their vision with Lil. Through wolf eyes, Lil saw that a sharp bend in the path caused the calf to be hidden from the herd. At his order, Mika and Erjat dug their heels into their mares and raced from hiding to divert the startled baby toward their trench. The bull and female rounded the bend, drawing close, hesitant to diverge from the migration route. Tamiel emerged from the trees and gave each mastodon a low-level soundgun blast. The frightened bull resumed its flight, and the female followed. The herd thundered behind, maneuvered by hawks and wolves. With the boulder wall growing taller and the winding path ominously narrowing, the lead bull slowed, sensing danger. Azazel dismounted, his muscular legs jumping from boulder to boulder. Eyeing him, the bull skidded to a stop. Feeling cornered, it put its massive head behind a small boulder and began pushing it to clear a path to flee from Azazel.

Azazel waved and shouted by *mencomm*, "Tamiel, look out!" Having shoved the boulder aside, with a snort the angry bull charged Tamiel. His horse reared frantically, its eyes wild with fright. Even with the leggings' grip, Tamiel wasn't able to hold on. Before he hit the ground, his tunic transformed into a protective cushion. Hesitating only a second, the avenging bull charged Tamiel. Azazel jumped. He thumped on the ground between Tamiel and the bull, aimed his gun, and shot a stream of condensed sound waves. Stunned, the bull's head bounced as if he'd run into an invisible tree. He staggered and his eyes became glazed, blood dripping from his damaged ears. Azazel didn't lower his gun. Recovering after a few moments, the bull shook his injured head and bellowed defiantly, ready to resume the attack. Azazel shot again. The bull, yielding to his pain, reluctantly trotted away. The approaching herd, too frightened to slow, thundered past. Azazel called his horse and swung on its back, racing to catch up.

As the gaping trench came into the escaping bull's view, he skidded, attempting to stop before his left foot reached the edge, where the soil crumbled under his weight. The bull grabbed a sapling with his trunk, but the limbs snapped. Sliding over the edge, he tumbled with a loud thud, breaking his neck. The baby and its mother, skidding and unable to stop, shrieked and plunged, the mother breaking her legs and the baby falling on her, moaning pitifully with pain. Dismounting by the trench, Rameel shouted aloud, "What in Zeya's name have we done?" Chest heaving, he ended the animals' agony with a soundgun blast set to kill. Rameel dropped his arm, slid to his knees, and vomited.

The approaching herd separated and slowed in time to avoid falling, a few by diverting a run around the hole. Others confronted the snarling wolves.

"That's enough for one day," Lil ordered, riding down the steep slope to the trench. His stomach was churning with revulsion, but his face showed no sign of it and his mind blocked Grandfather Zeya's castigating voice in his head. *I merely do my duty,* he thought to dispel the unwelcome taunts. Of all the voices ringing in his head, criticism from Zeya stung the most. It had been Zeya who'd returned immense tracts of Alterran land to harmony with nature. As if provoking him, the ravens filled the branches of a giant oak tree. "Jared, I want those disgusting ravens destroyed at once."

"Yes, Captain," he said, concentrating on the menacing birds, abhorring their taste for blood. He exploded five implanted ravens before the frightened flock flew away. "One got away, sir."

"Evil things," spat Lil, listening to the snarling wolves. "Call off the wolves."

On Jared's order, the wolves stopped attacking, gradually leaping to the boulders to wait for scraps. A surviving bull bellowed menacingly and skirted the trench, joining the others who trumpeted in mourning. Gathering along the trench, the hunters congratulated one another, abandoning *mencomm.* Rameel shook his head, sending disgust throughout their minds. He overheard Kamean exclaim, "That was amazing!"

The guardsmen weren't accustomed to physical danger, protected by the shield of their rarely malfunctioning technology. Lil showed only by the clench of his jaw that he'd perceived the joy in Kamean's voice. For millennia, his family had dampened people's passions and steered them into a peaceful, harmonic frame of mind. Scientists had frequently proclaimed that Alterrans' peacefulness was conclusive evidence of having attained evolution's supreme level. Sadly, his action might inadvertently prove that the seeds of violence still lay dormant within them.

"What a day!" cried Tamiel, patting his horse's sweaty neck and delighting in his bond with the beautiful spotted mare. He could sense his fellow guardsmen's warm feelings for their horses, even for the hawks and wolves; to a man, though, they hated the bloody ravens and were glad to see them gone. Feeling grimy from the sweat and dust, he made his tunic cleanse his body. His unsoiled tunic returned to its original shape. Yamin dismounted, trailed by the floating recorders, which he repositioned to capture the animals' corpses. "Hey, Yamin." Tamiel touched his finger to a small wound on his forehead, which trickled blood down his cheek. Taking a thin tubular device from his tunic, Yamin touched his forehead, causing the wound to vanish. "Thanks."

"Lucky for you that Azazel was close," Rameel grumbled, shaking dirt from his gloves while his tunic cleaned itself. His unhappiness that it had been up to him to kill the squealing animals pervaded his companions' minds. Kamean or Azazel, he believed, would have been unbothered. Lil had had to have Jared persuade Rameel more than the others to participate, designating him to organize the project. Concerned that they'd underestimated the danger of primitive hunting, Rameel agreed to participate only when Lil permitted them to carry soundguns. It'd been odd to negotiate with one of the House of En, and he'd been astonished when Lil had listened. Primitives were highly skilled, in their own way. Lil hadn't commanded anyone's participation because his plan intentionally violated their law.

Abandoning *mencomm*, Lil wanted nothing more than to end this disgusting experiment. Rameel assumed his usual management of operational tasks. He directed the first craft, now uncloaked, to hover directly above the trench. The cargo doors opened, and devices were lowered lift the carcasses. Azazel removed the scabbard and sword from his back and slid into the trench. As he guided the straps probing the animals' bodies, like snakes slithering to grasp the proper spot, they became rigid to lift the animals. Rameel dangled them, letting blood drain before taking them back for dissection. Shouting came from the hilltop. The young Earth women, spilling plants from their bags, slipped and slid down the steep slope, yelling and waving.

"What do you suppose they want, Captain?" Jared asked.

Azazel, covered with rapidly disappearing blood, peered up over the trench's edge and grumbled, not intending the captain to hear, "You know my position on this."

Annoyed but choosing to ignore him, Lil activated his tunic's universal translation device. He held out his gloved hand. "Stop where you are. What do you want?"

The women, taken aback by the stranger's sharp tone, not in the common tongue but their own language, quickly slowed to a stop. The black-haired woman, little more than half as tall as her companion, was wide-eyed with fright. She lowered her eyes and tugged pleadingly at her friend's arm to flee. Lil studied them, taking the opportunity to discover what these hominids would do when his people permanently revealed themselves. On Alterra, the Net would have told him their names, full histories, and physical readings, and he could have easily converted their essence to nanobots and hurled them away. Here, he had only his eyewear to detect cursory physical readings, he thought with irritation. The women showed no sign of virus or harmful bacteria; Ki had coated the Guard's skin, although he hadn't been sure whether Earth people could be infected by Alterrans when outside their shield. The shorter one's blood pressure was spiking with fear, but the tall one's readings, matching her firm stance and determined facial expression, showed that she was angry, not frightened. Planting her feet firmly, with hands on her hips, the tall one raised her chin haughtily in challenge and glared through emerald green eyes into the covered eyes of the white-haired strangers. Flicking away her companion's arm, she openly studied the line of hunters, not wincing at the sight of their pale, luminous skin or superior weapons. As if reprimanding servants, she demanded, "Strangers, this part of Albion is *our* land. You've stolen our animals! My people need these large ones. They're becoming harder to find. Give them to us, thieves!"

The shorter woman whispered, "Alana, run. They'll take us to be slaves!" She steadied her stance, guarding against movement toward her, her hand slipping to a chiseled stone knife tied in sinew encircling her tiny waist.

The astonished men didn't respond, ignoring the women's intrusion and making no outward sign of the surprise and curiosity reverberating in their collective *mencomm*. Not having been visible to Earth people before and with no villages nearby, they hadn't planned for this contingency. Lil, self-assured, relaxed and continued to study this unique specimen. He'd known that the filthy Earth people staying in this area planned their hunts, a slim sign of intelligence. But so did wolves. This well-proportioned woman with clear skin and delicate facial features, he supposed, would be considered beautiful even by his own people. She bore weapons but had the hubris to feel that her mere words cast a sufficient attack. She reminded him of his saucy little pets.

Unaccustomed to being ignored, the woman narrowed her eyes indignantly, pointed her ivory-ringed finger and scolded, "You've not even thanked the animals' spirits for giving their lives for yours." Growing bolder, she pointed to the trench and admonished, "You don't know what you're doing! You'll ruin the kills unless you dress them right away." She folded her arms, replanted her feet firmly, and stared icily.

Wondering if she spoke a grain of truth, the hunters glanced at one another until Azazel began a low growling laugh that infected them all. The young woman's eyes darkened at the men's disrespect, glaring as if throwing daggers. Lil had thought his men's appearance would scare away any Earth people crossing their path; she must perceive sufficient resemblance to mistake them for mere travelers. Remembering the women who followed the Earth hunters, he reasoned, these creatures could be of use, furthering their experiment. "We mean your people no harm," he said in a courtly manner, but without smiling. "We traveled from afar and don't know your customs or that you claim these hunting grounds. We, as well, need these animals for our survival."

"You have trained animals and that, that...thing," the taller woman argued, waving her hand toward the soundgun. "You couldn't possibly need these animals the way we do!" She put her fists on her hips, expecting to be obeyed.

Unaccustomed to arguments from Alterrans, let alone primitives, Lil became amused. If he were to rule this world, he'd need to manage the primitives, no matter how much he disliked it. Forcing a smile, he changed his tone and said as if to a small child, "If you help us prepare the animals for transport, we'll deliver one to your village."

The guardsmen were nervous. Among today's many violations of the law, this one could have the severest consequences. Her tribesmen might well believe her tale after seeing, tasting, and feeling a huge animal that had appeared in their midst. Unknown pathogens could plague either of their peoples. And violating the direct orders of Ama would result in painful punishment if Lil were to abandon them to save himself. The guardsmen distrusted the House of En, and Lil's unorthodox command style, although welcome, wasn't yet proven. Unable to stand idly, Azazel leaped from the trench in a single bound, projecting through *mencomm,* "Captain, you've no idea where this will lead." Lil sent a flash of anger at the man who'd dare confront him. Tempted to inflict punishment, he knew that

Azazel was his best guardsman and that guilt weighed heavily on them all. He'd asked his most trusted men to violate the law to fulfill his vision. Accepting the consequences, Lil suppressed his ingrained habits.

"We all agreed to this experiment," Lil said sternly through *mencomm*. "Now its success is in jeopardy. When I deliver the animal, the ship will be cloaked. When the carcass becomes visible, her people will assume the animal was a miracle sent by one of their gods."

Turning to the women, Lil spoke aloud as if to small children, extending his arm toward the carcasses in the trench. "Will you help?"

Rameel lowered the animals, and Azazel jumped in to position them. Exchanging suspicious glances, the women inched forward to see into the trench. Flies already swarmed. Finishing, Azazel raised his arms, scowling at the sticky mess from the animals' blood. He backed away and caused his tunic to clean itself. After wiping his bloody hands on the tunic, the new stains disappeared. The taller woman picked up his short hunting blade with the jeweled handle and marveled at the strength of the metal, gleaming as it reflected the sun's rays. Touching it, the short woman exclaimed, "Ouch," when she pricked her finger while barely brushing against its sharpness.

"How will you carry the entrails?" the tall woman demanded, shielding her eyes in the bright sunlight.

Rameel, having planned to discard them, now thought better of it and gave Yamin an order to find something. Yamin returned from the ship carrying a container that he handed to the women. The tall one felt the container, puzzled by material that was neither stone nor clay nor made from animal parts. She nudged her friend to follow her. They slid down into the blood-soaked trench, climbed around the dead animals, and motioned for hunters to follow. With gestures, the tall one directed where to make their first cuts. Smirking, Azazel sliced dissecting lines through the animal's belly. The shorter woman gasped, "Like a knife cutting water!"

When Maya fumbled with the skinning knife at her waist, her friend touched her hand to stop her. "Use theirs." Seeing Azazel's sheathed short knife hanging from the strap of his scabbard, she vigorously motioned for him to give it to her, while tugging to separate the hide that he'd slashed. Smirking again, he handed it to her. The tall one narrowed her eyes, displeased by the men's smirks and bad manners since she was doing them a favor.

The women expertly expanded the cuts of each animal, reaching in to extract the intestines, which spilled out on the ground with undigested leaves from the animal's morning meal. The removed organs were placed in the box, and the excess was drained and reinserted into the body for transport.

"Yamin, include everything in the record, no matter how uncomfortable it is for us," said Lil. "We need to examine the events of this day in detail."

"Yes, Captain," he replied, repositioning the spherical recording devices that hovered over their heads.

Completing their work, the women shook blood from their hands and delicately stepped across the slippery rocks. Rameel lowered the cables, but they slipped and the animals fell and had to be reattached. But one by one, the animals were eventually hoisted into the holds of the hovercrafts.

"They're making a mess," the tall woman whispered to her companion, studying the men and their goods carefully, trying to remember the shape and use of each strange object that they used. "They have fantastic tools, but they must not have done this before."

Holding up her bloody hands and pointing to her legs, the shorter woman said to a guardsman, "I'm sticky with blood. I need to be cleaned." She expected to be ignored, having heard stories of slaves who were treated worse than animals. These strangers with their superior ways no doubt owned many slaves. Instead, the guardsman handed her something he called a towel and demonstrated by rubbing it on his arm. She looked at him skeptically. Did these men not know anything? Still, not wanting to be impolite, she took the towel and hesitantly wiped as he had shown her. "Aggh!" She sucked in her breath with fright. Magic. The blood and grime instantly disappeared, leaving her skin and clothing as if they hadn't been blood stained. She put her head down and whispered, "Look, Alana, it's magic! Stronger than Drood's." She finished wiping her clothing, looking askance at the guardsmen, who studied her as well. "You try it!" she exclaimed, shakily handing the towel to her friend. She rubbed her hands over her clothing with a look of desperation, attempting to remove any taint of magic.

"Much here is magical," Alana muttered as she climbed from the trench and cleaned herself in long, deliberate strokes. Studying the guardsmen, she noticed that their clothing was clean. "Maya, their clothes clean themselves." After she watched the last carcass disappear into a flying ship, unnatural shadows caught her attention. "Maya, look where the horses were. The Droods are watching. The strangers don't see them, or they don't care." Alana's hand unconsciously touched the pouch around her neck with her talisman, and she whispered, "Protect me from the Droods." Funny, she thought, she was more afraid of the Droods than of these strangers with their magic. Maya simply shrugged her shoulders dismissively, her mind too numb to comprehend what the Droods might do. If Alana weren't with her, she'd have run away the moment she'd seen these men.

A loud bellow rang out; a bull had snuck back. Seeking revenge, the bull pawed the ground, shook his head, and charged. Azazel started for his gun that had been carelessly tossed near his horse, but the raging bull was too quick. He snatched Kamean into the air with his trunk and hurled him into the trench with all his might and fury. Reaching his sword as the closest weapon, Azazel slashed the bull's side. Having scrambled to retrieve their soundguns already packed away, Rameel and Tamiel came running, blasting him. Trumpeting defiantly, the bull reared, absorbing the pain. After continuing blasts, he succumbed and ran, shaking his injured ears. The hunters leaped to rescue Kamean. During his fall, his tunic had transformed into a cushion that protected his body, but his exposed head had a deep gash, from which blood flowed profusely like the mastodons they'd killed.

Reaching him first, Yamin laid a finger on his bloodied neck. "He has no pulse!" he cried out, eyes searching for the captain. With confusion, he felt Kamean's limp body and worried about his deadly pallor, with no clear idea what to do. He'd never known anyone to die, and the thought petrified him. Rameel climbed down, began lifting the injured man, and picked his way over the blood-soaked ground.

"Put him in my *tri-terran*," Lil ordered, standing at the edge of the trench. "It's fastest. Quickly! Tamiel, get Kamean to the infirmary before his aura expires." Rameel transferred the injured man into the arms of Erjat, who disappeared into the invisible ship with Tamiel. Within moments, there was a whirring sound followed by a blast of wind as they flew away.

"Wrap this up," Lil commanded, his voice and expression never changing from his constant calm, self-assurance. Inwardly, he felt as if he were caught in an Alterran mud pool, slipping and sliding uncontrollably among a sea of mud snipes as he sought to maintain his balance—it had been one of Jahkbar's favorite training exercises during his first youth, to teach him control under the most unpredictable of circumstances. Nothing was going as planned today, and he wanted to leave before anything else happened. "Rameel, fly the bull back to Hawan and deliver it immediately to the Ministry, to Ki himself. Azazel, you fly the ship with the calf and deliver it immediately to Ki as well. Jared will take care of the animals. The rest of you return with one of them." Rameel motioned for most of the hunters to board his larger ship. It soon disappeared, and the women again heard whirring followed by a blast of wind.

Regretting his commitment but unwilling to break his word, Lil strode to the women, speaking rapidly. "I'll deliver one animal to your village, as I promised. Return there immediately." He abruptly turned toward his ship, ordering it to prepare for takeoff.

Alana caught up with him and matched his stride. "You can't do that. It'll take us at least two days to get back. The animal must be promptly handled or it will be no good. You must take us with you!" She stamped her foot and glared at him.

"Sir," Azazel warned, "one mistake is leading to another! You can't!"

"Azazel, you're of course right," he replied shortly, using all his control to hide his agitation at both the primitive and Azazel. Although he wouldn't admit it, he needed Azazel, the only guardsman with a pure military background and unique skills. As a hobby, he studied ancient battles, martial arts, and weaponry. It had been Azazel who had produced their sharp swords and knives, although they'd originally been created as theater pieces. Worse, he couldn't deny that Azazel was right.

Lil curtly informed the women, "You must return on your own," and resumed his stride, wondering how his father would react if he learned about today. With his father's usual detachment from operational details, Lil counted on him to overlook their routine reports, just as he overlooked the rapid depletion of their food inventory, making Lil bear the burden of finding a solution.

"You asked me to help you," Alana shouted angrily, catching up to him again, "and I did, even though the entire kill rightfully belongs to my people. Right now, my entire village is out tracking mastodon." She ran before him and walked backward to see his face, but was frustrated that she couldn't see his eyes. "You've stolen the very herd that they hunt! You can't give us one animal and then let it spoil!" She pounded her fist into her side and again stamped her foot, with visions of flies and maggots filling the carcass, followed by scavenger birds. This man was more stubborn than even her father, Ewan. But she knew that she always won him over in the end. "You're obviously well fed. We're not. I demand that you take us, as well."

Lil ignored her, preparing to leave and expecting her to give up.

The women whispered to each other. Instead of abandoning their pleas, Alana matched Lil's stride and walked beside him. Maya struggled to keep up behind them. Softening her tone and leaning her head closer with her long tresses blowing in the breeze, Alana whispered, "I know you don't want my people to know about you. I'll create a story that I prayed to the gods for help; they answered our prayer with this animal. I give you my word that I won't tell my people. They won't look for you if you take us." She waited, expecting him to relent.

With Lil ignoring her, she firmed her lips with determination and pursued him. "You probably live far away from here, anyway. Perhaps even up there." She pointed to the sky with a knowing smile and raised eyebrows that implied that she knew his secret. In her childhood, she'd loved the hearth stories about the mystical creatures that appeared in the starry sky. "However," she dictated with authority, "you may never hunt in our land again."

A flash of exasperation crossed Lil's face, and he glanced at Jared, who stood nearby with the horses, awaiting the captain's order. "Wait here," he told the adamant woman. He spoke quietly to Jared, "We've made a mess of this, I'm afraid."

Jared nodded thoughtfully, surprised but honored to be the captain's confidant. "We've interfered with her village's food supply."

Lil thought for a moment and shrugged with resignation. "Regardless what my father might say about our actions today, I'd prefer to honor that portion of the Code that I haven't yet offended—to help the weak and cause no harm." He paused to give a rueful laugh. "I've offended all my family today, so it won't matter if I give these women a ride. At least some good will come of this if we help her village survive. Our fellow residents of this lonesome planet."

"No one but you, sir, would dare do this," Jared replied with a deep breath, glad that Yamin had taken all the recorders with him. If blessed Anu heard this conversation, nothing would save him.

"For that reason, I'll do this alone." Returning to the few remaining men, he ordered, "Azazel, we're done here, go back now. Take the remaining guardsmen other than Jared with you. I'll bring the last ship."

Azazel looked at him quizzically but said no more. After the men boarded, the ship disappeared. When the whirring and wind ended, Lil said to the women, "We didn't intend to cause you any harm. As a sign of our honor, I'll take you as well."

Alana folded her arms over her chest with a pleased glare. "Good."

Lil studied her indignant stance. He'd been certain that if any Earth people saw them uncloak, they would die of fright, their hearts bursting. Or they'd scream uncontrollably and run away. Nothing like her reaction, which was more than simple bravery. It was almost as if she'd seen his kind before. Not all Earth people were evolving at the same level. She had the self-assurance of nobility. "You were right. I don't want your people to know about us. We must deliver this animal without being seen."

"Everyone is out tracking the herd," she said, putting her finger to her lips in thought. The wind blew her hair, and she pulled it back from her face. "Other than us, that is. We've been gathering plants for preserving the meat and for medicine." She felt the pouch slung around her waist and was dismayed that most of her medicinal plants had been lost. "Ugh!" She scrunched her face in dismay and gazed at the trail she'd taken for any trace; this place was far away from her village, and she might not make it back before winter. If her people became sick, how would she take care of them? But there was no time to search. The captain was far ahead, and she signaled Maya to catch up.

Approaching the hovercraft containing the last mastodon carcass, the captain extended his arm to herd his charges inside quickly.

"Is it safe?" asked Maya, pulling back, her lower lip trembling. "The others disappeared."

Lil laughed, thinking that if this one had been alone, she never would have had the courage to leave the bushes. Taking her readings, he saw that blood pressure was spiking again and her heart was racing. "I assure you, they're fine. They were there. You just couldn't see them. If you've changed your mind, I understand," he said, hoping that was the case.

"You go first," said Maya, crossing her arms over her chest and planting her feet. Alana was always talking her into things, but not this time.

Lil walked up the ramp and turned around with his arms up. "See?" He was amused that the tall one came along as if it were an everyday occurrence. Lil was amazed that her readings showed perfect calm. The black-haired woman, alarmed at being left alone, closed her eyes and followed, one trembling step after another.

Lil called to Jared, "Bring back the wolves and the horses." They'd created a barn at the base of their mountain colony for these animals where Jared would keep them, out of sight of the other colonists.

"Yes, sir," he replied. "I'll check on the injured wolf on my way."

The last hovercraft was relatively small, its cargo hold barely large enough for the mother's body. After removing his helmet and gloves, Lil pointed to the seats in the rear and made a sitting motion to explain, and then went to the cockpit. The women exchanged surprised glances at seeing his elongated forehead. They sat for a moment in the dim light. Already the animal was beginning to smell. With no windows in the cargo hold, they snuck out and boldly slid into the rear cockpit seats, careful not to make a sound. Lil grimaced, although he smelled their floral scent, not a foul stink. It doesn't matter, he told himself shaking his head; this disaster will be over soon. They had to fumigate anyway because of the carcass. On his command, the ship rose vertically and smoothly flew at low altitude. Lil glanced over his shoulder to see if they were frightened by the flight, but he found their big eyes intently studying only him. He quickly looked straight ahead and pretended to be busy directing lights on the control panel.

As the ship left the ground, the women gasped with astonishment as they whizzed over the treetops, the images changing so rapidly that they became a blur. After a moment, the tall, light-haired woman tapped him on the shoulder. She withdrew her hand quickly, surprised at a strange energy emanating from him. Undaunted, she asked without fear, "What do they call you?"

"Sit back." Lil snapped with a slight turn of his head, irritated at the trouble they were causing him. Nevertheless, he unwillingly noticed the minty smell of her breath.

The coldness of his command startled Alana. Tempted to lecture him on manners, with restraint she haughtily raised her chin in offense and slid back, folding her arms under her breasts.

Lil resumed pretending that the controls required his constant attention. Nonetheless, he wished he were cloaked to study this fascinating pair. It was like finding diamonds when you were looking for coal. Earth people were disheveled and dirty, yet here were specimens that were clean, their clothing was well made of sewn hide and furs, and they spoke in sentences with clear diction. Sneaking glances as he moved around the control panel, he noticed that the taller one's intelligent green eyes were framed by long, untangled golden hair. The shorter woman's darker complexion and black hair more closely fit his expectation, although she, too, was well groomed and her long, curly hair was untangled. Even their fingernails were trimmed and clean. Each had a tiny bag tied around her neck, and they touched them from time to time, silently moving their lips as if it gave them solace. Each carried a spear made with thinned, pointed stone, and in their leggings, he could see a hidden stone knife. How many other knives might they have hidden?

The golden-haired woman peered over his shoulder, almost touching him but drawing her hand back cautiously, saying in a conversational tone as if she'd not been rebuffed, "My name is Alana, daughter of our leader, Ewan, Earthkeeper acolyte to Zedah and Yoachim, and the medicine woman of my people. This is my friend Maya, daughter of Gwi, granddaughter of Marita the Midwife. Maya is our village's Caller." Pausing to await a response that didn't come, she demanded with irritation at his poor manners, "Where are you from?" Even the most isolated tribesmen knew the common courtesies. She wondered whether all his village's women had died, leaving no one to teach his tribe of young men.

Not waiting for him to answer, Maya giggled shakily. "I've never seen men as tall as you. You're even taller than Ewan and Alana."

Alana leaned over his seat, trying to peer into his face. "Your hair is very light, lighter than mine, and so is your skin. It almost seems to glow." Refraining from poking him, she thought that he looked very clean, unlike the Albion tribesmen not taught by her father. Alana had never been able to tolerate the smelliness of the men living nearby. She sniffed him and thought that he smelled like her scented soap. Lil grimaced at her sniffing and shifted forward to distance himself. Behind his back, Alana returned the annoyed face but slid back into her seat.

"All your men are good looking!" Maya ventured, emboldened by Alana's move. "Nearly everyone looks alike, especially with that white hair. Why do you cover your eyes? How does your clothing change shape?"

"Your clothing *is* unusual," Alana interjected when Maya paused for breath, "and your weapons are made of a metal that I haven't seen since I was a small child. It's not found around here." Her last remark piqued his interest, but he remained silent. "How did you control the animals?" Undeterred by his silence, Alana observed. "Only Drood can do that. And the machine that shoots sound..." Her voice trailed off, thinking of the litany of strange things that she'd seen today.

Growing tired of his silence, they turned their eyes to the changing landscape passing outside the window. The distant glacier appeared at eye level, and the plain before it was flat. Lil flew at a low altitude over an area rich in game among the small, scattered lakes left behind by the melting glacier. "Look at all those reindeer, Maya. We should tell Maliki to hunt there."

As Alana had promised, her people weren't home. She pointed to a spot near the center hearth to leave the carcass. Lil opened the cargo bay door and mechanically hoisted it. Before leaving, Alana said, "As I said, I'll tell my people that our prayers have been answered by the gods. No one will look for you." She reached into her bag and handed him something, determined to show better manners than he had. "Thank you. May the Mother guide your way, stranger. Please accept this gift—the bark of the white willow tree. It's valuable as a painkiller."

He took it from her, nodding curtly.

"Oh, I need to fix this," Alana remarked with a broad smile, pointing to her legging and crouching down before he could respond.

Smirking with annoyance, he folded his arms, crossed one long leg over the other, and waited. Alana pretended to tug at her legging, casting innocent glances to study this inscrutable man. *His voice is not harsh, yet he acts with the firm authority of one whose words are never questioned. He's the most beautiful man I've ever seen, but he's so arrogant with his constant smirking. He thinks he's superior to us, like an experienced warrior treats a raw apprentice. Even so, he's young, no older than I. He wears no beard, like the men of my lost island. His forehead is very long. I wish I could see his eyes. He's only a head taller than I am, and he's muscular yet slender, not stocky like most in this land. Of course,* she chided herself, *he isn't from here. No one here has these magical things!*

"Are you ready yet?" he smirked impatiently, gently waving her to the door.

"Good-bye." Holding her spear, she reluctantly slipped down the ramp. *The first attractive man I've ever met, and he pays no attention to me.* Maya giggled with relief and hugged Alana when her feet touched the ground. To the eyes of the only unseen villager present, a woman too old and infirm for hunting, Alana and Maya had floated down from the sky, and the mastodon carcass had simply appeared out of nothing. The old woman peeked through her hut's entrance flap and trembled with fear. What magic was this? Was this evil or good? "Are they working with the Droods now?" she whispered aloud with a scowl, shaking her gray-haired head. Perhaps the rumors that Alana would mate Drood's son were true.

Sighing with relief, Lil commanded his ship to depart. At last, he had time to reflect on the day's events. The huge mastodon barely took the wolves seriously, although the birds had performed feats he hadn't anticipated. The wolves would be more effective with smaller prey like elk or reindeer. The horses easily became one with the rider. Even though he hated the hunt, he looked forward to riding again. Today was a start. Nothing about this path would be easy. He would *never* use ravens again. He needed to review the records to study those mysterious shadows. He had to check on Kamean's resurrection. Why had Alana seemed more intelligent than others? An Earthkeeper acolyte and medicine woman must be positions of some significance. Perhaps that was why she had the temerity to confront him, he thought, laughing.

CHAPTER 2
LIL

Lil flew the hovercraft indirectly back to Hawan, their Earth colony. He needed more time to think, having deliberately violated the Non-Interference Directive. Through the fog of his conflicting emotions, he marveled at Earth's beauty. To calm himself, he played one of Yamin's symphonic pieces and headed north to the glacier, his favorite route supported by the Earth's electromagnetic flow. His regular ship, the *tri-terran*, was smaller and faster. In it, he frequently came here to race along the glacier's edge and dive over the high cliff. Now, flying the bulkier transport hovercraft, he limited himself to descending into a narrow icy crevice that gradually widened into a river raging with glacier melt, whose waters splashed and leaped over the great rocks strewn throughout the riverbed. Following the river as it eventually flowed into flatland, Lil raced over the fledgling vegetation, where huge herds of reindeer and elk, a few rogue mastodons, and other hoofed animals took advantage of the new growth. He noticed a saber-toothed tiger lying in wait in the tall grassland, stalking a reindeer. It was exciting to witness a planet awakening from its long, cold slumber with life blossoming in incredible variety.

The deep-blue skies south of the glacier were filled with flocks of birds, some heading south for the winter. On the southern peninsula, where the glacier had receded centuries ago, trees had burgeoned into deciduous forests, now showing the first tinges of autumn crimson and gold. To Alterrans, immersion in pristine nature made them one with the universe, and he religiously drank in the sight.

Devoted to harmony with nature, the Alterrans had preserved natural beauty when constructing Hawan. Carved out of the largest mountain on the peninsula, far from the Earth tribes, the entrance was camouflaged by the illusion of a steep waterfall flowing over the original rock. The exquisitely beautiful setting never ceased to fascinate Lil. The waterfall appeared to be bouncing from rocks and pummeling a half-mile into illusory waters swirling below. Uncloaking before entering the energy field that created the waterfall illusion, the ship nestled itself among the mixture of hovercrafts and the smaller *tri-terrans* that were used for exploring this world up to the upper atmosphere. The huge hyperspace transport ship that had brought the original crew and the portals eons ago had long since been dispatched to return to Alterra. Hawan's landing port led to a courtyard constructed as a perfect isosceles triangle, whose floor was laid with tight-fitting white granite blocks forming a triangular pattern. The colony had been built by his half-brother Ki, assisted by the best builders. Duplicating Alterran architecture, they'd infused it with their family's religious symbols. Multistoried buildings lined the courtyard, narrowing as they reached the triangle's point, at which a tall tower stretched upward, disappearing into the clouds. The buildings had been chiseled by lasers from the ages-old mountain granite, long ago heaved from the Earth's mantle. They coated the granite with their own sky-blue crystalline glaze, which served as an energy seal filled with heating nanobytes while contributing to the ethereal beauty. Although high in the misty mountains, Hawan was topped by a transparent energy shield filled with nanobytes that collected and stored solar rays and shielded the colonists from the frosty mountain temperatures and high winds. From the balconies on the upper floors hung hydroponic gardens, heavily laden with a variety of colorful vegetables and flowers and tended by Dalits, who were small creatures specially bred for service work. Colorful, exotic birds brought to Hawan from Earth's southern forests flew from balcony to balcony, skipping about the garden trellises. As a research colony, they'd gathered many diverse specimens from throughout the planet. Glowglobes of changing colors floated through the courtyard to provide serene lighting in the deepening shadows of late afternoon. Lil had always thought Hawan, a giant work of functional art nestled in this breathtakingly beautiful setting, had a wondrous charm that was missing even from his beloved Alterra.

As Lil landed, a lone figure awaited his arrival, dressed in Hawan's silver tunic with a green sacred triangle glowing near his left shoulder. Greeting him with the salute of peace and harmony, he said formally, "Captain En.Lil, Anu commands that you meet with the Council of Elders tomorrow morning."

The dreaded dark cloud had descended on him sooner than he'd anticipated. Returning the salute, he replied without trace of emotion, "Understood. How is Kamean?"

"Kamean was deceased upon arrival, sir. He was taken immediately to the rejuvenation chamber. I understand that he's doing fine now."

Lil went to his suite across the courtyard. At the door, he said his name, "En.Lil." The sensors recognized his voice, and the door slid open. Inside, the glowglobes automatically lit and the heat sensors whirred, quickly warming his room. "Alterra—nature," he said, causing the wall panels to light up in a collage of homeworld pictures. Seascapes accompanied by wave sounds changed to a view of the narrow cone of a dormant volcano rising miles above the surface. Cessation of their volcanic activity should have been a clue, he thought, of the troubles that lay ahead.

Exhausted, he plopped on his bed. Using his tunic controls, he lay a moment massaging and toning his stiffening muscles, eliminating the ache from the unfamiliar ride. Within his suite, his tunic recharged itself through the Net. He wasn't surprised by the summons from his father. He'd detached from the Net, and the automatic alarms would have been given despite his best efforts to disengage them; the systems were too redundant even for him. No one was ever disconnected in his world. Yet it had its advantages. Touching his tunic controls again, he caused it to refresh itself, removing any taint of the hunt's dust and blood and transforming its shape to his usual silver uniform. Watching the blood disappear, he uncomfortably reflected how exhilarating the day had been—detached from the Net, taking their lives into their own hands—even though they'd lost control of the ravens; they needed to study what had happened there. It seemed to him that a strange darkness, what was once called evil, had permeated the flock. Otherwise, though, things had gone well, and his men had come to life to a degree he'd never seen before. And they'd all felt a special camaraderie that Lil hadn't known in all his lives except perhaps with Jahkbar. They had planned the hunt only for the best of reasons, for the benefit of all the colonists. He hadn't expected that they'd enjoy any part of it. The killing was the worst, and his stomach still felt queasy. Could they survive without consuming meat? His own people had consumed it in ancient times, eons before the enlightenment when substitutes were found. Was hunting a bad thing because they had violated the Alterran Code? Or, was it a good thing because they were developing skills that he hoped would permit his people to survive on Earth? He didn't know what to make of his conflicting emotions.

When Lil entered his suite, he hadn't seen his new personal Dalit, a member of the underclass of service workers. She bumped a chair. "What are you called?" he asked without taking his mind from his work.

The Dalit, shocked at his attention, responded with hesitation, "363, sir." Having originally come to Earth to work in the gold mines, she was less than half the size of the guardsmen and stockier for greater balance.

Being in an oddly reflective mood after the day's events, Lil asked, "363, what's your favorite story of Alterran history?"

Agitated, 363 responded, "As you must know, sir, Dalits attend only religious ceremonies."

"My mistake," said Lil, focusing; he hadn't fully realized that he'd spoken to her. "Proceed as you were. Peace and harmony."

"Peace and harmony, sir," she said without interest, her mind calmed by the perpetual Dalit haze.

Sitting dutifully at his workstation, he ordered, "On," and the wall panels transformed into replays of recorded messages. Kohdrai, an anthropologist, delivered an update on his observations of plains nomads traveling with small animal herds. His eyes alighted on the phrase: *The hominids lie with animals at night, living like little more than animals themselves.*" Lil winced; no matter how many reports about primitive behavior he read, he couldn't suppress his disgust. Yet, in pockets of development, the hominids had large settlements, even building boats for elemental trade. In the warmer climates, they had begun to use baked mud for building. And then, the greatest puzzle of all—the island that had sunk into the sea, where the hominids had used geothermal heat to fuel a seafaring civilization with impressive temples and harbors. What was driving such uneven advancement? Lil skimmed through other anthropological reports of hominid tribes, which constantly warred against one another or simply preyed upon any burgeoning development. As the population increased, they'd noted an increase in wars. Bloody battles, with heads left on spikes in celebration. Wars fought with stone weapons that were savagely effective.

Jared's image appeared, and he reported that the horses and wolves had made it safely back, but the hawks and ravens had not yet returned. Tamiel appeared and said that, as ordered, he was transporting Mika and Erjat back to the mines. Yamin noted that the recording equipment had worked properly and everything was now in the system as routine field information. He noted that the Net had detected unknown genetic forms in the hovercraft, and that he'd edited the logs to record the routine collection of specimens for the Ministry of Science; their experiment should be hidden in the daily flow. Lil rapidly skimmed through the panels reporting daily scientific missions and scanned general colony news, finding an item of interest. The scribes reported comets entering Earth's solar system. Their orbits were being studied. He marked the story for investigation. Azazel reported that he had resumed his monitoring of competing bands of marauders, one of which camped fifteen hundred miles east of Hawan along the continent's longest river. Most recently, he'd found that the group had torched one of the nascent port cities sprouting up on the coast of the middle sea, murdering all the inhabitants. Lil sighed, how would civilization take hold if the lawless ones—covered with grime, matted and filthy hair, green teeth, disgusting sexual habits—consistently destroyed the hard-working efforts of the peaceful ones?

He accessed Yamin's holographic report of the hunt and sped through the details. He froze an aerial image of the hunt and noted aloud, "There! Shadows. They seem to float, but they're not shadows caused by clouds. That must be what I saw in my peripheral vision. What are they?" Viewing the aerial footage again, he saw that the shadows followed them through the forest and lingered along the perimeter during the hunt. These same shadows covered the ravens before they dived into their prey. "It's almost as if they're intelligent. Evil, but intelligent." This planet wasn't as predictable as he'd thought, now that they'd ventured beyond their protected spheres. He sent Yamin a note to follow up on this and to show it to Azazel. Azazel was always interested in anything extraordinary.

Scrolling until he found his encounter with Alana, he paused the program and caused her full-sized, three-dimensional image to appear. Circling, he noticed that her body was muscular but lean, like a runner, yet her breasts were full. Her hips showed no sign of childbirth, even though she was older than first blood; his scientists had determined that most tribes mated shortly thereafter. Her furs were of high quality, and he knew that getting the first pick was a sign of high status, which was further confirmed by her ivory ring. The pouch slung around her narrow waist held freshly picked flower tops, mushrooms, roots, and bark. Touching her silky, golden hair, he caught a floral scent. Opening the bag around her neck, he found flint, a stone carving in a circular shape with a large middle hole, and other trinkets. He noticed a bulge on her side, above her hip. He felt something hard. Lifting up her clothing, he discovered the hidden pocket and removed the contents—a silver headband. No one on this peninsula could mine silver. Even if they'd found it by happenstance, no one here could mold metal, especially not of this quality and with the intricate carved designs. More puzzles. His people had observed Earth's only advanced civilization, on an island not far from Albion, but it had sunk into the sea at least a decade ago. Perhaps she was a survivor. If not, how could one hominid be so different from creatures like those grimy marauders that Azazel observed? Intrigued, he called up her biologic profile. "Hmm. Her merclorian count is as high as ours." Was she a leap in their genetics? He sent a note to Ki that she'd be an interesting specimen for study. A fleeting thought entered his mind that even by Alterran standards, she was a beauty, despite his repugnance for Earth people. "Off," he said, getting up, and the panels darkened and the heat stopped whirring as he left his suite.

The Ministry of Science was located in the majestic tower at the pinnacle of the triangular courtyard. At its top was the observation deck, used for stargazing. The transparent roof whisked away wind noise and controlled the temperature, permitting peaceful communion with the cherished universe. Below this level worked the scribes who deciphered the star messages. On several floors below, scientists studied the specimens gathered by guardsmen. The next floor down housed the neural net known as the Teacher. The Ministry's low middle floors held the rejuvenation and medical treatment chambers, and the bottom floors were devoted to energy production.

Entering, Lil removed his eyewear in the dimly lit building. Stopping first at the infirmary to check on Kamean, he found him resting comfortably. Having been rejuvenated, Kamean's appearance now was that of an adolescent boy, and his hair had resumed its natural color of dark brown.

"Peace and harmony, sir," he said, making the sacred triangle, honored by the captain's unexpected visit.

Lil nodded. "You were rejuvenated. How are you feeling?"

Kamean replied with an enthusiastic smile. "Doc put me in the chamber and fixed me right up, sir. It's great to feel young again. Not all my prior memories have been restored yet, but Doc will finish downloading them tomorrow. I'll be back on duty then."

"That's good to hear. I need you back as soon as possible. Peace and harmony." He made the sacred triangle and left. In the hallway, Lil said to Kosondra, the doctor's assistant, "Thank the stars that the resuscitation chamber still works properly."

"The chamber should function awhile longer without replacement parts, but nothing lasts forever," she answered. "As I've discussed with your mother, we must develop other treatment methods. I understand that they assigned scribes to examine the stars for insight." Lil's adoptive mother, Uras, was the chief medical officer.

Lil masked his frustration with their lack of progress, replying, "Thanks for your report. Please ask Mother to keep me advised if you begin experiencing problems."

"Will do, Captain," she replied blandly, eyes downcast in the Alterran way. "Peace and harmony, sir." Lil moved away, oblivious to acknowledging her.

He ascended in the tube to find Ki, his half-brother and head of the Ministry. The bustling research floors were filled with scribes working within the many open research stations. Some studied holographic screens creating detailed Earth maps. His guardsmen assisted with gathering the data, and they had installed monitoring devices at critical planetary locations to track geological developments. They'd learned much about the inner structure of this planet, its tectonic plates, and its electromagnetic flows, which connected with the magnetosphere. At the station before which Lil stood, scientists monitored seismic data from a volcano thought to be near eruption. Because of the volcanic activity that once existed on Alterra, their scientists were expert in this field, and they'd discovered that geologic activity on Earth adhered to the same scientific principles.

After lingering a moment longer, he ascended to a floor filled with noisy caged monkeys, cows, foxes, and small, furry, four-legged creatures. At a workstation, Lil watched a snarling dire wolf suspended invisibly. Alongside the wolf appeared a diagram in which a scientist sequenced its genetic code. The double helix resembled the genetic code of Alterra's creatures, a fact that had mystified their scientists when Earth creatures were found to be so similar. Intense arguments had erupted in the Supreme Council when they'd received the initial data indicating that the genetic design of one strain of Earth hominids was nearly identical to Alterrans'. Some furiously denounced the data, certain that further study would prove the Alterrans' unique superiority in the universe. Nevertheless, additional studies, anonymously delivered, confirmed the similarities. Lil said to the scientist, "I understand that the Earth creatures' genetic code is remarkably similar to ours. Do your data continue to confirm this?"

The scientist, surprised that someone of Lil's rank had spoken to him, replied with a bowed head, "Sir, yes! Generally, the code is similar, although we have nothing comparable to this animal. It's long been extinct on Alterra, but then of course, sir, you know that." He laughed nervously. Excited enough to shift his feet and fumble with his hands, he rushed on, "We don't cage the hominids, of course. But we've found from the dead ones that, genetically speaking, they're nearly identical to us, although I know that's not a popular conclusion," he said looking down again, laughing nervously. "And their organs function the same as ours. It's truly amazing. Many think that our experiments offer proof of the principles of universal creation." The scribe, suddenly realizing that he'd said too much, glanced up to see if the captain would inflict punishment. Was the captain merely testing his loyalty? The Supreme Council had considered it blasphemy to hint that the genetic code of these primitives could be similar and had ordered the information to be suppressed, imposing stiff punishment for violations.

It's astounding, Lil thought, to travel this immense distance to find things as they once were in one's own ancient history. No wonder this notion had caused their rulers such turmoil. He could see that the man before him trembled in fear of punishment. With so few Alterrans left alive, Lil routinely disregarded his family's punishment protocols. Ama would be angry, but it was unlikely that he'd ever know. Lil needed these people as much as they needed him, even if his father didn't realize it yet.

Ignoring the cowering scribe, he walked by other research stations, seeing the scientists tense when they saw him. He enjoyed the Ministry's activity, with his brother's scientists busily conducting a huge variety of experiments. When he found Ki, he stood by a transparent cage displaying the baby mastodon carcass, where he examined it with his primary assistants, Laurina and Mikhale. Having already electronically scanned the animal, they viewed its holographic internal image. When Lil approached, he lightly slapped Ki's hand in brotherly greeting. "Ki, old man, glad you're finally earning your keep. I'm tired of being the only one carrying the load around here."

Ki was slightly shorter than Lil, but the nourishment bars and continual toning had produced a similar body build. The most striking difference was that Ki's forehead was even more elongated than Lil's. The colonists' white hair and luminous skin were the telltale signs of entangling their bodies' atoms for space travel. Lil's hair was clipped short in the guardsman fashion, while Ki's hair looked perpetually unkempt, and he had Uras's brown eyes, which frequently gave away his cynical outlook.

"Flying around the countryside is not working, little brother," Ki joked as he put down his electronic notepad filled with graphs. "Spend some time around here and maybe you'll put that tunic to work. And don't call me 'old man' any more. You only look so young because you can't fly right. If I wrecked as often as you, I'd look like an infant."

"Hey, don't be so sensitive. This place is too boring for me, but at least you've got all the good-looking women," Lil said, smiling at blue-eyed Laurina, her hair drawn back and secured at the nape of her neck. "The Earth women are just little, short, dirty things."

"Since you were sent to Earth to uphold the directive, it's a good thing for you that they're short and dirty," Ki responded dryly, seeing a weakness.

Lil winced; Ki was teasing him for violating the directive he was sent to Earth to enforce. "You know, Ki, you need to get out more. You need a sense of adventure."

"Maybe," he said, narrowing his eyes. "Anyway, with the hominid population increasing, it's no wonder that the mastodon numbers are dropping, but we'll search for a physical problem."

"Have you discovered anything useful yet?" Lil studied the suspended mastodon, picturing the resourceful uses that Earth people made of each part. "When I'm questioned by the Council, it'd be great if I had new data that they'd consider worthwhile."

"Let's go to my space." As they walked, Ki said quietly, sensing a rare opportunity to influence his half-brother, "We don't have much yet. Preliminarily, this calf is diseased, and it may explain their decline." Entering Ki's office, Lil sat down and put his feet up on his brother's neat desk, which caused Ki to scowl and comment, "You're in a good mood." As with anyone other than the supreme leader and named successors, Ki could access Lil's brain waves to verify his emotions. But he didn't need it. Lil was relaxed, and his face glowed with emotion—if living on Earth had this effect, it would benefit all of them.

Lil's mood was rare, indeed. Ki wished that he could synthesize the mountain air, the adrenaline rush, whatever had caused his euphoria.

"Ki, I had serious reservations about that hunt, and I still don't condone killing animals, but, well, the entire event was amazing—being one mind with the animals; riding as if I were one with the horse; exposed to danger and seeing the world unencumbered. It was incredible."

"I get the image," chuckled Ki, enjoying seeing his self-controlled brother feeling emotion. It wouldn't last, he was sure. Still, it would be interesting if the changes that the guardsmen were experiencing affected Lil as well. It would make it easier for Ki to influence him. Mikhale brought in a small plate of cooked mastodon. Ki smelled it and wrinkled his nose, holding it out to Lil. "Since starting with mastodon was your idea, you have first rights. Would you care to taste?"

Lil grimaced. "I guess I'm the test subject. Am I going to like this?"

Ki deadpanned, "Oddly enough, the Teacher didn't have any tips on cooking this beast. Perhaps while you're flying around enjoying the scenery, you could stop at the local village and ask the chef for some recipes."

Lil bit into it, then spit it out, exaggerating his disgust. "Ugh! Tastes like boot leather. Earth people might have different taste buds. I think I'll stick to the vegetable and fruit concoctions you've created." Secretly, Ki had been experimenting with wild items gathered by the guardsmen, copying what interested the Earth people, making such items an increasing part of their diet.

"Hold still." Ki grabbed Lil's arm and stabbed him. "I'm giving you an injection just in case that meat had any bugs that we failed to detect." Putting down the device, he said, "Look, I'm sure there are decent ways to prepare it. We'll keep working on it." He paused, adding with sarcasm, "If the Council permits, of course."

He waved his hand for Mikhale to leave and shut his door. "In all seriousness, thanks for taking this risk. I know with the value you place on tradition that it's not easy for you to violate the directive, but all our lives are at risk. This is an important step to solve the food shortage."

Lil's expression regained the inscrutable blankness that belied the growing knot arising in his stomach. He resented the reminder of failing in his duty. If they'd been on Alterra of old with its vast resources, the thought of violating any syllable of Ama's order would have been anathema to him. The decision to violate the directive had come only after long hours of solitary contemplation on the observation deck, debating with himself what was the higher law to be obeyed—preservation of his civilization or adhering to an edict that had been issued in another time, on another planet they would probably never see again, an edict embodying a viewpoint that no longer made sense. Yet, tradition was ingrained in every fiber of his body, and violating the directive ripped his insides and left a huge flame of guilt. There was no need to go further than necessary, however. "You *are* complying with the Council's directive to create a molecular substitute, aren't you? Father believes it can be done."

"Right. You know we don't have the raw materials." Ki said, undeterred that Lil had so quickly slid back. He offered a beverage from his replicator, hoping over time to break down those mental walls. After Lil nodded his head, Ki willed the replicator to produce two drinks with a rosy color, a molecular synthetic of Alterran juice accented by herbs to calm the mind, and handed one to Lil. "I understand that you've been commanded to appear at Council tomorrow morning. I'll be there to support you."

Taking the drink, Lil stood, shaking his head. "Thanks. I think they know only that I detached from the Net." Ki's presence would exacerbate the delicate situation since the Council members frequently doubted his respect for their tradition and philosophy. Growing uncomfortable, he excused himself. "I'll go over the examination results with you when you're ready. I'd like to catch up with my men." Lil walked away, feeling the unpleasant taint of conspiracy with a half brother that he barely knew, sometimes admiring his accomplishments, yet painfully aware of their rivalry for the Alterran leadership. Jahkbar, his lifelong tutor, had counseled him to rely only on his own judgment. Trust was not a luxury that an Alterran leader could afford.

Ki nodded, smirking behind Lil's departing back. "No problem." He was smugly pleased that his star was rising over Lil's since their survival now depended upon his unique skills. It amused him that a civilization based on the elitist philosophy of the Great Awakening couldn't survive without the scientific advancements of that ancient individualism that they hated, but which Ki now subtly infused into their systems to preserve their lives. The Great Awakening disdained money and competition, preferring to assign each individual an occupation even if redundant, providing equal but low-level sustenance in return. Although incremental improvements to existing technology were sometimes developed, the Alterran system chose status quo over innovation, disavowing the creative destruction of the ancient capitalist system. Progress and innovation had become hate words, synonymous with waste and chaos.

When Lil entered Guard Hall, a Dalit changed the blaring, pulsating beats chosen by the guardsmen to the soft, melodic music that Lil preferred. As he passed the tables, his men respectfully saluted with the sacred triangle, which he graciously returned. The Guard totaled about two hundred. At any given time, a little less than half would normally be found at Hawan, with the others working around the globe gathering scientific information, supervising mining operations or transports, and conducting whatever special tasks they were given. Some mines had been closed since they'd stockpiled more than enough in case Alterra could reactivate the portal. On a daily basis, they lived as if the reactivation might occur at any time. Of those with duties at Hawan, most provided security or performed surveillance activities. Lil had had to make special arrangements to have his chosen men available for the hunt, and those men now relaxed at Guard Hall. Some were seated at a circular table around a tube system extruding into its center, while others lounged about in casual conversation. A montage of colorful, full-length holographic images of Alterra and the ruling family, including Lil and Ki, appeared on the walls. Lil's men took turns entering small rooms with special holographs capable of recreating their Alterran loved ones.

Lil took a seat with Jared at a table next to Azazel and Rameel, who played a game of *treschet*. A small carved figure on the board danced from one square to another at Azazel's direction. "Checkmate," said Azazel, grinning broadly, his gray eyes sparkling with amusement.

Frustrated, Rameel slapped his hand on his leg. "Three in a row. I'm not playing with you anymore. I beat everyone here other than you."

Lil cleared his throat and raised his eyebrows. "Except for the captain," Rameel added hastily, glancing at Lil uncertainly. "No offense, please, sir. It's not the same. You never lose at anything!"

"If there's any doubt, Rameel," Lil said with an amused smile, "I'll play you later this evening." Lil filled a cup from the center tube, and in an unaccustomed attempt at camaraderie, he held it up and addressed all the guardsmen. "Join me in one of the few pleasures permitted by the Council of Elders!"

The men lifted their glasses. Characteristically, he blamed the Council, rather than his father, for any discomforts.

Rameel stood and said, "I toast Captain En.Lil for his vision, and especially for leading the hunt day. What an extraordinary experience!" The other men enthusiastically joined the thanks.

Lil nodded slightly in acknowledgment, with conflicting emotions about whether the hunt had been ill considered. He added another toast. "I also toast Azazel for those amazing swords and knives. It was as if we were part of the ancient legends of Alterra! And, of course, I toast him for saving Tamiel's life."

"Agreed!" shouted Tamiel, with the men taking another sip.

"And I toast Kamean. May he return to us as a baby!" joked Tamiel.

Although a plate of Earth foods lay on the center table, the men relied primarily on their Alterran food, a nourishment bar extracted from the center delivery tube. On Alterra, the carefully balanced bars had been their sole diet, causing the guardsmen to have nearly identical body types, although occasionally, someone like Azazel grew differently from the rest; his mother had accidentally been administered a larger dosage of reproductive stimulation. As a member of the House of En, Lil consumed a different formulation, and he knew that the difference was more than just flavor. Not wanting his men to see, he selected vegetables and fruit from a plate on the table. Lil felt a pang of guilt in permitting his men to fill part of their food requirements with Earth foods. Being carefully prepared on Alterra from molecular ingredients for proper nutrition and emotional conditioning, the nourishment bars were tolerable, coming in several flavors. Still, when he and his men had discovered the Earth foods, they'd found their taste buds awakened, and they approached their work with a new spirit and energy.

"How much longer will the bars last, Captain?" asked Tamiel, his tongue being loosened with wine.

"The provisions will last for a little while yet," replied Lil with a casual look, not wishing to cause anxiety. "There's enough time for us to learn a new way to survive on this planet. For now, let's enjoy what we have. Yamin, how about some music?"

Yamin had been permitted to become an extraordinary musician. At various times through the long years of different lifetimes, his appearance varying slightly, he had recorded himself playing the same music on different instruments. He had combined the recordings so that he was, in essence, a one-man orchestra. He chose his prize selections and played his holographic concert while the live, young Yamin conducted. When it was over, the guardsmen gave him a standing ovation.

Lil applauded enthusiastically, slapping him on the back. "Yamin, among the many things we owe Alterra is our gift of long life. You've certainly utilized your time well."

"Thank you, sir. To Alterra, may we see it again," he toasted.

"To Alterra," replied Lil, hiding his painful fear that he might never see it again.

Not everyone used the long Alterran life as productively as Yamin. Their occupations were assigned at birth by the House of En through, it was said, determination of the baby's divine destiny. However, some individuals found, after rejuvenation, that their divine destiny was reinterpreted. Had the universe changed? The population was too complacent to question why the House of En issued a destiny certificate with a new occupation. Many guardsmen had had a career at home, but had volunteered to be stationed on Earth during one of the rare occasions when choice was permitted, seeking adventure in an alien world. A few, such as Jared, were assigned to Earth because of their skills; Jared had been an architect. He'd had no explanation, but he had long felt that his work on Alterra was pointless, since there were too many architects and the plans they worked on daily were never implemented. Other guardsmen, such as Azazel, had been so suited to being a guardsman that the Alterrans had reassigned him to the Guard in each successive life; his forebears had taught him unique martial skills.

"Excuse me, sir," said Jared as, trailed by Erjat and Mika, he came to Lil. "These two men request permission to speak."

Lil, feeling relaxed, nodded. "Permission granted."

Erjat poked Mika, amazed. "My name is Erjat, sir, and this here is Mika. We were on the hunt today."

"Yes, I certainly know that," said Li evenly, masking his amusement.

"Of course, you do, sir," said Mika, poking Erjat.

"What we mean to say, sir," said Erjat nervously, "is that it was something that we both enjoyed, more than anything. If you do it again, well, we want to, if you don't mind, sir, volunteer."

"And thank you for today!" interjected Mika, stiffening his back to make a formal salute.

"You're welcome, Erjat and Mika," Lil said pleasantly. "I'll keep that in mind."

As they left, Lil heard Mika say, "I'd told you he would. He's not like the others."

Had it been a mistake to come here? Improving camaraderie with his guardsmen was a benefit of being stationed on Earth, even though he felt constrained to maintain a reserved distance. On Alterra, running the world preoccupied his family full-time. His social life had been limited to the extended family members of the House of En to avoid the influence of others. Jahkbar had lectured his pupil throughout his life, *The supreme leader's decisions must be untainted by the opinions and philosophies of others. Prolonged contact with the mass of humanity will inevitably produce subtle shifts in your viewpoint that won't be recognizable to you. Best that you keep to yourself. Meditate to discover the true path. Much depends on you.* A leader couldn't be completely isolated, and he'd spent stints in military service and other leadership positions. But friendship outside the House of En was unknown to him. With few family members at Hawan, Anu had relaxed the traditions, knowing it would be lonely for Lil, who had no wife. To preserve the House of En's strategic options, no marriage would be arranged for him until his ascension many ages in the future at the time of Cancer. Until then, he could take concubines, although even those were carefully screened. That evening, Lil called upon his holographic concubine, Nersis, known for her skill at interpreting sacred hexagrams. Lil went to a private room, where her image appeared.

"Nersis, you're looking lovely as ever," he greeted her with a warm smile, with the ease of knowing that holograms told no secrets and made no judgments.

"Lil, my love!! I've missed you *so, so* much!" she gushed, with the animation and sexual inventiveness that Ki had programmed as a joke. He said it would counteract the tempered emotions bred into Alterran women. After she flung her arms around his neck, Lil nuzzled his nose in her hair and then gave her a lingering kiss, while he ran his hands up her transparent dress. After his difficult day, he was relieved that holograms were always willing, without being emotionally demanding, even though they were solid and anatomically complete.

* * *

After having sex, Lil poured a glass of wine. "Nersis, my pet, give me a reading." Sex hadn't been the diversion from his worries for which he'd hoped. In forging his own path to save his colonists, he yearned for the comfort of grounding his actions in established Alterran tradition, drawing upon the sacred geometry that infused his family's religious views.

"Of course, I always have one ready for you, my precious." Nersis produced a canister containing sixty-four yarrow stalks and carelessly tossed them into a seemingly random pattern. Through the spiritual procedure of dividing and selecting stalks, they formed a complete hexagram that foretold his fate. Sixty-four was the base number of their mathematics in harmony with the foundation of the natural world. She studied the results carefully before saying, "You have Hexagram fifty-five, no transforming lines. Your situation is abounding, full and exuberant, with hidden renewal. You have been in a powerful emotional field, but you must not grieve that this cycle is ending and a new path is beginning. You must be like the sun as it reaches its zenith, shedding its brightest rays as it begins to set. You must convert any inner sadness you feel in this transformation into positive radiance. Let it permeate your new path."

Nersis circled behind Lil and rubbed his temples and shoulders. She said softly, "My love, your new path is of great and noble purpose and will culminate in good things for you and your people. But the burden troubles you. Now you must sit back, close your eyes, and imagine the new path. As leader, your focus must be on fulfilling your destiny so that you may provide wise direction."

"Thank you, Nersis," said Lil, leaning back with his eyes closed. "Do you believe it?"

"Believe what?" She frowned with confusion, searching the internal net for some clue for the proper response.

"That there's a wave of time, pulsating and cycling through the universe, creating and recreating conditions for the same events, just as it creates the same pattern within patterns in an ocean wave or the leaves of a tree? I feel trapped in a vortex. Can I take comfort that this is a choiceless destiny, not really my fault? However does one know?" Bewildered whether he truly sought a scientific answer, she'd been programmed for empathy, and she remained silent, rubbing his shoulders and then moving her fingers to his temples. After a while, he gently took her hand and sighed, "I'm tired, it's been a long day. I think I'll go back to my suite."

Nersis began gathering up the stalks. "My love, we're at the end of an Alterran timewave. The cycles of change are compressing and becoming ever shorter and more intense. The normal hexagram reading could be completely disrupted during this time. I'm sure that everything will turn out fine for you—after all, you're a named successor! The scribes will read the star messages to guide you wisely." Sensing that he'd turn off her program, she quickly added, "Please don't forget me! I can only come to life for you!!"

Lil gave her one last kiss and murmured, "Off." Sitting alone, hearing the muffled conversation of his men in the antechamber, it comforted him to know that his true destiny lay in the path he had set for himself.

CHAPTER 3
ALANA

The mastodon carcass lay in the village center beside the large cooking hearth, which was bordered by stones and contained a large stone pot for boiling water. Nearly fifty huts were scattered throughout the gently rolling hills surrounding the hearth, varying by whatever material had been accessible at the time, even tree branches and small rocks. Small pools trapped from the bay to their north provided bathing water and easy fishing. Drinking water came from a spring around which the villagers kept tree limbs to fend off animals. Over a small hill was an area reserved for disposing of their waste, emptied from vessels made of tightly woven reeds kept in their huts. Wild goats and sheep strayed throughout the area, having become used to receiving tidbits from the villagers.

Giggling over their good fortune, Alana and Maya examined the carcass and prepared to preserve the body parts and dry the meat, using salt and other herbs that they'd gathered. It being a pleasant sunny day, warm for autumn, they disrobed and slid into worn, stained hides to perform their work.

"Who do you think they were?" Maya asked. She was six years younger than Alana. Only last spring, she had had her first blood. The Elder Women, led by Yanni, had taken her outside the village, then encircled her around a young apple tree, in a grove populated with many gnarly older trees that she'd climbed to pick many apples during her childhood. Yanni instructed her to spread her first blood at the tree's base, and Grandmother Marita chanted the words to make the tree produce fruit, like Maya the babies that Maya could then give birth. Alana, substituting for Maya's long-dead mother, had held back Maya's hair as she made her offering to Mother Earth, digging into the dirt with a sturdy caribou bone. Recognized as a grown woman, Maya then joined the Elder Women, singing songs to thank the Mother for giving her the precious gift of creating life. Now, with Maya old enough to choose a mate, the Elder Women scolded her for scorning the Mother's gift. At this year's Summer Meeting, she'd refused because she couldn't bear to leave Alana. Her decision had angered Jonk, her close childhood friend, who was now a developing teenager and promising hunter; he'd played her protector in countless hunting games when they were too small to accompany the hunters. Dark-haired Jonk, thoughtful and pleasant, but unwilling to adopt Ewan's grooming instruction, had always assumed that Maya would be his mate. Despite her refusal at the Summer Meeting, Maya's favorite topic had become finding ideal mates from the same village for her and Alana.

Alana shook her head. "I've no idea." She tried to look uninterested, but a stranger who wasn't threatening was always a welcome distraction. As a stranger herself who'd been welcomed into this village long ago, she felt an obligation to help others.

Playfully shoving Alana, Maya said, "Maybe you shouldn't have told them never to hunt here again. They seemed nice, much better looking than the men around here."

"Even Jonk?" Maya frowned at her. Playfully tossing a bit of fur at her, Alana said with a knowing grin, "Oh, I don't think we've seen the last of them."

Maya giggled and twisted a ringlet around her finger. "Who knows? In that invisible flying ship, they could be looking down on us right now." Maya spun around, swinging long black curls, her curious face searching the sky. Suddenly, she shivered and stood still, grasping at the pouch around her neck, feeling her fox totem for protection. "You know, that's spooky."

"I don't think they're here; there's no wind that doesn't move the trees," Alana reasoned while pulling a wooden drying rack into place near the carcass, where it would have direct sunlight. "I'm glad it's a warm day, or we'd have to smoke this meat to preserve it."

After putting a moistened finger in the air to check again for the absence of wind, Maya continued her dance, unable to contain her joyous energy. "It was fun to look down on the land, don't you think? We now know what birds see." Maya stretched out her arms and twirled around the hearth like a bird.

"Yes, silly, but it's our secret. No one would believe us anyway. Either they would think that we're lying or they'd be frightened," cautioned Alana while she examined the hide, determining where to place her cuts. Large cuttings of hide were useful as roofs, and Nosti, who protected her when she was in a trance, needed a new one. Maliki and Yanni needed an entrance flap for their new, larger hut, which housed their growing family.

"Or that we've had too many mushrooms?" Maya giggled. Although Alana had let her have only a little taste of her potions, Maya's senses had been heightened; when she'd seen the fox sneaking out of the woods, she thought it had spoken to her. Maliki killed it before she could reach out to it, but he had given her its paw as her protective totem. *A fox is wily and smart, just like you, pretty little Maya*, Maliki had told her.

"That's right. So stick to our story and don't speak about those men or their weapons, even to each other. And, *especially* don't speak about flying. Someone might overhear us." Alana gathered stone bowls made by villagers, as well as a few clay ones for which they'd traded furs at the Summer Meeting of the Albion clans. She picked up reeds and swatted at the flies hovering near the incision. "Help me, Maya. The flies are here already."

"You're probably right; you're always the practical one," said Maya, pouting. Turning away, she muttered, "It's a shame, though, I'd *love* to do that again." Giving in to the mundane, she began gathering wood from the nearby pile and stacked it in the center of the hearth for a fire.

Looking above her and shading her eyes from the sun, Alana said, "It's already midafternoon; we're going to need to work fast. I hope the hunters come back soon to help us." A flock of birds flew noisily overhead, heading south. "It'll be winter soon. We need to save every scrap of this animal." The sky was clear, and Alana gave thanks for the good conditions for preserving the meat.

They picked up a large, two-handled clay pot and headed to the spring to draw water. "Our people are going to be *so* surprised," gushed Maya. "And happy. Maybe Maliki will let me keep a tooth this time!" But she frowned. "They might not believe a Hunting Ceremony could bring a dead mastodon, though." They moved a branch and crouched to scoop up fresh water, stopping to take a drink.

Carrying the pot back, water sloshing out the top, Alana cautioned, "Just stick to our story, Maya, that's all we can do." She didn't think they'd believe it either, but she hoped they'd be too happy to care. "We promised the strangers that we wouldn't tell. They don't want us looking for them. I suppose that means that they must be camped somewhere nearby."

"But if our people come back empty-handed, couldn't we tell them we saw reindeer herds by the lake?" Maya tried to envision the conversation, and then shook her head. "I don't know how to tell them."

"Oh, we'll think of something," said Alana, waving her hand. "Maybe I can do a Seeing Ceremony." At the last Summer Meeting, she'd passed Zedah's difficult initiation test known as the Black Night of the Soul, where she'd confronted her painful memories of the destruction of Atlantis and loss of her mother. She was stronger now, free of the guilt and heartache that had tugged at her young heart. In a candlelit ceremony, Zedah had fastened around her forehead the cherished headband of an Earthkeeper, although her headband was exceptional. Whereas the others' bands were made of rawhide strips painted with animal figures, Alana's was made of silver with beautifully carved Atlantean symbols, from which dangled tiny silver trinkets. It had been a gift from Priestess Petrina upon her acceptance as a temple acolyte. Little Alana had loved her precious headband so much that she'd sewn hidden pockets in her clothing to carry it close even when she wasn't fulfilling her duties at the temple. Since she'd had it with her the day that Atlantis sank, she believed with her whole heart that its magic had saved them that day. At the initiation ceremony, Zedah also had given her the ingredients for healing potions and had told her that even the most powerful potions wouldn't work without her inborn talent from the Mother. In taking the potions during the practice rituals, she'd rediscovered a talent for traveling outside her body. It was a talent possessed in this land only by Zedah, although as a young girl she'd known that Priestess Petrina had had the mysterious talent. Her burning desire was to be anointed to serve Zedah and eventually become the land's head Earthkeeper. At the next Summer Meeting, as she completed her initiation, she hoped to take the next step in her journey by winning the breastplate honoring the Mother.

Maya emptied the pot's contents into a huge stone kettle whose sides had been painstakingly whittled until they were smooth and narrow, and which sat on a flat-topped stone within the hearth, and tied back her long hair. Using a flint piece taken from the small pouch around her neck, she lit on fire the wood and mastodon dung below the kettle. Alana examined the rock knives that her father, Ewan, and the village's chief hunter, Maliki, had spent long hours carving and sharpening. Before today, she had thought them to be cleverly made, the best of her land. Now, they seemed crude. But they were all she had and she would make do. Before cutting, they extended their arms, thanking the brave animal for giving up its spirit so that the people could live. They breathed deeply with closed eyes so that their fingertips would absorb whatever might linger of the animal's spirit. It was a short ceremony, but under the circumstances it would have to do.

The young women carefully pulled back the hide and sliced into the meat, cutting thin slices that they salted and hung on the wooden drying racks. As she cut into one of the massive legs, Maya asked slyly, "Alana, can I ask you something?"

"Of course," she laughed. "As if it would matter if I said no."

"Well, this is personal," said Maya, her voice low, avoiding Alana's eyes.

"Oh, it's that subject." Alana lost her smile.

"Alana, I care about you! You've been my mother *and* my sister my whole life." Alana had taken Maya under her wing ever since her mother, Gwi, had died giving birth to Maya's stillborn twin sister. Feeling so helpless at her death, Alana had renewed her vow to learn healing powers. "We've heard that Drood wants you to take his son as your mate. But," she paused and looked askance at Alana, nervously flicking her knife, "you wouldn't do that, *would* you?"

Alana slammed down her knife and stamped her foot. "You know that I'm to be an Earthkeeper. And Ewan would *never* make me go with that nasty, smelly, painted…ugh!" She made a face and shuddered. "His breath would stop a saber tooth clear across a canyon!"

Maya giggled. "His hair is so stiff that you could break rocks with it!"

Alana giggled too, but she'd sobbed over the years about a mate, tears of sorrow that she hadn't met an acceptable man, even though she'd received many offers at the annual Summer Meetings. But their hair was matted, and they smelled worse than mastodon; she grew nauseated at the thought that such men wanted to touch her. After she'd decided to become the

Earthkeeper, she no longer cared. Donning the white robe and distancing herself from daily tribal affairs suited her just fine. In a way, she'd always known that was her destiny. On Atlantis, sensing her unawakened talent, Priestess Petrina had permitted her, though only a lowly daughter of her personal attendant, to partake as an acolyte with the nobly born, and she would gladly have joined the ranks of the Daughters of Poseidon when the time came. Little golden-haired Alana had sat entranced at Petrina's jeweled-adorned feet, admiring her exquisite poise and dignity, as well as her ability to control others with a mere glance. In confronting the strangers, Alana had imagined herself as Petrina.

Stripping hide employing long, agitated strokes, Maya tensely pursed her lips. She'd rather be beaten with stones than offend Alana. Maya closed her eyes a moment, thinking, *Alana must be told.* Clearing her throat, she timidly said, "Some—not me, of course—say it's the only way to save ourselves. Drood's power is growing. Some think he's becoming more powerful than Shaman Yoachim."

Alana spun around in anger, her eyes brimming with tears. It stung that the old women criticized her for being proud. And now this. After loving her for all these years, these kind and gentle people would throw her at a vicious savage to save themselves? Her chest heaved with anger. No! "So, I'm to be sacrificed? If they're so afraid of Drood, let them band together and fight! Or we can move far away from Drood—maybe closer to the reindeer herd by the lakes."

Maya hid behind the carcass to avoid Alana's angry eyes. "That may not be far enough to be safe. Some say Drood has magical powers, and that it would be a privilege to mate with his son, especially with your talent."

Alana threw up her arms in exasperation, and she came around to Maya's side of the carcass and put a hand on her shoulder. "Maya, 'some' say? Drood's people have strange beliefs, not like ours. They're cruel. They even eat people! They absorb the power of the strong to make themselves stronger, or wiser, whatever they want to possess from their victim. Whatever talent Drood has, it's not like an Earthkeeper—our powers are gifts from the Mother. Drood's power comes from somewhere else; it's dark and destructive."

Maya, too upset to look at Alana, focused on her hide stripping. Alana shook her head in disbelief, dried her eyes, and told herself not to worry; Ewan would never make her marry that wilder. She glanced at the sky and frowned that the sun was nearing the horizon with so much work left to do. From a reed basket nearby, she picked up a bladder from a prior mastodon kill and pulled fat from the carcass, letting it slide into the pouch. Ewan used the fat to make soap and to light his lamp.

"I don't think that's true," said Maya, her eyebrows drawn together skeptically. "Is it?" She stretched a strip of hide on the rack and shooed away flies. Noticing a buzzard flying overhead, she hoped that she wouldn't have to fight away *that* nasty bird.

"For ceremonies, as if that matters," snapped Alana with disgust. She picked up a stone and threw it at a raven staring hungrily at the carcass from a low-lying branch not far away. Why wouldn't people listen to her warnings about Drood? They made that twisted little man sound as if he were a trusted elder. Last year, she and her father had once encountered Drood in the forest where she gathered her medicinal mushrooms. He had made himself appear immense, leering down at her, and when she blinked he was somewhere else, and then somewhere else again, all the while making that inhuman cackling laughter that gave her chills. She'd thought that her eyes were playing tricks on her, but her father had told her that Drood used the secrets of dark magic. Only the Mother's magic could defeat him—he'd told her to twirl her silver headband in the air above them. Sure enough, he shrieked and was gone. With that memory still haunting her, she picked up her knife and hacked at the hide in anger, a warm tear escaping her brimming eyes. "I'm sorry, I just can't do it. The people will have to find some other protection from Drood."

"Good," said Maya, peeking at her with loving concern, regretting how much she'd upset her. "I don't want you to leave. I'd miss you too much." She gave Alana a big grin, hoping she'd forgive her raising the subject. Maya tossed aside her knife, ran to Alana, and put her arms around her. "I love you, Alana. I'd *never* want to see you hurt."

Alana sniffled and hugged her, stroking her long, curly, dark hair. "I know, sweetie, I know."

"We'll always be together, won't we, Alana?"

"Always," she said softly. After a moment, she straightened and added, "But only if we don't starve to death first. Let's keep working. We need to save as much of this animal as we possibly can." Maya nodded, wiping her eyes. After working for about an hour, Alana poked into the rib cage, where she stood without bending, examining the massive lungs and heart. After placing pots and tightly wound baskets lined with bladder underneath, she cut muscle, and working together, they tugged out the organs, which thumped into the vessels. "Look here." Picking up a broken rib bone, she poked at the lungs. "I'm glad he gave us this one. I think she's healthy."

"I know," said Maya, holding her long hair back to look down into the bowl. "That poor baby was spitting blood. I hope they know what they're doing with it."

"As smart as they are, they must know." Alana shrugged, and focused on extracting the bladder and stomach, which she set aside to purify for holding liquids. Sinew would be used for thread or tied together for rope. Small bones would be carved into needles for sewing or used for jewelry, and the largest bones would become digging tools or used to reinforce the walls of their huts. The hide would be dried and softened to be wrapped around huts as warm, protective insulation or used in strips for litters. Little by little, every part of the animal would be put to good use. Maya prepared the cooking pit so that the hunters would have a good meal upon their return.

Rayna, her wispy gray hair uncombed, hobbled out with the aid of an antelope bone and screamed at them from her deeply wrinkled face, "Evil spirits! This animal is from evil spirits! Evil spirits! I saw you, you came from the sky!"

"Rayna, calm down. Where did you get such an idea?" asked an astonished Alana, for the first time realizing she and Maya were not alone. Her eyes quickly searched the village for others. "We thought everyone was out hunting. This animal is a gift from the gods. You've known me a long time, and you know I'm not evil."

"Since when do you walk in the sky?" she demanded, her eyes scrunched up and her bony arm pointing her bone walking stick where they had appeared from the cloaked hovercraft.

Alana chuckled with a big smile, and dismissively waved her hand. "Rayna, your eyesight is not so good. I certainly can't fly." At least if someone had to see them, it was nearly blind Rayna, who frequently saw spirits that no one else did.

"Rayna, how could you say such a thing?" Maya pouted, her pretty face looking as hurt as she could make it. "We're getting ready to make dinner. Why don't you help us?"

Putting her hand on the remnants of the carcass, Alana explained, "Maya and I performed the Hunting Ceremony. What you saw were the gods answering our prayers, certainly not us."

Rayna thrust out her wrinkled chin and narrowed her dark eyes. "I'll check the traps. But you don't fool me! I'm going to tell the others what I saw," she said, hobbling away, calling after her, "You must be learning from Drood."

Maya whispered, "Better she think that than know the truth. I'd better set out the things for the Hunting Ceremony," and she left and brought back the carved wooden statues of animals and Mother Earth that they used. They filled the cooking pot with meat, water, and wild carrots for that evening's stew, and continued placing other strips of salted meat on racks to dry. Rayna returned with three rabbits that she deftly skinned and prepared for roasting. They'd barely completed half the carcass when the men and older boys drifted in, quiet because of their failure to find the herd, trailed by the women and young girls dragging small, tired children by the hand. A few men carried sleeping children or empty reed baskets with rope handles that had been intended for bringing back the kill. Smelling the cooking meat, the hungry hunters looked into the big pot suspiciously but salivated at the delicious smell. To test if the carcass was real, Maliki poked his spear into its rump. When he removed it, he tasted the clinging tissue with a puzzled look. He next picked up a bone lying on the ground and tapped it to assure himself that it wasn't an apparition. "Alana, how?"

Stirring the contents of the pot with an antelope bone to avoid his eyes, Alana answered as if he'd asked her if the sky is blue. "Maya and I performed the Hunting Ceremony, and Mother Earth heard our prayers."

Pointing out all the ceremonial ornaments, Maya added with a flourish, "We prayed *very* hard, and the Great Mother blessed us."

"We'll eat well tonight and have new hides for winter," Alana said, a little too eagerly in Ewan's view. Glancing at him, she saw him staring at her, and she averted her eyes, uncomfortably calling to Rayna to add more salt.

To Alana's relief, Yanni gave her infant to her older daughter and said, "Let us help you, dear." Assuming control, she motioned with a sharp stare and a wave of the arm to those gawking at the carcass to get to work. Yanni's stare never left room for argument. Vesta, a pretty pubescent girl with large dark eyes, hugged Maya for the meal and then brought her basket and began sorting through scraps, particularly any useful for decorating clothing or hair. Others picked up knives and began trimming the remaining meat off the bones. Maya's Grandmother Marita assumed control over the cooking pot. With the evening sun too dim for drying the meat, the women began smoking the last bits. The men disassembled the skeleton and divided up the bones. Alana supervised the work, trying to avoid Ewan, who stood staring in disbelief. Although he encouraged religious ceremonies for the people's comfort, he didn't believe in unseen spirits gifting them with a mastodon.

"Alana, I want to see you in our hut immediately," he said, brusquely striding away through the evening shadows.

As she followed him, Alana overheard a high-pitched older woman's voice say, "Rayna said Drood's followers helped them. It must be a betrothal gift!" Feeling relief, yet revulsion, Alana was glad to distance herself, even though she dreaded Ewan's questions. With darkness approaching, she lit a torch to guide her along the narrow path toward the hut she shared with Ewan. Thanks to her father's skills, their hut was the largest and best made, being situated in a hillock overlooking one of the small springs that laced the area. Ewan had excavated one side of the hillock, and then stacked the walls with flat stones from the riverbed, which he'd gathered during the hot, dry summer months when the river became a mere trickle. He'd even dug a small alcove in which he'd collected soft feathers for their beds, and he'd dug into the earth, below the stones he'd set down as a floor, to provide a small hold for storing roots, nuts, and vegetables. Overhead he had erected poles, which he covered with mastodon hide but which could be drawn back in pleasant weather.

Ducks noisily flew away as she approached, and a nomadic goat greeted her, expecting a scrap of food. Taking a deep breath, she pulled back the hide flap and entered, forcing her voice into an everyday tone. "Father, you wanted to see me? Are you injured?" Her torch unevenly lit up the inside, revealing Ewan sitting on a mat, where he had lit a small oil lamp. He sat with his arms crossed, his face as scolding as when she'd run away with Maya and Jonk to spy on the Droods. He'd always see her as a child, she thought, not for the first time. After momentarily studying her, looking for clues, he said sternly, "Alana, sit down and tell me the truth of what happened today."

Settling herself, Alana wondered how she'd honor her promise to the stranger, a stranger whom she'd probably never see again.

Impatient with her hesitation, he demanded, "You can't expect me to believe that wild story, although I can't conceive how you got that animal here. I deserve the truth."

Her father wasn't a primitive, but an educated survivor of Atlantis. He'd been fishing with Alana the day the volcanoes erupted. Barely surviving when their boat reached the coast of this peninsula, they'd walked inland in a daze. The kindly people of this village had let them stay and nursed them. Although Ewan had lost his possessions, he'd been able to pass along to his daughter knowledge of medicinal herbs, and he'd taught the tribe sanitation and grooming practices, bringing a bit of civilization to those willing to accept it.

He'd also taught her the virtues of honesty and integrity. Distressed about breaking a promise, she pleaded, "Father, don't tell anyone else. I made a promise."

"I'll make that judgment," he retorted, staring at her with his piercing gray eyes. Even now, despite her status as medicine woman and acolyte, she squirmed and felt queasy from his disapproval.

Alana's resolve melted, as it always did, at the thought that Ewan was disappointed in her. The two of them, alone among these people so different from them, had forged a bond far stronger than a father-daughter relationship. As best she could, Alana recounted her magical day. Hearing her description of the men, Ewan felt the bag he carried around his neck with his last memento of Atlantis, his golden coins. Filled with hope, he whispered, "Could they be from Atlantis?" No one else could have metal weapons; he was sure that Alana exaggerated the so-called magic.

"They're tall like us, but paler, and their hair is nearly white," she concluded, slumping her shoulders and hanging her head with guilt at not keeping her promise.

"Did they do anything at all to frighten you?"

"No, nothing," she admitted. "The leader treated us like small children. He didn't want to help us, but I persisted."

"Yes, I know how that it is." Lost in thought, Ewan stroked his neatly trimmed gray beard. "I guess there's nothing we can do, but I don't want you going back there unless I'm with you."

"I'll need to go soon," said Alana. "I lost most of the medicinal plants we need." Taking his hand and gently pulling him to his feet, she said lightly, "Come on, let's go. I'm hungry, and it smells delicious." Ewan, lost in his imaginings that a band of Atlanteans was passing through, stood and embraced her. Returning to the hearth, they found that the villagers had had no problem accepting Alana's explanation; they happily consumed their meal and disposed of the remaining tidbits of the carcass.

Grabbing her arm, Maya gushed, "Alana, Koko's just arrived!"

"Koko? Where is he?" Alana cried. Like all women throughout the land, she was enthralled by the old, wizened storyteller, who was richly dressed and adorned with mementos from his vast travels—teeth, feathers, bones, and shells, to name a few. When she found him, Koko sat surrounded by women. Seeing her, Koko smiled and greeted her, "Alana, my favorite. It's good to see you."

She pranced about behind the others, waving to him, and gleefully called out, "We've missed you, Koko."

"I've missed you, too," he said, grinning and throwing her a kiss. "I have a wonderful new story to tell this evening." He turned back to the other women, putting his arms around those nearest to him.

That evening, gathered around the hearth for their celebration, the villagers drank fermented berries. Maya, Vesta, and their friends danced to Yanni and Tomin's melodies played on flutes carved from bird bones and mastodon tusks. Older women sat together talking and laughing with Koko, who wore a soft, woven flax shirt, pale yellow in color, that he boasted came from a city far to the south, across the middle sea. Fondling Tia's ample breast, full with milk for her newborn, he laughed and kissed her cheek. Although most women were mated at a young age, husbands routinely indulged wives who flirted and fussed over him. He was offered food and drink, as well as gifts of knives, pottery, and needles as an incentive for return visits. As the moon rose higher in the heavens, they settled in to hear evening stories. Extra firewood was added.

Families sat together, with mothers cuddling young children on their laps.

Maliki rose and stood on a flat-topped rock near the fire. He thanked Alana for obtaining the gods' favor granting them the mastodon.

"It's the gods who must be thanked," protested Alana. She hushed them and knelt, placing her forehead on the ground and her arms outstretched. "Great Mother Earth, thank you for sending us this food. We are grateful to you for watching over us." When she arose, the villagers' chatter resumed.

Maliki was short, but his powerful legs enabled him to run faster than any other hunter. Born in Albion, he resembled the other tribesmen, but being tutored by Ewan, he bathed regularly and his clean, black hair and beard had been trimmed. He wore a necklace proudly displaying teeth of the many mastodons and saber tooths that he'd killed. "As you know," he began, "our hunters couldn't locate the herd. Alana tells that the mastodon we're feasting on was a gift from the gods. I'm not proud. I accept the gift!" He raised his arms the heavens. Many laughed and agreed with him. "I'll tell you about the last hunt, in which we killed five mastodon—"

"There were only two!" a villager interrupted. "The number grows with each telling!"

Maliki, looking hurt as the laughter died down, continued. "As I said, we killed five mastodons," putting up his fingers to emphasize five, as Ewan had taught their people. Acting out the hunt, he recounted, "We paddled downstream through the night to reach the watering hole. In the morning, we found the herd. They were immense. We were only men with spears and knives. How could we bring down such huge animals?"

"Yes, Maliki, tell us how you did it," a male voice called out.

"We had a plan," he said, pointing a finger to the side of his head. "We had a good plan." He crouched as if hiding.

"Who created the plan, Maliki? Was it Ewan?" Everyone laughed.

Maliki straightened his spine and feigned astonishment. "My good friend Ewan was, of course, part of our fine group of hunters!" Returning to his story stance, he told, "We waited for a female and her calf to stand out from the herd. We hunters surrounded them and threw rocks and jabbed at them with our spears, drawing blood. We made them angry, so angry that they chased us. We ran as fast as the wind. Before a steep hill, we grabbed a tree branch, but the animals couldn't stop. They fell, hitting their heads on the rocks and breaking their legs. We put our spears into their eyes." He put his arms up in victory to the cheering audience, as he stepped from the speaking stone.

Ewan cupped his hands around his mouth and called out, "Koko, *please*, everyone is eager for your latest story."

Koko stood, tearing himself away from the arms of several women, and strutted to the speaking stone. He passed Maliki, overhearing him ask Ewan, "I know we don't have time for an Atlantis story tonight, but I was telling my son about the gold coins you have. Could you show him?"

Ewan shook his head no. "Not tonight. Bring him to my hut, and I'll be happy to show him."

"I'll do that," said Maliki, sitting down beside his well-groomed mate, Yanni, who held their youngest baby and sat beside their oldest son, Tomin. "You're not playing tonight, my love?"

"No, I'd prefer Koko's drums over my flute tonight. I'm tired."

Vesta gently pinched her and smiled. "But Yanni, your playing is so beautiful! And Tomin's too." Yanni smiled and shrugged her shoulders, rocking her baby.

Standing on the speaking stone, Koko smiled and bowed ceremoniously. Gazing at the audience, he began, "In case you don't know me, my name is Koko." When the laughter subsided, he continued, "My friend and I travel this country far and wide, and have seen many villages. And we kiss many women!" he added slyly, chuckling. "We've just heard a story about hunting a great, hairy beast. What is left for me to tell?

Should I tell of battles? A tale of love? Or a story of adventure?" He paused, holding his hand to his ear.

"I think adventure has it. But first," he pointed, "I have news. The people of the south mainland have built new, larger boats. They plan to sail to your southern coast with things to trade at the Summer Meeting. If you have extra skins and hides, take them with you. They have many sharp knives. You may well need the new knives because," he paused dramatically, "the Dane ships have been seen again."

Gasping filled the air, and a female voice exclaimed with anguish, "Not again."

"Yes, unfortunately," he said, frowning, briefly casting his eyes to the ground. "Their boats were seen off the coast. The people there blew conches and gathered in great numbers on shore, shouting and threatening with their weapons. The Danes decided not to fight. Those bastards prefer to sneak up on you! But rest assured, they may be gone, but they'll be back! Everyone should be prepared."

"Don't worry," Ewan assured them with a smile and a short wave of his hand. "They won't travel this far inland!"

"You can certainly hope. Now, back to the adventure." Koko strutted gallantly across the hearth while his assistant tapped a drum. "This is a story of a rich people with plentiful food, who were ruled by a wise king, named Cletus. Every-thing was perfect except for one thing. The good king had a nasty younger brother, Pronius. The king paid him a large sum of gold to leave his kingdom. He took the payment and left, escorted by loyal warriors. Traveling to the maritime cit-ies, they drank, gambled away all the gold, caused trouble, and were thrown out. As outcasts, they wandered, foraging for food and robbing travelers. One day, while Pronius watered his horse in a forest spring, he chanced upon an old man sit-ting outside a cave, cursing and throwing rocks. When asked why he made such noise, the old man replied that his gold was in the cave, but a wicked beast now dwelled there. If Pro-nius would slay it, he'd gladly share his fortune. Pronius had never met a foe he couldn't defeat. Not wanting to share, he told his men to ride ahead.

"Carrying a torch but holding his sword ready to strike," said Koko, demonstrating the stance, "he entered the cave. Much to his surprise, he walked far without encountering the beast, going deeply. The cave floor led downward, and a glimmer of light from above illuminated a large cavern. Neither hearing nor seeing a beast, he descended. Reaching the cavern floor, he found golden vases and chests strewn about. He couldn't believe his good luck. Maybe the beast was gone. He cried out in joy, removed his helmet, put down his sword, and filled chests with golden coins. But his cry roused the beast! It roared from the shadows. Glowing red eyes peered at him. When the beast came into the light, Pronius saw standing a giant clawed lizard, with huge teeth pointed like daggers. Terrifying! With another roar, it pounced between Pronius and his sword, blocking his way out. Desperately searching for a hiding place, a swordless Pronius ran deeper into the shadows. In the dark, he felt around for something to use as a weapon and felt debris. Picking something up, he felt the smooth surface and felt its outline and length. Human bones! He'd been tricked! The beast roared, blocking the way. Fumbling through the bones, searching for strong ones to use as a club, he discovered a sword. Lying low, he crept along the shadowed wall and threw a bone across the room. It clattered and echoed. As he hoped, the beast lunged at the noise, opening the stairs.

"Pronius ran quickly. He might have reached the stairs if he hadn't slowed to grasp the gold-filled chest. The beast pounced. Pronius swerved. The beast gashed his shield arm with his fang and chased him as he tried again to hide. Faintly, he heard his men calling. 'Here I am,' he called, the roar of the beast nearly drowning out his words. Circling the beast and jabbing with his sword, Pronius ducked under its great tail. A spear flew through the air, piercing the beast's eye. Howling in pain, it reared up, knocking Pronius on his back to stomp him. With swords drawn, his men ran to save him. The beast withdrew into the shadows.

"The men lifted Pronius to his feet, not seeing that he'd hidden a golden chest—a small one, this time, since Pronius was serious about escaping. When the beast roared and snorted again, they sprinted with the injured Pronius the length of the cave. At the entrance stood the old man with his back to them. Pronius, furious, held up his sword as if to strike. 'Let me see your face before you die,' he demanded. Slowly turning, Pronius saw his eye had been pierced. Laughing, the old man disappeared in a puff of smoke. Petrified, the men jumped on their horses and galloped fast away. After a time, not being pursued, they rested their poor, exhausted horses. Pronius withdrew behind a tree to open the golden box he'd stolen. Prying it open, he found it to be empty except for a mirror. Angry, he began to throw it, but caught sight of his image in the mirror. A strange feeling came over him, making him ill. He fainted. When he awoke, he lay alone. His men had abandoned him. Steadying himself, he picked up the box to examine it again. He couldn't avoid the mirror. But," Koko paused, "this time, the face in the reflection was," he paused, "the old man from the cave."

The villagers politely gasped. Koko ceremoniously bowed, and the villagers called out their thanks to him. Calling it a night, they began to gather children and drift back to their huts.

Before leaving the hearth, Koko whispered to his assistant, "Without drawing anyone's suspicion, find out whatever you can about those gold coins of Ewan's and Alana's silver headband." He whistled as he walked away, and then muttered when he was alone, "This might have been a *very* profitable trip indeed!"

CHAPTER 4

LIL

Knowing this day would come, Lil had rehearsed his arguments to Hawan's Council of Elders, hoping to persuade them. The coming confrontation left an uneasy feeling in his stomach, since he respected all these close relatives. But there was no way it could be avoided. They didn't have his vision. And it wasn't his fault that they were stranded here.

* * *

After discovering Earth's biosignature long ago and eventually finding that this planet had a breathable atmosphere, the Alterrans had sent small scientific missions, which had grown larger and more well established over time. Alterra was slightly smaller than Earth and farther away from the primary star in its solar system. With the lessened effects of gravity and the dimmer light, Lil's people were taller and slimmer and had larger, more sensitive eyes, than most Earthlings. Both being hominid, they had many physical similarities. When the genetic code was found to be nearly the same, some scientists thought that, in the distant future, the Earth people might create a civilization comparable to Alterra. Some had suggested that they nurture the Earth people. When the Alterran Supreme Council had caught wind of this, the scientists were denounced; sacred knowledge should never be divulged to unworthy primitives.

Lil, in training as the second named successor, had been captivated by the Council's deliberations many years ago. The twelve members, adorned in their traditional shimmering silver robes, were seated at a round table in their white, marble-walled chambers. The supreme leader, Lil's grandfather Ama, stood before the Council wearing the sacred triangle around the crown of his brown-haired head. He addressed them in his baritone voice: "Honored members of the Supreme Council, it has come to my attention that the scientists staffing our Earth outposts, most notably, I'm sorry to say, En.Ki, have proposed that we nurture the early stage hominids. Even a proposal to make genetic enhancements has been made." He paused, waiting for the inevitable reaction. He was not disappointed.

Jumping up, a Council member, Lil's great uncle, shouted, "No! Our civilization is sacred. How dare anyone think of giving our divine gift to these primitives?"

"In my term, we firmly rejected the notion of transforming other planets. We decided never to interfere with the divine order of the universe!" protested his great-grandfather, a former supreme leader.

"They are out of control. We should end the Earth mission and recall our people immediately," advised another Councilman, Lil's uncle.

"Let's discuss this calmly," admonished Councilman Trikon, striding confidently to the center. He was the supreme leader's brother and was known to be his principal ally. "I totally agree with your concerns. Let's remember, however, that there are many useful things to be gained from Earth. I certainly don't want our mining operations there to end because of a few misguided souls. I think we all agree that we need those raw materials since we don't know what will happen with our planet's core growing cooler. It's only prudent to preserve our presence."

"Yes, we need raw materials," protested a Councilwoman, Lil's distant cousin, "but we can't disrupt the universe by turning a blind eye to what our scientists have been doing."

Councilman Trikon replied smoothly, "Of course not, you're absolutely right. Let's keep in mind that these are mere proposals. We have it within our power to firmly put an end to this matter."

"What do you have in mind, Councilman Trikon?" she asked suspiciously.

Grandly outstretching his arm, he proposed, "We can impose discipline by sending a Guard unit to watch over our scientists. This way, we'll continue to get the metals and raw materials we so desperately need, while ensuring obedience to the Code."

Seeking to curtail the debate, the supreme leader quickly intoned, "Since we're of the same mind, you'll approve of a proclamation I've drafted." He quickly read as the words materialized beside him,

Proclamation 299,577-34
Non-Interference Directive

"WHEREAS the Alterran civilization is unique in the universe, and therefore sacred,

WHEREAS having established a colony on Earth for research and mining purposes, the Supreme Council finds it desirable for Alterrans to continue our missions on Earth in a manner that preserves the sacredness of Alterra.

BE IT THEREFORE DECREED that no Alterran may make contact with or reveal him or herself to the hominids of Earth, share knowledge with or instruct them, genetically manipulate them, or in any manner interact with or assist them. The universe has an

unfolding plan for the destiny of Earthlings, which will be revealed at the proper time, and no Alterran may interfere with that plan.

Violation of this law shall subject the perpetrator to the severest of punishment to be determined by the Supreme Leader."

"Well done, Supreme Leader," said the councilwoman with an approving clap. "Although I request a small clarification. We'll continue to study Earth and its inhabitants, will we not? This began as a scientific mission, and the results have been most interesting."

"Yes, of course. Nothing in this proclamation affects our research or mining operations," he answered. "Our ships can easily cloak for invisibility while performing their work. Around the mines and our facilities, we can project illusions that mask our presence."

The supreme leader stiffened as Banallo, his rival from the House of Kan and only one of two non-family members on the Council, rose to speak. "Illustrious Supreme Leader, it is well that you have rightly brought this important matter to the attention of the honorable members of this Council. This is shocking, and I wholeheartedly endorse the Non-Interference Directive. I'm wondering, though, whether you, as Supreme Leader, can ensure compliance with the directive, both its detail and its spirit, from so far a distance. After all, the allegations of genetic tampering with the Earth hominids by your grandchildren Ki and Ninhursag necessitated this action. I would hate to see us forced to abandon these valuable mines as the only way to avoid offending the Universal Consciousness. So, I ask you, if we adopt the Non-Interference Directive, how do you propose to enforce it?"

The supreme leader set his cobalt blue eyes on him and announced with a warm smile, "Quite right, Banallo. You have anticipated my next announcement. The rule of law is of paramount importance. Decrees are nothing without enforcement. To demonstrate my commitment to ensuring compliance, I'm sending to Earth to assume command my son and first named successor, En.Anu, as well as my grandson and second named successor, En.Lil. A brief stay on another planet will give them additional insights into the eternal design for the universe."

Although not consulted in advance, Lil and his father had been delighted by the prospect of an adventure. Having dignitaries of their stature on Earth, however, represented a significant commitment. Along with a large contingent of colonists came eleven Elders of the House of En, so that their Council, with Anu, would contain the harmonious number twelve. Because Alterrans feared their planet was dying, Earth was becoming increasingly important. Since early times, Alterra's ecosystem had been sustained by volcanic activity that warmed its atmosphere and made it a fertile garden planet. As the core grew steadily cooler, the volcanoes became dormant, and their magnetosphere was faltering.

A few centuries after Anu and Lil had traveled through the portal to Earth, Alterra's core cooled to the point of causing its magnetic poles to deteriorate. Coincidentally, as if the universe were jealously reclaiming its crown jewel for the mysterious dark matter of space, Alterra's star bombarded it with high intensity plasma waves. An extreme solar wind ripped huge holes in its atmosphere, causing it to rapidly leak away. Many died, unable to reach a rejuvenation chamber. Survivors took refuge in emergency underground facilities that had been hastily constructed in the hysteria that swept the planet when their inability to prevent the destruction became known. With power sufficient only for the maintenance of life support, the Alterrans could no longer activate the portal to Earth. Thus, for the Earth colonists, what had commenced as a research and mining expedition had become the last hope of the Alterran civilization.

With their home planet decimated, the Elders stranded on Earth obsessively sought to preserve their highly evolved philosophy. Before discovering Earth, the Alterrans had searched for life, finding only microbes. From this, they had concluded that their uniqueness, their sacred singularity, represented the culmination of the evolutionary path of the universe. Ever since the Great Awakening, which marked the beginning of worldwide adoption of the principles of harmony and stability, Alterrans believed the Universal Consciousness, which they sometimes called Quantum Consciousness, had left clues in nature meant for them, which they'd be capable of interpreting when they reached the final developmental stage of wisdom and knowledge. Then they'd be able to predict what lay before them. They studied the smallest elements and meticulously charted the movement of heavenly bodies. The messages, they believed, were to be found in the mathematical principles organizing quantum particles, as well as galaxies and the universe itself. Star movements implemented fundamental design and revealed the purpose of life. If they properly interpreted these movements, they would learn their past and their destiny. Through their perpetual surveillance of the stars, they discovered the universe's central axis and the waves emitted from its center, and they strove to find its purpose. Thus, it became the House of En's passion to mimic the universe's elemental purity through global policies imposing harmony with nature. To symbolize their passion, the Ens adopted an insignia in the shape of an isosceles triangle, representing a fundamental fractal formation, with a diagonal line representing the universe's central axis.

But the star messages proved to be inscrutable. Interpretation was required, which became the ultimate purview of the supreme leader. To seal the relationship with the Universal Consciousness, as well as to keep ambition in check within the ruling family, the position of supreme leader was ordained to be hereditary. Since permanent death no longer occurred thanks to the rejuvenation chambers, the supreme leader's child of pure lineage ascended to become the leader when his zodiac sign entered the new age; it was the Universal Consciousness, or Creator, selecting the birth and time of succession, so there could be no human dispute. To prevent manipulation, public monuments were built aligning each ascending ruler's time with the zodiac.

In truth, the star messages defied the ability of flesh and blood creatures to interpret them; they didn't predict the coming catastrophe. The supreme leader, like the other survivors, fled in his planet's waning days to a hastily equipped underground facility, and communications now had become fainter and less frequent. The once invincible Alterra no longer functioned as a civilization. For the colonists, the way home was closed, perhaps forever.

* * *

On the morning of the Council meeting, Lil gazed resolutely into a mirror and smoothed his white hair, still not used to the color. Before coming through the portal to Earth, his hair had been light brown. Since the white hair was a valued mark of space travelers, it was customary to accept it. Nersis had told him that this color made his blue eyes appear even more penetrating. The deep cobalt signified his pure genetics. Looking in the mirror, though, his eyes appeared tired. *Mencomm* was exhausting. Before leaving, he stroked the purple insignia on his silver tunic. Trusting that it wouldn't be stripped away, he hoped to convince them of his plan's merit. As Anu's son, he was confident that he would avoid physical punishment even if they rejected his vision. Filled with courage, he left for the Council chamber. Crossing the plaza, he found it deserted. As a research and exploration mission, Hawan had been sparsely staffed, primarily with military men and scientists, who were usually busy exploring the planet and analyzing the results.

Jared, waiting outside the Council building, greeted him with the sacred triangle. "Peace and harmony. Speaking for all guardsmen, we want to wish you good luck, sir."

Returning the sign, Lil nodded in appreciation, and said, "En.Lil" as the password to gain entrance. Like all colony structures, the walls of the Council building were made of smooth stone that had been carefully formed and decorated with the interlocking "PHS." Lil removed his eyewear in the chamber's dim lighting. In his many previous visits, the Elders had received him warmly, lauding him for his meticulous work. This time would be different.

With the Council meeting already in progress, Lil was asked to enter the center space within the circular table. Standing erect, shoulders squared, he faced his father, Anu, the Council Leader, in his ceremonial flowing silver tunic; he wore the sacred triangle over his white-haired head.

"Captain," intoned Anu with stony formality, staring at him with the same piercing blue eyes of his son. "I have a report here that you and your men went on an excursion yesterday that is characterized as a hunt. It says that you facilitated this so-called hunt through *mencomm*." Anu, barely containing his rage, threw his electronic tablet on the table. "You slaughtered animals, violating the long-standing prohibition, and you even brought them here to be consumed." Rocking back in his chair in his fury, he continued, "Not being cloaked, you permitted yourselves to be observed by two Earth women, thus revealing our presence here. And not only were you observed, but you interacted with them, even allowing two Earth women to ride in your ship while you did an errand for them. Needless to say, you committed multiple violations of the Non-Interference Directive. Captain, is this incredible story true?"

"Yes, sir, it's all true," Lil said firmly, locking with his father's eyes. "Since we're going to be living on this planet for a long time, we need to find food substitutes. The Ministry is working on adapting wild grains for agriculture, but that will take more time and land than we have. Since, in our research, we saw how Earth people hunt animals and rely upon them for their sustenance, we experimented with hunting. Cloaking wasn't possible. It was most unfortunate that we were observed." Lil stretched out an arm to Councilwoman Barian. "The women approached as we were harvesting the animal. They passionately argued that their people rely upon such animals for almost all of their diet.

They said that they have had little success lately in hunting, and that they desperately needed the animal."

"So, you were arguing with Earth people? Don't look to me to endorse this, Captain," chastised Councilwoman Barian, shaking her head and putting up her hand. "You know that this violates the Non-Interference Directive, a wise directive that I fully support. We simply cannot interfere with these creatures' destiny. Whether they are in harm's way or not is not up to us. We do not play God, Captain."

Lil walked around in the circle, carefully examining their faces, not finding an ally. "Since helping those less fortunate is a fundamental concept of the Alterran Code, I honored its spirit by helping them. The only way to do so, while preserving the animal, was for me to take them to their village."

"Who authorized this mission?" Anu asked, his voice icy and his face contorted, weakly attempting to control his anger.

"I did, sir. My men are totally blameless. They only followed my orders."

"Captain," said Anu, crossing his arms over his chest, "unless you've forgotten every bit of your training, you are aware that we abandoned the disgusting practice of consuming animals in the Great Awakening, are you not? Would you have us regress?" He slammed his hands on the table, glaring. "Would you have us become like these primitive Earth people? You were sent here by the supreme leader for the very purpose of ensuring compliance with the Non-Interference Directive! I'm aghast at what I'm hearing." Unable to sit still, the unusually unflappable Anu swiveled his chair to face the wall.

"Sir," argued Lil, "our food stores are dwindling. For our survival, we *must* adapt to life on this planet. Consuming animals may be the only way to achieve a balanced diet."

"Captain," interrupted Councilman Pilian with disdain, "I for one would rather starve than become a carnivore. Respect for other sentient beings cannot be thrown aside because of a temporary ache in one's belly. We have unassailable principles here and a strong legacy that must be preserved at all costs. If we abandon these, we are no longer Alterran."

"Maybe you'd rather starve, Councilman, but you can't sentence everyone else at Hawan to death by starvation," argued Lil, wishing he could shake sense into the old man. "That's why we used the *mencomm*—

Councilwoman Arawan interrupted, "Captain, have you ever received the history memories about the time before the Age of Wisdom? Specifically, are you not aware of why the *mencomm* was prohibited?" One of the youngest elders, she peered at him kindly. She was his only hope for an ally.

"Absolutely, Madam," he said, emphasizing the point with a wave of his arm. "I have absorbed every one of the Teacher's history programs. The *mencomm* was outlawed after it was used by extremists in a series of attacks that caused global chaos. There were enormous casualties."

"Have you received the history memories regarding the killing of animals?" Arawan asked.

"Yes, Madam. In the time before the Age of Wisdom, Alterrans dined on animals and engaged in other savage acts. Society was undisciplined, and individual greed and ambition caused constant warfare. As part of the Great Awakening, we came to associate these things. We banned carnivorous eating, imposed discipline, and enforced strict population control to prevent the social conditions that gave rise to the extremists."

"Well, Captain," interrupted Councilwoman Barian, her lips forming a tight circle, "if you have this knowledge, why did you commit such atrocious, uncivilized acts?"

"Madam, you mischaracterize our actions." Lil burst with exasperation, pacing back and forth, locking eyes with Councilwoman Barian, the natural leader of the Council. "I did engage in those acts. Why?" He stopped and placed his hands on the table before her. "Because our home is no longer Alterra. Soon our systems will deteriorate, and we won't have access to the ancient knowledge. We won't have food; we may not have full power and—we may not be able to rejuvenate."

Pacing again, he said, "For us to survive, we have no choice. We must change," hitting his fist in his palm. "We *must* adapt to conditions on Earth, just as the original Alterrans, whom you obviously disdain, had to survive. We *must* use whatever resources are now available."

"Don't be so dramatic," Councilman Pilian scoffed, waving his hand dismissively. "The Ministry will think of something. It always does."

"That's unrealistic," chided Lil. "Our supplies are nearly depleted. The Council has closed its eyes to the threats we face." Stopping again for emphasis, he warned, "We can't remain secluded in this granite tower and blindly hope that things will remain the same for an eternity. I'm certainly in favor of developing agriculture, but that will take time we don't have. We have no choice but to supplement our food supplies in the short term with animal products, no matter how odious. You can't sentence everyone to starvation. We owe it to Alterrans to preserve our civilization!"

"Enough!" shouted Anu, springing to his feet. "I can't listen to any more of this drivel. I can't believe my ears. You're actually proposing that we abandon fundamental principles of our civilization in order to preserve it. So, you're worried about perpetuating our civilization." Anu himself paced, and stopped suddenly, his voice dripping with venom. "I suppose next, in case the rejuvenation chambers become inoperable, you'll want to mate with these Earth people."

Lil threw up his hands in exasperation, "I assure you that nothing is further from our minds," looking at each member for emphasis. "We're simply looking for a way to survive to preserve the best of Alterra." Quietly, he added, "If we perish, the universe will never know about us or our achievements."

Councilman Trey cleared his throat. "Although I don't accept this, I think what I'm hearing you address is the slaughter of the animal. I don't believe anyone actually ate it, although I could be wrong. Have I missed in this impassioned plea your explanation of the use of the *mencomm*?"

Defensively, Lil shrugged and said, "We're novices at hunting. It's much more difficult than you might think. We're experimenting. There's nothing inherently evil in using *mencomm*. If the colony fuel cells become depleted, there will be no long-range communication available. There may come a time when *mencomm* will be the only method available to us for critical communications. We used it only in the best interest of the colony."

Councilman Trey derisively answered, "Oh," pausing for emphasis by scratching his ear. "Might I remind you, Captain, that abilities like *mencomm* present a slippery slope? One minute the use is for a noble cause; but soon, you feel euphoria of power over others, and then you can't resist using it for not-so-noble purposes, telling yourself that the infraction is trivial or isolated. Then one day, bam," he said clapping his hands, "you're hooked. It's like an addiction, Captain. This is the hard-learned lesson of history. Don't forget that." He wagged his finger to make his point.

Lil shook his head. "Sir, undoubtedly things could have been done better. But please understand that there is a growing frustration in Hawan at the Council's inability to plan for the future."

"Growing frustration? By whom?" said several Council members at once. All eyes turned toward Anu as he replied angrily. "This is the first I've heard of this. Captain, I think you're the only frustrated one. The situation with our food supplies will be worked out, as it always is." After the Great Awakening, to support their highly developed command economy, the Ministry of Central Planning had taken care of all details for the procurement, production, manufacturing, and distribution of everything their life required. It was an immense job that employed a great many people relying upon a battery of highly developed quantum computers. The Council had forgotten what a complex job this was, and they'd taken no action to fill the void, blindly leaving it to Ki to take action but asking no questions how he managed it.

"I can see that this is going nowhere," said Lil dejectedly, turning his eyes away from his father's. He vowed that, when he was supreme leader, he would be different. He'd be open to new ideas.

"Don't be insolent," snapped Anu, incensed. "Nowhere is precisely where you're going. You shall be confined to Hawan for three months. During that time, you'll limit your activities to supervising only the most essential operational matters. If you don't comply fully, all the guardsmen who went hunting will be subjected to the punishment protocols. Most importantly, during your confinement, you'll devote your time to re-absorbing Alterran history. And you should hope that the Earth people don't try to find us. In their simple minds, they're likely to think that we're gods."

"Imagine that!" said Councilwoman Arawan with an exaggerated frown, shuddering. "Disgusting!"

Anu waved his hand, dismissing him. "That will be all."

Disappointed, Lil left. They hadn't understood a single point, he thought. The Great Awakening, which had led to the Age of Wisdom, had truly produced a golden era of harmony and stability on Alterra. They had thrown off the chaos of the capitalist system for the steady state directed by the House of En. It had been a victory of protection of the environment and enlightened principles of living over individualism. As a patriot, he deeply loved Alterran philosophy, and he always strove to adhere precisely to the Code. Was he wrong in his analysis of Hawan's situation? Facts were facts, and someone needed to address their problems. A veil cloaked the minds of the Council, including his father. Philosophy was a useful lens for viewing life, but didn't it need to be tweaked when circumstances required? They automatically rejected anything that didn't fit their worldview. Walking across the courtyard, he wondered if he could be wrong. Why did he see things differently? Would the scribes' star analysis actually reveal a solution that escaped him? But he stopped cold. What if they divined that the Alterrans' destiny was to become extinct, ended like so many animal species in their past? Is this what the Council knew? Could they serenely accept such a destiny, never lifting a finger to change their fate? Could he?

CHAPTER 5
EWAN

Ewan arose before dawn the next morning, eager to get started. The strangers Alana had met could only be fellow survivors from Atlantis. Nowhere else on Earth had people the knowledge Alana had described. He lit a small cookfire outside their hut to boil water for tea, put a mixture of nuts and dried berries into a pouch, and tightly rolled his sleeping mat to carry it on his back. Unable to contain his energy any longer, he gently awoke Alana as the first glint of rose-colored clouds arose in the east and brought her some hot tea. "Alana, dear, please get up. We should get moving early this morning. If we try, we might be able to find these strangers. It's been so long since I've seen anyone from Atlantis. I want to reach our forest shelter by dusk."

Alana rubbed her eyes and sat up, yawning. "Father, I don't think they were from Atlantis," she protested, but he wouldn't listen. She arose, washed her face with water from a small pottery vessel that Ewan had obtained by trade at a meeting one summer of all Albion's tribes, and drank her tea. When she was ready, Ewan grabbed a sturdy spear, his favorite knife, and the overnight packs, and briskly strode out of the village with Alana trailing sleepily behind. Whistling, he hoped for a clue that would help him discover his kindred spirits. The area Alana had described was near the shelter he had built for her plant gathering trips. It was far, but they could travel part of the way by canoe.

Alana ran with her spear to catch up and laughingly poked him with her finger. "You're certainly happy today."

He grinned and gently pinched her arm. Although grateful to the good-hearted people who had long ago befriended him, he nevertheless yearned for the days of spirited conversation with friends over a moral principle or politics. Ewan had done his best to impart his practical knowledge to the villagers, and by most standards, they were unique because of his efforts. But creating a civilization with simple backwoods people was beyond him. He had spent hours reciting stories of Atlantis to Alana, hoping that perhaps some history of the island and her family would be preserved for their descendants. He never let his change in circumstances get him down. Despite the great sorrows of his life, he found a joy in being alive each day, an attitude he shared with Alana.

The day was sunny and pleasant, and they made good progress. Whenever they could, they followed well-worn animal trails, keeping an eye open for predators. Reaching a stream, Ewan said, "I'll get the canoe for us." He searched behind the bushes and brought out a canoe dug out from a birch tree. An elk leg bone had been carved into a paddle. Although Ewan was in his sixtieth decade, the constant exercise and lean diet had made him healthy and vigorous. As he paddled, he hummed tunes from his youth, and Alana happily joined in. Nearing the long trail to the forest, he pulled ashore and hid the canoe. They climbed steep hills and reached one of the many long ridges running through their land. It being cooler at this altitude, Alana put on a fur that Ewan had packed. With few animals traveling the high ridges, they would be safer, which allowed them the luxury to stop occasionally to admire the scenery.

"Look, Alana," he said, pointing north. "No treetops. That's where the ice mountain is that I told you about. It's magnificent."

"I'd like to see it one day," she said, standing on tiptoe to see over the treetops.

"I wish you could, but the way there is long and treacherous. Near there is where our hunting party killed the cave bears for our sleeping furs."

"I love that fur, Father. It keeps me warm at the *coldest* of times."

"Yes, we're fortunate to have it." Ewan's heart warmed that Alana didn't take his efforts for granted, that she accepted this primitive life and sought to make the best of it, as if she'd never known the wonders of Atlantis. If only he had more to give her. Fingering the gold coins in the pouch around his neck, he thought, *Alana, maybe there remains hope for the life that you deserve.* Coming through a clearing in the trees, they stopped at a spot where they could see for miles. "It's magnificent, isn't it?" he asked, and Alana nodded with a smile and put her arm through his, feeling his warmth. "The glaciers are becoming smaller. You can tell where they've been by the scratches on the rocks. Things are changing all the time. The mastodon becomes scarcer, but other, smaller, animals take their place."

"Such as those herds of caribou."

"Exactly. This land will one day be very different after I'm gone." Looking up to observe a flock of birds, he said, "The birds are finally returning to the numbers I remember from my youth. I think the ash from the volcanoes killed many of them." As he had told Alana many times, the time immediately after the destruction of Atlantis had been difficult. The volcanic ash spewing into the air rolled across the ocean, even reaching the shores of Albion. The vegetation and wildlife were nearly back, although he noticed that some plants and animals had not yet reappeared. Maybe they never would.

Pointing out some of the new vegetative growth to Alana, he observed as if lost in another time, "See here, Alana, the

Earth is always renewing itself. The old must die off to make way for the new and the young. That is the way of it." Clapping the dirt from his hands, he continued, "But not this day. This old one is still here, and I'm going to enjoy myself," he chuckled. "Especially because of you." Although hesitant to bring up a subject he knew would be unpleasant, he felt he must. "At the next Summer Meeting, you'll be choosing a mate and then moving into another hut. I'll miss you, but I look forward to my grandchildren!"

She grew angry and frowned. "I'm not choosing that awful son of Drood, Father."

He stopped in surprise, cocking his head. "Where on earth did you get that notion? Of course, you won't. It's completely out of the question. You've been raised to rely upon the power of reason, not the wild ideas of fanatical mystics. Black mysticism, especially."

"Where does black magic come from?"

"I have no idea. It's best to stay as far away as we can."

Relieved, Alana cheered up by remembering the glorious fun of the Summer Meeting. It took them almost a month to travel to the far southern plain. Because of the distance, her village didn't attend the winter meeting for the solstice. To honor the ancestors, they had instead erected their own stakes, as a modest replica. Always counting the days until the summer solstice, she dearly loved seeing old friends, attending the ceremonies, and getting new things through trading furs. She had made many acquaintances at the other villages and had become the special pupil of Zedah and Yoachim, the Earthkeepers. Yet she couldn't help but be annoyed that Ewan had brought up the subject of a mate, a source of frustration for years. Being a good head and shoulders taller than the men of this land, she felt awkward. More importantly, men from other villages smelled, and their hair was usually matted. At her village, her father had taught anyone who would listen to take care of themselves. And men from some villages mistreated their women. They were not kind and thoughtful, like her father and her villagers. In many ways, her father had unknowingly spoiled Alana and raised her expectations too high. She enjoyed being her village's medicine woman, and she wasn't ready to lose her independence, as she feared might happen with a mate. She wanted more. After Alana completed the first tests to become an Earthkeeper, Zedah had praised her and chosen her as her only pupil, saying, *"Always seek to help those around you, Alana. It's not always easy to put aside one's own interests for the many, but it is the path that an Earthkeeper must pledge herself to take."* Zedah, whose powers were far more powerful than Yoachim, could travel in a timeless dimension that no one else could see, and she taught Alana that Earth people shape this world through their dreams and desires. Alana yearned to see the invisible world and to follow in Zedah's wise footsteps, but that would require her to leave Ewan and live far to the south. Living so far apart would break Ewan's heart, and her own. And she'd have to leave Maya, too. Unless she could find a way for Maya to go, too.

Ewan, however, had not given up hope that his daughter would be mated and that he'd have grandchildren. "You're very special, and I'm *not* just saying this because you're my daughter. I've thought about this constantly over the years. When you were young, you went with your mother to the temple, where Priestess Petrina noticed your talents and let you study with the children of noble birth, even letting you become her acolyte. The only day I took you with me out on my fishing boat was the day of the destruction, because your mother was busy preparing for the Ceremony of the Light. And so you escaped the destruction of Atlantis. One of the few, as far as I can tell. Here, Shaman Zedah recognized your talents and picked you to follow her as an Earthkeeper. And, lastly, you've waited this long for a mate. All these things happened for a reason; a *very* good reason, it must be. Trust Mother Earth, my dear. All will become clear in time, I'm sure of it. Some day, there will be something important that you'll be called upon to do for your people."

"Father, I love you, but I'm just an ordinary girl," she protested, laughing uncomfortably. Throughout the years since their escape, he'd made it a point to console her that she was special. Nothing ever changed. Although becoming an Earthkeeper was her heart's desire, she couldn't tear herself away from Ewan; if he weren't near, she'd worry about him constantly. And she'd miss Maya. Outside of clan ceremonial gatherings, Zedah's solitary life seemed lonely to Alana.

Ewan bowed slightly, gave her a reassuring grin, kissed her forehead, and then strode happily ahead, twisting his way through a patch of prickly bushes. He whistled an Atlantean sailing song, waving his arm to keep time, and laughed when it ended. "Oh, to smell the salty air again…" Where the trail widened, she jogged to his side and slid her arm through his. Ewan patted her soft hand and gave her a big grin. "Things certainly change during our life in unpredictable ways. My childhood was spent going to school, playing games, and preparing for a life on the sea. All that changed in an instant." Snapping his fingers, he said, "The volcanoes erupted, the island sank, and now I live in a primitive village."

"Do you mind it that much?"

"Oh, no, I'm observing, not complaining. Everyone I knew died. Other than you, of course. I'm lucky to be alive at all. My only real regret is that you'll never know the wonders of Atlantis."

"Why was Atlantis unique?"

"Ah, it was a rare jewel. The last survivor of a far older Earth civilization that was destroyed through wars and catastrophes," he said thoughtfully. "Mother Earth and the oceans have a way of swallowing all trace of the ancients. The maritime cities along the middle sea preserve only a smidgeon of the old knowledge; they're infants compared to what once was. Such a shame," he sighed.

"And, then, Atlantis was destroyed," she said sadly, her memory hazy of the marble temple where her mother took her while she served Priestess Petrina. It had been so clean and airy, and food was always plentiful.

He shrugged and let out a deep breath. "Perhaps in the future mankind will create a civilization that can tame nature, or at least survive the worst that it throws at us."

"They'll need to be smart."

"Yes, indeed. And if those future people can do that, they'll surely be smart enough to avoid wars and killing." Ewan was silent for a long time, wondering what such a future would be like.

"Father, I've always loved your stories, but sometimes they make me sad because my life would've been *so* different if I lived on Atlantis. So much easier. I barely remember my childhood anymore."

"You still remember your mother, don't you?" he asked gently.

"Her face has grown a little fuzzy, I'm afraid." She frowned, ashamed to admit that her mother's memory was reduced to a warm feeling of love, rather than a discernible image.

"Oh?" said Ewan with dismay.

"What I'll never forget is her kindness. And I remember the fun we had going to the temple. I might be a priestess today if…" Alana was quiet, remembering what she'd lost. After a while, she continued, "I remember school. I liked learning new things, and I'm glad that I'm able to count. No one I've met here has been able to use numbers as we learned to do. When I have a child, I definitely want to teach these things."

"Sometimes, my dear, I feel sad for you living here, even though the people are kind. I understand that it will be difficult for you to find a mate, and I understand why you've put it off." He himself had never found a suitable mate among these primitive people.

Alana admitted, "It doesn't seem fair, even though I do love the people of this land. I try not to think about it. I'll make do somehow. After all, Yanni found Maliki, and he's a wonderful man."

"Yes, he is, my dear. We simply need to keep looking," he replied gently. If the strangers were from Atlantis, he might have the perfect solution. He had brought his pouch with the Atlantean coins that were in his pockets the day of the disaster. Being made of gold, they were highly valued. Perhaps he could find her a mate or, if they were just passing through, persuade them to take Alana with them. At the very least, they might have news or something interesting to trade.

In early evening, they reached the shelter. Ewan said, "Let's quickly gather dried logs and twigs for a fire." Ewan took from around his neck a flint rock strung on a length of sinew and flicked it against another rock to create a spark a fire in dry leaves. Looking around and alert for padding feet, he warned, "There are wolves and other predators in these parts. We must keep the fire going. I'll pull the hides closely around us and add foliage for protection."

"Yes, the way you taught me. I'm tired." Alana yawned, rubbing her eyes. "I'm going to sleep." She kissed him on the cheek, unrolled her sleeping mat, and pulled her furs around her. After ensuring that sufficient logs were nearby to feed the fire and securing the shelter's hides, he lay down to sleep as well.

When Alana awoke, Ewan was already gone. He had discovered the hoof prints of the strangers' horses. Kneeling down to study them carefully, he measured the prints with his hands. He frowned and sat back on his heels when he concluded that the horses had been shod, knowing that no one in this land shod horses. Finding a boot print, he examined the outline and measured the depth to determine height and weight. After a few minutes with the boot markings and finding a snip of tunic torn on a thorn, he stood up, eyebrows furrowed in the realization that these strangers may not be from Atlantis.

Occasionally, an Atlantean would wander through this land with stories of other survivors. His distinctive people always drew attention, and news of their visits quickly spread throughout the villages. He remembered hearing long ago, shortly after he and Alana had made it ashore, about priests from the main temple who had escaped before the final, devastating volcanic eruption—in a magic bubble, the stories went. Some said they had built a replica of their temple on the other side of the world. Atlantean temples had had a geometric purity that couldn't be matched. Ewan had had no idea where the distant land with the new temple might be, nor did he have the means to get there. So he had reluctantly dismissed as sheer folly any attempt to uproot Alana in an uncertain quest to find them. No, it had made more sense to count their blessings, such as they were, and stay put with villagers who accepted them.

After further studying the tracks, he stroked his beard with puzzlement. "Boots of this quality and material aren't available here." Ewan pointed out the path of the horse tracks down the steep embankment to the river. Where the land flattened, they walked along the mastodons' well-worn path. He saw where the herd had been diverted.

"The trench is just ahead." Alana pointed south, eyeing the hillside for her lost plants.

When they reached the trench, Ewan traced the outer rim of the huge crater and was baffled at its depth and length. "It would take an Atlantean army to dig a hole this deep!"

"Not with the things they had, Father." Alana was frustrated that she didn't know the words to describe their tools. Even more so, that he still believed that they were from Atlantis.

"I don't even see the dirt that was removed," said Ewan, amazed. "But if they had things to create the hole so easily, they were certainly careless not to fill it in. It's dangerous to leave this." Standing at the edge of the trench, looking in, he repeated in wonder, "How, by the Mother's blessing, did they dig this thing?"

"Father, I hope you'll believe me now," pleaded Alana.

Ignoring her, Ewan mused, "Whoever these strangers were, they had advanced clothing, tools and other things, but why didn't they fill this in? Perhaps they were planning to use it again." He scratched his head. Climbing down a jagged portion of the mostly straight and smooth trench wall, he found a larger piece of the strange fabric. Although he stretched it, pulled it, and tried to tear it, the fabric's shape reformed, adapting as if remembering what it had been.

"That cloth was torn from the stranger injured by the bull. I saw his clothing change shape to protect his body when the bull tossed him in. It didn't cover his head, though, which had an ugly gash. He lost much blood. His body was lifeless, but they hurried as if they could still save him."

Eyes wide, Ewan looked from Alana to the strange cloth. He tried new ways of tearing and ripping the cloth, but it constantly changed shape—even its texture and color transformed to match the ground where he laid it. Becoming frightened, he let it slip through his fingers.

Alana said quietly, "The strangers went into their ship and disappeared."

Ewan was speechless but was beginning to believe her. On Atlantis, he had seen magnificent buildings that were lit at night by luminous globes powered by huge machines. The Atlanteans had built giant ships that sailed the mighty oceans. He had even seen something resembling a large bird, which his friends said was actually a man with wings tied to his arms. But to his knowledge, Atlantis had never had anything resembling the flying ships that Alana described, nor did they have clothing that changed shape.

"There's something I forgot until now," Alana said slowly.

"What else could there be?" muttered Ewan, unable to absorb more mysteries.

"The strangers had long and short knives that were made of a shiny metal." She measured the length with her arms. "The sun danced off the blades, and I had to shield my eyes. The blades were so sharp that the men sliced through the thick mastodon hide effortlessly, and Maya pricked her finger by brushing the edge."

Ewan stroked his beard, finding this new piece of information more manageable. Objects of gold, bronze, and other metals had been plentiful on Atlantis, but he hadn't seen any such metal since leaving there. Metal couldn't be forged in this land. If they had more, perhaps they'd trade furs for such a knife. It would be priceless to his people, but of little use to the strangers.

Seeking a wider view, Ewan climbed to the hilltop with Alana following him. They sat for a while eating their food. Hearing a strange whizzing sound, they felt a vibration and a breeze, but could see leaves a short distance away remain still.

Alana held her hair in the wind. "Their flying ships did this after disappearing."

When it stopped, they stood up and looked about, seeing no trace of anything to explain the odd wind. A short while later, they gazed at the distant Magic Mountain, as the villagers had named it, although Ewan had scoffed at villagers' stories of strange occurrences. A silver triangle, glinting with sunlight, momentarily appeared and then vanished through the waterfall. He blinked in disbelief.

He touched her arm and whispered, "Alana, I saw something vanish into the waterfall."

"I saw it, too," she whispered. Would he finally believe her?

Fear filled his mind. "Let's get out of here," he said tensely, picking up his things.

"Couldn't we stay the night and leave tomorrow?" Alana asked, perturbed at his haste. The danger was over in her mind. "I need to gather more herbs and mushrooms. Some are only found here, and I lost what I had chasing after the hunters."

"Alana," he insisted in a strong tone that she'd rarely heard in her many years with him, "you'll need to make do this winter with what you already have. I have another hunting shelter that we can stay in tonight."

She gave in. Her father never raised his voice to her, but his tone was firm. She followed as he headed home.

CHAPTER 6
DROOD

"What, Drood?" asked Weena, a short woman whose chunky body reflected her large brood of children and relative prosperity as Drood's mate. She gazed at him from beneath long, dark matted hair, intertwined with pieces of foliage. Several dirty, barefoot children, ranging in age from toddler to middle years, hid behind her, afraid of their unpredictable father.

Drood jumped down from the tree, grumbling to himself. He irritably brushed the debris from his bushy hair and hobbled over to pick up the caribou bone he used as a cane. Ever since he'd seen the giants, he had wanted to catch one; their long femurs would make a much better cane.

Following him, she persisted, "New dream?"

"Tonight," he mumbled, hobbling away. This vision had been overwhelming; he was troubled and needed to think. He had had visions ever since an accident in his youth. Before then, his physique had been strong. He had spent his time watching nature in a nest he'd made among the branches of a large tree. He watched the animals foraging below, birds soaring purposefully through the skies or skipping among the limbs hunting food, the squirrels burrowing, the insects busily working in his tree, and the different types of clouds in the sky, the winds; he watched everything. Day after day he watched, sensing that there must be a great meaning to it all. Carefully listening to animal and bird noises, he began mimicking their language. He began to decipher the patterns of nature.

Believing he'd see messages in the clouds, he sought an unobstructed view by climbing a tree high on the ridge. Large, dark, pillowy clouds raced across the sky. He stood on one of the tallest limbs, facing the approaching storm, feeling the strong wind's power blowing against him and sending his wispy hair flying. In the distance, lightning flashed. He admired its power and the music of the thunder, first barely perceptible, then gradually booming. A thunderclap close by startled him. Nearly losing his balance, he grabbed the trunk to steady himself; becoming secure, he laughed at his fear. He waved to his fellow tribesmen passing below, heading for the crystal cave to wait out the storm. Suddenly he felt oddly tingly, as if his hair were standing on end. With a deafening crack, a lightning bolt struck his tree. Surreally, he felt himself flying through the air as a spirit. From above, he saw himself falling, hitting evergreen bushes and then rolling to the ground. His tribesmen rushed to help. They circled and pounded his chest, trying to trap his spirit. In an instant he rejoined his body and opened his eyes. Smoke rose from his singed hair. They rolled him and threw dirt on it to extinguish the smoldering fire and found that his leg was broken. Fearful of the lightning storm above them, they carried him to the crystal cave, which was used in religious ceremonies. The crystals lit up with strange lights when they brought him in. Becoming more fearful of the cave than the storm, the tribesmen offered to carry him back, but Drood insisted that his leg was healing already. But walking on it too soon left him with a limp.

Shortly after the lightning strike, his visions began. At first, they scared him. Closing his eyes, he relived the piercing white light that flooded his mind in the initial strike, when he felt oddly at peace. Animal images exploded in collages before him, and he woke up to find himself trembling on the ground, his scrawny mother sobbing by his side. When he became still again, she put his head in her lap and gently rocked him, joyfully wiping away the tears that left tracks on her dirty face. Becoming fully alert, he arose and told her not to worry. At the evening hearth, he told the skeptical tribesmen of his vision of the caribou herd and how they should hunt by painting themselves green, tying small tree branches to themselves, and rubbing themselves with caribou dung. When the hunters returned, they marveled how everything had happened as Drood had foretold. Many times over the years, Drood's visions had helped them, and the tribe treated him with reverence.

Not only had Drood received the gift of foresight within the power of the crystal cave, he discovered healing. Once, he had extended his arms over his dead mother and touched her forehead; she returned to life. He couldn't always heal, but he succeeded often enough for his tribe to hold him in awe.

Today, Drood's vision was the most powerful one of all. Lying in his favorite tree, he witnessed a monstrous, flaming red dragon flying through the sky, shooting great breaths of searing hot fire. Terrified people ran to escape, seeking shelter from the mountain-high span of its dark wings. Stopping, flexing its muscles to suck in a deep breath, the dragon blew white strings of fire, forming in the air a monstrous ball of flames, which it hurtled to the ground. It exploded into smaller fireballs that danced across the land, igniting everything they touched and incinerating a great forest. Pleased with its work, the dragon squawked and circled. The world was doomed. But it abruptly stopped in midair. Flying toward it was the very white-haired giant he'd seen hunting the mastodon. The giant threw a lightning bolt, piercing the dragon's heart. As it fell from the sky, its great claws grabbed a boulder from a mountaintop, dropping it into the ocean and causing great waves that doused the fire. Drood saw a great wave coming toward him, wiping away his village. Fear for his people jolted him. Becoming conscious again of his surroundings, he lay trembling, overwhelmed by a feeling of dread. Something terrible was about to happen. Fire and flood. Many would die. Was there a way for him to save his tribesmen? He must get them to higher ground, among the rocks.

Feeling a special affinity with the mighty giant who had slain the dragon, Drood directed his tribesmen to follow him, casting a spell over them so that they'd move with the wind and travel as shadows. They were to be his eyes and ears observing the giant, but do nothing more until the time was right.

CHAPTER 7
ANU

After the Council meeting ended, a deeply troubled Anu returned to his suite near the Chambers. A small portal had been chiseled through the granite to afford him one of the few windows within Hawan. Throwing his tablet on his table, he gazed westward, where the fir trees yielded to the sea on the distant horizon. Nature couldn't placate him today. Not having the energy to change from his official robe, he eventually flipped through the scribe reports, but couldn't focus and put down his electronic tablet. Calling for his wife, Uras, he painfully reported Lil's perplexing actions. "What's happened to him? Have I been too lax? How did it come to this?" Anu asked, closing his eyes and rubbing his temples. His head ached and he was embarrassed. Thank the stars that Ama wouldn't learn of his behavior.

Uras suggested wryly, "Perhaps the entire Guard would benefit from modifications to their nourishment bars."

Anu paused, considering this possibility, but shook his head, replying, "I don't think we need to go that far yet." He admitted this might be a possibility; but temporarily he'd have to give Lil the Guard formula, which would hinder his leadership abilities.

Anu was frustrated. It was imperative that his son be a role model who strictly followed Alterran law and tradition. After Lil's ascension, Alterran lives would depend on his interpretation of destiny. In difficult times, he needed his son to be strong and steady, as he'd always known him to be.

Anu had been perfectly content to turn daily operational matters over to his son. Preferring loftier pursuits, he spent his time studying philosophy and meditating. Before communications were disrupted, he had frequently consulted with his father, Ama, the supreme leader, on home-world governance matters. It wasn't truly consultation, though—Ama's mind saw a black-and-white world in which an iron fist was required to preserve peace and harmony. Ruling by an iron fist made Anu uncomfortable. Alterrans were highly intelligent and talented people; why was it necessary to quash all opinions not held by the House of En? Yet Anu's time to ascend at the beginning of the Age of Leo was fast approaching, and he had to be ready to fit seamlessly into his father's shoes. Here, he was trapped, cruelly denied the destiny for which he'd spent thousands of years preparing. Instead of a plush life enjoying the full resources of an advanced technological civilization, with hordes of ministries snapping to obey his every command, he headed a sparsely staffed, ill-equipped colonial outpost. At home through the Alterran Net, his thoughts would have controlled equipment, people, virtually everything; his replicator would have instantly created whatever he commanded, and he could have transformed himself into an electronic packet, traveling instantly through the Net, materializing anywhere in any form without warning. Ki hadn't had time to create the full capabilities of the Net here, and now the resources weren't available. He felt like a prisoner. If Lil were stripped of his rank, Anu pictured himself taking personal command of the Guard, assigning mission details, flying observational missions, filing reports, and monitoring other operational matters around Hawan—he shuddered at the thought. He would have scant time for his all-important mental conditioning to be supreme leader, having never abandoned hope. After all, the scribes' star analyses still reported his ascension to be his destiny, and the universal star messages were infallible. Of course, Anu could act decisively when duty so required; but he had evolved. He now thought the great thoughts that would link his mind with the Universal Consciousness. Everything else was a wasteful distraction. He couldn't permit this to happen. It was of the utmost importance that he persuade Lil to get over whatever was bothering him. As the one chosen by the stars, Anu couldn't simply replace Lil, at least not entirely.

Anu picked up his tablet and read the latest star report, assuming he would find comfort in the constant timelessness of the universe. Thankfully, the scribe's report began with the standard interpretations of good will. He read with mild interest the description of a large comet that was entering the Earth's solar system and would pass close to Earth. That should be interesting to watch, he thought distractedly.

Next, he turned to the status of the food supplies. He'd never before bothered himself with this detail, but was there any truth to what Lil had said? Stopping abruptly, he threw up his hands. What was he doing? He couldn't start second guessing things just because his conscientious son had gotten into trouble. Turning off his tablet, he sought to relax through a nighttime stroll around Hawan. Everything seemed to be in its place. Looking up through the clear roof, he saw the comforting blanket of the Milky Way extended across the sky, providing assurance of eternal constancy. Anu looked longingly toward Alterra in the Pleiades, and he began to calm down. As he walked, he remembered when, during the second of several youths, he had rebelled against his family's choice for his bride. He had glimpsed Uras attending a ceremony at the main temple. Being smitten with her loveliness and poise, through the Net he had surreptitiously viewed her identity, learning that she was a physician from a modest but respectable family. Later, he had secretly sent his holographic twin to her, materializing through the Net in her bedroom. However, his indiscretion was discovered by the nanobots that moni-tored the Net, which alerted the supreme leader, and he was sternly warned by his father and uncles to put the interests of his people above his personal wants; the House of En needed him to enter into a strategic marriage with the Southern Alli-ance to control the last of the great independent families. Anu had been so depressed that he'd stayed in his room for days. The life of a political leader responsible for the global population hadn't been his choice and never was his desire; he frequently envied the low-level, carefree positions that the supreme leader assigned to newborns. When the family con-sigliere suggested that he take Uras as his concubine, he'd been appalled at the hypocrisy. Fortunately, the matter had resolved itself after the Southern Alliance went to war, claim-ing that one of their members was the rightful successor to the supreme leader. Despite his preference for peace, Anu had caused the replicators to create the Dalit army and, using powerful weapons available only to the House of En, force-fully eliminated the usurper. Having order restored, the grate-ful Council of Elders had rewarded him by permitting him to choose his wife.

What had been his true destiny: the strategic marriage or Uras? Had Anu sent the House of En, and with him all Alter-rans, hurtling down the path of an alternative destiny? Had he doomed them, and would this unstable alternative universe fade away as a stray spark from a fire? He felt his face and arms; everything felt real. No, Uras had been his true destiny, and now he had to find a way to fix Lil's rift with the universe. He wondered, though, who the third named successor would be, since the few women at Hawan were committed and none were of Lil's rank. He'd need to keep faith that Alterra would recover.

As dusk approached, he went to the observation deck high atop the Ministry of Science. On a clear night, the sky was magnificent. One of the Alterrans' initial tasks on Earth was to organize the night sky into twelve named zones to deci-pher signs from the Universal Consciousness as if seen from their home. When Leo was overhead, Anu would ascend to be supreme leader. When it was Cancer, Lil would, and so it would follow for his children throughout the millennia. All this was preordained, leaving no room for uncertainty or conflict. Truly a sign of an advanced civilization, he thought.

Someone behind him cleared his throat. Looking through the darkness, he saw Lil's face become illuminated by a glow-globe. "Good evening, Father."

Now calm, Anu amiably greeted his son. "Hello, Lil, excellent night for star gazing."

"It certainly is," Lil replied with formality and cleared his throat, followed by an awkward silence. He tensed, not knowing Anu's mood.

Anu sighed, deciding to make the first move. "Your mother and I are concerned. You don't seem to be yourself. You've always been such a dependable son. I've never had a moment's doubt in your ability to lead our people."

Lil chose his words carefully. "Father, I don't want to argue with you. Please believe that I have the best interests of the colonists at heart. Times are tough and I can't see where we're headed. For once, the past may not serve as a guide to the future."

Anu put his hands on Lil's shoulders, searching his face for a clue to his mind. "Lil, I wish I could shake some sense into you. Your destiny has been written in the stars. When you are the leader, your people will rely on you to embrace harmony and stability. To whom much is given, much is expected."

Lil gazed into his father's eyes, no longer feeling the icy chill of the Council session. "Father, the scribes' interpretation of star signs must take into account present conditions. The path envisioned on Alterra no longer applies to us. There's nothing wrong with advance planning for the new path we're taking. Adapting to life on Earth won't interfere with the harmony of the universe. Isn't it our destiny to survive?"

He's speaking nonsense. Anu drew upon his meditative calm to reply evenly. "This isn't a question of survival; it's merely a matter of having faith that the supreme leader will lead our people to recovery. Then they'll bring us home."

"Recovery is a fool's hope, father."

Anu let out a deep breath, refusing to revisit the morning's argument. "Never forget that you're Alterran, Lil," he replied sternly. "It's a great and noble heritage. Of all the planets in the known universe, only Alterrans have achieved a great civilization. Only Alterrans are able to travel to other worlds and rejuvenate themselves at death. The leader of a race that accomplishes such feats must mirror that greatness. He can't be cavorting around the countryside and breaking rules. Showing kindness to Earth people can only lead to interaction, and one thing will lead to another— "

"I wasn't cavorting," Lil interrupted with irritation. "I was assuring a food supply for our people! And it's consistent with our Code to show compassion to inferior species. You're incensed about protecting a mastodon, but not a conscious hominid?"

"Whatever actions we take to promote the common welfare must be consistent with our philosophy," Anu lectured, reminded of his own tirades against injustice; Jahkbar, the family's mentor, would patiently mold his young mind to accept his House's principles established by Zeya. His years of meditative reflection as an adult had thoroughly convinced him of the rightness of that path. "If not, we lose the meaning of being Alterran and risk evolving into something else. We stand for something, and that line can't be crossed." He wagged his finger. "As was said this morning, *mencomm* leads one down a slippery slope to other transgressions. Before you know it, our civilization will be back where we were before the Great Awakening, and I shudder at the thought." He straightened his posture, tilted his head, and slightly turned. "I will say no more." With that, he lit his glowglobe and left.

Lil remained. He too received comfort from the astral blanket overhead. Shuffling feet behind him caused him to turn to see one of the scribes who worked in the observatory, keeping his head down to avoid forbidden eye contact.

"Sorry, sir. I didn't mean to disturb you."

"You didn't," Lil replied absently, absorbed in thought. He scanned the starry heaven, hoping for some sign that he was on the right path. "Tell me, is there anything of particular importance in the stars tonight?"

The scribe replied, "Oh, yes, sir, indeed. Look through the telescope, and I'll show you." Peering through, he said, "Ah, here it is, sir. Look at this."

Lil put his eye to the telescope, seeing an unfamiliar bluish light. "Is this the comet that I read about in the reports?"

The scribe was surprised. "I didn't think anyone in operations read our reports. Oh, forgive me, sir, *please* don't take offense."

"Go on."

"Yes, sir, this indeed is the comet. Actually, we've discovered that there may be several comets traveling closely together. We're greatly concerned. By our calculations, the cluster will pass extremely close to Earth. In fact, there is a fairly high probability that a piece of it or something disturbed by it will enter the atmosphere."

"Keep me informed as soon as you learn more," ordered Lil.

"Yes, sir. I'm grateful, sir, that you're taking an interest in this problem."

CHAPTER 8
EWAN

Returning to the village in late afternoon, before the first hut came into sight, Ewan smelled smoke and rotting flesh. Casting a panicked look at Alana, he sprinted through the last trees leading to the edge of the village and stumbled in grief, his legs wobbly from the horror. Hoping himself to be in a dream, he numbly stumbled down a narrow lane that led to the central hearth. Fires still burned from the smoldering, charred huts, some already reduced to ash. From a tree near the center hearth hung a male body, old gray-bearded Zerk, an axe handle protruding from his chest, his bloodied body already covered with flies. In the center hearth, amidst the red embers lingering from a bonfire, he could see a charred body clutching an infant. In horror, Ewan's body trembled and he spat with hatred filling every cell of his body, "Danes! The bloody Danes!" His eyes wild with hysteria, he rushed to the heaps remaining of huts, kicking through burning debris, frantically searching for anyone alive. Nearing his own hut, he found that the mastodon tarp was gone and the poles had been stolen. Inside, what was left of his pottery was strewn in pieces on the floor and his oil lamp was gone, as were the furs and hides that he'd been collecting for trade. Worst of all, gone were his prized bear furs, thick and soft, which they used for keeping the wintry chill away. With Maliki and his brother, three autumns ago he had traveled to the caves near the glacier, and they had bravely challenged the bears with their spears and nets. Even Maliki hadn't heard of people being so bold; the cave bears were nearly as large as a mastodon female and more vicious than a saber tooth with their sharp claws. Now, all that remained intact of his precious hut were the riverbed wall stones, which the Danes hadn't taken the time to steal, only knock about.

Running frantically through the village, Alana circled the cherished hillocks, choking out names that did not answer. Her heart pounded with the fear that she'd known as a little girl, helplessly watching from the fishing boat as Atlantis was torn apart and eventually sank from her sight, leaving them to drift helplessly without water in the searing sun. Once again, her life was sinking. Spying Maya huddled like a baby, sobbing by Rayna's bloodied, lifeless body, she sprinted to her, pulled back her heaving shoulders, and poured all her tension into her hugs. "Oh, Maya, I'm *so* glad you're alive! Are you hurt?" She slid her hands over Maya's body but could find no wounds. "I can't believe this happened. Poor, darling, Rayna. Come away from her body, Maya, we can't do anything for her." For a long time they cried into each other's shoulders.

When she could form words, Maya sobbed, "I spent the day gathering apples near the lake," before again burying her head into Alana's shoulder. Alana rocked her as she listened to Ewan's curses.

The Dane raiding parties presented a constant threat to the Albion villages, although Ewan had moved their village farther inland into hilly lands more elevated than Shylfing, the Danes' leader, customarily raided. According to Koko's stories, the Danes preferred to strike fast, leaping from their moored boats along the seacoast or river's edge, to kill and plunder.

"Until the huts stop burning," Ewan said, "we can't be sure how many have died. Turu must have died trying to defend them. Poor Rayna. Shylfing must not have wanted to bother with one so old. He's no doubt taken the captives as slaves."

"I don't see many bodies," said Alana, sniffling, tears running down her cheeks. "Maybe they escaped?"

Shaking his head, Ewan said, "No bodies and no signs of a fight. I think the men must've been gone. If I'm right, they'll probably return at nightfall."

When the fires began to die down, he found the Danes had stolen or destroyed everything useful. "My god, how ever will we make it through the winter now?" he wondered. "Even if we work day and night, it'll be impossible to find everything we need before the first snow." He searched through the rubble to save what he could. Finding a few smoldering furs, he covered them with sandy soil while repeatedly thanking the gods for his foresight in stashing emergency supplies in a highland cave.

When he could find nothing further to save, he collapsed near Alana, sitting hunched over with his head in his hands. Listening to the crying women, he could think of no truthful words of comfort. Eventually, he looked up and stared vacantly. "Winter is coming, and we have few supplies. Those whom Shylfing didn't kill today may soon be dead from starvation or cold."

"Father, don't talk that way," cried Alana. She gently removed herself from Maya and put her arms around her father. Trying to be calm, she reassured him, "We've started over before. This isn't any worse than when we landed here from Atlantis."

"I'm too old," he groaned, letting his head roll back, until he shook himself.

"No, you're not. Why, we can go south to the mainland, where it's warmer."

"My dear," Ewan said, patting her hand, smiling at her optimism, "I know you mean well. But we don't have time to travel to a warmer land, and even if we did, the people we'd encounter are hostile and won't accept newcomers."

"But we can't just give up," she protested, growing alarmed and exchanging worried glances with Maya. She gripped Maya's hand. "We can't let Shylfing win!"

Maya nodded approvingly, her large, dark eyes carefully watching Ewan, sensing his lost heart and feeling the panic rising. Ewan had been her champion; if he despaired, what chance did she have?

Ewan stood and sighed as if his heart were breaking. Reflecting his despair, cindery logs collapsed, sending sparks swirling into the frosty air. Alana was so like him, as he'd been once. He couldn't let her down. "No, of course we won't give up," he said softly. "But our only hope is to stay here, hunt, and gather new supplies as fast as we can. I'll take you to a cave in the high country. I've never told anyone other than Maliki about this but, as a precaution, I've stored some emergency supplies there. One never knows what will happen, does one? Those supplies will be enough to sustain us while we gather food for the winter."

"What's happened here?"

"Yanni, where are you?"

The returning hunters discovered the smoldering heaps of rubble. Maliki strode to the hearth with Agar, and quickly threw down the caribou doe that they'd caught. As Ewan had done, the frantic hunters searched for their families in vain. Defiantly thrusting his spear in the air, Maliki shouted, "I see their tracks. I go after them! Who's with me?"

"I am!" said a villager, his face contorted with rage.

"Let's go," cried another, picking up his spear and jogging to Maliki's side.

Ewan raised his hand and shouted, "Wait! Listen to me."

Maliki scowled but stopped, huffing deeply. Ewan thought that they resembled the mindless caribou herd that they had once stampeded over a cliff. However, if Alana had been taken, would he do anything differently? Of course not. "My friend, you're angry and you aren't thinking things through. You're famished. You can't just pick up and run, and you can't track in the dark. They're well armed and have horses and boats. You need supplies and above all, a plan. All of you, sit for a moment, and we'll decide what to do while Alana makes us a meal."

In this territory, captured people could rarely be rescued. The men might be alive only because they had been out hunting. They didn't have the weapons and skills to fight the heartless Danes, a fierce tribe whose daily existence was devoted to military training and pillaging. It would be risky, and his men would be killed, perhaps facing a tortured death. On the other hand, they had to do *something*. Ewan didn't want to make the decision. The men lit a fire and helped Alana and Maya cut the caribou into chunks for boiling into a stew. Whatever they decided, they would need food. As Alana tended the cook pot, Maya gave the men her freshly gathered apples.

With the men huddling to make their plan, Ewan, with heavy heart, grimly recounted the difficulties. "If any of you decide not to go," he said shaking his gray head, his wrinkled skin seeming to have aged a decade since they'd last seen him, "don't feel bad. It's unlikely you'll succeed. You'll just die trying. If you stay, it'll be hard to make it through the winter without our supplies. Even if you rescue your families and bring them back, with little food or provisions when you return, you might starve or freeze to death."

Maliki, whose wife, Yanni, and two children were missing, snarled, "Ewan, my friend, you are wise. But I can't live without my family. I go!" He thrust his fist in anger.

"Me, too!" shouted Jonk, jumping in rage, with others joining him. Glancing at Maya, Jonk thrust out his chest and pumped his arms to show her he was unafraid.

"Ewan, our hunting knives are sharp," cried Maliki, pulling his from its sheaf and holding it as if prepared to strike. "I swear to the gods, I will kill the Danes!"

"Kill the Danes," others cried, jabbing imaginary enemies with their stone knives.

Ewan silently stared into the fire, racking his brain for a plan. Not knowing where the Danes lived, how could these peaceful villagers take on bloodthirsty warriors? The usually resourceful Ewan sat mute, unable to offer encouragement.

Alana watched the men building their courage while she prepared her herb and mushroom mixture for the Seeing Ceremony. The ingredients had been gathered that afternoon, over Ewan's protests; surely, that must be a good omen. Maya laid around the branches that had been shaped into the circular form that symbolized the Mother's endless cycles of birth and death. Gradually, the men ended their frenzied jumping and dejectedly sat with drooping shoulders, weighed down by the enormousness of their task. Ewan spoke quietly, "Maliki, I thought you'd feel that you must go. At my age, I'd only slow you down. I'll remain here and gather supplies for your return."

Staring into the fire with his chest still heaving, Maliki said, "Good." His mind raced, remembering the trails leading around the eastern sea. He knew of a ferryman who could speed their passage, but the man would need to be paid. The man was crafty and kept wolves for his protection, but maybe they could overpower him and steal his raft.

"You'll need to take something to trade," continued Ewan. "You can't go that far without food. And you'll need something to pay the ferryman."

Maliki, startled that Ewan might be reading his mind, stood and nervously circled the hearth fire, seeing nothing but smoldering huts. "There's not much here." He kicked the rubble of his old hut, and it collapsed into ash.

Ewan looked at him grimly. "No, there's not. At least Alana may be able to help find them. Alana, dear, please begin."

Alana knelt beside Ewan, laying out shells filled with ingredients. Nosti, his hair a curly dark brown like Maya's, squatted by her side, ready to hold her if a vision during her trance might cause her to do something harmful. Maya helped her put on the smooth silver headband with its shiny dangling trinkets, which clinked hypnotically as she moved her head. As Nosti began to rhythmically beat a bone against a hide drum, while Maya began a soft chant of an ancient song in her light soprano voice, Alana added water to the mushroom mixture to make a thick liquid. Tilting her head back, she drank and then brushed her finger in the bowl to find any remaining sediment to consume. Finishing, she hummed along with Maya to the drumbeat, her shoulders swaying and the silver trinkets of her headband clinking. Suddenly stopping, she gasped, wide-eyed, and slumped to the ground, with Nosti easing her fall. She thrashed at the painful images exploding in her mind. A horde of warriors with great horned spikes on their helmets ran screaming into their village with their spears raised, chasing the frightened women. They ran over a child and stood laughing. They cornered the screaming women and crying children and forced them to stand while some warriors guarded them and others ransacked the huts.

A leader waited in the shadows. When the women were gathered, the leader strode into the village, and the warriors became silent. She saw the long dire wolf tail protruding from the leader's helmet and streaming down his bare, muscular back. From Koko's stories, she knew it could only be Shylfing. "Shylfing removed his helmet," she said in her trance voice. "Jewels hung from his beard and tinkled as he walked. He sneered, walking around the women and children. They trembled with fear. He demanded, 'Give me your golden treasure and I'll leave you alone.' The children cried with terror when he looked at them. When he tired of waiting, he tore Tia's child from her breast, and threatened, 'I'll kill this child unless you bring me your gold.' But, they had no gold. Angered, he ran his spear through the child's head. Yanni pleaded, 'We are peaceful people. We have no gold.' Shylfing's guard struck her in the face, and she fell bleeding."

Maliki stopped eating and threw his food away, his chest heaving. He took out his knife and twirled it in his hands.

"Furious at finding no gold," she continued, "they bound their hands, stole our supplies, and set the huts on fire. They killed Agga and hung his body for the crows." Hearing their screams in her head, she gasped and covered her ears with her hands.

Maliki snapped a twig, threw it on the ground, and grumbled, "She must tell us which way they went, or I leave."

Ewan frowned at Maliki but decided not to argue. Reason doesn't exist when it comes to one's family. Looking at Maliki's burning eyes, he knew that he'd pursue the Danes for the rest of his life; he only hoped that his life would last more than a few short days. Ewan softly coaxed, "Alana, dear, do you see which trail they took?"

Alana slowly lifted her head, her eyes red and wild. "Shylfing made them march north to the great river leading east to the sea. Their boats are there." The images of the cruel march gripped her mind. Unable to speak, she watched the future unfold. Crossing the great eastern sea, the women and children were drug onto a narrow beach surrounded by mountains. As if floating through the sky, she observed the coastline, with small fingers of land jutting into the sea like the veins of a leaf. She collapsed with fatigue. Maya shook her and held her head as she emerged from her trance. She told of the Dane village and whispered with exhaustion, "I'm sorry, that is all I can see."

"Enough!" Maliki howled, leaping to his feet, his face contorted with rage. Securing his knives in the holders around his waist, he grabbed his spears, thrust one in the air, and shouted, "I leave now. Who's with me?" He bent down, ran his finger through the cold ashes of the fire, and wiped the blackness under his eyes as he'd seen Drood's men do.

"I am," they shouted one after another, jabbing their spears above their heads and then taking a swipe of the soot for underneath their eyes and outlining their faces.

"Come!" Maliki waved his muscular arm toward the path leading to the great river. Maliki had only been to the great river once, but he remembered that it led to the sea, water as far as they could see. "We run. Catch them before they reach the dragon ships." If not, without payment for the ferryman, he knew they'd need to run through the mainland; it would take two full moons, maybe more, to reach them. They'd have to kill and steal for food to reach their women.

"I'll rip their hearts out!" Agar shouted, uplifting his fist to pull out an imaginary heart, and throwing it on the ground and trampling it. Picking it up from the ground, he pranced around the hearth to the cheering men. "This is what we'll do to the flaming Danes!"

"We'll torch them!" shouted Kutu, a thin, sickly man who customarily followed behind the hunting parties with the women. Agar smirked at Kutu's enthusiasm but turned stone faced at receiving Maliki's icy glare. "All may come," spat Maliki.

Maya caught Jonk's eye, and she motioned for him to come to her. Jonk stood a head taller than her, his bare chest glistening with sweat. Ignoring his smell, Maya stood on her tiptoes, wrapped her arms around his neck, and brushed his dirty cheek with her lips, running her fingers through his wooly, matted hair. Jonk looked into her eyes glistening with tears and then pressed her close, kissing her lips. "You *will* choose me!"

Maya nodded with a smile, wiping a tear from her cheek. "May the Mother protect you," she whispered hoarsely, barely able to speak.

Watching the hunters-turned-warriors circling the hearth in a war dance, Ewan ran his hands through his hair, rose slowly, and said quietly to Maliki, "Could we speak privately? I won't keep you, my friend, I promise."

Maliki sighed impatiently but nodded. Away from the others, Ewan pulled the pouch from around his neck and handed it to him. "Take this. It will buy food, horses, and boats when you need them."

Taking the bag, Maliki looked inside, and his eyes widened. "Ewan, the gold coins! You saved these coins for Alana's mating day. Are you sure?"

"Maliki, of course I'm sure." Placing his hand on Maliki's arm, he assured his friend, "My adoptive families need this. Alana is strong, she'll make do." He paused and cocked his head, suddenly realizing, "Somehow Shylfing must have known about these coins. Let them be his death!"

"A painful and slow death for Shylfing!" Maliki spat. "Thank you, Ewan, my brother." Maliki solemnly gripped Ewan's arm, locking eyes before he trotted back to his men.

"May Mother Earth bless you and bring you all back," Ewan called to Maliki's turned back, motioning for his warriors. Maliki set out at a sprint, taking the familiar trails chosen because of Alana's vision. But Shylfing's party, with a head start, moved quickly as well.

Moving slowly with their minds deep in melancholy, Ewan, Alana, and Maya gathered wood and lit a fire to burn the bodies of the dead. Holding hands, they chanted prayers to Mother Earth to reclaim her sons and daughters, the funeral pyre dancing in the chilly wind that whipped around them. Wearily, they struck torches and began to search the rubble for anything salvageable. They had much to do before the first snow.

CHAPTER 9
LIL

Striving to be the model leader that his family expected, Lil dutifully arrived at the Ministry of Science early each morning over the next two months and pored over the scribes' reports of star interpretations, research explorations, and mining production. Much to Ki's irritation, Lil grilled him on the Ministry's research projects. He always found it fascinating to listen to Ki, whose wealth of knowledge was unequaled. Lil admired his resourcefulness and work ethic, feeling inspired to achieve greater excellence. During his true youth, Lil had diligently absorbed the Teacher's entire repository of Alterran history. Nevertheless, he dutifully attempted it again, following the Council's directive. Putting on the Teacher's electrode net, he selected a history program as a refresher. The Teacher replied that his memories were complete; there was nothing new. Searching a directory, he discovered obscure references to a Library.

Lil asked Ki, as he passed by, "Hey, old man, I see here a reference to the 'Library.' Do you know what it means?"

Ki squinted, appearing shocked. "It's not something you'd be interested in."

Being bored, Lil pursued it. "Why not? I have another month of confinement, and I've been through everything. If there's something else, I'd like to see it."

Ki ran his fingers through his unruly hair, which struck Lil as curious; it frequently meant he was nervous. Ki looked at him askance and shrugged his shoulders. "All right, come this way." Ki led him to a floor that Lil had thought to be unused and stopped at a door with an old-fashioned lock that didn't open at Lil's verbal command. Seeing Lil's puzzled look, Ki explained, "Not many know about the Library. You see, as a precaution when they detected unusual atmospheric readings, the Alterran Science Ministry sent us a duplicate set of all knowledge from the time before the Great Awakening." Producing an old-fashioned key for the lock, he opened the door to a dark room. Lil smelled mustiness and heard machinery whirring softly. Ki said, "En.Ki," and the glowglobes lit up throughout the large room with shelves lining the walls and forming columns in interior rows.

Lil exclaimed, "No! There are actually real books on these shelves? How did they ever make it through the portal?" Lil had never seen a paper book since information only came on electronic readers. He reached to pick one up.

"Wait," cautioned Ki, holding him back. "They're delicate. There's machinery running in here to maintain the right temperature and oxygen level to preserve these ancient beauties."

"I'll be careful," said Lil, wandering around. "These are real antiques. They must be many millennia old, perhaps more. What else is in this place?"

Ki led him to a machine in the center. "Actually, the books are here just for safekeeping. All the information was digitized long ago and can be accessed through this ancient computer system. Almost everything here dates prior to the Great Awakening," Ki said with reverence. "Lil, there's probably nothing here you'd be interested in. Are you sure you want to bother with all this old stuff? Everything that you need to know is available through the Teacher."

"I thought you said that you've found useful information here."

"I did? Well, it's true that all the important scientific breakthroughs occurred before the Great Awakening. Some of the old-time entrepreneurs made amazing discoveries. One discovered the wave absorption technology and wireless energy transmission that we use. Another created the technology for the rejuvenation chamber. But harmony and stability eliminated their kind; their inventions were too disruptive." Ki cautiously watched Lil to determine if he understood the meaning beneath his words.

Unsure if Lil grasped the Library's significance, Ki thought it would be amusing to see his reaction. He explained, "For a person of advanced rank, such as you, these records are accessible if you have nothing better to do. To read them, you need to insert one of these old disks here. When the main screen loads, there is an antiquated searching program to find things."

Lil grabbed a directory and plopped down. "Thanks. I'll look around a bit. I do have one other question before you go." He paused. "How is it that only certain people are able to use the Teacher?"

"What? You've never shown an interest in this before."

Lil gave him an insistent look.

Ki pulled on his ear lobe. "Let me show you something." He typed in some search terms, which brought up a chart containing a numerical ranking of Alterran society with a description by rank of those permitted access to the Teacher. "This is an old decree issued when they reorganized the government during the Great Awakening. Before then, children spent their childhood in schools; access was unequal, and it was expensive for society—entire segments of the economy were devoted to education. At the time, the Teacher was an absolutely revolutionary development; all those years of formal schooling were eliminated."

"Coupled with digital manufacturing and the replicator, the Teacher disrupted life for many people," observed Lil.

"It certainly did. Some people had spent their entire lives working as educators, and then the need for them disappeared almost overnight."

"I seem to remember that they were caught by surprise."

"Well, actually, I've found articles hinting that there was another significant advance before then." Ki rummaged through some files and brought out some old print materials that he'd been saving. "They invented an electronic book, which was basically a shell, and they sent individual books and other prints to this shell. Pretty soon, this device could hold the text of everything ever written right in the palm of your hand. That's when paper books and newspapers became obsolete—"

"—which saved trees," Lil interjected.

"Uh, right." Ki nodded in agreement. "Once all knowledge was contained in the same place, it was a short leap to transmitting it directly into the human brain—"

"—through the Teacher's neural net," Lil finished his sentence.

"That's right. It was adapted from a neural net developed for communicating with comatose patients. They became like junkies. After only a few sessions, encyclopedic knowledge was instantly absorbed. No more time spent reading books or going to class." He paused and glanced at Lil's face. "No more forcing students to learn things unnecessary to the career path."

Oblivious to Ki's searching glance, Lil leaned back in his chair. "If everyone had the exact same knowledge, it must have been difficult to make employment decisions. One of the great failings of the old system was that the government didn't assign people to jobs; they were forced to find their own or face starvation." Lil smugly thought how their system eliminated that chaos. When he was supreme leader, he would find this duty particularly rewarding.

"Yes," said Ki, shaking his head out of Lil's eyesight. "Most unpleasant, to be sure. Even without the terrorists, society was undergoing significant change. This happened at about the same time that the old nation states were yielding control to global institutions. If you're interested, you can find materials where they debated policy changes. Fascinating reading, really."

"Sure, I might take a look."

Ki paced around him. "One thing the new global Ministry of Education did was to recognize an opportunity to standardize and direct learning of only, shall we say, *appropriate* information." He paused, searching for any sign that Lil grasped his irony. Lil's face was blank, long practiced in his successorship training. "Among other things, they thought they could eliminate discrimination and religious factions that way."

"Yes, a significant step forward to achieve worldwide harmony," remarked Lil, reciting the Teacher's explanation.

Ki smirked behind Lil's back. "It was efficient to learn only what the supreme leader thought necessary. If additional knowledge was later required, it was simply obtained in another session with the Teacher." He wagged his finger. "Even then, it was prudent for someone to have access to everything. So they created the ranking system, and those with a high rank are permitted to absorb any program."

Lil listened intently but masked his reaction. He uncomfortably sensed that Ki's words held a hidden meaning. Lil never joked about the Alterran Code or the great traditions of harmony and stability, and he'd discipline any guardsman caught doing so. With Lil's silence, Ki cautiously continued, "As you know, under harmony and stability, the vast mass of the Alterran people are in the exact same social class and have the need only for the knowledge and apprenticeship of their forebears. Since those in control didn't want each person to know everything, they needed a way to control information and thus the population. At birth, the baby receives the same rank as the parents, along with a destiny certificate; the baby receives an implant giving the child access only to Teacher programs necessary for that destiny."

"Yes, I know all that," huffed Lil impatiently. "That was an important achievement of the Great Awakening. But there are some with greater access than that."

"You're right. An Alterran whose family has a minimum rank of ten is given an implant at birth, permitting the child to access the full range of the Teacher. Electrical stimulation is applied to develop the complementary skill set."

"Which families are those?"

"Lil, I'm surprised you don't know; Jahkbar must avoid the unpleasantries. Only the extended family of the House of En and two Council members of the House of Kan have a rank of ten or higher."

"But there must be exceptions," Lil said with annoyance. "My guardsmen get greater access."

"Yes, but it's not that their rank has changed, only that they've been given an expanded destiny certificate. For their duties at Hawan, they needed to be more versatile. They needed more than military learning. So, they received programs to, for example, gather scientific information. Conversely, those like Jared and Rameel, who hadn't been in the Guard, received military information."

In closing the chart, Ki added, "Only the Dalits with a rank below two have no access to the Teacher. Their knowledge is carefully limited to religious ceremonies and menial duties." Rising, he said, testing Lil, "The Teacher represented a vast improvement for society, don't you think?" He quickly strode away, not waiting for Lil's reaction.

Lil strummed his fingers on the table. Given Ki's position, he was puzzled by his odd behavior. Beginning to review a directory, he remembered the Teacher's instruction that the ages before the Great Awakening had been a dark time; people were unenlightened about social welfare and preservation of natural resources. Society had been divided into classes with tremendous social, economic, and political inequality. Since they didn't rely on star messages to choose their leaders, there was perpetual upheaval and violence. Thus, the Teacher's instruction for the age before the Great Awakening was limited, retaining only a full account of ancient legends.

Lil searched, not expecting to find anything worthwhile but dutifully complying with the Council's mandate. He scrolled through unfamiliar entries, choosing at random a published work that had been mass distributed. Numerous protests and riots were reported, confirming the Teacher's program.

He yawned and continued to a page marked "Editorial." Someone objected to the plan for restructuring society. This piqued his interest. The author said that the Great Awakening plan gave too much control over citizens' lives to the government and criticized the plan for being vague and using obtuse language. Further, the plan was denounced for endangering traditions of liberty, self-determination, and democracy, which were described as "sacred." Odd language, he pondered, since his society downplayed the individual in favor of the collective, which everyone agreed was an enlightened attitude. Before the Great Awakening, many unemployed and penniless workers had gladly accepted the safety net offered by the House of En, he thought. He proudly recalled that his family had eliminated unemployment. How dare the author criticize an improvement of such magnitude! He was perplexed by the author's emotional opposition. Continuing to read, he found that the editorial also referred to widespread protests against the plan. Puzzling; Alterrans were taught that people had overwhelmingly adopted the principles of the Great Awakening, having become disgusted with the severe social injustices of the old system.

Well, perhaps this so-called editorial was an aberration, he thought as he searched further. The next document was another mass distribution piece from a decade earlier than the last one. The initial page reported serial mass disasters, resulting in huge casualties. The author depicted the events as a worldwide, coordinated terrorist attack. Not surprising, Lil thought; the Teacher taught about the era's extreme violence. He froze, however, when the article identified the terrorists as a previously unknown fringe group called the Party of Harmony and Stability, which promoted a radical form of environmental and social activism. The group's philosophy was not well understood, according to the author, but they were quoted as advocating for the destruction of all existing industrial, political, and economic systems in favor of a fundamental restructuring of society. The author quoted the group's manifesto: "a state of harmony with nature and the universe, while concomitantly providing for social and economic equality, which would be attained by a social reordering and depopulation plan." The author was openly contemptuous.

Lil drew back, blinked, and shook his head. It was not what he'd anticipated, and he had difficulty comprehending the context. Perhaps this was a fictional work, or some psychotic writer promoting lies and propaganda. He thought it best to try an entirely different disk. He found an earlier piece in newsprint that had been widely distributed. He recollected that paper had once been made from trees, which had destroyed the forests and led to an increase in carbon dioxide that would have destroyed the planet if the people had not wisely adopted the principles of the Great Awakening. Returning to the disk, he read that a new leader promoting radically new policies was preparing to take over the government. He looked for background describing the battles won by the conqueror, but the paper referred only to an "election." He didn't know how this could be reconciled with the standard teaching about great violence that had cyclically occurred before the people recognized divinely chosen leaders. He shrugged and thought that perhaps there were brief interludes when new leaders didn't obtain power through death and destruction. Surely, he thought, if he looked only a little further, he would find everything as the Teacher taught it.

He felt his body grow stiff, since he customarily received considerable exercise during his observation missions. To compensate for being sedentary, he toned his muscles with his tunic. He relaxed, sitting back with his eyes closed, and felt his tunic's nanobytes massaging his body. Feeling refreshed, he sent a message to his mother asking her to meet him for lunch.

Being at the Ministry of Science meant that he could satisfy both personal and professional obligations.

Having excess time, he stopped by the Teacher and attached the neural net. He examined the listing of available programs, looking for a language program to permit him to communicate more effectively with Earth people. Although fully intending to honor the Council's edict, as a commander he was accustomed to working on backup plans; given the proximity of Alana's village and their dwindling food supplies, it was possible that communications with the Earth people would become desirable, even by the Council. He found a program that presented a rudimentary Earth language called the "common tongue," which had been derived from an old maritime culture they'd discovered. Lil ran the brief program, which sent waves creating new memories.

As he left, he asked Ki for an extra key to the Library so that he could return later. Ki observed him curiously and handed him a key, asking, "Did you find anything of interest?"

"Not sure. I'm having lunch with mother. I'll be back later." After walking over to Guard Hall, he found Uras waiting by the door. "Mother, good to see you, as always."

"Hello, darling son," she said, putting her arm around him. He winced, glad that no guardsmen saw him, and he kissed her on the cheek. After entering, she gazed at the images appearing as a collage on the holographic panels. "It's charming here; I've never ventured in before."

They sat down at a table, where Lil punched a code into the center tube, and the nourishment bar for their rank appeared. As he took a bite, Uras looked at him with concern. "I hear you've had a difficult time lately. What's been going on with you?"

"Just trying to save the colony, Mother," Lil replied casually, diverting his eyes, not wanting to explain himself again. "Have any interesting cases?"

"Seriously, what's going on?" his mother insisted, surprised by his reticence.

"I am serious," said Lil. With deliberateness, he looked around the Hall to avoid her motherly gaze but caught the eyes of guardsmen and turned back. No wonder the House of En was sequestered, he thought; leaders shouldn't be seen this way.

"All right, I believe you, although I don't understand you," she said with exasperation, putting down her bar and throwing up her hands. Grabbing his elbow, she pleaded, "*Please,* tell me exactly why and how you're saving the colony!"

"Mother, quiet. You of all people should understand that we can't continue for long here doing things the way we have. We can't get new supplies from Alterra. The few survivors there live in underground bunkers. We can't go back. You know this, and Father and the Council know, but none of you will take the next step. It's obvious that we'll spend the rest of lives here, so we *must* adapt."

"I see," she said thoughtfully, folding her wrapper. "Did you actually eat the mastodon? Did anyone?" She'd never tasted meat and couldn't imagine degenerating that far. Surely, with a little effort they could find sufficient wild fruits and vegetables even on this primitive planet. After all, the hydroponic garden was developing nicely.

"Yes," he said, wincing. "Okay, I admit it wasn't so good. We've much to learn. But that doesn't mean that we should give up. We'll need food. It would be great if we could live entirely on agricultural products—believe me, I'd give anything if we could. We can't feed all these people entirely from those hanging gardens. Do you think I like the thought of eating meat? But right now we have no means of farming unless, of course, we enslave Earthlings to farm for us. Would you prefer that violation of the directive?"

"No, of course, not."

"Well, then, we're in a box, and one must choose which evil is more acceptable."

She patted his hand. "Calm down, darling. You have a point, but you must find a way to comply with the Code."

"The Code will just need to be bent for a little while until we can bring things back into harmony," Lil huffed a little too loudly. Glancing around, he found guardsmen staring at him. He cringed and said more quietly, "Mother, can we change the subject? I need to ask you about something."

"Of course."

"I was reading in the Library–" Uras knitted her eyebrows, puzzled. "–old records that Ki showed me, and I was randomly choosing history articles from before the Great Awakening. Each item seemed to contradict the Teacher. I'm pretty confused. How likely is it that the random articles that I selected would be the only ones in conflict?"

Uras again raised her eyebrows. She didn't know about any of this and had never heard about the Library, but her long years as a political wife had given her an acute sense of the forbidden. She feared that her son had unwittingly stumbled onto another path to trouble. Lil was the second named successor, but if he proved to be undesirable, the Council might reinterpret the star signs to designate another. She needed to deflect Lil from these dangerous thoughts. "Darling, I believe that Ki received some fascinating field reports, and he's hoping that, with your experience, you'd help him interpret the data."

"I get the message."

CHAPTER 10
MALIKI

Near midnight, when the wind grew blustery and heavy clouds concealed the gibbous moon, Maliki grunted with grim hope. Still jogging familiar trails, he led sixty warriors—the faces of nearly a third wore only a youngster's fuzz, but every hand was needed. Knowing every twist in the winding path, he had no need for moonlight. He knew the feel, smell, and nighttime sound of each stream and hollow along the way and could read the minutest of signs. The sharp edges of branches that brushed against their arms had been broken by a large, careless party rushing by, and their feet felt impressions left in the moist dirt by the hardened Danish boots. With their powerful legs, made muscular from continual running and climbing, the men could jog for hours without slowing and barely make a sound that even a trained ear could distinguish from the gentle pattering of night animals. All except for Kutu, whose weak legs stumbled as he struggled to keep up the unforgiving pace.

Slowing, Maliki hooted like an owl in three crisp notes, signaling the men to stop. The narrow path was nestled against the steep hillside crested by the miles-long ridges. Even in the blackness, Maliki recognized the upward path through the thick brambles. "Climb," he whispered in the ear of the closest man, who passed it along to the next as quietly as possible. The warriors felt their way up to the ridge, and on the worn flatness of the ridge trail, which permitted greater speed, Maliki would close the gap. After Maliki reached the top, breathing normally despite the exertion, he helped others scramble over the top rocks. Older men, like gray-haired Bowd, his wife's father, breathed heavily, and Maliki was glad that it was too dark to see Bowd's proud face; he knew that the old man's dark eyes glared with the shame of needing help. Kutu scrambled last after Bowd, huffing and suppressing a coughing spell as best he could with his hand. If Maliki's face had been visible, the men would have seen him scowling. He and a few others had no need for rest, but Bowd and Kutu were exhausted, and he reluctantly let them rest a few moments. Soon, he could wait no more. "Run by twos," Maliki whispered so all could hear, less fearful of making noise at this height. Maliki took his place at the end of the line with Taku, the brother of Maliki's wife, who was also an excellent hunter. "We make good progress." Maliki heard Taku's voice through the darkness in which he could only make out a trace of his nearby body.

"Yes," Maliki's gravelly voice betrayed his tension. "We are too few." His head having cooled since leaving the village, his frantic mind raced to devise rescue plans, drawing upon the learning from the countless hunting expeditions that he'd planned with Ewan. As a boy, he'd learned the invaluable lesson that bravery was only one component of success. A sneering older boy had mocked him, calling him timid when he crouched hidden in the brush observing a grazing caribou with a full rack. The older boy ran at the animal in full view, raising his spear as he approached to plunge it into the animal's side. The grazing animal ignored the boy until he drew close. Suddenly, he snorted, put his head down, and effortlessly butted him with his sharp-tipped rack, barely moving more than a few paces. The buck had cut a mortal gash through the boy's chest. Ewan had taught Maliki that there was honor in waiting for prey to be careless; then the hidden hunters could pounce. If the Danes' ships remained harbored when they caught up, the men would hide in the bushes and silently overpower one at a time. If the ships had sailed, they had no choice but to cross by ferry and pursue by land, a long, arduous trek that would take a moon or more. He touched the pouch with the gold coins hanging around his neck and silently thanked Ewan for his foresight.

An unnatural wind swept down the trail, and the men felt their body hair rising into goose bumps. Taku touched Maliki's arm and warned, "My body tingles."

"Drood." *Mother, don't let him attack us now,* prayed Maliki. Drood was a menace, but the villages had had an uneasy truce that neither would attack the other. No doubt Drood sensed their vulnerability, as his hunters had done so many times with the weaklings of herds they had hunted. Hooting two short bursts, the men trotted closer together. They had no time to form a tight circle hiding their backs against the attack. How could Drood have known they would be here? Maliki heard a grunt, followed by the rustling of bushes. Were they to be picked off? Maliki's heart swelled with anger. When mistier clouds let through beams of moonlight, he glimpsed a short, scrawny man standing a hundred paces before him. The man wore long robe of soft hide and held a staff topped by a human head. Quickly hooting three bursts as an owl and skidding to a stop, Maliki demanded, "Move! No time for you."

"Oh?" sneered Drood, his menacing voice reverberating in the wind as if spoken into each man's ear. "I have time for you."

"What do you want?" If Drood wouldn't let them pass, Maliki prepared to stab his puny body and swing at his hidden warriors.

"I know where you go and why." Clouds again covered the moon. In the blackness of the trail, Drood's skull-headed staff glowed eerily, and Maliki heard shocked gasps behind him.

"Then you know that the Mother guides our steps, and we must run like the wind to catch those who have captured our families. Let us pass!" Maliki took a step forward, his spear ready. His tribe had heard many rumors over the years of Drood's cruelty, but Drood hadn't harmed any of their village.

"Not so fast. I must get something in return."

"What is it you want? Our village was destroyed, and our women and children were taken. We have nothing left to give!" spat Maliki, his chest heaving with impatience and anger.

"You know what I want. It's the same reason why I've never attacked you. I want Alana to marry my son. Ewan knows and so do you, as well as those who are, or should I say were, of your village."

"What madness is this?" shouted Taku, but without taking a step forward, fearing Drood's dark magic. He'd seen the bones discarded by Drood's tribe, and he, like all his tribe, knew about the mysterious shadows that encased Drood's warriors. This time, though, his fear for his family overrode his fear of Drood. "This is no time to speak of mating proposals! Let your son woo her." To Maliki, he whispered, "This one truly has a black heart."

Drood pounded his staff in the ground, and the skull beamed its eerie light on them. Maliki could see Taku's face as bright as daylight. "Vow to me that she'll be my son's bride, and I'll not only let you pass, but I'll help you." The men behind Maliki gasped and cowered, putting their hands over their eyes for shade.

Quivering, Taku whispered in Maliki's ear, feeling his brother as steadfast as ever. "For love of the Mother, Maliki, vow to him! We can't die here and leave our families to be tortured. A forced promise to a black heart is not binding, and Ewan will dispose of him later." As Maliki hesitated, two more cries rang through the night, followed by the rustling of bushes as bodies were drug away. Taku whispered fiercely, "Maliki, you cannot wait!"

Maliki felt acid rising in his throat at the thought of betraying Alana and Ewan. Where was the Mother's mercy this night? Had she herself been captured by the god of darkness? Thinking of Yanni and his children, he said softly, "I vow." This is truly a dark bargain we make this night. We are cursed.

"Louder, so all will swear to the seal of this bargain!" Drood's voice hung in the air, as if spoken above the entire line of cowering men. "Say, 'I vow that Alana is to be mated to Maku upon my return.'"

Maliki wet his dry lips, forcing the words through his dry throat as loudly as he could.

"I take you at your word," growled Drood. He hovered his staff in their direction, and Maliki felt the tingling in his body grow greater. Men cried out in terror until their voices faded into the stiffening breeze. All went black. Maliki weightlessly floated, sensing that he flew with the wind. Through the blackness, he could see the rosy fingers of the coming dawn, and he gradually felt the weight of his body return. Feeling the sloping, pebbly ground beneath his feet, he felt his body and found that his arms, legs, and torso were as before. He heard the sound of waves, and he peered through the thin morning fog, outstretching his arms to feel for his friends. Taku was near, and when he touched him, he groaned. Maliki quickly shushed him. Feeling farther through the fog, he touched Jonk and Agar, who each gave his arm a reassuring grasp. From the low grumbles, the others seemed to be there as well. With two short bursts, he gave the crow signal, meaning that they should be still and alert. If Drood were true to his word, as black and repulsive as it was, the Danes might be near. In the distance, he heard voices muffled by the fog. Putting his ear to the ground, he heard feet, but not as many as he'd expected with the women and children. They must be boarding their long ships. He squawked as a crow once, signaling that they should move forward with caution, prepared to attack.

Accustomed to sneaking up on wary prey, the men kept their footsteps soundless while they crouched forward, spears and knives ready. Through the fog, the outline of two tall, muscular Danes wearing hide helmets became visible. Maliki signaled that he and Jonk would take the larger one on the right, and that Taku and Agar should take the other. Maliki and Taku crouched. They sprinted at their prey, leaping up with knives drawn. In one fluid motion, they pulled themselves up the man's back and drew the blade across his throat, preventing him from yelling as blood gurgled from his throat. Jonk and Agar each speared a man before he could turn with his weapon. Beams of sunlight streamed through the clouds, illuminating the long ships that were heavy with exhausted women desperately holding on to babies and toddlers, unused to the tossing of the ships. Older children, left to fend for themselves, were coerced into paddling. Three ships had been pushed away from shore, and Maliki could see two more out in the channel. The last Dane warriors were preparing to jump into the remaining boats. His eyes scoured the nearest boats for Yanni and his sons, but he couldn't find them.

"Rush them before they're gone," urged Agar, his voice full of the emotion they all felt.

Maliki had planned for small ambushes, not a frontal assault against these huge, well-armed men. Seething, he reluctantly said, "Small animals do not attack mighty ones without cover." Nosti, seeing his wife and baby in the last boat, bolted past him, followed by others who ran to save their families. Sprinting and sliding down the steep incline to the small beach, they were seen by the burly Danes. A scar-faced man with long, dirty hair cascading from under his helmet waded from the water and drew from his side a handle to which was tightly tied a large stone cut with spiky protrusions. Nosti charged him with his spear. The scar-faced warrior grabbed his spear and cracked open Nosti's skull with his hammer-like weapon. Nosti's body staggered from the blow and fell in a bloody heap. The six men behind Nosti bravely poked at the scar-faced warrior's back, but he flung his hammer around in a great sweep, knocking them all to the ground with crushed skulls. Laughing heartily, the Danes jeered and pushed their boats away, with the last warriors jumping in.

Ignoring the jeering Danes, Maliki snorted and exhorted his men. "Good men fell today. They let their hearts rule their heads. If we are to rescue our families, we must be smart. We must not forget the lessons of hunting." Through the lessening fog, he could see the smoldering campfires, with roasted meat carelessly left on the spit. "Even if it turns your stomach to eat food left by the Danes, food that should have been eaten by our wives and children, we must eat to have strength to save them." He picked up a discarded elk leg from the spit over a fire where only a few embers glowed, took a few bites, wiped his drooling mouth with the back of his hand, and handed the still-meaty bone to Bowd. To the men who stood squeamishly gaping at him, he said loudly, "Eat. Refill the water pouches. Then we run to the ferryman. We'll make him take us close to the Dane village; I'm sure that he knows the way."

"But he won't take us without payment," protested Jonk.

"Ewan gave us gold," said Maliki grimly, disgusted that, if he lived, he would betray his friend's generosity.

* * *

"Get up." Drood poked his sleeping son Maku with his antelope bone cane. He squinted in the moonlight, hearing the first birds chirping the dawn chorus. Impatient that the body below him had not awakened from its slumber, he cracked his cane against the boy's legs and grabbed him by the ear.

"Ow!" Maku sat up, clenching his fist and drawing back his arm in preparation to fight until he met his father's cold stare. No one crossed Drood. He brushed aside the patchwork of sleeping furs and arose, grabbing the spear that lay beside him. "Are enemies near?"

"Good news," said Drood, nearly smiling at his eldest son, confusing him with the rare event. "Come." Drood had already aroused his pregnant wife, Weena, to light a fire to make tea. Sitting down on a log near the fire, he waved for his son to sit beside him. Unlike his father, dark-haired Maku was a strong boy in his late teens who towered above his father in height, if not in stature or ambition. Like all the tribesmen, he felt a mixture of dread, awe, and adoration for his father and his magical powers. During the summer, Maku had crudely hacked his beard; with the approaching winter, he was letting it grow again, and he tugged on it now, searching his mind for what his father intended.

"It is settled. You are to be mated to Ewan's daughter, Alana." Drood sipped his tea and stared with satisfaction into the fire. Not only would the marriage give him legitimacy as a ruler, but he'd witnessed Alana's Earthkeeper powers. The girl had promise. More promise than even Elaine, the Earthkeeper hermit who dwelled in the glen. By harnessing Alana's powers, he could control the peninsula without a war.

"When?" asked Maku, wrinkling his nose in disbelief. His father had hinted at this marriage for years, not wanting to risk humiliation if his formal overture were rejected. In truth, Drood had been perfectly blunt with his intentions, even demonstrating the wonder of his powers as an enticement, but Ewan had rebuffed him.

"Soon," he cackled in the throaty laughter that petrified those not of his tribe. "*Very* soon." He planned to wait for a while, to see if Maliki and the other men returned. Witnessing Maliki offer her to him would be sweet, a sweetness worth waiting a few months for. But he wouldn't wait forever. Against the Danes, they were unlikely to return. "Weena, plan a mating ceremony for the winter solstice. As well as a huge feast befitting our new status."

CHAPTER 11

KI

The first small Alterran expedition arrived millennia before Hawan's construction, following an arduous flight through space during which they skimmed through a vestigial ribbon of primordial light that flowed at this universe's creation speed. With them, they brought the first portal. Alterrans on their home world, at that time having fully operational solar collectors capable of capturing their sun's immense energy, opened a temporary rift in space-time that permitted a traveler to pass directly from the portal on Alterra to the one on Earth. Among the first scientists to travel through the portal was Anu's son, Ki, who eagerly sought to escape the rigidity of Alterran life. After surveying the planet, he established a base that he named Eridu in the middle latitudes at the river delta leading to an inland sea, which was fed by the melt of the glaciers stubbornly gripping the northern mountains. In those early days, glaciers buried whole parts of the northern continents. Under his command, the first explorers scouted available land for natural resources, identifying subsurface deposits of the rare metals that Alterrans sought. They needed metals for their delicate electronics, having nearly exhausted their own supplies. Drilling into the planet with lasers, they opened mines, staffed by short, stocky Dalits who had been specially bred for the low, dim tunnels and uneven footing of the mines. The primary mine, from which gold and diamonds were extracted, was at the far tip of the large southern continent that was free of the glacier's grasp. Beryllium was mined on the other side of the planet from Eridu. In light of this planet's harsh, icy conditions, few Alterrans were interested in Earth so long as the mining shipments arrived, and Ki had it to himself.

To Ki, the early days had been an exhilarating time of discovery, blessedly devoid of Alterran intrigue. He had found the emerging hominid population to be fascinating, and after many centuries on Earth, he had invited his sister, Ninhursag, to join him in studying their development. A geneticist, she had been delighted that Earth was a natural laboratory. Eventually, with the glaciers receding and the ambient temperature rising, the hominid population became highly mobile and rapidly evolved. She analyzed their genetic code and concluded that the dominant hominid species was nearly identical to Alterrans. When she submitted her research findings back home, however, she landed herself in a political maelstrom by proposing that they facilitate the Earthlings' development. Her work had been misinterpreted and deliberately manipulated for political purposes, she thought. Accused of genetic tampering and unable to defend herself from afar, she was ordered home. A new policy was now in force, and Ki had been directed to construct an elaborate, permanent colony to house Anu, Lil, and the others who would enforce the new Non-Interference Directive.

Under Ki's microscopic supervision, Alterran engineers chiseled Hawan from the walls of the highest peak in remote mountains formed from one of the earliest upheavals of Earth's crust. In choosing this inaccessible spot on the distant peninsula, he had sought to avoid the burgeoning Earth population of the middle latitudes. In constructing Hawan, he planned a special place for his precious Library. Ninhursag had told him of the ancient store of knowledge preserved in the backrooms of the Alterran Ministry of Science. There, she had learned genetics principles that were not taught by the Teacher. She had smuggled him works that she knew would interest him, and he'd been able to advance his scientific knowledge far beyond the Alterran Teacher. This was knowledge that was ignored and disdained by the House of En and, thus the Ministry, because it was created in the time before the Great Awakening. The Ministry was even considering destroying the Library to redeploy the space. Transforming herself into the visage of the Ministry's head, Ninhursag had snuck into the backroom and coated it with an electronic replicator net. She copied the entire room's contents, and she then sent them to Ki through the portal. Being forced to read, since the ancient books couldn't be absorbed, Ki nevertheless found the science and the philosophy of the ancient times fascinating.

When, upon Hawan's completion, Anu and Lil had arrived through the portal, Ki sulked at their assumption of control and secreted himself in the southern hemisphere on the shores near their gold and diamond mine, in the enclave where he'd worked with Ninhursag. He was Anu's firstborn, and he should have been named successor of Alterra—and he would have been in any rational system not based on the nonsense of a pristine bloodline. Coming to Earth when no one else was interested in this distant, primitive planet, by all moral rights in the universe, Earth belonged to him. He bitterly sat slumped in his chair on his veranda, watching the waves and the seagulls. Anu soon found that they couldn't dispense with Ki's unique scientific skills. Somehow, he knew more than other scientists taught by the Teacher. Anu had insisted that he return to assume control over Hawan's scientific operations, as head of the Ministry of Science.

Despite a demotion from governing all Earthly operations, Ki unleashed his creative energies, aided by a full complement of those who had absorbed extensive scientific programs, but always supplemented by the secret knowledge that he gleaned from his private Library. He captured the wave energy boundlessly available through the constant geologic processes of Earth, and converted it into usable power, which he wirelessly transmitted throughout the colony. Since Anu and the Council of Elders limited their thoughts to loftier concerns of universal harmony, Ki took satisfaction that disdained details such as energy production, maintenance, medical facilities, and food creation were the true lifelines of Hawan, making him the ruler by function, if not by name. Under his direction, the Ministry had measured the Earth and identified the ley lines of electromagnetic pathways. The harmony fundamental to Alterran beliefs meant being one with the planet, with the planetary dimensions serving as a system of sacred geometry based upon the sacred number of twelve and the multiple 360. Although Ki admitted to being cynical about the Alterran government, he felt that Alterrans brilliantly understood the connection between sacred geometry and the universe.

Now, with Alterra unable to generate sufficient power to activate the portal, Ki worried particularly about their food supply. Incapable of replicating the molecular composition of the nourishment bars with the available resources, he might need to resort to old-fashioned bionic ingredients. Teams worked on converting Earth's wild grains into varieties suitable for agriculture, but the successive generations took time, and there were insufficient Dalits for natural cultivation. Having recruited Lil to begin hunting, Ki was relieved that he was committed. The punishment given to Lil would be far lighter than that given to anyone else.

* * *

Returning to the Ministry, Lil checked with Ki. "Old man, what do you have for me this afternoon?"

"Well, here's something that may interest you. A comet will pass close to Earth and—"

"—I'm aware of that," Lil interrupted, making a self-satisfied smirk. "I read the report."

"I'm glad the operations unit is on top of this," Ki replied wryly, wondering if, being marooned on this planet, they would ever stop competing against each other.

"Sounds serious." Lil was no longer flippant; he pressed his lips, knowing that Jared and Rameel couldn't handle an emergency of this magnitude during his punishment.

"Very." Ki displayed images captured the previous evening. "A piece of this comet has already broken off and crashed into this solar system's sixth planet. It's gaseous, but the explosion was so large that it was easily visible to our observers. If a much smaller piece hits Earth, it would be devastating."

"If Earth is threatened with a direct hit, our options will be limited. On Alterra, we could have launched a deflective device to alter its course. Here, we'll have to come up with something else."

"Yes," Ki agreed, "we're studying our options."

Lil thought for a moment and added, "Keep me posted. At least, we should have the Guard stationed around the planet watching from a safe altitude. They could record whatever may happen."

Ki nodded. "I agree, although you should leave sufficient hovercraft nearby in case it's coming straight at us and we need to evacuate quickly."

On Alterra, they'd smugly thought that they could control anything. The universe had taught them otherwise. Grimly, Lil gave the necessary commands to his men to commence preparations. Still being confined for punishment, for now, he'd need to depend on them. "Ki, be sure that Father reads this report. Suggest that he end my banishment so that I can deal with this." Ki nodded, uncomfortably agreeing that Lil would be needed. "You can find me in the Library if I'm needed."

Ki was apprehensive; he didn't want Lil suspecting what lay in his heart. Ama, who woodenly enforced the principles of the Great Awakening, would grant no quarter to individualism, branding him a subversive enemy of the state. Seeking to deflect Lil's further attention, he said as casually as he could, "Too much time in the Library can be bad for you. Those old books might transmit extinct viruses." Seeing Lil's upraised eyebrows, he quickly added, "The books might contain traces of ancient bacteria or spores that we've eradicated."

Controlling his emotions, Lil studied him, noticing how he pursed his lips and ran his hand through his hair. Oddly, Ki seemed more concerned about his going to the Library than the comet. *How much does Ki know about the old society?* The supreme leadership belonged to Lil as the second named successor unless he made a serious mistake. He and Ki were rivals; assuming, of course, that Alterran society survived and they made it home. He reminded himself that there were limits to confiding in Ki. "The Council directed me to learn more about Alterran history and the dangers of *mencomm,* and I've exhausted the programs of the Teacher. Doing as ordered, old man," he said airily with a broad smile that did not match his wary eyes, turning toward the Library.

Uneasily, Ki took a deep breath as he watched Lil walk away. He didn't like Lil's learning his secrets; no matter what facts he learned, Lil would never interpret things the way he did. Lil couldn't have his respect for individualism; it wasn't in his best interest as named successor. In the past, many had valiantly fought to save the old system, believing with religious fervor that self-determination and freedom of choice were innate human rights. But not all, and those others were the victors. Having spent considerable time in the Library, Ki knew that the official history offered through the Teacher had been rewritten in favor of the victor, the Party of Harmony and Stability.

CHAPTER 12
ALANA

Over the months since the rescue party had bravely set out, the last leaves had dropped from the now-bare oak and ash trees, and the winds had grown bitterly cold, nipping at Alana's nose and chilling her bones. In the mornings, she broke the icy film atop the spring and brought water to be heated for washing in the last pot ignored by the Danes. Reluctant to leave, she slept with Ewan and Maya huddled in the alcove within their smashed hut, over which they hung thick fir tree branches. During the cold rains, at least the alcove kept them dry. She held back tears whenever she remembered the comforting warmth of the thick mastodon hide or her stolen giant bear sleeping fur. Since the tiny cellar below their floor hadn't been found by the Danes, they still had a few summer vegetables. Keeping her faith until the villagers' return, Alana steadfastly gathered plants and caught wild sheep, trimming their wool with her knife and then boiling it clean and hanging it to dry in the late autumn sun. Ewan built a wooden trap for catching fish, but the pots that he'd used for smoking it had either been destroyed or stolen. Maya skinned trapped rabbits, sewing the skins together into garments and making stew. Despite Alana's optimism, Ewan knew these supplies wouldn't be enough. They needed warmer clothes and sleeping furs.

Alana sat with Maya by the fire in the evening, making a reed basket for storage and listening to Ewan's ideas for capturing and killing a cave bear by himself. "Father, you can't possibly be serious," she laughed, confident that he'd drop this idea when the other men returned. He didn't respond, and she grew worried about his black mood. Her father had always been cheerful and steadfast, and she needed the old Ewan now. Why didn't he believe in Maliki and the others?

"Alana, it's dangerous to be alone," Ewan said darkly, barely above a whisper, as he hunched beneath his few rabbit furs, supplemented by the thickest fir branches they could find. But it wasn't enough, and his teeth chattered with the cold despite his best efforts to stop shivering. He'd given all the other new furs to Alana and Maya, claiming that his leathered skin protected him from the cold. He stared vacantly into the fire, overwhelmed by the cruelty of the world. "To be alone without provisions is near certain death. In winter, it means a cruel death." Never before had he yearned so intensely for Atlantis and his wife; his stomach was in knots. Closing his tired, red eyes to escape, he dreamed of a happy time, playfully chasing his green-eyed betrothed through the bush-lined labyrinth between the torch-lit porticos that opened into the magnificent expanse of a terraced courtyard. An illuminated statue of reclining Poseidon, smiling, amused, and joyous no doubt at some entertainment in that delicious pre-catastrophe time, arose before the pillared temple where his love served as an enslaved attendant to the priestess, the priestess who had sensed Alana's openness to the Earth Mother's energy and had begun her apprenticeship. The night was warm, and the salty breeze caressed her long, curly blonde hair. She was two decades younger than he; it had taken years of backbreaking work to accumulate the coin to buy a wife's freedom. As she moved, the seashell necklace that he'd given her betrayed her location. A few steps ahead of him, the strap slipped from her silky long gown clinging to her slim, curvy figure. Teasingly peeking at him through the marble pillars, she lingered, watching for the silhouette outlining the broad, muscular shoulders wrought from his seafaring life. He pretended to lunge at her, missed, then caught her, whirling her to his chest to hold her tight, burying his face in the sweet-smelling fragrance of her hair and skin, enmeshed by her soft laughter, and feeling the rising excitement as she caressed his neck. They kissed. He shuddered with long-suppressed desire—.

Shaking his shoulder as if he were a naughty urchin caught stealing their evening meal, Alana cried, "Father, you scare me." She set down her reeds and put her arm around his shoulder. He grumbled and frowned at being snapped back to the bleak present. Glancing at her frightened face, so closely resembling his cherished wife, he softened his tone. Shivering again, he stretched to throw more stubby logs into the fire, sending embers swirling in a dance through the crisp night air. As they disappeared, he longed to follow them. Alana noticed in the flickering light that he looked haggard and stressed. Fear welled up in her at the wandering of his mind; an old villager had once lost his senses and become bedfast until he wasted away, losing the will to live; she couldn't stand to see that fate for her fearless Ewan. First praying to the Earth Mother for composure, she lectured, "You know how hard we've worked." Having trapped and fished, working night and day, their stores were increasing, and Maya had accumulated a mountain of apples and nuts; their reed baskets were filled with wimberries and elderberries. "Don't worry so much. We have all this wool and the new furs from the traps to lay over us for warmth. When our people come back, we'll have enough until they can hunt. The caribou will be coming down from the high country soon." She refused to give up, vanquishing the horror from her mind. "Cheer up!"

Ewan lifted his head and attempted a weak smile to rouse himself from his dark thoughts. When Alana again picked up her reeds and resumed her light-hearted chattering with Maya, he sank down, letting their fantasy plans to surprise the returning villagers drift over his numb ears. It was as if nothing were wrong, he thought irritably, annoyed by their innocence and undying hope. Alana didn't remember the difficulties they'd overcome after Atlantis imploded. He sank deeper into melancholy, unable to bear the inevitable day when his daughter would finally be crushed with the loss of all hope; if not for themselves, then for the others. He couldn't endure that day.

Despite his exhaustion, Ewan tried to keep one eye open at all times, fearful that the cannibal Drood might take advantage of his weakened condition to prey on them. But he frequently found himself dozing off in days-old exhaustion. Why did life need to be so hard? Throwing another log on the fire a little too strongly and seeing the rising sparks snuffed out as they vainly struggled against hope to survive in the brisk night wind, he knew he couldn't sit there and freeze to death. He probably was scaring Alana; he could see that now. He had to take action. He would either kill a cave bear or die trying.

As the temperature plummeted and the days became shorter, he could wait no longer. Sitting on the frosty ground near the hearth, sharpening his knife, he announced, "Tomorrow, we gather together everything usable and move to the cave. I need to get you settled in case it snows." He watched his breath dance in the air before him.

"You mean, get all of us settled," admonished Alana absent-mindedly, thinking him merely imprecise. She plucked at the fur from the rabbits then roasting on the spit.

"Hmm," he said, taking a drink of water from his travel cup to avoid her gaze. He wished the Danes had left him a kindly drop of his fermented berries.

After thinking it over, she protested, "But father, the villagers won't know where we are when they return." Looking at the firelight shadowing his face, she saw wrinkles and dark lines below his eyes that she hadn't noticed before. He looked more unkempt than she'd ever known him to be. She vowed to boil water for his morning grooming rather than let him wash in the chilly stream.

Tapping her arm for reassurance, he said gently, "Maliki knows about the cave. He'll surely look for you there." After brooding for a while, he took a deep breath. It was time for her to acknowledge the truth. "Alana, I don't want to destroy your hope, but I don't believe anyone will ever return. You'll believe that too, soon."

"I'll *never* give up hope," she insisted, refusing to entertain any thought of failure.

"As you wish." He shrugged. Never? There's only so much an old man can do, he thought. She was like him when he was young and foolish, not willing to accept defeat. How else could he, a lowly seaman, have had the temerity to woo the attendant to the priestess, or to survive in this beautiful yet forbidding land? Ah, back then he was naive.

Several days later, having completed the arduous move, Ewan announced as he sharpened his short knives and the tip of his long spears, "Tomorrow, I go hunting."

Alana, accustomed to her father's absences, didn't object; she thought that his mood must have improved because they were away from the spirits of the dead now inhabiting her old village. The caribou must be near, and she'd enjoy the fresh meat. She felt claustrophobic in the smallness of the cave's main chamber and assumed that he did as well. He'd shown her the passageways that led deeper into a large cavern, where they stored the apples and other food they'd gathered. But the deep passages were narrow and dark, and she hated going there, resolving to return to rebuild her village at the first sight of spring. She simply replied, "All right. I'll prepare a pack for you. How long do you think you'll be gone?"

"A couple of weeks," he muttered as if distracted, testing the knives' sharpness.

"Oh? Why so long?" she demanded, dread welling up inside her.

He didn't want her to worry, but he'd always been honest with her. He put his hands on her shoulders and, in case he didn't return, drank in the sight of her creamy skin, straight, delicate nose, and green eyes narrowed with concern. Seeing her eyes tear, he had to escape. He straightened and announced, "I'm going to the far north to kill a cave bear. The fur will keep all three of us warm this winter when the temperature drops further."

"A cave bear, Father?" Tears streaming, she pushed away the knives to hug him. "You can't possibly do that alone. Please don't go." A younger Ewan might have succeeded; she didn't want to hurt him with the obvious—he was too old and slow.

He said firmly, "My mind is made up. If anything happens to me, the two of you have enough food if you ration it and watch the traps. When it's frigid, go deep down in the cave where the temperature is constant. In the spring, make your way south to Yoachim." He closed his eyes, afraid that he might never see her again. Alana held him tightly and sobbed.

In the morning, she said good-bye with dry eyes and kissed his cheek, promising one last time to gather whatever they could and to check the traps.

"Always remember how much I love you, Alana," he called back as he began his journey, his voice drifting into the winds.

"I'll look for you every day!" She desperately stood on tiptoe as she'd done as a small girl, calling to his disappearing back.

As soon as he was out of sight, Alana said frantically, "Maya, help me with the Seeing Ceremony. Maybe Maliki is close and he can go after Father." They mixed the herb and mushroom paste, which Alana hastily gulped. Maya sang and watched over Alana, who began rocking and speaking gibberish. When Alana's vision became clearer, she saw a village with a long house near a harbor with long ships and concluded that it was the Dane village. Her mind flitted around as if flying above. "The women and children are so thin!" she exclaimed in her trance voice. "They sleep outside in the cold. I see only a few of our men. They're wounded." She saw guards kicking and poking them with spears. Their bodies were bloody. Alana sat upright with wild eyes. "Maya, they throw the men to the wolves!" Glimpsing them being dismembered, she screamed, losing the vision. Running outside the cave, she vomited, and when the contents of her stomach were exhausted, she heaved. Maya followed and pulled back her hair and held her while they sobbed.

Unable to stop the horror flashing in her mind, Alana spent the day clinging to Maya. "It was sickening," she shrieked hysterically, her eyes bloodshot. "They won't live long."

A worried Maya, her own stomach in knots, fixed Alana a strong herbal tea, remembering the ingredients from the countless times when she'd helped Alana heal the sick. The tea sent Alana into a nightmarish sleep, in which she sprinted away from the dark, shadowy Danes only to be cornered by a cackling Drood.

During her fitful sleep, Maya went into the nearby woods to check the traps for small animals. She felt an unnatural coldness and screamed at the shadows that seemed to vibrate transparently near her. She grabbed a fawn from her trap and sprinted back to the cave, not daring to peer behind her. When she reached the cave, Alana's blankets were empty. Maya searched frantically, screaming as loudly as she could. Forcing herself to calm down, she made sense of the tracks and discovered Alana down at the stream, filling their travel pouches. "Alana, you scared me!" she panted, sinking down on a rock and putting her hand over her pounding heart. "Drood's men are close. What are you doing?"

Alana, knee-deep in the cold, swirling water, had a strange glint in her eye. "We need to move fast."

"What do you mean? Did you see shadows here?" Maya narrowed her eyes, afraid that Alana had taken too many herbs. She might drown. She must be freezing. "Get out of there. Give me your hand."

Newly invigorated, Alana waded back to the stream bank and strode past her, dangling the water pouches. "Hurry, Maya. We'll get the strangers with the invisible ship to rescue them."

"But Alana," Maya said, grabbing her arm but barely slowing her down, "we've no idea where to find them."

"I have an idea," Alana said, breaking away and resuming her stride. "After the strangers' hunt, Father and I went back. Near the trench, we heard that whirring sound and felt the wind as we did that day. A little later, we saw a strange object disappear into the waterfall at Magic Mountain. It must have been the flying ship!"

Running to catch up to her, Maya cautioned, "That's not much to go on and, it's a long journey from here."

"I know. We don't need to go the forest path. This time of year, we can paddle through the streams," said Alana, handing her a bag of water. "Here, make a travel pack."

Seeing her gathering things, Maya frowned. "You don't mean through the glen, do you? I'm scared of that place."

"I'll ask the lady of the glen to help us," said Alana casually. Attempting to downplay her remark, she busily gathered a mixture of dried berries and nuts, as well as the rabbit furs that she'd sewn together for a wrap.

Enraged, Maya threw down the furs that she'd been collecting. "I won't go. You're not thinking clearly. Even Drood's people warned us never to go there."

"Drood's people," Alana scoffed with a wave of her hand. "What do they know? They're jealous because they think the lady of the glen has greater magic."

Shaking her head, her face turning red with anger mixed with fear, Maya spat, "I'm *absolutely* not going there." She marched out of the cave and plopped on the ground. What would she do if Alana went mad? The thought of living alone in this cave all winter was too stark even for tears. A freezing wind swirled her hair, chilling her to her bones, causing her to shiver and her teeth to chatter.

Alana knelt beside her and smoothed her hair. "Maya, you've known me a long time. You have to trust me. Going through the glen is the only way to reach Magic Mountain quickly. We can't paddle through the rapids. We would need to leave the boat and climb over all those steep rocks. You know that might take a week. We must ask the lady to help us. Think of our people, Maya."

Maya's lower lip trembled. "We should stay right here." She grabbed Alana's arm. "Alana, I know it's hard for you to accept, but we can't help them. Ewan knew it was hopeless. We must think of our own safety!"

"Maya," Alana admonished, pulling her up. "We'll be all right, you'll see. It's safe in the strangers' ship. If they won't help us, we'll return. I promise you. Help me get ready. We leave at sunrise." Maya stared at her walking away, hoping by morning that she'd change her mind.

Before dawn, Alana awoke her and prodded her to get dressed. From the highland cave, it was a brief walk through the sparse trees and boulders to the ridge. They walked the windy ridge top until they glimpsed through the heavy brush the river below, twisting like a snake. Descending an animal trail, Alana explained, "Ewan always kept the boat behind a clump of bushes. Fortunately, the river is low this time of year. Paddling should be easy."

"Until we pass the glen," Maya sullenly reminded her. "How will we ever get through the rapids?" worried Maya, but Alana pretended not to hear.

Finding the dugout boat and the antelope-bone paddle, Alana slipped the boat into the shallow river and climbed in the rear to navigate. Paddling with the current, they saw the woods gradually turn to steeply graded grasslands strewn with boulders, where wild sheep and goats grazed. After paddling by gently sloping meadows with herds of caribou, they turned into a narrow tributary.

"Oh, no," complained Maya, shivering with fright, again ignored by Alana.

Working against the current, they increased their paddling. The tributary's banks became increasingly rocky and were soon lined by steep, moss-covered boulders.

Maya said, voice trembling, "This is spooky already, and we haven't even reached the glen yet."

"Keep calm, Maya. Everything will be fine," whispered Alana bravely. As they entered the narrow gorge between the high rock walls, they could barely see the sky above them through the overhanging trees. The deep water became eerily calm. Alana hadn't noticed the sound of the paddle splashing in the water before, but here, in the quiet, it sounded deafening. "Maya," she whispered.

Maya jumped.

"Maya, don't you think it's beautiful here?"

"I'm too scared to notice," she whispered.

A splash. "What's that?" Maya jerked, rocking the boat in her panic.

"It's just a frog," whispered Alana, desperately swaying to still the boat. "Keep paddling."

"Who goes there?" A sharp female voice broke through the calm. A glowing pink light illuminated the rock wall ahead, where they needed to pass. Alana couldn't discern a point for the light, which cast a long shadow in the waters behind her. Standing on flat, mossy stones where the glen walls turned sharply right was a slender figure of medium height in a floor-length, dark-green woolen cape, her head covered by a hood that obscured her face. The river to her right splashed over the stones as the waters narrowed. Alana steered their canoe to the left, close to the rock wall, where a series of pointed rocks rose from the stream to create a still pool leading to where the lady stood above them.

The voice sounded older, and Alana guessed her to be at about Grandmother Marita's age. She gripped Maya's hand, closed her eyes, and inhaled deeply, seeking to control her fear. Everything depended on convincing the lady of the glen to help them. She'd heard Drood once call her Elaine. "I am Alana, daughter of Ewan, medicine woman, acolyte to Zedah, and this is my friend, Maya, our Caller. We are people of the village, from over there, where the sun disappears at night."

"Why are you here?" the lady asked shrilly, her distinct voice echoing off the walls, only faintly muffled by the moss. She stood erect, stonelike, her arms folded in the ample sleeves of her robe.

"Blessings of the Mother," Alana replied with her best manners for greeting friendly strangers. She strained to speak clearly, in the common tongue. "We travel to Magic Mountain to ask the strangers to help us," Alana explained. "Our people were captured by Danes. Only the strangers can help us save them."

"Ha!" the lady's voice spat such scorn with a single word that, for the first time, Alana felt her plan foolish. Her stomach muscles tensed, and her throat felt dry. She was glad she was sitting so that her legs didn't tremble. "What makes you believe they'll help you? They think we can't see them."

Feeling Alana tense, Maya pressed her grip assuredly and whispered, "Courage. You can do this."

Alana nodded at Maya, and she envisioned Priestess Petrina, standing regally before an assembly and enthralling her audience by the command and tone of her words. "We met them hunting," Alana spoke with command, imitating Petrina. "Their leader gave us an animal and took us in his flying ship. I know that he'll help us. You need not concern yourself."

"Yes, I know you went in his ship. I watched you." Her last words were spoken less shrilly, softer, with a hint of something else. Was it suspicion? Or grudging respect? Encouraged, the women stopped paddling, daring to let their canoe drift toward her. The lady was silent, as if listening to the sound of the gentle waves lapping against the stone walls.

Breaking the silence, Alana said, as steadily as if asking for help stirring a pot at the cooking hearth, "We need your help."

"You need *my* help?" the lady snapped, her voice again echoing; Maya's eyes were wide with panic. She sounded offended at this demand from a young stranger.

Alana wished that she'd had time for the greeting pleasantries, but she was desperate and had no choice but to plunge ahead. "I mean no disrespect, but my duty compels me to act with great haste. We *must* get to Magic Mountain quickly.

We can't paddle through the waterfalls and rapids up ahead, and climbing the rocks would take many days." Alana paused. "We've heard that you have powerful magic."

"So?" The lady took her hands from the folds of her sleeves and a staff appeared, curved at the top with intricate carvings that resembled those of Zedah's staff. Alana's mood lightened with hope; those who served the Mother would surely assist those in peril.

"Noble one, for the sake of those who honor the Mother and praise her name, we ask that you cast a spell and send us to the base of Magic Mountain," Alana spoke quickly, breathing a sigh that her request had been completed. She drew upon all the powers that she knew to direct her mental energy in the lady's direction, hoping that she could influence her. If only she had been initiated to Zedah's powers, she lamented.

"Hmmph!" The lady smirked and tapped her staff impatiently. "You're impertinent. What makes you think *I* can do that?"

"Drood told—"

"Drood?" the lady shouted, her voice reverberating off the walls of the gorge. Her cloak shook with her anger. "You follow Drood?"

"No, no, I don't," said Alana quickly, desperate to dispel the lady's rage. "His village is near mine, that's all. I promise you that I follow the ways of the Mother. I'm an acolyte to Zedah. I've been taught by Yoachim. I simply heard Drood say that you possess great power. He seemed to be in awe of you."

Although the lady failed to answer, she didn't move from the rocks.

"*Please* help us," Alana pleaded. "If you watched us with the strangers, then you must have seen Shylfing take our women and children. And now he's captured our men who went to rescue them. You must know what Shylfing will do to them!"

Not receiving an answer, Alana pleaded, "Are you a mother? If your children were being tortured, wouldn't you want someone to save them? The way of the Mother is to help others. You have a staff like Zedah's, so you know my words."

The lady replied, more subdued, "Your plan will fail. The starmen have many illusions at Magic Mountain, and their entrance is high. You'll never make it."

"My father and I saw a flying ship go through the waterfall. I'll start there."   "You're going to your death. You should turn around," warned the lady. When the women didn't move, she shouted and tapped her staff, "Now!"

"No!" shouted Alana back to her. After her echo died down, she continued in a softer voice, pleading, "If we don't try, there is no other way."

From within her hood, Elaine stared at the young, foolish girls below. Their faces were earnest, bearing the bravery of ones who had no idea what lay ahead. Yes, she had a duty to help those in peril, but with only a faint glimmer of a chance of success, these young girls were the ones in peril. Should she refuse and cast a spell to send them back where they'd be safe? Perhaps the Mother was calling them home, as she'd done with most of the other villagers taken by the Danes. Elaine didn't like involvement with people; she'd fled village life long ago to avoid the constant, petty requests for her magical powers. She did, however, admire these girls' selfless pursuit of their people's rescue. Sighing, she said softly, "For the sake of the children, I'll help you. Pull your boat up and lie before me on these rocks." They did as commanded, stepping carefully over the slippery rocks. The water was icy cold, but Alana and Maya didn't notice in their joy that she would help them.

"Close your eyes," Elaine ordered, holding her arms out-stretched above them, with the staff parallel. The staff emitted a soft light that engulfed the girls, and they felt drowsy.

In the late afternoon shadow of the mountain, Alana slowly awoke, becoming aware of a cushion of snow beneath her. Her hair whipped around her in the blustery wind, and she shivered uncontrollably in the icy cold. Opening her eyes, she saw the ominous rock mountain rising more steeply than she'd imagined, its distant pinnacle disappearing into the mists. The mountain's rocky base was covered with twisting green vines, and she heard the waterfall nearby. Finding Maya still sleeping a few feet away, half covered with snow, she shook her. "Maya, wake up. Put on your furs quickly. You'll freeze."

Startled, Maya cast cautious glances around her. Frowning at the cold and her own chattering teeth, she tugged at her furs while pushing back the cold strands of hair that stung her face. "I didn't expect it to be *this* cold," she yelled over the wind's drone, barely able to stop the chattering.

Rising, they brushed the deepening snow from their clothing. Alana pointed toward the waterfall and waved Maya to follow her through the snow. Alana could find no path that led through it, seeing only a hopeless, dark abyss. The waterfall seemed to fall from the clouds. Pulling her scanty rabbit furs tightly around her, Alana put her lips near Maya's ears to make herself heard, tinged with dejection. "I don't see a way through without a flying ship." She searched the sky above her, hoping that a ship would appear.

"I wonder where the water comes from," said Maya, peering with wonder at the misty top. "A river can't flow this high. Why isn't it frozen?"

Alana perked up. "You're right." Sliding her toe carefully to the precipice's edge, she peered over the edge. "An ocean of water tumbling down, yet it doesn't lead to a river. It's as if the bottom pool flows into the ground. Strange."

Fearing that she'd be blown by the wind, Maya slid to her knees to take a peek at the rapids swirling below. "We can't find out from here."

"Let's search the rocks. There must be another way inside." Alana climbed over the rocks at the mountain's base.

After searching for what seemed to Maya an endless time, and growing numb with cold, she whimpered, "Alana, this is hopeless. I don't see any sign of life. It'll get dark soon, and there's no shelter. This was a terrible mistake." A wolf howled as the early dusk approached, and another responded from the opposite side. A strong gust of wind knocked her off balance, and Maya slid down and pulled her thin furs around her. Sniffling and shaking from the cold, she rocked back and forth and complained, "I'm freezing! We're going to die here. Why did you make me come?" Tears ran down her face, and she refused to look at Alana. When her mother had died, she'd heard Grandmother Marita tell her to prepare to return to the Mother. She sobbed all the more because her mind was too numb to remember the words to make peace with the Mother.

Alana took her by both arms and thrust Maya's limp body to her feet. "Get up! No one's dying here. You'll be warmer if you keep moving. We just need to look a little farther." With desperation, Alana began running her hands over the sheer rock of the mountain wall, searching for an opening. Pounding it, Alana's hands became bruised and bleeding. Reluctantly, stumbling through the deepening snow to search farther away, Maya crouched to listen, and then she began waving frantically. "Alana, come here. I heard something coming from behind those vines. Hey, how could anything be green in this cold? I thought I heard a horse, but it's hard to tell with all this noise."

Alana cupped her ear. "I hear it, too," she said excitedly, pulling back the vines. "These feel real, but you're right, how can green things live up here?" Behind the vines lay the mountain's stone face preceded by a wide, dark crevice. Gingerly peeking over the crevice's edge, Alana moaned, "Oh no! I can't see the bottom. Not one more obstacle!" Furiously grabbing more vines, she found only more wall protected by that deep, dark, impenetrable crevice. In frustration, they madly tore at the sturdy vines until they were left huffing from exertion.

"We're getting nowhere," Alana shouted angrily, dropping to her knees. "We're never going to be able to help our women. They're going to die, and we are, too!" She picked up a rock and heaved it at the wall. The rock didn't crash. Instead, it disappeared, as if through a curtain. An irritated horse whinnied.

"Oh, Maya," she whispered, stunned, embracing her friend. "Did you see that?"

"I think so," Maya, astonished, replied with wide eyes, "but I don't believe it."

"Do you remember when the flying ships disappeared?" Alana asked, the excitement giving her new energy. "The leader said they were actually there, we just couldn't see them."

"Is this the same magic?"

"Let's see." Alana bravely grasped the vines and swung over the abyss. She dangled in the air, unable to touch the wall. Undaunted, she slid to her knees at the crevice's edge and gingerly extended her hand. "Hah," she said, drawing back in triumph. "This isn't real. I feel the ground even though I can't see it."

Maya blinked, unconvinced. "It's not really a hole?"

"No, it's solid. See for yourself."

"No. Oh, how can you be so sure?" Maya's lip trembled in fear of what Alana would do next. "Please don't try to cross. You'll fall. I don't want to be left here to die alone at night in this cold. I always thought that I'd have my friends around me when I died, and that I'd be buried in the orchard. Not like this! Not left for the vultures to pluck out my eyes."

Alana took her shoulders and shook her sharply. "Maya, I need you to stay calm." Maya slumped against her shoulder, and she hugged her and stroked her hair. "Hey, sweetie, I'm afraid too, but I'm more afraid that we won't be able to save our people."

Pulling at her, Maya whimpered, "I don't want you to do this. Let's look for a trail down. Or we'll slide through the snow."

Alana lifted Maya's chin with an ice-cold finger and glared into her frightened eyes. "Maya, listen to me. We have no choice. It's nearly dark, and there will be no moon to guide us. We can't climb down. Have faith in the Mother. She wouldn't have let us get this far only to abandon us, would she?"

Maya stared at her numbly, putting her hand to the totem bag at her neck. She closed her eyes and tried to be comforted by the feel of the fox paw.

Alana's hand went for her bear claw in her totem bag. Ewan would have surely have had powerful words to draw courage, and she missed him so much. It was so lonely being responsible for everyone's life. She shook off her sorrow. "Now, hold my ankles." With Maya holding her, she inched forward on her knees, seeing nothing below her. Nearing the wall, she stretched her body long and extended her hand. It disappeared in the rock. Maya gasped, but Alana felt no pain. She jerked her arm back.

Maya, breathing deeply, gasped, "Alana, are you all right?" The howling wolves were drawing closer.

In joyful wonder, Alana wiggled her hand and found nothing amiss. "Did you hear that?" She looked back at Maya, hearing a whinny. "That's definitely the sound of horses. And it's warm in there." She made up her mind. "I'm going through that wall. I'll signal when to follow."

When Alana stood up, hovering above the crevice, Maya giggled, incredulous. "You look as if you're floating in the air!"

Alana took step over step across the crevice, refusing to look down. "Here I go." Closing her eyes, she pushed herself into the wall, feeling a slight tickle as she passed through the illusion, surprised at the instant quiet. Smelling horses and hay and rejoicing in the sweet gift of warmth, she opened her eyes. Shaking her feet to dislodge the cold snow, she saw in the dim light a narrow, long room lined with small windows, through which horses poked their heads to watch her. She ran her hands over her body. Finding herself all right, she stuck her hand back through the wall to motion for Maya to follow. A few moments later, Maya smacked into her.

"Sorry," she shrugged. "I was afraid to go slow." Looking around, she whispered with a smile, "Ah, warmth at last." They cautiously snuck down the room.

Ahead, a voice talked to the horses in an unknown language. Crouching in a shadow, they saw a hunter holding a feeding bag. The women pressed tightly against the wall, but a horse snorted and butted Maya's head. "Ouch," she gasped.

Jared turned his head and stared in disbelief. Activating his universal translator, he demanded, "How did you get here?"

Both women spoke at once, trying to relay everything. It came out jumbled, but Jared understood that they were in a panic and that people needed to be rescued. "I can't help you," he said, shaking his head. It was so cold outside, how could he push them back out in the dark mountainside? Maybe he could let them spend the night here.

The women gestured, trying to persuade him. Alana felt the leader would be more sympathetic, or at least have the authority to act. Not knowing his name, she demanded, "I want to speak to your leader."

Jared couldn't believe her hubris. "You want to see the captain?"

CHAPTER 13
LIL

Lil resettled himself in the Library. In truth, he looked forward to reading the old stories about the *mencomm* attacks—just not for the reasons that the Council had directed. Like the hunt, he'd found *mencomm* to be intriguing, although he understood their caution that its use could be addictive. When controlled, however, it would be highly valuable. And it expanded his mind, similar in many ways to the sensations he'd had during the moments spent space traveling—the total immersion of his senses, floating through the wormhole, emerging through the portal, rematerializing in an entangled state, and capturing through his own eyes the first glimpse of an alien planet. Before then, Lil's life had been the epitome of stability, consisting of training for his successorship and absorbing nearly every program of the Teacher, punctuated by myriad monotonous rituals prescribed by their extensive calendar. Harmony and stability presented an excellent governing philosophy for civilization, but lack of challenge eventually became mind numbing, even without the emotion modulation contained in the nourishment bars. On Earth, his flights were never boring. So confinement was, he had to admit, a punishment.

Scanning the old Library index, he was amazed at the volume of secreted material. He decided to start with one of his favorite subjects, the timewave. He found an article reporting that, prior to the Great Awakening, the timewave had neared the bottom of its final trough before commencing the new cycle; this accounted for the quickening pace of change, although the change was always unpredictable, at least to humans. Rapid change wasn't limited to humans, he discovered. Certain animals had experienced an unexplained evolutionary jump, in which their language capabilities increased as well as their use of tools. Concomitantly, new scientific studies intimated that animals throughout the developmental chain, even single-celled ones, had some degree of consciousness; scientists raced to discover a consciousness particle thought to be entangled with the Universal Consciousness. Naturalists had begun, along with environmentalists, to advocate for worldwide mandatory vegetarianism. Finishing the article, Lil wondered if the Alterran timewave had followed them to Earth. Through his recorder, he accessed the colony's intricate program for calculating the timewave and plotted that it was approaching the final series of short troughs before renewal. He sat back, scratching his head—this was why the universe was so chaotic, forcing him into a disgusting course of action. If the Alterrans back home were to discover that his guardsmen were hunting and eating animals, they would call them degenerates. But what choice did he have? Destiny drove his actions.

He dispelled the contradiction from his mind and resumed searching, noticing the subject "terrorist attack, *mencomm*." "Ah, here it is," he said aloud. It was a mass distribution report of a governmental crisis investigation of colossal casualties. It described how terrorists had programmed mobile telephones to transmit codes that infected users' minds. After implantation, the codes lay dormant in their targets—people controlling critical infrastructure. Through *mencomm*, terrorists all over the world took control of victims' minds. Operators of major dams opened floodgates, drowning huge numbers of people. Others caused power systems, even a nuclear reactor, to overload and explode, sending surges through the grid, knocking out entire systems. Transit vehicles collided, planes came crashing from the skies, ships collided with bridges, causing them to collapse, trains crashed—the list was endless. In a single day, the whole of Alterra was plunged into darkness and chaos. Critical information systems were obliterated. No one knew who might have a controlled sleeper mind. Standard communications couldn't be used by emergency responders or governmental officials, many of whom had been compromised. Years later, when the article was published, the Alterrans hadn't recovered. The article noted that this crisis had come on the heels of the attack on global food supplies. Suspected in both was a little-known group called the Party of Harmony and Stability.

This latter fact alarmed Lil, and he sought more information. A link led to another governmental report. The members of the newly established global Food Ministry had adopted standards for a drink that the poor relied on as their primary source of nourishment. After deaths so massive in number as to be called "continental genocide," investigators discovered that the international standard had no nutritional value. Instead, the victims' drinks were filled with a chemical causing extreme lethargy and death. Reporters had uncovered evidence that persons appointed to the international agency had strong ties to the organization later implicated in the *mencomm* attacks— the Party of Harmony and Stability. After its plot was uncovered, the Party had issued a press release calling itself a new world order destined to restore balance to the universe.

Lil desired more information but found no additional links. Although it was ancient history, he was deeply disturbed. Even in his successorship training, he hadn't been taught these details. Recalling the article he'd read earlier, he searched for the Party of Harmony and Stability. An enormous quantity of information was available, but it was dated after the Great Awakening.

He limited his search to the period one hundred years prior to the Great Awakening. Oddly, the search produced only a few articles, and these he had just read. Thereafter, the Party of Harmony and Stability had won overwhelming victories in elections at all levels of government and was rapidly implementing its transformative policies, much to the grateful thanks of the populace. Party leaders announced that the change they'd been waiting for had come. The turbulence of free markets was over. Government would own all property, guarantee lifetime jobs and living quarters to all, and dispense all health care. Vast tracts of land were to be restored to their natural state and people relocated to densely populated cities. To end hunger and obesity, the Party unveiled a meal bar providing all necessary vitamins for an ideal weight. Because the bars were made through molecular formulas rather than from natural ingredients, the environment was promoted through the elimination of farming. With initial supplies limited, public rallies were held demanding a production increase. The author speculated that the rallies were staged by the Party and that there was something sinister about the solution-for-everything bars. In an interview addressing the global crisis, a Party member was quoted as saying, "You never want a serious crisis to go to waste. And what I mean by that is an opportunity to do things you think you could not do before."

A fleeting thought crossed Lil's mind. Perhaps the old articles had somehow been missed during a document purge. He knew that the Council sometimes ordered the purge of scientific reports that contained "errors." In attempting a few new searches, he found no other old articles on the Party. Another thought struck him. The walls in the Council Chambers contained scrolls of the letters "PHS" within the sacred triangle. So ubiquitous was this design that he had never considered its meaning. Did the letters stand for the Party of Harmony and Stability? Had it won and revised history to support its agenda? To the victor goes history, he seemed to recall vaguely.

His next search turned up a partially expunged fragment. "A command economy with centralized planning was tried a long time ago and failed. Although well intentioned, it was unsuccessful primarily because of the government's limited technology. In addition, competition from the surrounding market economies disrupted the more enlightened decisions of the central planners, making the populace unhappy with the steady-state consumer goods. We have solved these problems. Our quantum computing capacity is unlimited, giving us the ability to control every minute detail of the economy. Money is irrelevant, and we can eliminate all of our debt with a stroke of a pen. With global implementation, no annoying comparisons will be made to innovations in market economies. We also note that the old experiment was subject to corruption charges. These were largely attributed to the fact that the revolutionaries' philosophy had been that religion was the opiate of the people. Atheism therefore became a foundational principle. We, on the contrary, will embrace religion as a useful tool. To avoid the purges endemic in the old experiment, our Party will convert into a family dynasty fixing succession for all future time. Other advantages we enjoy over the prior experiment are that personal property is of less value in an electronic age, especially in light of new technologies for replicating matter. Ownership of the means of production by the government will seem natural. Most importantly, young people prefer comfort and a social safety net to any system that creates the smallest anxiety for them. Through their own habits, they have no expectation of privacy. They'll readily embrace our solutions. Our enlightened humanitarian system will be simple—from each according to his ability, to each according to his need. There will be a new world order. At long last, we shall have utopia."

Lil recalled that, just before the Great Awakening, the economy had still been a mixture of the old free market principles laced with the needs of the developing command economy, but that the mixture had caused hyperinflation. Therefore, the new global government outlawed money. Without it, people worked for the government, lived in government-supplied housing, received government-supplied health care, subsisted on government-supplied nourishment bars, and satisfied other personal needs from replicators with a menu dictated by the government. Simplicity and equality at its best.

What was his family's role? He had absorbed the family history taught by the Teacher, but he wondered if it was the sanitized version. Nothing contradicted the Teacher that terrorist episodes using *mencomm* caused mass casualties that led to the dismantling of economic systems and nation states. Even basic food supplies couldn't be grown and delivered. People were starving. Armed militias had sprung up. In countless ways, society underwent massive upheavals. He had always been taught that people had craved the harmony and stability offered by the principles of the Great Awakening. To achieve these noble goals, weren't the Party's actions tolerable?

Searching further, he found a brief history after the Great Awakening of the House of En. "Ah, this must be the real history," he said aloud. He learned that the new global command economy had initially given rise to great ruling families with private militaries and their own food supplies. Key members of the Party of Harmony and Stability belonged to the House of En. Through strategic marriages, alliances, and assassinations, over time the families' numbers were reduced to two: the Houses of En and Kan. After the last war, instigated when the House of Kan claimed the supreme leadership, only one ruling family remained. Led by Anu, the House of En soundly defeated the Kans and banished a usurper to the supreme leadership. Under the treaty ending the conflict, the Kans were left with only two seats on the Supreme Council, neither of which was in the succession line. In the war, the Ens had achieved strategic advantage by publicly advocating for full disarmament while secretly retaining their fearsome weapons. After having achieved full planetary control, the command economy was sealed and the House of En had the sole, undisputed right to the supreme leadership.

Lil sat back from his machine and reflected. The turmoil before the Great Awakening had happened long ago, and few of the people involved were alive because the rejuvenation chambers had then been outlawed for the general population. Even if, arguably, the extremists had been wrong in some respect, he couldn't turn back the clock. Society had moved on. It had been fundamentally restructured at every level. The population's philosophy of life had been irrevocably altered, and the Party's principles had been inculcated in them. As many said, humanity had been set free. The Ministry of Central Planning professionally planned and controlled every aspect of their economy, eliminating the painful dislocations caused by the ancient free market cycles. People were content to be taken care of by the House of En, and they were glad that their leaders were determined by divine right, without rancorous elections.

Lil breathed deeply, trying to reconcile the contradiction between the extremists' actions and the superior goals of the Great Awakening. The harmony-and-stability philosophical system had become ingrained in all Alterrans. If he revealed this history, would they continue to follow the House of En's Code? If there were not one central Code governing all Alterrans, would people follow divergent religions? The cycle of ancient wars would repeat itself. Equally bad, he thought, would be a society not based on any spiritual guidance. What kind of lawlessness and depravity would that surely bring? History had shown that certain fundamental truths were too important to be left to the whims of the masses.

Horrified by his vision of inevitable chaos if the truth were known, he shouted aloud, "No!" Terrorism was but one element of the change that had occurred. It didn't matter. The clock could not, should not, be turned back. The change might have occurred anyway; all the signs were there. As second named successor, he had been trained since birth to prepare for his ascension as supreme leader. It would be his mandate to preserve the beauty of the Alterran system and to provide for and protect those in his charge. He understood the heavy weight of this responsibility, but he was prepared to accept it for the good of the people. Whether the capitalist system or democracy had been good or bad was irrelevant. The philosophy of the House of En was now the way of Alterra. Everyone agreed that the Alterran Code embodied universal principles of goodness, peace, and harmony with the environment. The Supreme Council had been right to restrict access to the Library. He would continue that policy when he was supreme leader.

Sweating, he needed a diversion. He began contacting his guardsmen for status reports, beginning with Jared. At that precise moment, Alana was pleading with Jared.

"Good evening, Captain," said Jared, his voice strangely pitched. "Until a short while ago, sir, there would have been nothing unusual to report."

"And now there is?" Lil tapped his fingers impatiently.

"Uh…sir, do you remember the two young women from the mastodon hunt?"

There was a long pause on Lil's end before he tersely said, "Jared, get to the point."

"Sir, they're standing here in the horse barn," said Jared, turning his back to the women and wincing. He knew an eruption was coming.

"What?" Lil darted up from his seat. "How did they get in?"

"I don't know, sir," Jared admitted tensely. "I think they came through the rock wall."

"What's happening right now?" demanded Lil sharply, leaving the Library and striding down the empty corridor, wishing the Net here worked as it did on Alterra.

"They've been trying to tell me a story that I can't fully understand. I think they want to speak to you."

"To me?" Lil huffed, passing near Ki's office and the busy scribes.

"Yes, sir." Jared squirmed. "The best I can make out is that somebody has taken their people and they want us to do something about it."

Lil groaned. He had made progress extricating himself from the unfortunate incident with the women, and he had no intention of reopening his wounds with the Council. "Tell them to go back the way they came," he ordered. Ending the connection, he angrily strode at a near run through the Ministry's hallways to the transport tube.

Jared motioned for the women to leave in the most threatening manner he could conceive; however, Jared was by nature a builder, not a warrior. Maya smiled and pleaded with him. It had been years since Jared had been this close to a real woman, and Maya's sorrowful brown eyes affected him. He was relieved when Lil called, asking, "Jared, has the problem been handled?"

"Uh, no, sir. They're quite adamant."

As Jared's commanding officer, Lil was forced to intervene, however much it annoyed him. As he sped through the tube to the horse barn, he couldn't forget what he'd uncovered in the Library. Having discovered that a monumental lie shrouded the Great Awakening, he needed time to think. As the named successor, he would benefit from this lie. But to him, it wasn't a lie at all; he had taken no part in it. He would act honorably for the benefit of all. He vowed to be kind and fair, although when necessary, firm. Weren't people better off if he produced a better world? He could do nothing now about the loss of the old society. He couldn't recreate the nations in existence before the Great Awakening, nor did he believe that Alterrans living today had any desire to return to the old ways. So, he asked himself, did any of this matter? No, he concluded. He resented the distraction of Alana and Maya, who had lied to him and broken their promise. He vowed to dispatch them firmly and swiftly and then reprimand Jared, perhaps even demote him. Azazel would have decisively dealt with the women.

When Lil suddenly emerged from a transport tube camouflaged to appear as part of the wall, a startled Alana involuntarily jumped. Maya shrieked "Oh!" Alana, having journeyed this far and having overcome so much, soon recovered her resolve. Similarly, Lil resolved to be kind to these childlike creatures, just as he had resolved moments ago to be kind and fair to his Alterran subjects. But, he thought, kindness could not lessen the message. This was the task of a ruler. He had to be absolutely firm and clear in turning them away. Thanks to the Teacher, Lil was able to communicate with the women in the common tongue.

Lil stared at them, his cobalt eyes as cold as his father's had been to him in the Council session. Folding his arms over his chest with a firm stance, he broke the icy silence first. Speaking courteously in his best military manner, he said, "Alana and Maya, I don't know how you found your way here, but you should not have done so. You made a serious mistake. This is our home, and you're not welcome. You must immediately leave. I want no argument from you. Go." He waved his hand at them. Looking at Alana, he added sternly, "I'm disappointed. You promised me that no one would look for us. Did you lie? Does your word mean nothing?"

Maya trembled, but Alana moved toward him and attempted to grab his arm. Lil stepped back to avoid her. "I didn't lie. Please let me explain." Alana looked crushed by his accusation. He was so much colder to her than the last time.

Lil didn't respond, maintaining his steady gaze and stance, changing only by firming his jaw with resolve. Alana desperately continued, stretching out her arms to plead. "I'm glad I can see your eyes now. I don't know your name, but I feel in my heart that you're a good man. Please believe me, I wouldn't be here if this weren't a matter of life and death. I've nowhere else to turn."

Fearing that she'd made a terrible mistake, she looked for encouragement to Maya, who gulped with fear but managed to say, "Our village was attacked by Shylfing, the Dane. His people are evil and cruel." Maya was near hysteria that he'd force them back into the cold and certain death.

No, this had to work. Alana looked at Jared for sympathy. "Our women and children were captured and taken away to the Danes' village. They'll be tortured. Our men tried to rescue them, but they were also captured. Most have been killed. They've been torn apart by wolves!" She expected a sympathetic reaction, but with Jared staring at the ground, she turned back to Lil, realizing that only he could take action. "You're the only one who could save those who still live."

Lil held her gaze for a moment, reminding himself of the Non-Interference Directive before turning away. "I'm sorry to hear about your people. But as I said, you must leave immediately."

Alana again moved directly before him, as she'd done at the hunt. She managed a smile of supplication, as she'd seen from those seeking favors from Princess Petrina. "People capable of this magnificence must be wise and kind. I beg you to help us."

Without pausing, Lil ordered in a placid tone as if he was ordering tea, "Jared, please show them back to the place they entered." Jared took them by the arm and began pulling them, but Alana wriggled free.

"No, you must help us," Alana angrily shouted, marching back to Lil. "I know you don't want to concern yourself with the problems of my people. You think our lives aren't worth your attention. But when good people will be tortured and killed, how can you stand aside and let evil happen?"

Lil maintained eye contact. She thought she saw a slight softening in his jaw. Speaking as quickly as she could, she said, "If we act quickly, they can still be saved. But you must act now, tonight." She stamped her foot and met his gaze defiantly.

Lil raised his eyebrows with a hint of amusement. "Tonight?" He was again fascinated that this Earth woman was so brave. Or reckless. How could she have risked her life on that destitute mountain to find her way here? No, although impressed, he had to remain firm.

Alana interpreted his pause as reconsideration. "Yes, tonight. One of your invisible ships could destroy them. It would be seen as an act of god. You could then land, and I would get the survivors." She searched his face for a glimmer of hope.

Maya pleaded to Jared, who still held a firm grasp of her arm, "Please help us."

Alana pleaded to Lil, "I beg you. We can't let them die."

Lil was moved by Alana's passion. If they'd been Alterran, it would have been his duty to save these innocents. But, he reminded himself, they were not Alterran. They might look like them and their motivations might be similar, but they weren't Alterran. Thus, the directive, which was his sacred duty to uphold, mandated that he not interfere. This was clear, and he was still under punishment for his last infraction.

"Alana, I have sympathy for your people. We are, indeed, highly principled and honorable, but we have a directive that prohibits us from interfering in the affairs of others." Lil stopped, expecting them to appreciate his position.

Instead, Alana's voice grew louder as she pointed her finger at him, "How can any honorable person let good people die when saving them is so simple? All you need to do is fly a ship!"

Lil thought, this should be an easy decision. The directive clearly forbade any action to help them, and he had been sent to this planet expressly to enforce it. But he'd also been groomed since birth to take a paternal view of his subjects. He looked her in the eye and said softly, regretfully, "Alana, there's nothing I can do."

Alana became more incensed and argued, "Of course you can! You could destroy their village without anyone even knowing about you. It would be easy!"

Exasperated, he threw up his hands. "That's absurd. We can't indiscriminately blow up an entire Earth village simply because you want us to. We've had no trial and conviction. What you ask us to do might kill the very people you're trying to save. You don't know where your people are."

Alana brightened. "If my people are separate, would you agree to fly your ship? Don't destroy anything, just pick them up. You aren't causing anybody harm that way," she said, without knowing how she could segregate the villagers. She hoped the women were still held in the stockade.

Lil shook his head. "No, it's still interference."

Sensing that she was losing, she protested, "Why? What can I say to make you understand? Why you can't let innocents be tortured and killed?"

Lil replied evenly, as he walked several paces, "If such is their destiny, then it would be against the Creator's wishes for us to interfere. You don't know the grand design of the universe. Perhaps there's some value to the Danes or their progeny that you have no way of seeing. On the other hand, if your villagers were to live, how do we know that their children's children wouldn't be evil, perhaps causing even more harm than the Danes?" He pointed his finger skyward. "We don't know the Creator's grand design. We can't make value judgments that one group of people is better than a second. If we did, whose values would we use? Should we assume that our values, the values of an ancient, advanced people, should be applied to primitive people?" He looked distant, as if addressing an assembly. "These things are all relative, you see. If we start interfering in others' affairs, where would it end? Would we be called upon to be an enforcer for each person who believes he or she has been wronged, no matter how slightly?" He stopped, taking great satisfaction in presenting the traditional position so well. His logic was unassailable; the matter would be promptly concluded. He wanted to do nothing more than return to his suite and comply fully with the Supreme Council's Directive. But when his gaze returned to Alana's horrified face, he felt his resolve melting. He knew she found no morality in his position.

Jared felt Lil wavering. He understood that not helping her offended Lil's honor, so he tried to help. "Alana, you said the villagers were good people, but from another point of view, the Danes might be viewed as good people. By what standard should we judge goodness? This is a difficult question."

Alana strode up to Jared pointing her finger at him, huffing, "There's nothing difficult about this question! Our villagers are kind and gentle people who live peaceably, harm no one, care for their children, welcome strangers, and honor their ancestors. The Danes create nothing for themselves. They steal property and people. They destroy whatever they don't steal, and they mercilessly torture their captives for their own cruel pleasures. The difference between my villagers and the Danes is as clear as the difference between night and day. This is obvious to any thinking creature. All who are made by one Creator are subject to the same principles. If you do not recognize the difference between the two, then you're no better than the Danes!" Alana folded her arms over her chest, breathing deeply, staring defiantly from Jared to Lil.

Perhaps Alana had struck a nerve, or perhaps after the strange events of the day, Lil needed to prove to himself that the Alterran Code was founded on principles of goodness and honor. He found himself agreeing to fly a hovercraft near the Dane village, but absolutely and unequivocally nothing more.

Being under confinement by the Council, he had to devise a pretext for obtaining a craft. He found this a strange predicament for the named successor, but such was his life at present. He promised to repair the rift in the universe later. He asked Ki to request the largest hovercraft for him in preparation for the comet observation.

Ki cautiously agreed. He didn't know Lil's plan, but he thought that it would be good for Lil to be indebted to him, a favor he could call in at some future time. True to Ki's word, a ship was prepared for them. Lil slid into the pilot's seat and departed Hawan, stopping to pick up the women and Jared at the horse barn.

Lil cautioned Alana as she took her seat, "Alana, as I said, the most I will do is fly over the Dane village."

Alana nodded, knowing she would deal with the rest when they got there.

CHAPTER 14
SHYLFING

Shylfing, a lustrous black bear fur draped over his hulking shoulders, sat on his stolen throne in the middle of his long house, enjoying the merriment and noise while his men consumed some excellent mead acquired in a raid in the southern mainland. He himself drank a new beverage—beer, stolen in the same raid. A box holding his favorite golden coins, golden goblets, rings with large stones, and many similar treasures lay by his side, all the more sweet since so few knew how to mold gold. He fondly ran his fingers through his treasures as he held his beer cup in his other hand, delicately, as he'd seen his hapless victims drink it before he'd killed them. Those prissy cowards were no match for his manly, battle-hardened warriors. Those who forgot the ways of the land were ripe for looting. Barefoot slave women of various colors of hair and skin, their clothing tattered and filthy, served the men food and drink. The condition of these women didn't matter, he thought. After using them up, his men would easily set sail to find others. He enticed a matted, long-haired dog with a tidbit of roasted meat; instead of giving it the tidbit, he wiped his hands on its coat and then kicked the growling mongrel away.

He absently watched the night's knife-throwing competition. A noisy dispute had broken out, which was being settled by combat. He thought, let the best man win; he would never interfere. These little combats kept the men on their toes, kept them wary and always observant, hard and ready to die at a moment's notice. Good warriors all. Thor, god of war, must be pleased with them. Dying in battle with one's sword was the highest tribute a man could pay to the war god, and death in combat was the surest path to climbing the Tree of Life to Valhalla. Shylfing thoughtfully stroked his gray beard, which was cut short and carefully combed. He had personally led his men at the front lines of many battles, too many to count at his age. The spoils of war from his great victories lay around him. Yes, Odin must be pleased with him. He was sure to gain swift entrance to Valhalla. Eat or be eaten, that was the way of this world, and he had been the one doing the eating. Tonight, though, he was tired. His knees ached, as did old battle scars on his left hip and his neck, aches that he had to mask; his men would challenge a weak leader.

"Bring me more beer," he loudly ordered a passing slave woman, pulling her toward him, swaggering to hide his difficulty rising with his stiff knees. "I'm celebrating."

Hearing the snarling dire wolves in the pit at the other end of the long house, he chuckled at their trainer provoking them. Those would-be rescuers from that miserable little village would be suitable entertainment to feed his warriors' edginess, giving their people life. Having too many mouths to feed on this prickly flat land bordered by the vicious mountains that shut out the great herds roaming on the other side forced him to make raids against their more fortunate neighbors. The days were growing short, the waters would become too icy for their ships, and the restless warriors would soon be killing one another. Tonight's entertainment would compensate his disappointed men for the meager items brought back from the pointless raid on the peninsula—only tasteless dried meat, matted furs, and scrawny women and children. No gold and silver. Koko's runner had lied; Shylfing had tossed him to the wolves, and he'd toss Koko as well when he caught the little bastard. Right now, he'd punish these prisoners for being worthless. It was harvest time; let the women work in his fields—for as long as they lasted. Bursting out in laughter, he spewed his drink on a passing serving wench who listlessly didn't seem to notice.

He scowled, reminded that his scouts needed to perform. If the raids of that scoundrel Ragnar further east produced better treasures, his best men might sneak away to join his old enemy. Ruthless Ragnar was stiff competition, so feared that his victims, trembling with fright, gathered all their valuables and relinquished them without a fight. Well, at least the foolish victims thought there would be no fight, he chuckled. If Ragnar was in the mood, he torched the place anyway. Tomorrow, he'd whip his scouts; that would teach 'em. With proper treasures, he could bargain for more ships; his blasted land lacked the best shipbuilding materials.

The covering over the entranceway fluttered, and his elegantly dressed wife, Callendra, eyes downcast, gently pushed her skinny son into the long house. The boy, with the same delicate features of his mother, came forward at a slow, reluctant pace. The woman, hair of red-gold, with creamy, unmarked skin like goat's milk, was his prized captive from the south. When she was a young virgin, her father had offered her in exchange for their safety. She'd stood before him, accepting her fate with noble serenity, shedding not a single tear. She'd been so beautiful in her long white robe bearing her family's red crest that Shylfing had actually kept his bargain. Now a woman, Callendra took care of herself in a way that Dane women did not; it flattered him. Shylfing gave her the best pick of the clothing and jewels that he brought back, thinking himself a fine husband. This son of hers, Galen, with his womanly good looks, was another matter. Shylfing peered at him with disgust that the boy wasn't developing his own manly habits. Although he still tried to encourage the boy, his patience was over. Tonight was the final test. The boy had grown too old to continue excuses, and Shylfing needed a suitable heir. His warriors ridiculed Galen's bathing and grooming when they thought Shylfing couldn't hear. Unless he turned Galen, his men would mutiny and run to Ragnar or fight among themselves. As the woman and boy drew near Shylfing's throne, he greeted her by lifting his cup and saying with sarcasm, "Callendra, you're as beautiful as the day I first laid eyes on you. You're making a rare appearance. Are you here for tonight's entertainment?"

Woodenly, not raising her eyes, she replied, "No, my lord. I'm here only because you commanded me to bring your son to you. I do not wish to stay."

Shylfing sneered, "No matter, there are plenty of other wenches. Leave us. Tonight I make a man of Galen!"

Her eyes widened, but she refrained from betraying her feelings. She vaguely remembered her carefree and happy life in the warm and sunny home of her youth, not this cold, muddy hole of a place. She had tried to prevent her only son from turning into Shylfing, but she was powerless to prevent the future, and she resigned herself to her fate. If a kind god existed, which she truly doubted, Shylfing would kill them both in his disappointment. When she had first arrived she had been spirited and protested her treatment, for which she had received beatings and cuts, carefully placed so as not to mar the beauty of her face. Now she was broken, and her only motivation was to avoid unnecessary pain.

Tonight, Shylfing would end Galen's sissy ways or his life. Being the son of his official wife, Galen was his heir, but he couldn't rule if the men lacked confidence in him. Although Shylfing had sons by other women who could carry out his proud tradition, his failure with Galen gnawed at him day and night. He wasn't being a dutiful father unless he made his only legitimate son a worthy warrior. Ridicule so far hadn't succeeded with Galen, so Shylfing decided to try another tactic. Less gruffly, he made an effort to reach the boy. "Galen, I understand that you're doing well in your sword training. I'm glad to hear that. A warrior needs excellent skills."

Surprised that Shylfing wasn't hitting him, Galen replied politely, as his mother had taught him. "Yes, Father." He stood erect with his chin upraised, meeting Shylfing's piercing eyes, masking his terror of the snarling wolves; he'd heard stories that captives, as well as those who displeased his father, had been torn apart in the pit. He knew he disappointed his father, and he didn't wish to die that way. He had mixed feelings about seeing others subjected to this punishment. He knew that his mother didn't approve, but his mother didn't belong. She had died inside long ago. After spending the afternoon with her, watching her joyless grooming, he'd decided that the warrior life was the only path left; it would please his father if he tried, and he should make the best of the situation. He'd been practicing his swordplay with his tutor and could feel his new muscles. He might not have the Dane physique, but his slave tutor complimented his flowing motions and footwork. The sword had been a rare treasure—no other Dane possessed such a rare weapon, forged in Atlantis, a place of legend. Sometimes he even found the idea of being a warrior and traveling the coastline in search of adventure and treasure to be exciting. Standing before Shylfing, he was relieved that his father had taken notice of his effort. It encouraged him. For the first time, seeing his father through his own eyes and not his mother's grumbles, he noticed that his father had a powerful demeanor that brought him authority and respect. His eyes were intelligent and wise.

Raucous cheering from the knife game meant that a winner had been proclaimed and the drunken men sought new entertainment. Shylfing nodded to the wolf keepers. He stood, put his arm around Galen, and walked him over to their seats at the side of the pit. Galen gazed up and smiled warmly. "I hope to make you proud of me, Father. I'm going to be the best swordsman in this entire land!"

Shylfing smiled back—even his eyes smiled for once. He pressed his son's arm and admired his muscle. "I have no doubt you will, Galen. You'll make me very proud."

All the warriors noisily followed Shylfing to take seats, shouting at one another and throwing chicken bones and empty cups at the wolves to further incite them. They laughed when the snarling dire wolves lunged up the pit walls, clawing at the edges, but never getting a hold and falling back on the others, who bit them in return.

Shylfing signaled a guard to bring in the first prisoner. A tarp was drawn back, and Nosti, bloodied and beaten, limping and shaking uncontrollably, jerked when he was speared in the back. He tripped, landing by the pit. In the flickering torchlight, he peered over the pit's edge at the menacing dire wolves, jumping with their long sharp teeth to shred his arm. Noisily, Shylfing's men cast wagers how long he would last.

After watching the terrified man, Shylfing huffed and exaggerated a disgusted face. He put his thumb down, as he'd seen royalty do in the port city. "This creature is a coward. He cries like a baby. No knife." Shylfing gave him the ultimate insult; he would not enter Valhalla. The warriors hooted and howled in agreement.

Shylfing stood and quieted the men. To raise Galen's stature, he ordered, "Galen, tonight you will have the honor of pushing the prisoner into the pit." Snapping his fingers, he called, "You, there. Bring Galen his sword."

A warrior made a wry smile and winked at his friends as he handed the large sword to the boy, expecting him to drop it when feeling its weight.

Taking it, Galen deftly performed for the surprised, drunken crowd by twirling his sword and pretending to thrust, going through the fluid motions taught by his tutor and calling out the animal-like names. Encouraged by their cheering, he stopped pretending, focused on the kneeling prisoner, and nudged his buttocks. The prisoner accepted the prick rather than fall into the pit. Galen stabbed him in the arm, then the leg. The sobbing prisoner clung to handholds along the edge. Galen stabbed him in the small of the back and then kicked him. The prisoner teetered, and his knee slid. Losing his grip, he fell with a scream. Before Galen could catch his breath, the dire wolves had ripped open the man's throat and torn off his limbs.

The winning wagerer yelled, "Ah, I told you this one wouldn't last a single breath. Pay up!" Stone knives and stolen trinkets were laid at his feet in payment.

"Well done, boy," said one of Shylfing's fiercest, scar-covered warriors, patting him on the back.

Galen, who had long been the recipient of the men's cruel jibes, smiled broadly, happily enjoying the moment.

Shylfing stood and smiled, proudly raised his fist in triumph and cried out, "That's my boy!"

CHAPTER 15
THE RESCUE

"There it is!" Alana pointed, leaping with excitement. "Maya, look!"

Maya joined her at the window of Lil's hovercraft, following where she pointed to the fire lights in the distance. "I can make out the coastline. It's what I saw in my vision." It was lit by the full moon and a new, bluish-red object that eerily illuminated the sky. Alana pressed her face against the glass with Maya by her side.

Slowing the cloaked hovercraft, Lil saw smoke rising from a long, shabby building of roughly hewn logs. Shacks were scattered throughout the steep slopes leading from the mountains to the inlet where numerous dragon boats were moored. Lil said, "Jared, that bluish-red light is the comet we've been tracking. It's noticeably more visible now than yesterday." They studied the glowing light, now nearly half the size of the moon, with a visible tail.

"According to legend, comets bring disaster," he replied grimly.

"I hope not," said Lil as he circled several times at a low altitude above Shylfing's village so that Alana could look for her people.

With frustration, Alana said, "Oh, where are they? I don't see any of them. Can you fly any lower?"

"No," said Lil, "they're already questioning our ship's noise."

Alana tried a different window. "Maya, do you see anything?"

Maya, pressing against the window, said, "I see women carrying buckets by torchlight, but they're not our women." They watched them dump buckets into a large pile. Picking up binoculars, Maya gasped, "It's…" she stammered, "I think it's a bone pile." Shuddering as she remembered Alana's tale of wolves ripping apart their hunters, she put down the binoculars and whispered to Alana, "I'm getting sick to my stomach." Maya put her hands on her belly and looked dizzy.

Fearing that the captain would overhear and turn back, Alana whispered adamantly, "You've got to remain strong. Our people depend on us. Don't look at it." She squeezed her arm and gave her an encouraging look. Maya gave her a weak smile.

Maya closed her eyes to calm herself. "I'll be all right. I can do this," she whispered. She focused the binoculars away from the bone pile. In the distance, she saw shadows in a fenced area farther away. "Alana, in your vision, didn't you see our people in a field?"

"Yes." she answered excitedly. "What do you see?" She strained to see something in the direction Maya pointed.

"Look there. I think I see something, but I'm not sure." She handed the binoculars to Alana, who said in a louder voice, "Captain, can you fly toward the mountain?" She sighed with relief when Lil did as she asked, and the dark shape of the mountain came into focus. In the field leading to the mountain's rocky base, Alana made out shapes in the moonlight. Someone sat rocking a smaller figure. "There's Yanni, Maya. Look, there's Yanni!" Alana joyfully jumped and hugged Maya, who was too teary to speak. She pleaded, "Here they are. No one is around. You can rescue them without being seen. And you don't need to destroy anything or interfere with anybody!"

Lil exchanged concerned glances with Jared, who asked, "How can you be sure no one's around? There must be guards."

Looking with the binoculars through the shadows, Alana could make out two figures. "Over there, under that shelter, I see two figures who must be the guards. They're both lying on the ground asleep. Maybe they've been drinking."

"And they're passed out!" cried Maya.

"Let me see," said Jared. After looking, he said, "I only see two, and they don't seem to be moving."

"Yes," Alana exclaimed. "Why would they need more guards here? They're up against a mountain bounded by the sea. Besides, everyone knows the Danes are drunkards. They're surely passed out and won't hear us."

"We can pick them up quietly," said Maya excitedly.

"If you cross the field at a low level, I'll motion to my people to run to the far corner, and we can pick them up," Alana suggested.

"Absolutely not!" Lil replied, heaving his shoulders with irritation. "If you appear floating through the sky motioning to them, you'll terrify them. They'll scream and refuse to come. I'll land within the stockade by those trees. You run out and bring back as many as you can. We'll stay only a few minutes. If you're not back, I'm leaving."

Alana sighed in relief that he'd now agreed to the rescue. When the cargo bay door opened, Alana and Maya sprinted within the stockade and gently shook each sleeping figure awake, placing a hand over her mouth or putting a finger to her own lips for silence. Not all were from her village, but they were all prisoners, so she brought them. Lil's ship temporarily became visible. The captives hobbled, crawled, or were carried to the ship, but they all made it. The nearly dead prisoners asked no questions; they had faith in Alana. The guards remained fast asleep.

As Lil began shutting the door, Alana asked the women, "Quickly. Where are the men?"

Yanni moaned in a lifeless tone, "They're dead. All of them." Alana held back tears and didn't protest when Lil closed the door and took off.

"Alana, come here," ordered Lil after flying awhile. "You said your village was destroyed. Where I am taking you?"

"We moved to a cave in the highlands."

"Are there any landmarks so I can find it?"

"There's a high rock outcropping that overlooks the valley below," she said. "From a distance, the rock looks like a face."

"I know it," Lil said, keeping his eyes straight ahead.

Alana studied the bluish-red orb before them in the night sky. "That thing seems to have a tail. It looks like a dragon from a storybook that I had as a child."

Storybook? Once again, Lil's interest was piqued by her surprising background.

Alana returned to help the survivors, most of whom were now fitfully asleep with exhaustion, screaming when they dreamed. She comforted as many as she could.

Contacting Hawan, Lil learned that the entire Ministry was working late tracking the comet. Feeling guilty about his absence, he tried to gather useful information. The bluish-red orb was steadily growing larger and brighter. Whatever was going to happen to Earth would happen soon.

In the eerie light, he found the pale-faced rock that Alana had described. He landed by the cave and helped out the women and children. Some lay down while others limped toward the cave's entrance, looking back, not able to see the invisible ship.

"Alana, I'm needed at Hawan," said Lil, almost apologetically, when he'd helped the last injured villager reach the ground. "That dragon, as you named it, is a comet. It's far above the clouds right now, but it's coming closer, and a part of it will slam into this planet in three days. Take everyone as far underground as possible. And take all your provisions. You'll need to stay awhile."

Alana lifted a child, steadying her on her hip. "We'll stay down as long as we can bear it. It's so dark down there."

Lil fleetingly looked annoyed, then he popped open a panel and extracted two tubelike objects. "Here, take these. Press here." When he demonstrated, the object glowed with light. Alana smiled warmly, gazing up into his deep, blue eyes, which sparkled in the soft yet pervasive light. She found his expression less cold even though he stood straight-backed and formal as if prepared to preside over an assembly. "I can't begin to tell you how grateful I am for everything!" She stretched out her arm as if to touch him, but she thought better of it and masked her action by shifting the sleeping child whose head lay on her breast.

"Yes, thank you so much!" gushed Maya, filling the awkward silence. Flashing a huge smile, she waved good-bye and helped the limping Yanni, her arm draped over Maya's neck, slowly walk toward the cave.

"Your kindness and integrity show on your faces," Alana said as if in apology, seeking to make amends for her harsh words at the barn. Not that she regretted a single accusation, which had all been necessary to prod these inscrutable strangers into action. Men who could protect the peaceful people from the Danes' atrocities but instead chose to hide in their fortress and ignore what happened around them. Princess Petrina had taught her to help others, and Zedah had taught about preserving the Mother's bounty; of course, many didn't listen, even among her own people. But she didn't want the strangers to leave with ill feelings toward her; she might well need them again.

Lil nodded curtly. With his attention focused on determining his next actions to safeguard his people against the comet impact, he immediately turned to leave. Alana ran back up the ramp and lightly touched his arm, again withdrawing quickly.

"You've helped us twice now, yet I still don't know your name. I wish to remember you."

Lil paused momentarily, the edges of his lips hinting at a smile and his eyes softening toward her. After the comet impact, they might all be dead, so what did it matter if she knew his name? If he died and she lived, perhaps she would pass on his story to her tribesmen, creating a myth that would transcend time like their own ancient legends. "My name is Lil, of the House of En. This is my first officer, Jared." He lingered a moment, admiring how strong and healthy she appeared despite her hardship. Life sometimes clung on to little. He couldn't fathom how she'd been so resourceful under these harsh conditions or how she'd climbed the mountain to invade their colony, undeceived by their illusions. Beneath the filth and vileness of so many that had caught his attention lay beads of greatness and compassion that he'd overlooked. If Earth people survived the comet, would they thrive again? No doubt, fighters like Alana and Maya would eventually lead their people to create a vast civilization—would it mirror the Alterrans' mistakes of so long ago?

Alana held his thoughtful gaze, disappointed that he seemed so distant again. He must long for his mate. "Thank you, Lil and Jared. I wish you luck with the dragon." Having dawdled too long, she scampered back down the ramp, lifted onto her other hip another child who lay listlessly on the ground while juggling the lighting rods, and walked to the cave. She hadn't had time to prepare for the arrival of sick and injured patients, and now she had to prepare for a comet. Somehow she'd get by.

CHAPTER 16
ALANA

Taking a moment from adding her last carrots to the watery stew simmering in her one unbroken pot while keeping a careful eye to turn the nearby spits where fresh fish were roasting, and all the while worrying that it wasn't enough to feed the nearly one hundred emaciated survivors, Alana gazed up with red eyes to study the dragon. She and Maya hadn't slept, having spent the night tending to the wounded. When they dozed, she listened to the anguished screams of torturous nightmares. Since only the day before, the dragon had grown into a blazing second sun. Heeding Lil's warning, she rushed to prepare food so they could retreat into the depths of the cave where she could only make small fires for warmth. She was grateful for Lil's gift of light; without it, her skittish patients would have panicked in the darkness. Adding to their vast store of sweet apples, berries and nuts, this stew would need to last those who couldn't yet chew however long it would take until this latest crisis passed. Thanking Mother Earth for not abandoning them, instead leaving her full traps and fishing nets, she implored the Mother for one further favor—*Please, Mother, don't let Drood find us.* Later in the day, she put the leftover stew into a hollowed stone that Ewan had carved by hacking away during his despairing days, as if murdering the Danes. Maya made many trips to the stream, bringing water for Alana to brew her healing tea of herbs and white willow bark.

Through gentle but firm coaxing, Alana and Maya, aided by Morgana, a rescued outlander, guided the wounded through the narrow passageways leading to the deep cavern, the people being too dazed to wonder at the glowing light in her hands. The stronger children dragged with them Ewan's emergency food stores and the furs and other things gathered before the rescue. Once Alana had everyone settled in the large cavern, she cleaned their open wounds. The ribs of some children were showing as if they were skeletons. Seeing them lie listlessly, their eyes open but unseeing, she feared they wouldn't all recover. She spooned stew into their mouths and jiggled them to make them swallow before it dribbled from their mouths. Following behind her, Morgana lifted each patient's chin to sip the healing tea.

Her people couldn't stay permanently underground, worried Alana in a rare spare moment to herself. Having no huts and no skilled workers to rebuild the village, she and Maya whispered to themselves that, as soon as the winter snows thawed, they'd have no choice but to disperse to other villages. If they followed the coastline, they'd be sure to find someone. For now, the cave provided safety. Although it was chilly, it was warmer and drier than the wintry weather to come. Throughout her busy days, Alana never ceased to worry about Ewan. It wasn't unusual for him to be gone at length, but the weather was turning sharply colder, and even Lil was worried about the glowing object in the sky. Since the herbs and mushrooms she used in the Seeing Ceremony were the same ingredients for the medicine her people needed, she made the difficult choice to medicate the suffering women rather than use them to search for Ewan. If he returned soon uninjured, he'd be angry that she hadn't treated the injured instead of foolishly worrying about him.

Not all the rescued people were her villagers. There was a tall mother, Morgana, with a small daughter, Tara, who were both fair of skin and golden haired, like Alana. Overhearing Morgana consoling Tara, Alana's memories were stirred. Through the common tongue, Morgana offered their gratitude at being rescued. Despite her weakened condition, she smiled constantly and eagerly helped out.

Alana delicately lifted her friend Yanni by her bony shoulders, unsure if more than her nose and ribs had been broken, and brought tea to her parched lips. Yanni managed to swallow a few drops and licked her lips. "Yanni," Alana gently asked, "are you ready to tell what happened?"

With the soft glow of Lil's light revealing the deep purple bruises and crookedness of her broken nose, Yanni told her story, pausing at times to cough and gasp for breath. "We didn't see them. They ran from the trees like a swarm of angry bees. Their war cries were so chilling that I was paralyzed with fright. Their clubs were raised. Laughing, they grabbed us and threw us like apples into a pile at the hearth. There was screaming, terrible screaming. Older children ran, and the monsters clubbed them. I knew it could only be Shylfing's Danes; only they could be so cruel, worse than Drood. They laughed from their bellies when they trampled old Rayna. She moved too slowly. They cornered little Pedron," she choked, unable to complete her sentence. Alana held her, stroking her hair until she began again. "They took Tia's baby and threw it into the hearth fire. Tia reached into the flames, but a monster ran his sword through her back, and she fell, burned…" Tears ran down Yanni's face, leaving tracks in the dirt. Tia was her best friend, and her dying screams haunted Yanni. Morgana brought a moistened fur to wipe Yanni's face. Yanni, the women's leader, had always been meticulous about her appearance.

Alana whispered, her own tears flowing down her face, "Yanni, you don't have to continue if this is too painful for you."

Yanni struggled to raise herself on her side, overcoming the pain of her broken ribs. "Someone needs to know. I may not live. Those who died must be remembered," she said hoarsely, stopping for a coughing fit among her shivers. "They bound our hands and tied us together. The brutes shouted, 'Where is the treasure? Where is the gold?' They kicked us and spat when we couldn't tell them. They ransacked our huts shouting for 'treasures' and became furious when they found none. One wearing a wolf tail—must have been Shylfing—strutted before us, cursing the Mother until he was red in the face. They set our world on fire. They pulled on our ropes to make us stand and march. Some fell along the way. They were kicked or whipped until we moved again. Falaria, because of her limp, was beaten to death, and her body was left for the animals." She choked, her eyes staring wildly nowhere.

Alana sat holding her, stroking her hair. Morgana brought another drink of tea. Yanni closed her eyes. Alana thought she might be sleeping, but she suddenly twitched, as if feeling a poke. "We marched night and day, without food or water, until we reached their boats in the big river and set sail. We were far from shore when our men tried to catch the last boat—I don't have any idea how they followed so quickly behind. We were too far away for me to know who was killed. I think we slept most of the way. After dragging us off the boats, they lined us up. I couldn't understand them, but they seemed angry about the lack of treasure. Some men leered at us. I was sure they would rape us, but a well-dressed woman stopped them. In the common tongue, she ordered that we were needed for the harvest and were to be left alone; they couldn't have their way with us."

Yanni blinked several times, trying to hold back her tears. Alana sensed the worst was to come. Yanni continued more slowly than before, "After only a moon cycle, Maliki and other men of our village snuck in—we have no idea how they traveled so quickly. They tried to break us free, but they were discovered and were no match for the Danes. After they were captured and imprisoned nearby, we saw, we heard the beatings and their grunts. The guards ridiculed us, saying that our saviors were to be thrown into the wolf pit to be torn apart." Her lips quivered, and she sobbed.

"You don't have to go on, Yanni; we know the story." Alana didn't want to know more. Dire wolves weren't common around her village, but once, with a hunting party, snarling gray wolves had challenged her group for a caribou kill; their vicious, sharp fangs had been close to biting her. Yanni became silent and stared at the wall. She had lost her father, husband Maliki, and two brothers.

In the ensuing days, Alana's greatest fear was that some would lose the will to live. Life would be difficult without winter supplies. She needed them to have hope, to rise to the struggle. She and Maya couldn't possibly hunt, cook, bring water, comfort, and do everything else for nearly a hundred women and children. She felt overwhelmed. Yanni refused to eat, and her robust body had been reduced to skin and bones. Alana coaxed her, "Yanni, try to eat the stew, or at least sip the broth. You must get better to carry on for those you've lost. They'd want you to live. Tomin needs his mother." But Yanni simply stared with the wide-eyed look of one whose mind was dead. Over and over, she remembered seeing her poor Maliki, one eye gone and unable to walk on his broken legs, being dragged to the long house. She'd clung to the fence and tried to wave good-bye, but the guards laughingly beat and kicked him all the more. It pained her that she'd caused him agony in his last moments alive. He was too injured to have any chance to fight off the wolves. Yanni didn't know that men were capable of such cruelty. There was no point to living.

Alana knew better than to rush the healing process. To survive the winter, they needed more provisions and clothing. She and Maya, and maybe Morgana, would have to manage somehow. The snow would come soon. Thank the stars they had this cave with Ewan's hidden store of supplies, she thought. When Ewan returned, he might have more furs. But where was Ewan?

CHAPTER 17
THE COMET

Late that night, Ki and his staff were still working when Lil rushed to the Ministry of Science. Some conferred in small groups, and others intently studied the wall panels. "Ki, what's going on? Give me an update."

"It's about time you returned," Ki smirked, his eyes narrowed with annoyance at Lil's absence, wondering what could have been so important. "We've got a major situation developing." He pointed to many bands of pulsating strips of red lights overlaying maps of the Earth and its upper atmosphere. "We've been plotting the comet's potential trajectories. Two of the three will pass a safe distance away. The third will come *very* close. It won't hit Earth or its moon if it travels along this trajectory," Ki said as he outlined its path on the screen. "It'll come close enough that there will be a strong gravitational pull. We expect unusual tides. It could stress the existing plates and fault lines—so expect earthquakes."

"Is that the worst scenario?" asked Lil, knowing that Ki usually held the worst for last.

"No. We're most worried about this one." He pointed to a light trailing behind the comet. "It's a fragment that's headed directly toward Earth. We calculate that it will be captured by Earth's gravity within two days. Although small, it's still large enough to cause catastrophic damage."

"Where will it hit?" Lil asked.

"We think it will enter the atmosphere here, with this location as the impact point." Ki pointed to several locations in the western continent. "Incredibly, there's more. If this thing stays on course, it's likely to hit here. Laurina has been studying the geology. Tell us what you've found."

Laurina pointed to the impact site and produced beside it a holographic view of the multiple underground layers. "It's a volcanic caldera, a remnant of a super volcanic eruption many thousands of years ago, maybe more than one. The earlier super eruption would have affected the entire planet. The cone was blown away, and the top layer sank to become the caldera. Today, an extensive magma chamber lies deep below the crust, with a cone going all the way to the mantle, and heating the caldera's geysers and hot springs. This hologram presents the scale of the magma chamber. If it's hit by the fragment, the combined explosive force of the impact and the volcanic eruption it incites would be catastrophic. We've run simulations. We don't know for sure what would happen, but it's likely that the planet would wobble on its axis, possibly even be knocked on its side relative to the present pole positions." She showed this happening in a holographic simulation. "At the very least, Earth's rotation will be affected, changing the length of days and seasons."

"That would destroy nearly all vegetation and the wildlife," gasped Lil.

"Almost certainly," Ki agreed, shaking his head. "The planet could even be torn apart."

"I want to see that simulation again."

Laurina went over it all again, with Lil intently studying the smallest details.

"Obviously, this thing will be devastating to Earth," Ki remarked, nervously running his fingers through his hair. "There's no way that we'll avoid significant damage, if we even survive. Our simulations can't begin to capture all the consequences of a pole shift or rotation change. It will place unimaginable stress on the tectonic plates. At a minimum, we can expect major volcanic action, earthquakes, flooding, landslides, severe temperature variation, and perhaps even large landmasses breaking apart. You name it, it will probably happen."

"The loss of life will be massive. Extinction, including us."

"That's right," Ki said, barely containing his anxiety. "The Earthlings and animals may be nearly wiped out, as well as plant life. The temperature will drastically change. I wouldn't be surprised if this planet becomes encased in ice again."

"We've *got* to stop it." For a long while, Lil studied the screen, asking Laurina detailed questions. "We don't have a spaceship capable of escaping Earth's atmosphere, so we can't deflect it before it's captured by Earth's gravity. What are our options?"

"Time is running out," said Ki. "Without deflection, we can only mitigate the damage."

"We'll explode this thing as high as our craft can fly." Lil pounded his fist on the table, his jaw twitching with determination.

"That's what I'm thinking," said Ki, nodding, and Laurina agreed. "This close to Earth, it'll produce a blizzard of smaller hits, but that's nothing compared to the damage caused by a direct hit on that caldera."

"The highest feasible intersection point is here." Lil identified the northeastern continent, above a receding glacier. "The ship must be packed every inch with explosives."

Laurina interjected, "Based on our simulations, it's enough power only if the ship bores into the core before exploding." She and Mikhale had gone over the calculations repeatedly for hours and could find no room for error.

"We'll set the craft to self-destruct, which will provide greater explosive force," Lil said grimly. He drummed his fingers on the table. "Even with a direct hit, small pieces will rain across the continent."

"Yes," agreed Laurina. "Too many fragments to track."

"But at least the planet won't be torn apart, averting the worst of the disaster," said Lil with a deep breath.

"That's right," Ki agreed. "The ship's programming will be tricky with the need to account for turbulence caused by the fragment. We'll need a pilot nearby in case anything goes wrong."

Losing his legendary calm, Lil picked up a cup and threw it at the wall. "First, we lose Alterra, and now Earth is on the brink. I think the universe is out to get us." He called Yamin, waking him up, snapping, "Yamin, what pilots are available for immediate takeoff?"

"Now, sir?" asked Yamin groggily, not realizing he was speaking to the captain.

"Yes, now," Lil snapped. "We have a major emergency on our hands."

"I'll be right with you, sir," said Yamin, now fully awake. From his bedside, he checked his monitor and responded, "Tamiel is flying over the western continent in a *tri-terran*, but Azazel is scheduled to leave in one hour."

"Good," replied Lil. "Tell Azazel to be prepared to fly the largest hovercraft transport. Ki's team is loading it now. Advise him that it will be filled with explosives and a mobile portal. This mission is critical. Then come to the Science Ministry immediately."

When Yamin arrived, Lil pointed to the wall screen and commanded, "Patch in Azazel." When Azazel's face, conveying his guardsman's professional blankness, appeared on the screen, Lil ordered, "Azazel, it's imperative that we destroy a comet fragment that's about to hit Earth."

"Yes, sir."

"You will meet Tamiel at the coordinates Yamin is sending you. It's above a large fingerlike lake, half covered by glacier, in the northern part of the western continent. Circle until I advise that a comet fragment has entered Earth's outermost atmosphere. It's an electromagnetic hot spot, so you'll be able to repower the fuel cells in flight. Ki will make the final trajectory calculations, taking into account the entry turbulence, and transmit them to your ship. If he's confident that the ship has been programmed to make a direct impact, I'll order you to transport yourself into Tamiel's *tri-terran* and take over as pilot; it's going to be rocky after the blast. If it can't be programmed, you'll have to fly manually into the comet. In either case, the ship will be programmed by Ki to self-destruct."

Not flinching, Azazel answered, "Yes, sir."

"It's critical to the lives of every creature on this planet that the ship bore directly into the fragment's core and explode," Lil explained, locking eyes with Azazel. "Azazel, you're our best pilot. That's why I need you."

"Understood, sir. How soon do I leave?"

"One hour." Lil gave him the sacred salute, and Azazel returned it without showing emotion.

When Azazel's visage faded from the screen, Ki said in a low tone, so that others couldn't hear, "Lil, I need to speak to you privately."

Lil snorted in irritation but followed as Ki led him to an alcove, where he formed from the Net a filter to prevent others from overhearing.

"Yes?" Lil raised his eyebrows in surprise at the necessity of a filter.

"This impact could be devastating," Ki said in a hushed tone, despite the screen. "Shouldn't we warn Earth people?"

Lil's eyes went wide with alarm, and he turned his back to the scientists milling about the room. This was the last thing on his mind. He and his men had recorded many Earth tribes living throughout the planet, but they had always done so invisibly. Until recently, he'd been meticulous about enforcing the directive.

"There's no time," said an astonished Lil, shaking his head sharply with a derisive laugh. "I won't put my men in jeopardy for such nonsense. What good would it do, anyway?"

"But at least some should be warned," protested Ki, "especially if there's no risk to our men."

"This disaster isn't our fault." Lil crossed his arms emphatically. "We have our hands full trying to stop the comet. That's how we're helping them. Beyond that, whatever happens is their destiny. For good reason, we will honor the Non-Interference Directive. Not another word. Remove this filter right now!"

"But—"

"Don't waste my time. We can't warn all these tribes, and even if we did, they'd be petrified by the messenger and wouldn't comprehend. I won't risk the lives of my men." Raising his chin in defiance of Lil's furious glare, Ki nevertheless released the filter. Lil strode away and resumed giving orders, bringing an end to the matter.

Ki let him go; he also didn't have time to argue before he implemented his plan. Returning to his official duties, Ki ordered his team to keep refining the projected impact time. The countdown was displayed throughout Hawan for all to see. When Anu and the Council awoke the next morning, they received Ki's holographic report.

Anu's serene image, wearing his sacred triangle on the crown of his head, appeared on all the room's monitors. "I've read these reports and know that you're about to destroy the comet fragment. I don't want to distract you, Lil, at this critical time. Know simply that I have the utmost faith in you. On Earth as it is on Alterra."

After Anu's image faded, Lil confirmed that all guardsmen throughout the planet were on alert. A few were ordered to remain at their observational posts, and the rest were ordered to return to Hawan. In case the destruction plan failed, the colonists were ordered to remain indoors at their workstations, ready for action. Anu paced back and forth, peeking through his portal as the fragment grew brighter than the sun. He hadn't seen the point of bringing the Council out of stasis; if the planet exploded, they'd die more peacefully than those

awake. Displayed on one monitor was a countdown clock showing the hours, minutes, and seconds disappearing. All eyes in
the Ministry, Guard Hall, the infirmary, and every other nook
and cranny were focused on their monitors.

Having nothing left to do for the moment but wait, Ki, Laurina, and Mikhale separately stole into Ki's office, where he'd
formed an electronic filter to guard their conversation. Sliding
into a chair, Ki asked, "Are the holograms ready?"

Laurina nodded, eager for his approval. "Yes. When we
found that a tribe revered an animal god, I copied it to create an
identical hologram. Here's an example of a serpent, the tribe's
symbol for wisdom." Ki winced, trying to remain expressionless.
In the days when he was the lone scientist on Earth, he'd occasionally project himself as a serpent in order to visit primitive
camps; he'd always been an admirer of the Earth women. Laurina tilted her head, puzzled by his demeanor, yet continued, "I
made a composite showing the gods of thunder and lightning."

"Aren't they worshiped by those marauding savages?" he
asked, perplexed by her choice.

Laurina gulped, avoiding his eyes. "Yes, but it's all we had.
If we couldn't identify a meaningful symbol, we used a hazy
image of Mikhale in a long white robe."

"Mikhale in a white robe?" Baffled, Ki raised a single eyebrow, squinting. "I don't understand."

"He's an Anunnaki." She bit her lip, now seeing the absur-
dity of Mikhale's luminous white image. "We had no time to
plan."

"Okay, Okay, sounds reasonable," said Ki, not wishing to
wound her delicate ego. "How did you choose whom to receive
the message?"

"With such little time," Mikhale explained, chastened at Ki's
lack of enthusiasm for his Anunnaki image, "the most readily
available coordinates were those of the last tribes observed by
the guardsmen, which includes, unfortunately, the marauding
tribes. Many might be worthier of saving. This is the best we
could do."

"Understood. At least we did what we could," replied Ki dismissively, putting his hands on his hips. "Well, let's get started. Mikhale, you can't both be gone. Keep refining our calculations."

Launching her programs, Laurina sat back with Ki to watch them unfold. To a tribe in the western land, she projected a hologram of Chimantou, the Great Spirit, instructing the people to run to a bog and cover their bodies with mud. Other tribes were warned by softly glowing images of their revered animal spirits to move to higher ground, some to Earth's tallest mountains. Those living on high ground in the north of the western continent were told to dig deep pits and cover themselves, leaving only an air hole, or to move deep into caves, taking as much food with them as they could carry. Coastal tribes were advised to paddle far from shore and to flow with huge waves to come. Viewing the images, some tribal people trembled and refused to believe; some heeded the advice, gathering family and friends. The marauders laughed and returned to their mead. With time running out, Laurina ran the last program.

"Thanks, Laurina," Ki said, putting his arm around her shoulder with a smile. "It might not have been much, but at least we tried. I have no regrets about violating the directive."

"Nor do I," said Laurina, eyes glistening with pride. He hadn't touched her before, and every cell in her body tingled. After holding his warm gaze a long moment before he left, she fought to control the emotions sweeping through her— monitoring the ever-changing trajectories was her task, which demanded every bit of her attention. She had always proudly served under Ki, awed by his legendary talents. Even with all she'd seen, helping the poor Earth people to survive this calamity despite the directive was a defining moment for her. Working so closely with Ki over the years, she'd been one of the few to decipher his carefully concealed violations of Alterran orders; at times, she'd even been concerned for her safety if she were implicated. No more. If they survived, whatever path

Ki took, she wanted to be by his side. Mikhale, she knew, felt the same loyalty.

Forcing herself to focus on her calculations, she reentered the control room, now crowded with Lil's guardsmen, as well as the Ministry's full complement of scientists and engineers, all eyes riveted on the changing wall screens. Laurina slid into her seat beside Mikhale, where they huddled to complete their work. Seeing the glowing particle ignite as it became engulfed in Earth's upper atmosphere, Lil ordered Azazel to be patched in, and his steadfast image appeared on all the monitors.

"Azazel, the particle will be at the demolition point in twenty minutes. Are you prepared?"

"Yes, Captain," said Azazel evenly, his gaze steely and unwavering, giving no hint that, momentarily, he might fly to his death. Thinking of the legends of old, Azazel remembered with chagrin that the hero was always bidden farewell by tearful family members, followed by a lingering kiss from the soft lips of a lovely, sorrowful maiden in a long, flowing gown with a crown of roses scenting her luscious hair. Regretting that he hadn't been given more warning, he'd have created a maiden from his recorder; as it was, all he could do was imagine the kiss.

Tensely, Lil waited while Ki conferred with Laurina and Mikhale, hoping that he could order Azazel to escape to Tamiel's ship. If not, he'd do his duty, as would Azazel. Ki bent over, watching the simulations running on Laurina's screen, his face as calm as if he were watching an episode from his memory book. He tapped his finger on his pursed lips, seemingly oblivious to the tension of those surrounding him.

Azazel's transmission sputtered with interference. "Sir, the object has become so bright that I no longer have a visual."

Lil waited impatiently, his hands on his hips. After receiving nods from Laurina and Mikhale, Ki stood straight and put his thumb upward. "Lil, we're confident that we've calculated the final trajectory. We're sending the flight program to Azazel now."

"Azazel," said Lil calmly. "Confirm that the program was received by your instruments." Azazel's ship bounced, and the transmission sputtered. "Ki, resend," Lil shouted. Mikhale ran his fingers across his console to resend and sat back. The screen sputtered again. "Azazel, what is your status?" When the screen went blank, a soft groan came from the room. "Azazel, come in."

"According to our instruments, he received the program," said Ki. "His ship might be accelerating toward the fragment already."

"Azazel, we've lost visual contact. You're ordered to transport to Tamiel's ship, take manual control, and get out of there. Brace yourselves for major sonic waves."

After moments of static, Lil heard the faint reply, "Will do, sir. Azazel out."

Reaching Tamiel's ship, Azazel vowed that he would find his maiden.

High above the northern portion of the western continent, the explosive-filled craft bored into the fragment's core and detonated in a hot flash of blinding light. A fireball flew above the outermost atmosphere, and massive energy waves radiated from the blast. Large chunks of burning debris fell toward the Earth, some pieces large enough to make the surface, where their heat melted holes through glacier ice, ejecting fresh water and causing a sooty ice rain over the land for a thousand miles. A raging fireball incinerated the burgeoning vegetation rebounding from the glacier's recession, fueled by searing winds greater than hurricane force. Sonic winds and electromagnetic waves blew across the planet, rocking hovercrafts stationed on the planet's far side. Fires rolling southward ignited all the grasslands in streams leading to the continent's southern tip. Days before, Earth people there had seen a strange dragon in the sky and hid. A few heeded warnings of the "gods." Most were annihilated, along with mammoths and saber-toothed tigers.

Although Azazel and Tamiel had braced for the shock wave, they didn't expect their ship to be whipped around like Mika's glowglobe in the meadow; they passed out. The ship spiraled downward until its sensors took over. Eventually regaining consciousness, Azazel found his ship above the distant southern ocean.

At Hawan, the shock waves pummeled the granite mountain, dislodging ceiling stones and sending loose objects flying through the air. Screaming colonists were flung to the floor. In the control room, shelving toppled and computer equipment crashed; an electronic bubble sprang into existence, sheltering Ki and his staff from debris. Sparking power systems, overloaded by the wave energy surging from collection points, exploded with ungrounded electricity. The electronic shield holding the baby mastodon faltered, and it toppled out, taking with it vials of its blood; the blood splattered Aferiona, a scientist, and its leg landed on her. With Agnon's help, she was dislodged and taken to the infirmary with a smashed leg. Although animal cages tipped over, only monkeys and experimental rodents escaped, leaving the vicious tigers and dire wolves snarling in their metal cages. When the rumbling subsided, Lil and Ki dug themselves from the control room's rubble, assisting the injured. There and elsewhere in the colony, dusty survivors frantically searched the rubble to reach those unable to move, while avoiding chunks of loosened granite that sporadically crashed from the ceilings.

Even though Lil and his men sprayed foam on the smoldering communications and power systems, small fires nevertheless erupted. "Great. Nothing's working, not even the Net," spat Lil, breathing heavily, kicking a chunk of ceiling and causing dust to rise from the debris. He closed his eyes and used *mencomm* as his only resource to assess injuries and damage, seeing from the eyes of a guardsman that an entire building wall had collapsed, burying a cohort of colonists. After searching through the eyes of numerous guardsmen, he concluded that Hawan's walls weren't otherwise in imminent danger of collapse. "Rameel, get the injured to the infirmary. You men, come with me." Lil headed with his guardsmen to the collapsed building.

Rameel and Mikhale put severely injured colonists on mini-hovers and helped others limp down the stairs to the infirmary. Reaching the medical floor, they found their path blocked by smoke from a fire in a storage room, which Uras and her panicked assistants were dousing with improvised water buckets. Putting down their patients, Rameel and Mikhale caused their tunics to transform into protective bubbles. They ripped open emergency packs in the burning storage room and sprayed the fire with foam. Coughing and holding a cloth over her mouth, Uras lit glowglobes, which floated on the smoky clouds filling the room. She glumly picked through the damage.

Discovering communications coming online, Uras frantically called out to her son. "Ki, we've been able to quench the fire, but we have no power. Patients are streaming through the door, and I can't help them!" By light of the glowglobe, she began feeling patients, testing for broken bones.

"Sections all over Hawan have exploded," replied Ki as he and Laurina dashed about the control room trying to assess the damage. "I've blocked power to reduce the fire."

"They're bringing us injured people; some may have died. It's important that I get power for the treatment chambers as soon as possible!" pleaded Uras, her voice trembling. Kosondra and Schwara had the men put patients on the floors, where they caused the underside of their patients' tunics to convert to cushions.

"Understood. I'm doing everything I can. I'll get back to you." Ki examined his control panels, which operated with wireless connections. He pointed out damaged modules to Laurina. "The damage to these panels isn't as bad as I feared, and the surge seems to have passed through, although we'll need to watch for aftershocks. See these?" Laurina nodded, observing modules blackened by fire. "Replace them and we'll be able to bring emergency systems back online to areas that aren't blocked with debris. With the infirmary below us, with any luck, we can at least provide power where we need it most." They cut power from severely damaged areas of Hawan, diverting it to the infirmary through an alternative pathway. Nanobots were sent through the system to repair key junctures to reactivate the pathway to the infirmary. Soon the chambers began purring again as power was restored. The Net resumed, and it automatically began to freshen the infirmary's smoky air.

"Ki, thank the stars you brought the power back!" exclaimed Uras, her voice shaky. Immensely relieved and eager to get to work, she put her hands in an instant sterilizer and caused her tunic, drawing upon the Net's power, to be sterilized, and then rushed to examine her first patients. Kosondra organized the incoming stream of patients, while Schwara made small wounds disappear by touching them with a thin, pencil-like device. With the Net restored, Kosondra and Schwara caused each patient's tunic to draw upon residual power; they soon rippled, curing superficial abrasions.

Uras heard Ki's voice crackle through the still-damaged system. "We have extensive damage. I've had to cut power nearly everywhere else. Only operate essential equipment."

"We must use the chamber, but we'll try not to use other things." As injured colonists flooded the infirmary, Uras examined each new patient. "Kosondra and Mikhale, quickly, these three are dead from internal injuries. Get them into the chambers." Mikhale rushed each lifeless body to a bed inside one of the three chambers. Scanning lights swept over their bodies as Uras performed diagnostic tests, from which she programmed the treatment cycle. As each chamber began whirring and dancing arcs of electromagnetic energy encased the patient, Uras momentarily closed her eyes with a prayer. Patients cheered. Uras monitored the progress of each chamber's program while she continued to assess new patients. As the chamber restored each patient's health, Mikhale quickly removed the smiling patient to a bed in Kosondra's makeshift recovery area and placed a new patient in the chamber. After a short recovery, cured patients were directed to assist Lil with the collapsed building.

With a thud, an aftershock rocked Hawan, knocking Uras against a wall, sending more equipment crashing to the floor and causing power in the infirmary to sputter. "Oh, no," cried Uras. "Kosondra, help me with the chamber." Uras paused a moment before looking, closing her eyes with a prayer. They cautiously opened the door, and Uras examined her patient. "He's not responsive, but the program progressed far enough to restore his aura. Quickly, start it again."

While Kosondra reprogrammed the chamber, Uras examined the patient in the second chamber, whose treatment had been similarly interrupted. "Schwara," she ordered, "start the program again." Uras paced slowly outside the whirring chamber, sneezing at the dust settling on the normally immaculate floor. Vaguely, she was aware that her hip hurt where she had been hurled to the floor. She struggled to suppress the fear swelling in her mind by focusing on implementing triage for the wounded and myriad other emergency measures.

When the whirring of the chamber ceased, she closed her eyes and held her breath before looking through the chamber window. Letting out her breath in relief, she saw that her patient, Drigha, was sitting up in the chamber with a huge grin, running his hands over his formerly crushed legs. "Welcome back," Uras cheerfully greeted him, entering the chamber. "I'm *very* glad to see you." She performed a quick examination and checked the equipment readings. "Fortunately, the treatment cycle is complete, and you're fine. We're going to move you out for the next patient."

"Thanks, Doc," Drigha said. "I feel great. Was there much damage?"

"I don't know yet, but it can't be good."

"I'll help out around here." Drigha slid from the treatment bed, gingerly shaking and testing his repaired legs.

"Normally, I'd let you stay here to recover, but we need every able body to help," she replied, brushing a sweaty stray strand of hair from her eyes. She smiled briefly and moved on to another critical patient, calling hastily behind her, "Work with Kosondra, Drigha."

After Mikhale positioned the next patient in the chamber for treatment, Kosondra frantically screamed, "Something's wrong! I can't start the program." Tears streaming down her face, she jabbed at the controls, reinserting the program as quickly as she could.

Uras rushed over to examine the chamber's control panel, and tried several alternatives. The darkened chamber gave no trace of beginning the brightly lit sequence of healing rays. Putting her ear to the chamber wall, Uras detected a low hum. "The chamber still has power. We took quite a jolt. Check the outside. I thought I smelled something earlier."

Drigha ran his fingers along the outside casing and dropped to the floor, checking for cracks. "I feel something rough and uneven."

"Oh, no," cried Kosondra, dropping to her knees to run her fingers at the machine's base. "Cracks, large ones. I smell chemicals escaping. Drigha, get me something to stuff these cracks. Maybe we can seal them."

Drigha grabbed a discarded tunic and stuffed it into the crack. He heard a low creak, and he withdrew his hands just moments before the chamber settled, and the cracks radiated out in long fingers, widening at the chamber's bottom. "These are useless," spat Drigha. "This entire panel must be replaced."

Schwara shrieked as she tapped at the control panel while casting searching glances into the dark chamber. "Oh, this one's not working either. I think that last jolt damaged it."

"Lil, Ki, one of you, help us," Uras called, her voice far steadier than she felt. She hoped that the nanobots still worked to pick up her plea. "Lil, Ki, the chambers aren't working. They're cracked."

Lil ordered Rameel to rush with repair crews. They examined each chamber and found that none were operational. Fearing that the misaligned chambers might teeter and topple over, the men took rods from the smoldering storeroom to prop them up. The damage was too extensive for repair. They needed replacements from Alterra.

"This is too much." Uras sank to the floor with her hands covering her face. Rameel felt her pain but could offer no comfort. Having no hope, he nevertheless had his men recheck whether any fix might be available. After a few minutes, Uras groaned, "Even if we could repair these cracks, we can't replace the lost chemicals. This is delicate equipment. We can't make these repairs here on this blasted, primitive planet!" She lowered her head again, disconsolate, unable to think. Kosondra cut the power to the useless chambers and slid to the floor beside Uras. Stunned, the repair crew ceased working and mutely listened to the ominous hiss of the escaping gaseous chemicals, their faces in shock at the thought that they couldn't be healed if wounded. The assurance of healing, leading to multiple lifetimes, had been an essential, secure premise throughout their whole lives; it had changed in an instant. Tears streamed down Schwara's face as she leaned against the wall. Of the many disasters that day, the failure of the rejuvenation chambers hit them the hardest. Patients inside the chambers undergoing treatment permanently died, as would the dead and dying patients awaiting their turn. Having relied solely upon the chambers for their serious medical needs, Uras had no ready alternative for treating critical patients.

CHAPTER 18
THE DANES

Shylfing's guards, awakening the next morning from their drunken stupor, couldn't believe their eyes upon discovering that their half-dead prisoners were missing. Shorter and slimmer than those considered warriors, these men had been captured as young boys during Shylfing's southern raids.

"This is entirely your fault," the pimpled one complained, scratching his matted black hair and watching debris float to the ground. "You brought the mead. If Shylfing finds out the prisoners are gone, it'll be we who are thrown to the wolves next." He punched his comrade, who caught himself before falling.

The other, who wore a patch over one eye from which a jagged scar descended down his cheek, scowled and lifted his arm as if to strike back. "Oh, quit your bloody whining. You drank it, didn't you? I didn't force it down your stinking throat."

"Calm down, I didn't mean anything," said the pimpled one, feeling his throbbing head. "Hey," he pointed upward, squinting, "I don't remember having two suns in the sky." He blinked repeatedly and scratched his matted hair, wondering why he couldn't remember the second sun.

His companion punched him in the shoulder. "Forget about that. Think clearly now. Shylfing will get you, but that thing in the sky won't. If we find them women first, he'll never know, now will he?" He bobbed his head with a knowing smile.

The pimpled man took a bite of bread and said while chewing, "How can that ragtag lot have gone far?" Looking around in a daze, he concluded, "Why, they must be hiding in that woods over there. Why don't you go look?"

"Why don't we both go look?" demanded the one-eyed man, slapping the other's leg. "Ain't nobody could climb that steep rock over there, and there's no way they could've made their way past everyone to steal a boat. We'll get 'em back to work before anybody's the wiser, you'll see."

Setting out, they weren't concerned. The prisoners wouldn't have had the strength to go far. Making the search into a game, the pair jumped out from behind rocks thinking they'd scare their prey. As they lazily searched, they joked about the cruel punishments they'd inflict on the prisoners for causing them the inconvenience of missing a proper breakfast. But after searching for most of the morning without finding even a footprint, they grew alarmed. By early afternoon, they concluded that the prisoners had somehow eluded them, and they, too, needed to escape to avoid the wolves. They gathered what little food lay about, slipped through the woods, and began climbing the mountain.

When Shylfing's cook came to the field in late afternoon to get greens for the evening meal, she discovered that both prisoners and guards were missing. Her screaming about the escape was heard throughout the village. Warriors awakening from their afternoon naps were delighted to have a manly task to perform. Fortifying themselves with rounds of mead, search parties spread out to comb the wood and the beaches. Not finding them on land, they concluded that they had escaped by sea.

Galen, sensing another opportunity to prove his worth, assumed command in Shylfing's absence. With his horrified mother watching on the rocks above, Galen strutted on the beach and sent his mother defiant glances while he rallied the men with jibes to join him in catching and torturing the women. Now that the women were runaways, Callendra couldn't help them anymore. Under Shylfing's law, anything could be done to them.

A woman wearing a white linen dress, which had been pilfered from a southern port city, stood beside Callendra watching the horizon. "Where's Shylfing? He'd stop these fools."

"Shylfing beds his wenches, where else?" she replied without emotion, pulling her fox fur more closely over her dusty rose dress embroidered with a yellow crest and trimmed with tiny pearls. She observed the dark clouds on the horizon and noticed that the birds were racing away from the shore. The air made her skin feel prickly. She couldn't rouse herself to care.

An old Danish woman, wearing many necklaces of brightly colored beads, warned with a bony finger, "Strange, strange things going on. A dragon crosses the sky. Prisoners barely able to walk disappear. The ground rumbles. It's a sign of doom!"

"Silence!" Callendra ordered impatiently, her eyes distant and blank. Pointing to the beach, she said with venom, "These stupid men talk of going to sea. They're too drunk to see the black clouds coming toward us. The sea recedes, and they laugh. They deserve what befalls them." Galen, too, she thought. Especially Galen.

The Danish woman shrieked, "A great band of evil is coming. Stop those fools!"

Callendra held her arm to stop her from warning them. "Say nothing," she firmly commanded, clutching her fur as it blew in the increasing wind. Her long, red-gold hair swirled around her. "Let the fools do as they wish. The gods will determine their fate."

The woman was puzzled. Shouldn't the mother save her son? She had sons of friends and nephews down below. The men were noble warriors.

Callendra watched with a sinking heart as her son led the drunken men, blinded by bloodlust, to the boats. Although she had thought she was too numb to feel pain, it tortured her that those she most hated had won. Her eyes were dry; she had no more tears.

Not caring why the sea had receded from the shoreline, Galen and his drunken band carried their boats across the muddy seabed, the strong wind muffling their words. With the swirling current rocking their boat, their progress was slow despite hearty rowing. Ignorant of the strange currents, Galen obstinately stood at the helm to prove his courage, refusing to acknowledge any sign of danger. He, a mere boy, was not afraid, why were they? Over the drummer's strong beats, Galen shouted, "Row with all you've got. Row, catch those whores."

With the waves growing larger and choppier, their rowing hadn't taken them far beyond the shore, and it was still shallow below them. A panicked sailor stood, speechless, pointing behind Galen. "Sit down," Galen yelled. Laughing, he derided him, "You look as if you see a sea monster." Hearing the roar, he turned. The monster wave smashed the boat like a small toy. The women on shore ran inland in terror. All except Callendra. She moved forward, closing her eyes and extending her arms to welcome the cleansing wave. Her torture would finally be over.

The wave slammed over the coastline, wiping out the Dane village and destroying everything in its path. No one would know this tribe had existed except through the tales told by victims of their terror.

CHAPTER 19
URAS

Two critical patients died after the chambers failed. Uras held their hands, turning cold as life left their bodies. She wasn't sure why they died. Afterward, she sat there too shocked to move. With rejuvenation, her generation had been the first to live long, successive lives. True, permanent death had become unthinkable. Her mother and father had died many centuries ago, and she barely remembered them now, relying on holographic images to remind her of their faces and the events of her first youth. Over many lives and rejuvenations, memories faded, overwritten by those of the current life. To preserve their own full histories, Alterrans maintained electronic diaries, called memory books, into which they downloaded the memories of each life, thus preserving the sights, sounds, and feelings of significant events in their past, so as never to be forgotten. It seemed odd, but Uras remembered her early life only through her memory book, it had occurred so long ago. Distraught and feeling the need for human connection, she opened her parents' memory book, seeking happy times. The detailed holograms enveloped her, and she relived her own birth through her mother's eyes and feelings and watched herself through her mother's eyes celebrating her fifth birthday. How different life was then, she thought. Needing more memories, she opened her own memory book to relive her youth and her courtship by Anu; she hadn't believed at first that he was serious, since she wasn't an En. She'd been so proud of him defeating the House of Kan. When Anu came for her after the victory celebrations, announcing that his reward was permission to marry her, she'd cried tears of joy and embraced her dashing hero. She relived her wedding to Anu, which had been celebrated across the planet. She'd ridden through the narrow streets among the densely built, soaring skyscrapers of Daria, the capital city, with people happily cheering and waving to her, flower petals streaming down. Feeling much better after reliving the happiness of the births of Ki and Ninhursag and the adoption of Lil, she closed it. She didn't have time to grieve; the colonists depended on the medical team.

Without rejuvenation, their lives would drastically change. Death would have finality now. How inefficient! A lifetime spent acquiring a skill was gone in an instant, never to be reclaimed. What a waste. Who would order a universe this way? The constant threat of mortality would irrevocably change their outlook on life. Each day could be their last.

Long ago, she'd learned as Anu's wife that the Supreme Council had taken extreme measures to control the population. The meal bars had been presented to the public through a major address by the supreme leader viewed throughout the planet. Developed to supply the nourishment and caloric requirements of each body type, the bars were proclaimed to be the perfect, environmentally friendly food to eradicate hunger and obesity without consumption of self-aware animals. But the bars were also a means of birth control. Over time, the bars controlled the population so well that other ingredients were added to eliminate social ills, such as aggressive behavior, independent thinking, and other perceived disorders. The population became docile and easily managed. The House of En ate a formulation that didn't control personality but did control their births. They couldn't chance warring among their own house.

The introduction of the nourishment bars had happened long ago, and the colonists assumed that their inability to conceive was evolution or a by-product of their extended lives. The supreme leader even secretly commissioned pseudo-scientific studies that reached these conclusions to spread disinformation. Occasionally, the supreme leader determined that the population's genetic pool should be refreshed, and he ordered that women having desired genetic profiles should conceive. Upon receipt of a directive, Uras would summon the assigned women for medical examinations and give them a shot that counteracted the bar's contraceptive additives. The mother was counseled that the scribes had deciphered a special message from the stars that she was destined to give birth. Thus, genuine Alterran children were rare. Most, such as Lil, who had a youthful appearance, were enjoying another life thanks to the rejuvenation chamber.

Now, without the chambers, these strict population control measures would be disastrous. Since the colonists had been uniquely selected, death would leave Hawan without valuable skills, even though basic knowledge could be absorbed through the Teacher. Anu would need to permit access beyond each person's rank so that survivors could learn the basics for survival, let alone to thrive in this isolated place. Uras wondered what lay outside the colony's walls; she'd never ventured out. Oh, she would have to think about this later. She roused herself to resume doing what she could to comfort the wounded. Giving herself an energy shot, she felt her depression improve.

Many hours later, when she had brought the latest emergency under control as best she could with her limited resources, Uras searched the Teacher for the ancient death ritual. Although she felt disoriented, at the very least, she could perform these rituals honorably, giving her lost people their proper send-off to the Universal Consciousness. She thanked the stars that the Teacher hadn't been damaged, or they would have been truly lost. She had much to do, but she had little energy to resume her work. She felt like going to bed and never getting up, despite the energy shot she'd taken. The colonists were truly endangered. She shuddered to think of the massive numbers of Earth people who had died in the comet's aftermath; they would have barely glimpsed the fireball that incinerated them. No time and nowhere to hide. Even initial Earth survivors faced death, with their food sources destroyed.

Was this destiny decreed by the Universal Consciousness seeking renewal? A civilization endures for eons and is gone in the blink of an eye. Alterra suddenly loses its atmosphere, and even its survivors in another galaxy are struck down. What sensible divine plan was this?

CHAPTER 20
ANU

After absorbing the knowledge about the burial ritual, Uras went to Anu's chamber. Fuming at the static interference that prevented him from contacting his father, Ama, Anu struck his monitor. "This equipment is fried! It's useless."

Uras, herself overwhelmed and wanting comfort, embraced him. For a long while, they clung together, sadly gazing out his little portal at the oppressive gray clouds. People assumed that the supreme leader and the named successors had been bred into heartless, cold rulers. She knew such myths weren't true. Well, maybe a bit; Ama, she was sure, wasn't burdened by a single empathic emotion. Anu was different. Her husband felt guilt for everything bad that happened because he hadn't foreseen and prevented it; the universe, after all, had been made for Alterrans. Futilely, she'd remind him that the universe was like an ever-renewing biosphere and that not every creature came out the winner; in short, bad things simply happened. Through the star messages and his own meditations, Anu sincerely believed that deciphering the future lay within his grasp. At times, she wished that he possessed a smidgeon of Ama's indifference, just enough so that he could rest easy. "Don't worry about that now, my love. It's enough that you and our sons are unharmed."

Anu said softly, "If Lil and Ki hadn't exploded that comet at the precise coordinates, hitting the core exactly as they did, this entire planet would have broken apart. We came so close to not standing here."

Uras smiled through her tears. "We're lucky to have them as sons."

Anu was again silent, too overwhelmed to speak. He knew that she needed comfort, that it was imperative for the leader to offer all his people reassuring words, even though he too felt lost. What meaningful words existed after a disaster of this magnitude? First Alterra and now Earth. He put his hands on her shoulders and looked into her tired, red eyes. He forced a smile, practicing what he'd say to the others. "I have the utmost faith in my people. We'll fix the damage and rebuild. We'll repair the rejuvenation chamber, or we'll find another way. Yes, these are trying times. But these things will pass." Proudly, he intoned, "We are, after all, Alterrans."

Knowing that he needed her to be receptive, Uras weakly attempted to smile.

"That's the smile I love," he said, hugging her again. "We'll get through this. We're healthy, and Lil and Ki are unhurt. I hope the same is true for Ninhursag."

"Me, too," she sighed, pressing against him more tightly.

He kissed her forehead and gently pushed away. "Sorry, my love, but I've called the Council from stasis, and I've sent them a nanobot describing the impact. I need to monitor the disaster, however much I'd rather hide in your warm arms. You can stay, if you'd like." He began receiving global images of the disaster sent by the few remaining craft in flight.

Watching over his back, she sighed, "I think I will." Uras normally couldn't stand the boredom of Council sessions, but she needed to know what was happening. Would the Council have sage advice? A supreme leader indeed had supreme authority, but the wisdom of ancient ancestors was comforting at times like these.

Since Ki was overwhelmed, Anu had received star interpretations directly from his scribes. One stated that the signs were in favor of harmony and stability in the universe. Another that stormy weather may lie ahead. Did these scribes even read their own interpretations, he wondered with annoyance. A third stated that the presence of an unidentified object near the Orion belt may portend that this was not an advisable time to begin new ventures. He threw them away.

Entering the adjacent Council chambers, he found Ki's assistant, Mikhale, prepared to begin his presentation. With the Council taking their seats and expressing their concern, Anu began. "Earth has sustained massive damage. Although the glaciers have recently been receding, the Ministry of Science projects that the crystalline ash falling from the comet impact will reverse the glacial decline. The Earth will rapidly cool, and the glaciers will grow for perhaps another century. Let's get right to the latest reports." Nodding to Mikhale, he instructed, "Tell us what you've learned."

Mikhale projected images showing fires raging out of control across much of the western continent and giant waves rolling across the oceans. "To say we were lucky would be an understatement. This peninsula happened to be in a pocket that didn't take a direct hit from these giant waves, although smaller ones inundated our western shore. It was a function of where the debris from the comet hit."

Awed at the devastation for which he'd had little advance warning, Anu bowed his head. "The Universal Consciousness was on our side today."

"Fortunately," said Councilwoman Barian, nodding.

"It proves that we have an important, unfulfilled destiny," said Councilman Pilian, shaking his gray-haired head. "We must have faith that everything will work out for us."

"Yes, faith is imperative," agreed Anu. "Action will also be necessary."

Continuing, Mikhale presented more images. "The last remaining port cities of the Earth people are now deep underwater after a monster wave crashed through the middle sea." Changing the focus, he said, "We now have additional information about the blast. After our ship crashed into the fragment, the main body exploded. The two largest ones fell here and here." He pointed in the middle of the far north. "Both locations were covered by glaciers, and the falling fire and ice bored holes, spewing glacier pieces across the continent. The fire heated the glacier, causing instantaneous melting in the immediate vicinity of the blast. The glacier melt sent torrents of fresh water gushing in all directions, including a sizeable channel that opened all the way to this ocean."

Changing the images, he said, "Here's what we're getting from the southern continent. You can see vicious electrical storms due to the high level of electromagnetism remaining in the atmosphere. These storms are causing severe flooding in areas that weren't within the primary impact zone. The weight from the flooding is upsetting delicate fault lines, leading to increased earthquake activity," Mikhale concluded and looked around for questions.

The Council members sat stunned.

Anu, eyes downcast, said simply, "Thank you."

Councilman Pilian impatiently asked, "Anu, do we know the status of the power system yet?"

"Not yet," he replied. "Ki and Lil have their teams doing a thorough investigation, working as fast as they can. They'll get back to us soon, but we'll need to wait, I'm afraid. I've been told our first outpost at Eridu was submerged. Fortunately, the mines at the southern tip of the southern country were far enough away from the impact that they sustained little damage."

"What about the electromagnetic wave that caused our damage? Do you expect more aftershocks?" asked Councilman Pilian.

"The Ministry's report predicts that the initial blast waves have diminished. Now they're only perceptible to our instruments. The greater dangers from a planetary standpoint, as Mikhale mentioned, are consequential earthquakes and volcanic eruptions. We think it unlikely that the colony itself remains at risk."

"What is the status of the rejuvenation chamber?" asked Councilwoman Arawan. "I heard that it was damaged. Is it fixed?"

Anu replied softly, staring as if lost, "All chambers have been irreversibly damaged because of our inability to obtain replacement parts from Alterra."

The Council members whispered emotionally among themselves. As Alterran elders, because of the chamber, they'd led many successive lives, living even before the Great Awakening when the existence of the chamber had been a carefully kept secret. Over time, the chamber became less effective and, because of their extreme age, the idle portions of their days were spent in stasis chambers. Of all of the day's events, this one affected them most personally. For longevity to no longer be a cornerstone of Alterran life would send ripples throughout society in ways they couldn't begin to imagine. How would harmony be managed in this unstable environment?

As Anu called for order, Councilman Pilian asked, "Was this tragedy predicted in the star charts?"

"Is this our destiny ordained by the Creator?" demanded Councilman Djane.

Councilwoman Arawan demanded, "Have we displeased the Creator? Is the Creator trying to eliminate us? Or was the Creator eliminating the Earth people and we happened to get in the way? We should have the scribes do a full star assessment."

Anu stated diplomatically, "Interpretation of destiny is uncertain. The grand plan may be unfolding but not yet be apparent. I have some reports from the scribes, but they need further analysis."

Councilwoman Barian interjected, "We can speculate on esoteric matters later. We must have a concrete plan to repair our facility. Our people expect this of us, as well they should. Anu, do you have a plan?"

"We're working on a plan. Lil has ordered all guardsmen back to Hawan because of fear that the electromagnetism and the comet ash make it unsafe for flying. This will free up guardsmen to work on the repair of the infrastructure. I've authorized engineering sessions from the Teacher for them. They'll begin immediately to make an assessment of the structural integrity of all buildings."

Councilwoman Arawan cleared her throat for attention. "How soon will they be back? Are we in danger?"

"They are expected soon." Anu pointed again at the screen. "Another team will remove debris from these collapsed buildings, and they will determine what may have been lost. The Ministry is monitoring whether there are other comet fragments likely to hit the Earth, and they'll report immediately if they have concerns."

"If I may speak," said Councilman Trey. "The honorable Councilwoman Arawan posed the question, in essence, whether it is our destiny to perish. I concur with the request for updated star readings. The Alterran civilization is the crowning achievement of the present universe. As such, I think it is vital that we survive—not only survive, that we thrive! Any proper reading of the stars, I'm quite sure, would show as much. We must look at these events as presenting an opportunity for renewal. Everything in nature undergoes periodic renewal—why not a civilization? Longevity, harmony, and stability have been the hallmarks of our civilization. I have great faith that Ki will find a way to restore longevity. Harmony and stability are, after all, states of mind. We must approach this crisis, and all solutions, to preserve our philosophy. Nothing else is acceptable."

"I shall request that Ki turn his attention to completing the star reports." Anu hoped to conclude the meeting without making commitments that would divert workers from necessary tasks.

But Councilman Trey continued, "I quite agree with my fellow Councilman. It is also a noble Alterran virtue that we consume food to nourish our bodies. Before this crisis, our food supplies were dwindling, as the reports from the Ministry of Science show. We haven't discussed this, but with the massive destruction we've seen today, I fear that we have fewer options. Anu, do you have any update on our food supply?"

"No," Anu replied, "but you raise a good point, and I will look into it."

Councilwoman Barian said, "Anu, you've committed to obtain several reports. The Council cannot advise you until that additional information is in hand. I move that we adjourn and resume when the reports are ready."

"Agreed," he said, glad to conclude this.

Uras muttered to herself as she slid from the chamber to return to the infirmary, "Didn't accomplish much."

CHAPTER 21

LIL

Having gathered all guardsmen at Hawan for their safety, Lil held an emergency session to organize the inspection and reconstruction efforts. Ki advised that few of the far-flung global monitoring devices still functioned. Thus, they were now blind to the unfolding planetary developments. While waiting for the aftershocks to subside, Lil himself arranged for his men to gain the necessary knowledge from the Teacher to undertake required repairs. Access to the Teacher was as tightly controlled as if knowledge were a fundamental state secret; only Anu with the consent of the Council was authorized to grant individuals greater access. Yet, Ki had discovered a bypass, and Lil, now that he knew the true facts behind the rise of the House of En, was too annoyed by the Council's inaction to be concerned about a lapse in protocol; their being more concerned about control than people's lives hadn't changed. If he'd been on Alterra, he knew that Ama would have imprisoned him as a terrorist.

When the aftershocks diminished, Ki advised that it was safe for the crews to commence work. After giving final orders, Lil had his *tri-terran* prepared in order to assess nearby damage before the clouds heavily laden with soot reached Hawan. Accompanied by Jared, Kamean, Erjat, and Mika, they flew out from Hawan, seeing little damage around their mountain. With power partially restored, the waterfall illusion once again guarded the entrance to Hawan. Farther away, downed trees lay everywhere. Nearing the far west, they saw that the old shoreline didn't exist; the peninsula shoreline had been restructured, and the caps of the tallest trees were peeking from the water. Small coastal fishing villages had disappeared, the ill-made huts offering no defense against the raging waters. No doubt the bodies had been washed into the ocean. Circling back across the peninsula, they saw that the inland areas, being protected by the mountains, had experienced relatively little damage. Flying over the highlands close to Hawan, Lil wondered if Alana's cave had been flooded and their rescue efforts had been futile.

* * *

Alana thanked the Mother that she and the surviving women were deep when the Earth shook so violently. Strewn about before her were fallen trees and limbs. At least obtaining firewood would be easy. She cautiously ventured out with Maya, forced by necessity to gather fresh water and to search the traps. Morgana had organized everyone able to walk to head to the stream to fill pouches with water. The traps were empty since small animals were still hiding, but Maya reset them in hope that rabbits, at least, would soon forage. If not, she might have no choice but to kill some of the wild goats who hung around like pets. The two women, afraid to travel far, gathered all the edible plants, even the nasty-tasting tubers, that they could find close by.

Alana heard a noise and tapped Maya. "Maya, I hear the whirring sound. Look up there." She pointed. A breeze blew her hair as she squinted skyward. "I can see a shadow that looks like their ship. It must be Lil or Jared." They waved and shouted, "Hello, Lil. Hello, Jared."

* * *

Looking down, Lil and Jared saw the women waving. "How can they see us?" Jared asked with alarm, checking the control panel. "We're cloaked."

"With the electromagnetism in the air, our cloaking mechanism must not be effective," Lil reasoned. This would further curtail their flights. Circling, he didn't see anyone else. It would be useful to find out whether the cave depths offered sufficient protection. "Look there on the edge of the highlands." Lil pointed. "Those strange shadows again. With these clouds blocking the sun, they can't be natural."

"The monitors pick up no readings," Jared noted.

"They hovered near us during the hunt. We need to investigate." They faded away when Lil's ship passed overhead, and none could be seen after several more passes. Lil headed toward Hawan, but, to Jared's surprise, he hovered over the women and descended without explanation. When he opened the hatch, the women came running, and Lil was surprised that he felt glad to see them. He hadn't let himself acknowledge it before, but Alana was stunningly beautiful for an Earth woman. Despite the difficulties, she'd still managed to maintain her grooming.

"You're uninjured?" he asked when they grew near.

"Yes, thank the Mother, and you, as well?" she replied with a smile.

Maya waved to Jared when he followed Lil down the ship's ramp. "I'm glad to see you."

Jared stood stiffly, uncertain if Lil would permit him to speak.

To Lil's irritation, several women shyly stepped from the cave to investigate the strange voices. "Let's go." When Lil turned around, he saw that Kamean, Erjat, and Mika had left the ship and were staring with amazement at him with the women.

"Who are they?" asked Vesta timidly. She'd limped from the cave with a leg injury and now stood cautiously behind Alana.

Alana said gently, "You may not remember, sweetie, but these two are the wonderful men who rescued you."

"Oh, I'm sorry, I didn't remember. I was in such a daze!" She blushed. "Thank you, thank you, thank you! You can't imagine how horrible it was there." Unconsciously, she rubbed her bruised hip, remembering the painful kicks by her laughing captor.

"Yes, thank you so much," said Schwee, a woman closer to Yanni's age. Yanni followed behind Schwee, her eyes glassy as if in a trance, and her dark hair, tinged with gray, disheveled.

With a glance, Lil ordered his crewmen to depart. "Oh, please don't go so soon," pleaded Maya. "We weren't able to thank you after you rescued our people. Won't you sit down, if just for a moment?" She blushed three shades of red at being so forward. "Alana just made a new pot of her special tea."

Lil looked uncomfortably at Jared. If he'd known the other women were nearby, he wouldn't have landed. His crew now stood behind him. Before he could object, the women were busily bringing cups fashioned from birch bark, which they filled with tea and offered to each man. His surprised crew sought his approval. They had violated the directive again, he thought. So he found himself nodding that it was permitted.

"Lil, couldn't you introduce your men?" Alana asked uncertainly, not knowing the proper manners for men not of the peninsula.

Erjat whispered, "She knows his name? What's going on?" He and Mika had been at Hawan on special leave from the mines, and he wasn't anxious to be punished with a permanent deployment there.

Mika whispered, "Keep your head down and drink."

Vesta, her eyes cast down, shyly offered a cup to Kamean, who took it silently with a slight nod of his head. Thinking him a young boy about her age, she stood by his side on one leg, trying to mask the pain of her favored leg.

"Were you and your women safe down in the depths of the cave?" Lil asked, annoyed that his quest for scientific information had turned into a tea party.

"The Earth trembled and shook like an angry father punishing a naughty child," Alana said. "Of course, we were frightened about being trapped so far below the ground. Most of us. Some of our women seem to be immune to fright now. Thank the Mother, none of us were harmed. It actually wasn't until I came above ground and saw all the felled trees that I realized how lucky we were to be protected. Thank you for the warning."

After an awkward silence, Alana hoped she wasn't rude, but out of desperation, she said, "The Danes didn't find everything, fortunately, but we desperately need more furs or hides for warmth. I'm worried about my father. He went to hunt a cave bear to get us the warmest of fur, but he hasn't returned yet. Have you seen an older man by himself?"

Lil abruptly put down his cup, the set of his mouth firm. "No, I haven't seen him. If the stars are aligned, he'll return safely." He was not about to be drawn into another task.

"Yes, if the stars are aligned," Alana said softly, her eyes downcast with embarrassment, barely masking her disappointment that he wasn't offering to search. He didn't owe her anything, she knew. But it was so *easy* for him to help.

Lil stood, regretting having landed. "Thank you for the tea, but we need to leave now." Without another word, he strode blank-faced back to his ship, with his men trailing silently behind him, eyes straight ahead.

Alana was unsurprised by Lil's sudden coldness, as if a boulder had suddenly fallen in the man's mind, trapping his emotions. Different people had different customs, as she'd seen for herself. Even within Albion, some tribes raised their children peacefully, while others were mean and hostile to strangers. She'd been lucky. Vesta, Schwee, and the other women stood, mouths wide open with amazement, watching them take off in their flying ship. They immediately peppered Alana and Maya with questions, wanting to know how they knew such men, where they lived, and why their skin was luminous. The strangers were *so* handsome, Vesta gushed, sending Maya into a giggling fit. Gathering up the cups, Maya concurred, "They aren't smelly and hairy like men from the south."

Yanni, suddenly snapping to life, her eyes brimming with tears, objected angrily. "Maya, you ungrateful child, our men weren't like that!" She slapped Maya and drew her hand to slap her again before Schwee grabbed her arm. "Maliki is dead, Taku is dead, Jonk is dead—Jonk who loved you and wanted you for his mate—and that's the way you remember him! With insults?"

"No, thanks to Ewan, our men were unusually fine, not like the others of this land," admitted Maya with shame, rubbing her cheek. She regretted her words, and she tried to make amends by hugging Yanni, who had begun to sob uncontrollably once again. With a disgusted expression, Yanni shrugged her off and hobbled alone back to the cave, mumbling about her ungratefulness.

Alana put her fists on her hips, frowning and seething with frustration. Was she the only one with sense? The last thing she needed was for her women to start fighting. The strangers cared nothing for them and never would—her women were mere curiosities to ones of so much wealth. The nobles of Atlantis cared nothing for their servants, even good ones. She remembered the caged monkeys on Atlantis, and it made her shiver. She had more imminent dangers to worry about at the moment. "Don't dawdle! We must get everyone back inside. You know that I saw shadows down in the valley yesterday. Drood's men are searching for survivors, and not so that he can help them!" Maya nodded grimly and helped her return the women to the cave. Before going inside themselves, Maya helped Alana brush the ground with branches to hide their footprints and then pulled downed fir branches over the entrance. It might do little good, they knew. Predators like wolves would smell them, and they'd have little trouble crawling through the gaps. She didn't think wolves would venture down the narrow passageways to the large cavern where the women were camped. However, she posted two women as sentries at the cave's mouth, armed with only the spears that Alana and Ewan had had with them. It wasn't much, but at least they could shout a warning to the women below.

Maya whispered, "We have enough food for a while, but we can't hide from Drood forever. When they are stronger, we need to start chiseling stones into knives."

"Yes, and teach ourselves to fight, as well." Alana hugged Maya and closed her eyes with exhaustion. She'd never doubted her strength before.

* * *

In the hold of Lil's ship, Erjat, Mika, and Kamean whispered questions at Jared, asking how he knew the women; they recognized Alana and Maya from the hunt. Those two were stunningly beautiful. Kamean thought that little Vesta was pretty as well.

Sitting alone in the cockpit, Lil reflected on this chance meeting and his own unexpected gladness at seeing Alana. He'd been willing to let the future unfold in momentary episodes, but he felt uneasy that he was losing control of the grand design.

* * *

Another blustery night, and the huge bonfire in this place, little more than a crevice among the rocks, did little to warm Drood's bones. Terrified by his dragon dream, he'd led his faithful people to the rocky hills to escape the impending fires and floods. For saving them, they gratefully swore complete allegiance. While his people slept, he planned to return to the other place, like a dreamworld, but real—a place where he could shape the world the way he wanted. Tiny dark spots interfered with his view of the fire. The spots grew into smoke, eventually transforming into the shapes of his scouting party, all sturdy, muscular men. A man adorned with human teeth went to his knee and lowered his head. "Drood, as you foretold, Alana and other women stay in the cave at the rock face. We didn't touch them, as you ordered. The starmen watch over them."

"The starmen?" Drood exclaimed, perplexed that his usually reliable vision hadn't shown him this future. Their leader's mind was blocked from his view, but not the mind of the powerful white giant who'd slain the dragon. Drood could feel that one's growing discontent.

"Father, snatch Alana now," urged Maku, Drood's son, wiping his chin after taking a drink of mead from his skull cup. "The winter solstice draws near." The boy leered at the thought. Although he enjoyed overpowering his women, taming the beautiful Alana would be delicious fun. He'd try not to leave too many marks. Stroking his beard lost in thought, a strange twinkle in his eye, Drood didn't answer. "Father?"

Drood impatiently waved his hand. "You'll have to wait. A more interesting future is now possible." Convulsing in laughter, his people poked one another at their good fortune, whatever it may be.

CHAPTER 22

ANU

"I've received the reports that you requested yesterday." Anu cleared his throat and shuffled his feet, delaying the bad news. Coming out of stasis, the Council members had forgotten, or refused to recognize, the dire reports that Anu had given them the day before, blindly trusting that Anu, Lil, Ki, or some nameless aide would fix whatever the problem, as they'd done millions of times before. They had entered the meeting room joking and laughing, ignoring the depressed faces and downcast eyes of the waiting colonists. "The good news is that other than the buildings adjacent to the ones that collapsed, the infrastructure appears to be sound, although testing is continuing. The collapsed areas were the living quarters of our scientific staff and Dalits. The survivors will be moved to usable space in the Ministry." Anu cleared his throat so that his voice wouldn't quiver. "The damage to the power grid was systemic; some areas are damaged beyond repair." He paused and cast his eyes downward, tossing his recorder on the table before him. "As the last item, the stasis pods were unharmed, but the rejuvenation chambers cannot be repaired. They are unusable. Although Ki will search for alternatives, nothing will be available in the foreseeable future."

"What?" exclaimed Councilman Pilian, pushing his fingertips down on the desk so hard that they turned white.

"That's most troubling, Anu," said Councilwoman Barian, the disappointment in her voice causing the others to become silent. The usually sharp-witted Barian frowned so deeply that the wrinkles etched in her aged face seemed to connect.

"Our lives will never be the same," Anu said softly, gazing across the room at no one in particular. Normally unflappable, he ran his hands through his hair as if he were Ki, wishing that one of Ki's miracle solutions would pop from his brain. "Moving on down my list, the next item is that the star reports indicate that the universe was undergoing a time of renewal, and harmony and stability should be restored in the near future." Anu thought that Ki must heavily edit the reports. He kept his thoughts to himself since the Council members were reassured.

Councilman Pilian, pressing his lips with anxiety and feeling that something pleasant was needed, said, "Excellent progress on the infrastructure, Anu. I have confidence that Ki will be able to do something about the rejuvenation machine; he's a remarkable man." The other Council members agreed. Anu masked his smirk; the Council members had pilloried Ki on countless occasions for straying from the bounds of harmony and stability. For the moment, all was forgotten because Ki was their only hope.

"Yes, he certainly is. I'm glad that you recognize his countless contributions; I'll let him know. Even Ki can't work miracles, however. In my heart, I know that hope survives on Alterra, and that our trusted people are diligently working to restore our infrastructure, the portal included. In light of the deteriorating conditions here at Hawan, our only hope for survival is to make it home. That's where I will devote every minute of every day. Although we've lost our communications, I'm confident that if I meditate more deeply, I'll reach Ama to advise him of our plight. I'm confident that he'll help us." Anu gazed across the room as if half of his mind were already in a meditative state. He blinked, realizing that the Council members were still there, some frowning with puzzlement, but he focused instead on Pillian's broad smile and nodded in agreement. "Now, as a final matter, Uras has researched the Alterran death ritual. It is, of course, deeply regrettable that we are unable to send the bodies back home. We'll preserve them in the hope that a way will eventually be found to return. The ritual service will be held on the observation deck this evening. Although the clouds remain heavy, Ki will have them blown away just before our ceremony so that we may all take comfort in our universal harmony. An announcement will be sent shortly to the invited colonists. I'm sure that you won't mind delaying your return to stasis until after the ceremony. Unless you object, I'd like to adjourn."

Spending the remainder of the day preparing, Anu asked Uras to plan the ceremony's details. The contemplation required for the rituals would put him in the proper frame of mind for his delicate meditations. Whereas Ki was brilliant in deciphering the secrets of the quantum world and the principles of entanglement that permitted travel through the portal, Anu believed that his consciousness could also travel through entanglement. Although he'd not meditated into a sufficiently deep state to experience entanglement, scholars had reasoned that it was possible, and that Alterran brains held a physical key to accomplishing it. In his own meditations, he'd once fleetingly sensed a collective presence that could only have been the Universal Consciousness. It was, therefore, not beyond his abilities to attempt communication with Ama across interstellar space. Needing privacy, he turned off communications to everyone but Uras, striving to develop the proper message.

Uras jumped at the chance to keep busy with mundane details that she'd otherwise detest. Sitting with the dying had taken its toll on her. She had initially planned the ceremony to take place in the courtyard, which was large enough for everyone, even the Dalits, to attend. When she'd told Anu of her plan, he'd insisted that the observation deck had to be used. Although smaller, it provided the ethereal atmosphere that was crucial to uniting the deceased colonists' essence with the Universal Consciousness. That evening, glowglobes providing soft lighting guided the way for the invited colonists to the observation deck, which had been decorated with baskets of flowers. Holograph tubes had been installed for each deceased colonist. Uras and her staff had opened each colonist's memory book and created a holographic collage of his or her happiest memories. Small groups gathered to watch each one, occasionally pointing out their own images within the deceased's happy experiences at Hawan. The most striking images, all agreed, were the sometimes comical expression of each colonist emerging for the first time through the portal, catching a first sight of an alien world. The traditional music selected by Uras softly played, complementing the mood of universal harmony and oneness. When everyone had arrived, Anu directed them to form circles and join hands, and then he asked for the glowglobes to be extinguished, leaving the starry panorama above them.

Anu, flanked by Lil and Ki, began the memorial in his soothing baritone voice. "We are gathered here tonight to honor the spirits who have left us. Death is not unknown, but this generation of our people has been fortunate to not know permanent, finite death. Things have changed. Let us remember the spirits who now reside with the Universal Consciousness. It's not such a bad thing. In fact, they are blessed, since our journey to join those who have long gone before us has been long delayed. Perhaps we are simply being called home. Let us hope it is for rebirth.

"Now, let us raise our hearts upward to become one with the eternal universe. Let us deeply breathe the night air, absorbing the power of the Earth, the power of the universe, the power of the Universal Consciousness, our Creator. As we honor and remember our fallen comrades, we wish them well as transformed spirits. As above, so below."

The others repeated, "As above, so below."

Anu continued, "We bless them and wish them safe passage as they ride the waves of the universe to reach their final, eternal destination."

Waiting for his nod, the scribes lit the candles that each colonist held. When all were lit, he continued. "For those of us who remain, we feel the loss, and we cannot help but fear our mortality. This is new for us, and we will be mindful of it every day. Let us not waste whatever time remains. Let us enjoy the beauty of the universe and the beauty of this planet. Whatever our path in life, whatever the form of our destiny decreed by the stars, we must enjoy each day to the fullest, as a gift from the Creator. We must find beauty in all things, and we must live in harmony with the universe."

The holograms were darkened. When Anu read the name of each deceased colonist, only his or her hologram appeared, giving the good-bye message that each colonist left in case the unthinkable happened on this alien planet.

In closing, Uras led the colonists in singing the beloved Alterran anthem praising harmony and stability.

CHAPTER 23
MUTINY

Like the dark, oppressive clouds hovering above them in the skies, the thought of their newfound mortality weighed on the colonists' minds. In the days after Anu's death ritual, Lil kept his guardsmen working constantly on infrastructure repairs. During their limited recreational time, he found them slumped with despair at Guard Hall, whispering anxiously about the colony's bleak future. Although he'd ordered the Dalits to play uplifting music, the mood remained dark. Making the situation worse, his crews clearing rubble had extracted more bodies, and Anu had had to repeat his death ritual. Today, leaving the Ministry early, Lil went to Guard Hall and found it nearly empty. At the only table sat Jared, Erjat, and Mika; Lil chose to sit alone. Erjat and Mika peppered Jared with questions about the village women. Knowing that Lil overheard, Jared answered truthfully but briefly, telling them to forget the encounter. Lil considered interrupting him, but the hall was otherwise empty and he was relieved that his men weren't focused on the recent deaths. Exhausted, he decided the best course was to downplay his error. He ignored their discussion and returned to his suite.

Seeing Lil leave, the men grew silent. Lonely for homes that might no longer exist, Erjat and Mika drifted into a hologram cubicle and recalled memory book programs of old friends, who they assumed were now dead. Jared, from his memory book, viewed a favorite program with his parents during his first youth, when his father had won a lottery prize. They'd been awarded extraordinary permission for an excursion into the interior; under the Great Awakening the interior continent had become a nature preserve that was forbidden to ordinary Alterrans. They'd spent a wonderful day at a lake, far from the densely crowded megacity. It was a warm, wonderful memory. He hadn't realized it at the time, but it was as if humans had been punished by being shoved like vermin into those dense cities, with their high rises containing tiny, identical living cubicles. Reliving his memory, he envied his parents. According to his destiny certificate, when he finished this tour of duty, he would have been assigned a wife. He knew that few Alterrans could conceive, but he hoped that he'd be one of the lucky ones. Now, this dream was shattered. He turned off the hologram. Having no reason to return to Alterra, his thoughts turned to Maya, tiny in size, but with huge, liquid brown eyes that always seemed to be filled with laughter. She seemed so resilient. If anyone could survive these catastrophes, it would be her and her friend, Alana. He couldn't fathom their bravery in reaching the horse barn.

In his suite, Lil checked his monitor for the latest reports from Ki and then spent hours sending orders directing the repairs. Taking a break, he read the latest star reports from the scribes. He laughed at them, oblivious to his Dalit's stare. Lying down on his bed, he dozed off for a long nap while his tunic massaged and toned his muscles. His Dalit stole the opportunity to read the star report. She huffed, "Not even they believe this nonsense," and dutifully resumed her tasks.

That evening, with the guardsmen now off duty and congregating at the hall, Lil returned. Many stood before a wall monitor, complaining loudly about a message signed by Anu, stating that the daily ration of nourishment bars was to be reduced from four to three units.

"Captain, did you know about this?" Rameel asked with agitation. His normally immaculate hair and fingernails were filthy from his repair duties. "I've just spent two days working without a break, crawling through ducts trying to repair the energy coils that the nanobots couldn't reach, in order to prevent the electricity from spewing out of control and frying us all. I'm starving. And what thanks do I get? My rations have been cut."

Lil shrugged, unable to countermand an order imposed by Anu. He slid into a seat, averting his eyes from Rameel's disappointed expression. "You knew the food supplies were dwindling. That's why you agreed to participate in the hunt, remember?" Should he inflict punishment for this insolence? Lil wondered. On Alterra, that's what his family would have done if their floating holograms were talked to in such a rude manner. It was necessary to preserve order, Anu had lectured him when he'd questioned Jahkbar's instruction. Lil had disregarded the punishment protocols at Hawan, particularly after they'd lost communication with Alterra. He'd thought that allowances should be made. Was that a mistake? But he was also annoyed by Anu's sudden intrusion into his operations responsibilities. Anu should have discussed this with him before issuing such an order, especially under their extreme circumstances. Anu had never bothered to monitor food supplies before, why now?

Without being granted permission, Rameel slid into the seat across from him, with Azazel coming to stand by their table. Rameel assumed a familiarity that he'd never have dared before the group had engaged in the hunt. Lil frequently asked Rameel to manage projects because he'd been a Ministry of Central Planning executive who'd absorbed the Teacher's management programs. Rameel boldly complained, "Captain, I didn't realize things were this bad. If we'd known, we should've been learning to hunt much earlier. Everything is developing into a crisis. There should be better planning. Are we to wait for our stores to be empty before we're authorized to solve this problem? What have the Council and Anu been doing about this?"

Returning Rameel and Azazel's steely gaze with one equally as steely, Lil didn't speak. Internally, he answered, *they've been waiting for the stars to provide,* but he couldn't share that thought with these emboldened men. He was well aware that something needed to be done. To distance himself, he moved to an empty table. Lil didn't believe his family's protocols should be applied on Earth, but he wasn't sure where to draw the line. He wasn't comfortable with this closeness. All his men seemed more assertive than usual. Was this because they hadn't eaten their full ration and the conditioning was wearing off? Was it tension from the catastrophe? Or perhaps he was to blame. Rumors had no doubt spread that he had violated the directive by visiting Alana, on top of violating it for the hunt. They'd become fellow conspirators, he supposed. He wondered how the extremists who dismantled the political systems that existed before the Great Awakening had started down their fateful path. Was this how it all began?

Returning from his thoughts, he heard Erjat discussing with Mika the women they'd seen at the cave. He scolded, "Keep this to yourselves. No one else should know. In fact, it would be better if all of you forgot about them. Starting today, I'm adhering to the Non-Interference Directive."

But Azazel, sitting nearby, challenged him. Although he'd not been part of the crew visiting the cave, he'd repeatedly heard the men's whispered stories. "Why is that, sir? The way I see it, we have dwindling food supplies here, we cannot return to Alterra, and even if we could, there is no Alterra to return to, and the broken rejuvenation chambers mean that we all will die in a short life span. There are essentially no marriageable women here at Hawan, and without women we cannot have children to carry on our race. Am I missing something?"

In silence, all eyes turned to Lil. He considered walking out the door, but his loyalty to his men overcame that emotion.

He was conflicted with the knowledge that they were, essentially, right. After all, he had felt these things, even if he hadn't articulated them. As Alterrans, they had grown accustomed to waiting for destiny, comfortable with the routine, unhurried by their long lives. Everyone, he now realized, except for Ki, who had never been complacent, having been inspired by the old masters whom he alone had studied. After a long pause, he spoke slowly. "Some of what you say is true. What would you have me do? It's not my time to ascend to the leadership."

The men looked down. They didn't know what they wanted.

The nervous conversation turned to their usual banter, but it eventually found its way back to the catastrophe.

"Has any location on Earth been spared?" Tamiel asked. No one seemed to know yet. After another long pause, Mika asked Erjat, "Which one did you like? It sure would be nice to touch a flesh and blood woman, not a holograph."

Lil snapped, "End this discussion right now," at the same time wondering if Alana would be all right.

After another difficult silence, Jared asked, "Would there be any harm in paying them a visit once in a while? They might need help. We could help with heavy lifting." When the others burst out laughing and slapped Jared on the back, he protested.

"You, too, Jared?" said Lil with scorn, his eyes narrowed with annoyance.

"Captain, I'm serious," he protested. "We've things they might need to survive in this cold. Those shadow things might be preying on them. They're not safe." Jared told the other guardsmen about the rescue, and the theft and destruction of the women's winter provisions. They stopped laughing.

In this light, Lil felt uncharitable saying no. Although he didn't want to admit it, hadn't he acted out of kindness before? He ignored them by reviewing new reports on his recorder. Eventually, his thoughts turned to Alana as he took a sip of wine. He laughed to himself that she probably knew a better recipe for cooking mastodon. He caught himself smiling. As he looked around, the other men stared at him, and he quickly wiped the smile from his face. "It's not wise for us to visit. We have too much work to do. If we have some blankets and warm things, I could drop them off."

"You, by yourself, Captain, could drop them off?" Azazel asked suspiciously.

Lil looked from face to face. He was opening what an ancient legend called a Pandora's Box of unintended troubles. For a long while, he considered standing up, invoking his status as captain, named successor, and ordering everyone to disperse, never to speak of this again. But a part of him understood; he wanted to see Alana again. He realized for the first time that if he was going to die on this planet, he didn't want to die without ever having had the true love of a flesh-and-blood wife and children.

Needing to escape, he ducked into a hologram room. Desiring the comfort of his family's spacious suite at home, he selected a window view from his living room on Daria, the Ens' capital city. He watched transports zinging through the narrow, crowded streets filled with a million bright window lights of the wall-to-wall skyscrapers. His family's living quarters, complete with a port, were atop one in the central city. Below his balcony, he watched signs flashing for the theater, restaurants, and musical entertainments. The cosmopolitan Daria looked nothing like the pristine wilderness surrounding Hawan. His memory of a city that no longer existed didn't bring the relief he sought to his troubled mind. If the rejuvenation chamber couldn't be fixed, he sighed, they were now mortal. He'd been cruelly reminded of their mortality when, the preceding day, one of the engineers repairing the power system had been severely burned in a minor explosion. Having no burn units without the chamber, the engineer had died an excruciatingly painful death, and word of this tragedy had spread throughout the colony. The reality of a mortal life depressed every last one of them. Even Anu, who had never faltered in his belief in their return home, had finally accepted Ki's conclusion that the equipment was beyond repair. Anu was now sequestered in his suite meditating in an attempt to reach Ama, and the Council remained in blissful stasis, oblivious to the needs of the living. For all Lil knew, those at Hawan were the last survivors of the great Alterran civilization. When the last of them died, all of their wisdom and accomplishments would be extinguished as a flame upon the wind, as if they had never been lit.

Injustice caused his stomach muscles to tighten, and he pounded his seat cushion with his fist. It was up to him. The leaden weight of responsibility made his heart pound. All their lives depended on his making the right decision. He never thought being leader would cause him such isolation. When his time would have come to ascend as supreme leader, he would have had vast numbers of elders, relatives, counselors, ministers, and scribes to consult with, and there would have been the traditional ritual calendar guiding his actions. Here, with Anu and the elders abandoning their responsibilities, it was up to him alone. He could rely only on Ki, his sometimes rival, and his guardsmen, whom he had been raised to see as inferior. All that was changing.

Lil requested the coronation hologram of his great, great, great grandfather Zeya, the first leader of the House of En, who had inaugurated the Great Awakening. Zeya rode through the streets of Daria, waving to the cheering throngs on his way to the ceremony. Like all Alterrans, Lil had been raised to revere Zeya as the founding father of the enlightened Alterra, and pride swelled within him, as it always did, when he lived the coronation. The ethereal Zeya's triumphal words captured their people's new mission. "Today, we Alterrans chart a new, enlightened path, leaving behind hostile nations with divisive viewpoints. We are one people, with one government, one set of laws, one philosophy, and one religion. This path proves beyond a doubt that we have risen above the petty wars and conflicts that have heretofore plagued our planet's history. We now stand at the threshold of a great new beginning of true human equality, living in harmony with nature and at total peace with one another. No need for money and uncertainty, no need for competition, no need to suffer manipulation of the many by the few. This is a truly exciting time. Come, each of you, join with me and step forward into this human utopia."

A lump came to his throat as he was reminded of these powerful words. This was his legacy. The Great Awakening, through his forebears' foresight, had elevated humans to a higher plane of existence. With every ounce of energy in his body, he vowed with his fist thrust into the air that he would *not* let it perish so long as breath remained in his body. His chest heaving, he wondered what it had been like for Zeya to stand at the precipice, seeing before him the shifting currents of history, when old notions still prevailed, knowing that he alone held the power to fix society. What was it like to be the singular one who recognized in the swirling chaos the loose strands of the future? Strands he alone could reach in, pluck, and weave together to form the unrippable fabric of the future path. A glorious and magnificent path. Afterward, this path might seem self-evident, as truisms were known to be. Was it actually apparent before it happened, that the old was to be thrown out for the new? Or was it apparent only to the victors, who, after the fact, changed history to justify their cause? That was the lesson of his time in the library. Like Zeya, didn't he stand at a precipice before divided roads? Decisive action was imperative. To preserve the memory of all that was right and good about his people, he had to act before it was too late. But how? Apart from their immediate needs to stay alive, the only long-term solution he saw for their mortality was procreation. It would be a giant leap, but he saw no middle ground. Since they could not rejuvenate, preserving their civilization would require new generations. The only way for new generations to be possible would be for women to give birth to babies. The only women available would be those of Earth. The stars! His destiny had been tugging at him all along ever since the hunting experiment. He'd thought then that the day had gone awry; he'd been too steeped in tradition to recognize the totally new path for survival toward which he'd been drawn, an unpredictable and dangerous future. A future path that would require them to violate the Non-Interference Directive. But if Earth was now their home planet, would this be interference anymore? Would the directive be void? If so, there would be no violation. Even if there was a violation, who other than he would enforce it? Would destiny prescribed by the Universal Consciousness trump a human order? He blinked and shook his head. This was too complicated. Maybe it was the wine, or the Earth foods he'd been eating. The change in thinking was too fast. He had to check himself. Any action they took would be irreversible. Decisions should be based on detached, rational analysis, not the momentary heat of emotion. He had to carefully consider everything before taking any action.

Lil closed his eyes, seeking to empty his mind to calm himself. Unsure of success, he caused a mirror to appear to check if his face betrayed his inner turmoil. Before stepping from the cubicle, he heard Azazel loudly proclaim to two dozen guardsmen sitting before him, "Who of you wants to be the last one left alive?"

"Azazel," Rameel cautioned, sitting at the edge of his seat and gripping the table with his hands until his knuckles were turning white and whispering with urgency as quickly as he could, "you *must* plan…"

On another day, this mutinous scene would have incensed Lil to the point of drawing lightning from the Net to turn them into ashes. Hesitating, he approached the group, who sullenly slid back in their seats, casting their eyes away from him. In former days, they would have crawled away on their bellies, begging for forgiveness. Azazel braced his stance, his face hardened, preparing to defend himself. From secret trips into the Darian underground, he knew a few tricks to defend against a Net attack.

Lil ignored Azazel's icy stare, and his voice gave no hint of anger with Azazel's provocation. "Calm yourself, Azazel. Sit."

Slowly, Azazel lowered himself, his eyes steady as if Lil were an opponent at a fighting match. Lil drew up a chair beside him and sat down casually. Studying the men's tense faces, most eyes downcast to avoid his piercing cobalt eyes, Lil thought of the vows he'd made only moments before. He made his final decision to surrender to this strange, new destiny. "We must adapt to survive on this planet. In more ways than our experimentation with hunting. We must go much further." The stunned men alertly raised their chins to him, and one by one, he held their gaze. Azazel raised an eyebrow and rested his forearm on his leg, tilting his head with his eyes narrowed. "For love of Alterra, because we are now mortal, we must find a way to procreate so that our civilization, some part of us, will survive. We owe it to those we've lost." He paused to let his words sink in.

Perspiration beads appeared on Rameel's upper lip, but Azazel boldly held Lil's gaze, a look of grudging approval slowly transforming his face. Lil heard, "for love of Alterra," repeated in soft, reverent tones throughout the room.

"Think over whether you want to join me. We can't act rashly. There will be repercussions. If we choose women, whether ones at the cave or some others, it means leaving Hawan. Anu would never permit Earth women to live here in violation of the directive, and we can't go against him. Taking wives means abandoning our way of life."

Azazel smirked. "That life abandoned us!"

Lil nodded slightly. "Perhaps. Or we're being led in another direction for reasons we can't yet comprehend. In any event, we shouldn't start down this new path unless we're prepared to go wherever it leads us." Lil noticed the men's furtive glances. It was easy to complain but an entirely different matter to undertake a drastic course of action. "Don't rush your decision. If we all decide to leave, there would be much planning to do; the way will be difficult. We won't go unless all agree and swear an oath to one another to see this through. Agreed?"

Despite his words, he didn't truly think that they would vote to leave for life in the wilderness, at least while any bit of their pleasant amenities existed. No, their refusal would settle his internal conflict for him; it was a panacea. Later, he could rationalize that he had been pushing them to end this episode without blaming him. At least he could take comfort in the thought that he'd thwarted the mutiny without bloodshed.

"We'll meet here in one month for a final decision," he announced, leaving abruptly, not wishing to be swayed by their fear.

During the next month, he mulled over his plan repeatedly, inviting Jared to his suite for the first time, in order to discuss it endlessly. He gradually changed his mind. The vote wasn't merely a panacea. Leaving Hawan was the only path to assure their civilization's survival. Yet some days he was less sure. Jared, he soon discovered, was enthralled with Maya. Pathetically, had they all gone mad with carnal desires? As for himself, was he making a detached, calculated judgment? As much as he fought it, he thought more and more of Alana. No one had more to lose than he. As the named successor, all he had to do was to wait for his zodiac time to ascend—to ascend to rule a ghost civilization, if any indeed survived. Here at Hawan, no one would remain unless they embraced radical change. Alterran philosophy had worked in an advanced civilization, but it rendered those at Hawan unable to adapt to their present environment or to even see that change was required. This was a fatal flaw. Testing the purity of his motives, he reminded himself of the undeniable facts that their food stores were dwindling and Hawan was irreparably damaged. This situation could lead to death or life, it was their choice. Their precious traditions could be preserved by establishing an Alterran-Earth village, teaching these women and the children they'd bear to live civilized lives—a new Alterran utopia in harmony with the Earth. The entire plan depended on Alana, however, because he had no hope that another acceptable woman existed on Earth. She was clean and intelligent, with fortitude and leadership skills. Not to mention that she was the most beautiful woman on Earth. If she accepted him and this plan worked, any colonists who remained alive in the future could join him. It was the best he could do for Alterra. Change or perish, he concluded.

In one month, all guardsmen noisily met in the hall. They were groomed in proper fashion, and their insignias glowed on the breasts of their silver uniforms. Also present, although unnoticed or ignored, was Lil's Dalit, who had snuck in, hiding in the background. She had overheard Lil's discussions with Jared and feared for her life if the captain were to leave.

When Lil arose to speak, the hall instantly grew silent with anticipation. His own purple insignia proudly glowed on his uniform. "I appreciate that every guardsman is here. We are all proud and dedicated Alterrans. You all know the purpose of this meeting. As you can imagine, this is uncomfortable for me." As he paused, examining their faces, he felt conflicted at the glow of their Alterran insignias, to which he associated intense pride. The men squirmed, never growing accustomed to the intensity of his penetrating cobalt eyes. The only exception was Azazel, who stared back from his position at the rear, his arms crossed over his chest, his legs braced as if ready for battle. Lil could see in the firm resolve of every face that the men took the vote seriously. "We must be in this together, or not at all. Anu and the Council are not going to permit us to bring the women here, and no force may be used. We can't live two lives by just occasionally visiting our Earth families; that would be unfair, and it wouldn't solve our long-term problems. We must teach this new community the best of our Alterran ways if we are to preserve them. We must tell and retell them the stories that will be passed down from generation to generation to retain memory of us. I will not be a part of any plan unless we dedicate ourselves to acting honorably, in our best tradition. Does everyone agree?"

Azazel, his voice rising above the low rumble, said, "Captain, I believe I speak for all those here in saying that we agree with everything you've said."

"Thank you, Azazel. As I said, this must be a unanimous decision because if someone stays, he'll be assigned to hunt down those who go." He paused, and failed to find any less determined face, with a few merely shrugging their shoulders. "If we go, it won't be easy. We'll be living in a primitive wilderness. Although we've studied it, we can't be prepared for what might happen. Although our interactions with the women nearby have not produced any viral outbreaks, we can't be sure. There could, of course, be injury. In short, we'll be forced to abandon our old ways of life and find new, less comfortable ones."

He paused to take a drink of water and confirmed that the men remained listening attentively. "We may take a few things from here to ease our transition, but we can't leave the colonists without the means to protect themselves. That would be wrong, and I'm sure you all agree." The men nodded in agreement. "Since we won't have the ability to generate power, many of those things would soon be useless to us anyway. Every man must understand that if we vote to go, we'll face hardship, perhaps extreme hardship. Our risk of success increases if we stick together. So we must all agree. More than that, we need to take an oath on our sacred honor, that if the vote is to leave, all two hundred of us will plan together, and we'll leave when the time is right. We'll vote in secret."

They were speechless; they'd never voted for anything before.

Lil ignored their astonishment, and with a glance, Jared and Rameel withdrew ballots, which they passed down the rows of eager men. "These clay tablets and styluses are symbolic for the vote today for the primitive life that awaits you if you vote yes. Carve an X if you want to proceed, and leave the tablet blank if you do not. Then put the tablet in this jar here beside me." With unusual seriousness, the men accepted the implements and voted. Azazel came forward first, proudly displaying his X before slipping it into the jar. One by one, the rest slowly shuffled forward and dropped their ballots into the jar. When the last man had voted, Jared and Rameel poured the ballots onto a table and counted. Jared raised his thumb up, smiling broadly. It was unanimous.

The men cheered, slapped backs, and grinned. They had decided to proceed, but this was only the beginning. The cheering died to low murmuring. Erjat meekly arose, asking, "Captain, do the women want us?"

Azazel protested in frustration, "We go there and each of us chooses a woman!"

"No, no, no," the others loudly disagreed, and he sat down, shrugging his shoulders, a bewildered look on his face.

Jared put up his hands to quiet the crowd back to orderliness. "We're not like the Danes. We're honorable men. All of our actions *must* honor Alterra."

Azazel scoffed, sitting back with his arms crossed. "Well, then, how will our Alterran honor let us begin this dance?"

"Why don't we plan a meal near the cave and invite the women as a surprise?" Kamean asked earnestly. Everyone laughed, and Kamean smiled sheepishly.

"Kamean, who's going to do the cooking?" Erjat asked, feeling the tension in the room dissipate. "What are you going to make, crème de nourishment bar?"

"We'll give a course on a hundred ways to serve nourishment bars," joked Mika.

"Those women will fall into our arms after that meal," laughed Tamiel.

Erjat put his tunic over his head like a scarf and pretended to be a woman with a high-pitched voice, saying, "Oh, a nourishment bar, I think I love you. Come marry me!"

Lil, exasperated, shouted, "Enough! I don't know what we'll do. I'm the leader of a military unit, not a matchmaker." He was about to throw out the voting tablets, but Jared caught him, whispering, "Captain, calm down. This is new to all of us. It's a good thing that you're doing. We all need to get used to this new life."

Adjusting his shoulders, Lil asked, "Doesn't anyone have a serious suggestion?"

The men looked at one another, unaccustomed to being asked for advice. Yamin tentatively stood, clearing his throat and shuffling his feet. "Sir, you seem to have gotten to know the head woman. Why don't you ask her what to do?"

"Yeah, Yamin, good idea," said Rameel, gently pushing his shoulder.

Lil was pleased. It was reasonable, and it gave him an excuse to see Alana.

CHAPTER 24
MORGANA

As a child, Morgana had happily played in the Atlantean gardens. Although those memories were growing dim, she remembered Atlantis as a magical place. There were large cities with tall, stately temples with marble pillars, surrounded by beautiful gardens and clear blue pools of water, where the religious ceremonies were held. Ships filled with goods from foreign lands regularly arrived in their harbors. On market days, her mother took her with a basket that they piled high with pomegranates, olives, and grapes brought from the trading cites of the middle sea. She wore lovely, colorful clothing made of soft fabric, and attended school, learning to read, write, and add numbers.

Her father had been an honored shipmaster in a war at the far end of the inland, middle sea. After that war, which the Atlanteans had lost, her father had become a merchant trader. While he was at sea for months visiting the inland cities, she stayed with her mother and grandmother. When he returned, they would run to the harbor to greet him, and as soon as the shipped had docked, he'd climb down and lift her up and give her mother a bag filled with coins. He would remain there only while he purchased items to trade on his next voyage.

Her world changed forever in a few days. When the rumblings first began, the school sent the children home. Since for decades the volcanoes had occasionally experienced small tremors without consequence, no one was alarmed. Her teacher told the students to stay home and do their lessons. As if at a passing curiosity, her mother and their neighbors stood outside their doors pointing at the dancing ribbons of thin, dark clouds swirling in the air. Over the next few days, the ribbons thickened, and the wind blowing across the volcano became scorching. Morgana's father suddenly slammed open the door, yelling for them to leave everything and run to the harbor. Her mother stopped to throw her jewelry into a sack, and they faded into the crowds pushing toward the harbor. With the air growing thick with ash, Morgana's father gave her a cloth through which to breathe. Progress was slow because the crowds at the harbor found no available vessels. Morgana's father pushed and shoved his way along, holding Morgana's hand and trying his best to create an opening for her mother and grandmother.

With a deafening bang, the volcano blew its top, sending burning debris all around them. Fires erupted. The people panicked, stampeding to the harbor. Those at the front were pushed into the sea. With the earth shaking violently, statues and stele fell, followed by imploding buildings. When Morgana's father picked her up, he had to loosen his grip on her mother's hand. Her mother and grandmother fell behind in the panicked crowd, and Morgana never saw them again. Her father frantically called to them but was uncontrollably caught in the human tide heading for the harbor. When the crowd slowed to a stop, her towering father pushed through the people, angrily shouting at his ship's crewmen to let them aboard. Seeing him, they lowered a rope ladder. People desperately tried to grab the ladder from him, and he fought them off, lifting Morgana and then climbing up himself.

Reaching the deck, he again frantically tried to see his wife, checking different views with his long spyglass. His crewmen insisted that he set sail or all would perish. Greatly pained, he gave the order. Deafening booms from the volcanoes continued. In the chaos, Morgana was left to secure herself on the deck. She tied herself to the side so that she wouldn't slide back and forth. When her father dropped his spyglass, she loosened the ropes and picked up the spyglass to search for her mother and grandmother.

Bouncing against high waves, the ship finally succeeded in leaving the harbor, and the crew hoisted the sails, gaining speed when they caught the wind. Earthquakes below the ocean floor caused large waves to crash against the sides of the boat, rocking it. Through the spyglass, Morgana could see great lightning bolts in the volcano's smoky plumes, and hot lava streamed in huge clumps, consuming each of the beautiful buildings. What the lava didn't incinerate toppled into the abyss. Morgana felt as if a great bubble had burst underground, spewing magma up into the air and causing the crust to collapse into the hole.

Although the ship was gaining speed, a vortex was drawing it back to the harbor. Morgana's father desperately raced the length of the deck, calling for each crewman to row with all his strength. Great clouds of black smoke and ash rolled from what had been the land, over the ocean and toward them. Suddenly the wind shifted. It was as if the ash clouds were parted by some unseen hand and blown around them. The terrified crew was stunned.

"It's a miracle!" he whispered. Morgana's father knelt down and led everyone in a prayer of thanks to the gods for miraculously sparing their lives. The strong wind picked up their sails and blew them away from the vortex. With unceasing effort, the crew was miles away when, with a final gasp, the remaining land disappeared into the sea.

When it eventually became quiet, the crewmen lay in exhaustion. Since the ship had not been reprovisioned from its return voyage to Atlantis, there were insufficient supplies, and the tired crewmen called out for water, their dry throats throbbing from breathing the smoky air.

Their hardship was not over. A great thunderstorm spawned by the volcanoes moved across the ocean. The pounding rain battered the vessel, causing the masts to break and fall onto the deck. Morgana's father was killed. She rushed from her hiding place and sat sobbing by his side, futilely trying to push the heavy mast from his chest. She held him for hours as the ship careened.

When the storms broke, the damaged vessel lay adrift. The exhausted survivors could do nothing for the deceased other than to whisper small blessings before tossing their bodies over the side. Morgana, weeping with all her heart, tenderly kissed her father good-bye before the men lifted his body and dropped it over the side with the others. She was alone, and she felt lost despite the kindness shown to her by the surviving crewmen. On the third day, the ship drifted close to shore, and the survivors filled the small rowboats. They lay exhausted on the beach in the late morning sun near a small fishing village. Curious villagers ventured out to help them, bringing water for their parched mouths.

A kindly family that lived on the coast took Morgana in. Although she didn't understand the language, she learned quickly. The fisherman and his wife kept a small garden and raised chickens. His wife was skilled at making clothing, and she taught Morgana how to soften hides, stitch them together, and use tiny fish bones as decorations. Although they made a modest living, they had been happy.

Late one afternoon as she was helping her adopted mother harvest the garden, someone at the shoreline frantically shouted, noisily blowing a warning through a conch shell. A flotilla of long ships decorated with skulls, filled with huge, helmeted warriors with dire wolf tails, rapidly approached them. Having heard nightmarish stories about the vicious Danes, she waited, petrified. Her adoptive mother grabbed her hand and forced her to run. When the vessels skidded ashore, the warriors leaped out and executed the defenseless fishermen. Catching the women and children with a chilling laugh, they forced them onto their boats. When their hiding place went up in flames, Morgana and her mother came choking through the smoke into the burly arms of a sneering, scar-faced Dane.

They ransacked the village, stealing everything of value and burning all they left behind, including the fields and orchards. They filled the ships with captive women and children until they were full. Those for whom there was no room were slaughtered. The Danes sailed north near the shoreline to Shylfing's village. There, many of the women were repeatedly raped, eventually dying from their injuries, overwork, or lack of food. Being strong, Morgana lived there two years, giving birth to a daughter, Tara. She and her daughter were still alive when the women from Alana's village were brought to tend the fields.

Upon reaching the safety of the cave, Morgana gave an offering to the strange gods who had rescued her.

CHAPTER 25
THE PROPOSAL

L il looked in the mirror to comb his hair and then set his tunic to tone his body. Twice he refreshed both his tunic and his body. To his amazement, his Dalit brought him some sweet-smelling liquid and motioned that he should dab some onto himself. Did the entire colony know he was courting a wife?

His Dalit looked at him askance with anxiety, thinking that she had to find a way to get him to take her with him when he ultimately left. All of this talk of starvation and freezing had all the Dalits near hysteria; they knew that they'd be the first ones to be sacrificed.

Lil remembered when he'd first met Alana at the hunt. He had secretly been impressed with her presence and command of the situation, an unexpected trait in an Earth woman. He remembered that she had given him something, a piece of bark. Although it was all she had, she generously gave it to him. He considered an appropriate gift in return. Recalling her worry about warmth during the winter months, he decided to bring her blankets that had been specially woven for the early field expeditions in the glacial temperatures when the Net hadn't been available to regenerate their tunics.

Leaving his suite, he walked through Hawan's still-beautiful courtyard. The glowglobes were necessary even during the day since the heavily overcast clouds obscured the sun. With the sun's rays rarely reaching the surface, the days were growing markedly colder. As he set out in his *tri-terran,* it began to snow lightly, a dirty snow mixed with still-lingering soot. He wasn't sure that he would find Alana; it might take several trips. If she weren't outside the cave, he couldn't envision himself entering the cave and searching her out—the women might laugh at him, or she might not take him seriously. Even if he found her, he couldn't decide what to say. How would he propose that his stranded guardsmen court the destitute women of her village?

Flying low by the cave entrance, he saw snowy footprints leading down to the nearby stream. In the distance drawing water was a slim figure, which he recognized as Alana when he flew closer. The stars must have blessed his plan. She turned her head at hearing the whirring noise and saw the shadow of his ship. Uncloaking and landing, he emerged. Feeling the chill, he instantly caused his silver uniform to become the brown and green tunic that he'd worn for the hunt, even adopting his riding boots. When he strode toward Alana, she turned to smile at him confidently, putting down the water pouch. "Hello, Lil. It's good to see you again."

"Hello, Alana," Lil began, returning her smile. Up close, he could see deep anxiety on her youthful face. "I happened to be working in the area when I saw you. I hope you're doing well, and that the other women are recovering."

"I'm fine, thank you," she sighed with exhaustion. Her smile turned to a frown, and she dejectedly slung her water pouch to the ground, her eyes cast downward, and then glanced into the distance, the wind tousling her golden hair. "To be truthful, I can't say as much for the others. Although their bodies are healing, their minds aren't. Many have lost hope. Some worry me because they say they've nothing to live for. A few days ago,

Yanni ran from the cave. She was delirious with fever, and she screamed that she wanted to drown. Morgana and I were able to prevent her from reaching the stream, but it took all of our strength to drag her back. I gave her one of my calming teas. She slept for a while, but who knows what tomorrow will bring? I tell them that they just need to survive through the winter." Alana shrugged her shoulders and continued to gaze distract-edly into the distance. "They say they don't see the point. They complain that surviving the winter isn't worth the struggle." She paused a moment, choking back tears, putting the back of her hand to her mouth.

Lil moved closer, tempted to put his arms around her to console her, but being unsure of her reaction, he held back. Too soon. Surprised and irritated at his uncertainty, he focused inwardly to regain inner calm. He *couldn't* fail at this task.

Alana misinterpreted his hesitation, thinking that he was looking down on her again as too primitive. Irritably, she picked up the water skins and strode back to the cave. She was too tired and too overworked to waste precious minutes being one of his specimens, no more than a research report for some distant, mysterious people. She paused and looked back, think-ing she would give one last try, "I'm frightened about my father. He's been gone for months now. I look for him every day. Have you seen any sign at all?"

Lil caught up with her and lightly touched her arm. "I'm terribly sorry, Alana, I've seen no one, but I haven't been out much; the soot might damage our engines. If I see any tracks in the snow, I'll look. I couldn't search when I was with my men. I certainly understand how upset you must be."

She drew closer and put her hand on his arm, searching his face with her eyes, imploring him, "Please search for him. Please do whatever you can. It's been so long. I'm afraid that his spirit now rests with Mother Earth. My father was a skilled hunter, but it was foolish to attempt to kill a cave bear by him-self."

"Why did he try it?"

"Because the Danes stole our sleeping furs, and he didn't want us to freeze." Tears ran down her face as she turned and brushed snow from a rock, plopping down. Lil sat close beside her, not knowing what to say. After sitting awhile in respectful silence, she asked, "How are things at Magic Mountain?" She smiled through her tears to break the tension, wiping her eyes.

"Magic Mountain? Oh—" He suddenly remembered one of their earlier conversations. "What we call Hawan. Actually, we've had some bad luck ourselves. We sustained significant damage from the comet." He paused, took a deep breath, and looked away, saying quietly, "Some things may never be the same."

"I'm so sorry to hear that," said Alana with surprise. "I guess this is a difficult time for everyone. It never occurred to me that *you* could have problems."

Lil stiffly looked straight ahead, nervously moving his hands. "It's a good thing you were in this high cave."

"When we felt the Earth shaking, Maya and I thanked you many times for warning us to go deep." Alana wanted to touch his arm, but was certain that he'd again reject her, remembering how he'd coldly snapped his arm away before the rescue, as if she were vermin. Lil patted her hand, and Alana's eyes narrowed with uncertainty. He thinks of me as my father does, she thought with disappointment.

"We exploded it in the sky across the ocean, but the blast caused an immense fireball and smaller pieces hit the Earth. Huge fires have been burning, and many have died. We grounded our craft in fear that the soot would damage the engines, although it's not a problem here," he gestured with his arms, "so we've flown short missions. But this land hasn't escaped damage."

"Damage?" she asked. "We've seen fallen trees, but I haven't gone far."

"The western shoreline has disappeared, including where your old village was. From the sky, one can see the tips of submerged fir trees."

"Those immense ones?" gasped Alana. "Our original village used to be along the coast, where the fishing is good. Ewan persuaded the people to move farther inland to be safe from the Danes; there, we had to learn to hunt game. It's a shame; the fir trees were so mighty and beautiful, it's hard to imagine anything powerful enough to destroy them."

He nodded. "A huge ocean wave crashed ashore after the explosion, drowning everything in its path. If it weren't for the mountains, this land would be underwater. It could have been worse, though; we were actually in a pocket. Areas to the southeast, throughout the middle sea, were flooded." He patted her shoulder. "This is incredibly bad for your people, on top of everything else that has happened. I'm so sorry."

She shuddered. "This is horrible. What else could happen?"

"Our scientists predict that ash will continue to fall in the western land. The ash will eventually reach us as well, but it will be much thinner. We don't expect all the plants around here to die, but the entire Earth will be dimmer and the winters will be colder for many years. Storms will be more fierce and dangerous until the energy remaining in the sky from the explosion dies out. These problems will not subside quickly, I'm afraid."

Alana put her head back and blinked her eyes, her stomach in knots. Getting her tribe south to Yoachim and Zedah in the spring had been the only thought that could calm her in recent days. And they might be gone? She rubbed her hand on her cheek and gasped, "I can't think about this, or I'll go crazy."

They looked at each other for a moment. Lil had wanted to avoid depressing talk, but the disasters loomed in their thoughts. Had he lost her already? Not knowing if it was wise to pursue his plan on this trip, he longed to at least comfort her. He refrained from touching her, hoping for a sign that she'd welcome his advance. Despite everything she'd experienced, she was so lovely, and he admired her perseverance. She had many of the best qualities of Alterran women. There was no one else for him on the entire planet Earth if she refused him.

Seeking a more personal conversation, he asked, "Alana, you're much taller than the other village women, and your skin tone is much lighter. Why is that?"

"I wasn't born here," she explained, stretching her shoulders to relax; perhaps she could spare a few moments. He was conducting a harmless study, she supposed. "When I was about ten, my father and I came from an island that was destroyed. It was long ago, but I remember how frightened I was. I was helping him in his fishing boat that day. We saw the volcanoes erupting. For a while, all we could see was thick, black smoke. I'll never forget the deafening booms of the explosions. Everything happened so quickly. The fast waves pushed us far away from shore, toward this land. Our island broke apart. It seemed as if we drifted forever. When we landed here, the village people took us in. They were kind, and we've lived with them ever since."

"Fascinating," Lil said with interest, fitting her story into place with some of their discoveries. "We observed an extraordinary island. The people had finely crafted buildings, even using marble carved to perfect proportions, and there was a fleet of merchant ships. The people attained an advanced knowledge of science and mathematics far above any other Earth people. About fifteen years ago, we witnessed its destruction. It's no wonder you're so different from the others." His eyes studied her with new fascination.

"I guess I am different," said Alana uncertainly, feeling discomfort. Would her difference simply make her a good specimen to collect? What did they do with specimens? She didn't want to be a caged monkey.

"In a good way," replied Lil instantly, smiling uncertainly and searching her face, not comprehending why she seemed to be offended; to him, being different than the primitives was too obviously good to require an explanation. He'd had more success when he was trying to avoid her. Didn't she value what he had to offer? He stood up, took a deep breath, and gazed toward the stream, making up his mind. They had no alterna-

tive; it was now or never. "Alana, I have something to ask you."
That didn't sound right. He turned back to her, forcing himself to speak to her in tones that he'd used with his cousins.
"Actually, I'd like to ask your advice. I hope you won't think me
insensitive."

"What is it, Lil? You can ask me anything." Alana cocked her
head, answering with warmth in her voice, thinking that he was
acting *much* friendlier than before.

Lil was encouraged, and smiled warmly, a big grin that had
always worked with Nersis and his dates at home. "My men
think your women are beautiful, and…they are…interested."

"What?" In her exhaustion, she feared that her thinking
was muddled. She should have recognized the reason for
his newfound nervousness; the strongest men who'd barely
noticed her while hunting suddenly became tongue-tied at the
Summer Meeting when they vied for a mating invitation. If she
hadn't been so tired, she might have laughed. *You can't appear
eager simply because he's so handsome,* she told herself. "Your men,
they're the ones who are interested?" She tilted her head and
raised an eyebrow, permitting herself only a faint, teasing smile.

He smiled nervously, unaccustomed to banter. "We're interested in getting to know you, that is. This is a difficult time. We
want your advice how to do this in an honorable manner, so
that our intentions won't be misunderstood."

Alana thought it over, kicking her feet in the dirty snow;
her body had been cold for so long that she barely noticed
the frigid temperatures. Her optimism was slipping with every
day that she heard the anguished cries of her women, every
day that she saw their food supplies dwindling, yet she was too
tired and too afraid of the Droods to attempt hunting solo any
distance from the cave. At least thinking about Lil's proposal,
no matter how fanciful, was entertaining, like the rescues in
her childhood storybooks, if a rescue was what he proposed.
She was pleased because she was attracted to Lil, despite her
doubts about his motives. Maybe this was a trap; maybe they
were secret cannibals, or they kept women locked up; after

all, she'd only seen men. Anyway, how could all her worries be cured with a few words uttered by a stranger? That was a foolish wish, and she wasn't a fool. True, the day of the hunt, she'd been fascinated by him, but later, she'd been repelled by his coldness, and she hadn't let herself think about him. In a few ways, he might be an acceptable mate; maybe even the only one who might tempt her not to stay with the Earthkeepers. She didn't know him well enough. She'd like to see him again, without pressure. She was surprised that all the men would want to come. She scratched her cheek and squinted. "I don't understand. Don't you have women at Magic Mountain?"

Lil didn't want to reveal too much, especially if they weren't interested. "Our group came here as the escort of a research expedition. The men far outnumber the women. We expected to return upon the completion of our duties. Regrettably, things have changed. We no longer expect to return; we must adapt to permanent life here. More things will be revealed in time if we move forward."

"What about you, Lil?" Alana asked, studying his face for his true thoughts, not wanting to be hurt if he felt too superior to participate. She was a medicine woman, she couldn't be the mate of just anyone in his tribe. What was she thinking? Her people *needed* an Earthkeeper in these trying times. If the other women chose mates, she would be ecstatic for them, and she'd be relieved that she'd be free to travel south. Surely, Yoachim and Zedah survived. If they'd died, she would be needed even more.

Reaching for her hand and drawing her to him so close that she felt warmed by his cloak and could smell the freshness of his breath, he said softly, "Alana, I think you are beautiful and intelligent, and I want above all else to know you better. Only you." He removed his glove and stroked her hair. She tingled and breathed a sigh. "This is difficult for me, for all my men. On our home world, marriages are only late in life, and then they are arranged. We have strict rules. In light of what has happened recently, we believe that these rules no longer apply to us. Others in our colony disagree, however, so we can't take you there."

Unexpectedly, Lil's powerful arms encircled her. She lost herself in his warm embrace and felt him nuzzling her hair with his nose, leaving her scalp tingling. Not wanting him to think her a primitive fool, she insisted, "Tell me something about yourself. I don't even know where you're from."

"If we move forward, I promise that I'll answer all your questions. If we don't, it's best if you don't know."

Frowning, she slipped from his grasp. "We're not fools!" *We've suffered too much to let it happen again.* Her duty compelled her to protect her people, not turn them over as slaves merely because she'd grown weak from weariness. She kicked her feet in the deepening snow, narrowed her eyes with hands on hips. "Since you won't tell me of your home, I don't even know how your people treat women. You know everything about us. I *must* know more about you!" Her lips were pressed with determination, and she adjusted her furs over her chest in a deliberate manner, creating a barrier. She looked away, becoming increasingly incensed. "You said that marriages are arranged, but that your rules no longer apply. These are good women who have suffered brutality. They loved their mates, and they're deeply grieving. I hope you don't want to simply visit occasionally for sex." Glancing back, she adopted a regal stare that she'd learned from Zedah. "Lil, what *are* your intentions, *exactly*? I can't even see the truth of what you say in your eyes through that band!"

He snapped off his eyewear in the overcast light, moved quickly to her side, and gently took her hands. Looking into her eyes, he said earnestly, "I understand your hesitancy. I don't ask lightly. For over a month, we thought this over and voted. We've agreed that leaving and starting a new life is our best path. We're uncertain what to do next. Our society is structured. Everyone has a place, and that place is dictated. Our population is small, and people live a long time, or at least they used to. At a time decreed by destiny, a marriage would have been arranged for each of us. So we don't think about choosing a wife. Also, few babies are born. Now, facing the rest of our lives here, our rules must change. We will need to grow our own food, provide housing, and…" he hesitated, "marry and plan for the perpetuation of our race."

Alana gasped for breath. "Are you suggesting that your men desire us to be permanent mates?" She had eagerly sought Lil's help to find her father; this was too much. Completely unexpected. Her mind raced. She'd been in despair for her women, knowing that only a few strong ones would survive the winter. Now, she saw a glimmer of hope. But a lifetime commitment after only a few words?

"Isn't that the best way to provide for children? That's what your people do, I believe," Lil said defensively, standing behind her and caressing her arms. Her furs slipped, and she pulled them close, noticing the heat generated by his tunic.

Trying to calm herself, to think things through, Alana pushed her hair from her eyes as the wind tousled her hair. "I am an Earthkeeper acolyte. Most don't choose mates; if one is chosen, he must be special and I must be a virgin at the ceremony. As for the others, my people have customs handed down from our ancestors. It is important for the success of the village and the protection of children that a man have a single mate, or wife, in your words. The ancestors decreed that the couple should be officially joined so that children will receive proper care. In this land, a woman chooses her mate at the Rite of Summer. That is," she sighed, choking back tears, "if we survive the winter, and if the women regain an interest in life." Wiping her tears, she said, "A chosen man customarily comes to live with the woman's village. Since our village was destroyed, we must choose men from other villages and go there." She paused. "If we choose your men, would we live at Magic Mountain? Would you build a new village?"

Lil hugged her tightly to his chest and stroked her hair. "I can assure you that our intentions are honorable and that we won't mistreat you. We seek wives to build a life here with children. Our leaders won't accept you, so we'll need to live elsewhere. Beyond that, I have no answers yet. If your women say yes, we'll work this through together."

"I'm so overwhelmed, I don't know what to say."

He released his arms and pointed her chin up with his finger. "I hope you see by now that I have the deepest concern for you. I'm sorry if I'm rushing things."

"This is too fast!" protested Alana, pulling back. "What does 'deepest concern' mean? Our people speak of love."

Lil gently drew her to him, gazing into her green eyes. "It means that I care about you. I think about you constantly. I worry about you. I want to touch you and comfort you. Alana, we must face the situation we're both in. Your women are living alone in a cramped cave, hiding from invaders, facing a severe winter with insufficient provisions, and as harsh as this sounds, you may not survive. Love can come later."

She turned her ahead, tears brimming in her eyes, but he gently turned her back. "You're incredibly strong, but even you can't possibly shoulder this entire burden yourself. You told me that a woman tried to kill herself. We can help you through this."

"But why must we decide so quickly?" she pleaded.

"If we are to abandon our colony, we need your commitment," he replied curtly, reverting to Lil the ruler. "Living under these conditions is foreign to us, but I promise you, we'll obtain the necessary knowledge for survival here and do whatever it takes to make this work."

She felt hypnotized by his beautiful, deep-blue eyes and was enticed by an offer that relieved her burdens. In her weariness, she was tempted to say yes; anything for good meals and nights of peaceful slumber. *Why isn't Ewan here?* He would prod her to think things through. "Our people are obviously different." *With their magic, they might not even be from our world, and he's not being honest.* "How do you know that we can mate and have children?"

Lil replied while pacing, "Our planets' chemical components are roughly the same. Amazingly, or inevitably, according to your point of view, life initially developed on both planets along similar evolutionary paths. Some say this is a sign of the universal constant, or more metaphorically, the Tree of Life. In our research, we found that our bodies have the same genetic code—uh, birth instructions—the same organ systems, and, with our planets' gravity and orbits nearly the same, our systems function and have rhythms that are fundamentally the same. Our skin luminosity is not genetic. That is, it is not an original part of us; it is an effect of the way we traveled here. We live longer than you, but that should benefit our offspring. The primary differences we have recorded are that my people are much taller than most of the Earth women, and our eyes are larger and more sensitive to sunlight because of how light appears on my home world. Does this matter?" He shrugged. "I'm a ruler, not a scientist."

She understood little but admired his confident, intelligent tone, his authoritative movement, his eyes' alertness, and his beautiful, clean face housing those dazzling eyes. Most of all, she was impressed that he thought her sufficiently intelligent to understand. If she weren't so tired, she could follow his thoughts. She yearned for someone strong, a leader she could admire and trust, someone who would not be intimidated by her abilities; he was such a man. She was drowning in his beautiful eyes, the melodic sound of his voice, and his warmth. How could she know this was his true self? Was she simply exhausted? *Don't act like a silly child, this can't be true; he's tricking you.* Her body ached to disrobe and have him take her. Yet, if she had a child by him without honoring the mating rituals, Zedah would forbid her from being a full Earthkeeper; she'd be ruined if he abandoned her. She was Alana, daughter of Ewan, medicine woman and Earthkeeper acolyte. She said scornfully, "You must think me a fool. You were so cold to me at the mountain! Are you the same person? This a trick! Do Alterran men not know affection?" She hoped with all her heart that she was wrong, and that he would prove her wrong. He had a powerful magnetism, and she was touched by his concern for their feelings. For once, she had met someone with her father's qualities. *Please let him be true.*

"Yes, of course we show affection," he defended, cross at her question. *Why is she so difficult?* Any Alterran woman would swoon at his touch. "Like any ruler, my duties demand my attention. You'll need to understand." Catching himself, he shook his head and adopted a more affectionate tone. "You are *definitely* no fool. Much has changed since the mountain. Let's not rehash the past."

She tapped her foot and looked at him haughtily. "How do they show affection?"

He hesitated at the coldness in her voice, but when her eyes softened and her lips quivered with fear that he might leave, he enveloped her in his arms and slowly lowered his lips to hers. Alana surrendered. Seeking breath after a long moment, she gasped, "What's all that energy I feel?"

"It's our auras joining. Two are stronger than one."

"Auras? What are they?"

"Our life energy. It's only visible through my glasses." He picked them up from the ground and handed them to her.

She giggled. "I see it growing stronger when we touch!"

Lil whispered in her ear, pressing himself against her, "See, we're meant for each other." He kissed her soft lips again, lingering as he felt a mind-numbing passion well up in him that he'd never felt for Nersis, unsure if he could keep the promise to be honorable.

Reluctantly drawing back, feeling as if she'd drunk too much berry wine, she said dreamily, "Do all Alterran men smell so nice?" Lil smiled warmly, melting her heart. "It's *so* nice seeing your eyes. They're such a beautiful blue! Bluer than the sky, with deep blue specks." Alana said thoughtfully, "I can't speak for the other women. I'll ask them. I'll even encourage them to say yes. I believe you when you say you're honorable, and it's no secret that we could desperately use help. If they agree, the men should come here for a meal of introduction that we'll prepare. Your men must supply the kill in advance. We expect you to be true to your word at all times. Do you agree?"

"Of course," Lil gasped with relief, perplexed how she had, once again, gained the upper hand; did his mother act this way with his father? No doubt. He felt the time was right for the words he had prepared. "Please say that we realize that they've recently lost their mates. We understand your deep grief, and we don't take it lightly. In normal times, our proposal would be insensitive. But these are not normal times. If we wait, all may be lost. In the midst of tragedy, we must preserve life. Our men can help you thrive. We are not beasts like the Danes."

"I'll tell them. How shall I answer?"

"I'll fly above tomorrow at this hour. If you say yes, have a small fire burning." Remembering the blankets, he asked her to wait. Fearing it unwise to levitate, he made several trips, laying the blankets outside the cave entrance.

Examining one, she found it lightweight, yet tightly woven using an unknown material. She exclaimed with delight, "There must be one for everyone!"

"Each will provide sufficient warmth no matter how cold it gets."

"Oh, Lil, thank you so much!" She threw her arms around his neck and sobbed with relief. He put a blanket around her shoulders and held her, stroking her hair, surprised at how pleasurable it was to comfort her.

"Do you happen to have anything to protect us against Drood?"

He retrieved an extra recorder from his ship. "This is temporary." He created an illusion of impenetrable rock to hide the cave entrance. "This isn't real. See? You can pass through. If you are in danger, press here, and it becomes real. Nothing will pass through, not even light, until you press here."

"Oh, thank you!" she said, relieved at having a defense against the Droods. She smiled, tears brimming in her eyes.

* * *

The next morning, Jared cried out with joy, and Lil silently but cautiously did as well; flying overhead, they saw the smoke rising from the huge bonfire near the cave. The women had chosen life.

CHAPTER 26
THE COURTSHIP

"The women have agreed to a meeting," reported Lil, stiff with military formality, not breaking a smile, standing before an assembly at Guard Hall. He waited for the pleased chattering to die down. "There are more men than women, so I've selected those of you who will go." Azazel, arms crossed against his chest, cast an *I told you so* look at Rameel. "We'll look for suitable women at other tribes. In preparation for the meeting, we'll hunt for game, and they will prepare a meal. We'll get to know one another. *Everyone* must be on his *best* behavior. If you wish a wife, these things must be arranged properly. These women have strict customs, and they are also a bit unsure of our intentions given the rough treatment at the hands of their captors. I'm told that mates are chosen at a ceremony called the Rite of Summer, which, if we proceed, we'll attend in the southern plain. It's not until then that procreation can begin. If anyone cannot abide by these rules, then you should not participate in this plan. You may still leave, but you won't have a mate." Changing tone, he said with a hint of a smile, "Before the meeting, comb your hair and groom your tunics. Also, I suggest that you apply a few drops of the liquid in this vial," which he handed to Yamin to pass around. "The Earth women seem to respond well to the aroma." Lil finally cracked a grin, and the men laughed heartily as they passed it along.

In the days before the meeting, Jared prepared the horses, the wolves, and the hawk for another hunt. Dispatching the hawk to locate suitable prey, he learned of a caribou herd that had wandered into their territory to escape the increasingly icy north country. A hunting team led by Azazel with increasing expertise killed two dozen elk and caribou, preserving them in the manner that Alana had done with the original mastodon. They delivered the kill to the women, along with baskets of pears, apples, and legumes. They even sent unused tablecloth linen they'd found in their storeroom.

Preparing for the event, Guard Hall continued to serve as their base, which raised no eyebrows since all colonists had been crowded into undamaged space. Looking into a mirror, Kamean wondered aloud what he would say. Would that pretty little girl who gave him tea be interested?

Combing his hair nearby, Erjat joked, "It's easy. Tell every woman that you're the biggest stud in the universe."

Mika laughed. "That will leave all the women for the rest of us!"

Kamean slapped Erjat's shoulder, "No, I'm serious, Erjat, what do you say to a prospective wife? I wouldn't even know what to say to an Alterran woman, let alone someone from another planet." On Alterra, at the proper time, he would have received a notice from the House of En identifying his wife. Choice was something new. Kamean gazed in the mirror, attempting various smiles and pickup lines that he'd used on Alterra when making himself available on the Net circuit.

Once again, Lil's Dalit came to the rescue. "Nothing fake," she scolded Kamean with a disapproving frown. "You'll blow it. Compliment them. It could be their eyes, or their clothing, something they've made, and especially the food they prepare or the clothing they make. Tell them about things you've seen on Earth during your missions. You *must* have many interesting stories." The men were not used to speaking with a Dalit, but Lil's was unlike the others.

At the cave in the days before the dinner, Alana explained to Lil's assistant, Yamin, that the ground outside was too hard to dig a deep cooking pit. The women planned to suspend the meat in parts hanging from a tree over an open fire, but she warned that that cooking method would make the meat less tender. To their amazement, Yamin shot a beam of white light that melted the snow, broke through the frozen ground, and warmed the ground to create a cooking pit to Alana's requirements. The amazed women lined the pit with mastodon dung and covered the dung with tinder. Schwee, who served as Keeper of the Fire, brought her burning torch, which she touched to the tinder, igniting the fire. When the dung coals were burning red, they covered them lightly with ashes and then laid the prepared carcasses, laced with poles for lifting when done. Last, the pit was covered with the heavy mastodon hide. Since it was winter, they planned to continually add additional dung, which they asked the men to gather. The meat would be juicy and tender the next day, and leafy pouches with asparagus and wild grasses would be added to the roast in the final hours. Lil brought their camping heaters to supplement the hearth fire.

While the meat roasted, the women fussed over their appearance. Having regained little of their strength, they fretted that they looked haggard. Water was carried from the stream, and Alana made a mixture of dried flowers soaked in water and animal fat to produce a sweet-smelling soap for washing. They were pleased that the smell lingered on their skin. The women combed one another's hair with a broken seashell comb that Alana recovered from her old hut, and washed and repaired their hide clothing. Much of their clothing was in tatters, and they anxiously fashioned the hide from the new animal carcasses into clothing. Since the men had brought more meat than they needed for their special dinner, they preserved the extra. Deep in the cave, it was cool enough that the meat should last.

Combing each other's hair, Vesta and Maya teased each other about their interest in Kamean and Jared, erupting into endless giggles. Yanni couldn't suffer the merriment. Throwing to the floor the new clothes with which she'd been helping, she snapped, "Stop it! Stop it! You simply *can't* go through with this."

"Yanni, dear," Alana quickly said, picking up the clothes and shaking out the cave dust. "You can't blame them for being young girls. They've never had mates. We all agreed to this meeting, you as well."

"Alana, I know that we agreed, but I feel *so* guilty," she cried, choking back tears. "I've changed my mind. My Maliki, may the Mother bless him, hasn't been dead for long. The rest of you—your mates are barely cold in the ground! It's *wrong* to do this, *especially* before we've honored their spirits at the Rite of Summer!"

Schwee, a hare-lipped woman who, self-conscious about her looks, took on the unwanted projects, wriggled through the ogling women to where Yanni stood casting a stare so accusing that Maya hung her head in shame. The women nervously shuffled their feet, keeping their eyes cast downward. "Yanni, I," Schwee stuttered, wringing her hands, "I lost my man Kuku, as well. I loved him with all my heart, and I miss him, just as much as you miss Maliki. But I have two little ones. I'm not a looker like Alana or Maya. What chance do I have to be taken in, to find someone to help me raise my children? With my looks, I won't find a man among these strangers. If enough of you do, though, and it keeps us together as a tribe, at least my family won't be cast out to die! Alana and Maya could have left and saved themselves, but they're taking us along too. I'm grateful!" She choked with tears, and her friend Midri, also known for her plainness, put her arms around her.

Midri scowled. "Think of more than yourself, Yanni!"

Alana hugged Yanni, who turned her head, murmuring, "No."

"Yanni, of course you grieve for Maliki." Alana kissed the older woman's forehead and smoothed her graying hair. "No one questions that! Maliki was a wonderful man, the bravest of hunters, and we *all* miss him." Looking at the others, she added, "We miss all the men a great deal. They died trying to rescue you because they loved you. We can't bring them back, no matter how hard we wish or how much we grieve. They wouldn't want you to die of starvation or cold. You *must* live so that you can honor their memory and tell others of their bravery. Those with children must live for them. I agreed with the captain that no mating will occur until after we've observed our rituals. This meeting is only an introduction so that they'll be committed to help us and our children survive this winter. You *know* that we desperately need help. Do I have to remind you of all the ways that they've helped us already? There's *nothing* to feel guilty about! We've seen their good faith; they brought us all those fine blankets and the meat, as well as the light, and the hides for making these dresses. But, if you still feel this way after we meet for dinner, we can of course say no to further meetings." The women were comforted by Alana's words and slowly continued to prepare.

Maya whispered to Alana, "I hope they listen. If we don't starve, we'll be easy pickings for Drood's men. For me, the choice is easy."

Alana put her arm around Maya and sighed with worry, "For me, too."

* * *

Before leaving Hawan, Lil asked his Dalit whether she had more suggestions since the cologne had been well received. She was startled at being addressed but was happy for him; her feelings surprised him because he'd been taught that Dalits had been bred without them. She returned with flowers carefully wrapped against the cold. Lil also selected ample bottles of Alterran wine to relieve the awkwardness.

"Will you take me with you, sir?" 363 asked with anxiety, nervously keeping her eyes on the ground and twisting her cleaning rag. "You'll need someone to serve you, wherever you go, won't you?"

Lil was surprised at how much she perceived. "Only the guardsmen may go, for now." She nodded meekly in understanding and said no more, withdrawing as Dalits did.

* * *

To avoid suspicion, the men left Hawan wearing their usual silver tunics. During the flight, Lil permitted them to reprogram their tunics into Alterran leisure clothes of their choice. Lil chose a plush purple tunic embroidered with the sacred triangle, accompanied by his comfortable black riding boots. Upon arrival, Lil ceremoniously placed the flowers in Alana's arms. She gasped in delight, the women smiled their approval, and Alana gave him a long peck on his cheek. "I'm so glad that you're not wearing your uniforms," she said, laughing and latching onto his arm, claiming him as hers. Letting the less fortunate women have the new hides, Alana wore her rabbit furs, laced with boiled wool, revealing ample cleavage. Around her forehead, she wore her silver Alterran headband. "Your men don't look so much alike now. Does everyone from your village have white hair?"

"No, it happened when we traveled here." Perplexed, Alana raised her eyebrows, frustrated that he'd speak words again that she wouldn't understand. He patted her hand to ease her worry. "It's a long story. I'll tell you another time. Tonight is special—for us." He smiled so warmly that her heart skipped a beat. She held the gaze of his beautiful blue eyes, a color that no other man shared.

For the meal, the women had fashioned vessels of hide to serve as plates. At their direction, the men lifted the poles skewering the tender meat from the pit. It easily fell from the bones.

The cooked legumes were scooped onto the hide plates, while Azazel poured the wine into the cups they'd brought. Even in winter, the cooking pit provided sufficient warmth for them to mingle outside as the men moved about introducing themselves using the universal translators. Near another fire inside the mouth of the cave, older children, led by Yanni's surviving son, played flutes fashioned from mastodon tusks or, for a different tone, a long bird bone, accompanied by a hide-covered drum.

Standing beside Lil, Jared shyly exchanged glances with Maya. He'd chosen a blue woven shirt and dark pants. Her neatly combed dark hair was decorated with a bone and feather arrangement that matched the decoration of her new hide-fringed dress, which swayed when she walked. The crackling fire danced in her big brown eyes. Standing alone, she coyly gave him a big smile and beckoned him to her. Lil cleared his throat and said with a slight smile, "Jared, you're relieved of duty." Jared hadn't been on duty, but, with his sense of loyalty, had stayed near Lil.

Growing impatient, Maya boldly took his huge hand and coaxed him away from Lil. Smiling down at her, he gazed at how lovely and lively she seemed. She was so tiny. Would that matter? Searching for something to say, he stammered, "Dinner was delicious." He was lost in her exuberant smile and the perky way that she used her body to accent her thoughts. "And you look lovely this evening. Did you make your clothing?"

"Yes, thank you. Do you like it?" She twirled around and giggled at his grin. "I made you something," she said demurely. "Stay right here." Leaving him a moment, she retrieved an object hidden behind a tree. "Now, bend over." She placed a necklace of bone and feather pieces around his neck. He straightened and felt it, looking it over.

"It's beautiful, thank you." It had been a long time since a woman had given him something. Alterran women lived independent lives at their assigned professions, preferring uncommitted sexual contacts arranged by making themselves available through the Net. Touching her hairpiece, he said, "It even matches yours."

"Yes!" she giggled with a little jump, smiling up at him, happy that he noticed the detail. Would he understand that she wanted to choose him? "I want to thank you again for rescuing our people," she said shyly, gingerly reaching for his hand, which engulfed hers. Remembering how he had recoiled when she'd tried to touch his arm in the barn, she was relieved when she felt his warm fingers tighten over hers.

"Oh!"

"What?" he asked with concern, afraid that he was too strong for her. She was *so* tiny. "Are you all right? I'm clumsy sometimes, I'm afraid. I hope that I didn't hurt you."

"Oh, no, it's not like that at all. When I touch you it feels like, like the energy of a strong wind." She twirled hand over hand in demonstration of the whirlwind. Embarrassed, she covered her mouth with her hand, laughing. "Does that sound funny? But I can't describe it any other way. Do you know what I mean?" Oh, Maya, why did you say that, she thought. He already thinks Earth people are stupid. "It's good, *very* good."

Laughing, he said kindly, "I know *exactly* what you mean. That's our life energy coming together." Maya has such a unique way of expressing herself, he thought. She has the cutest dimples, and she's always giggling with the joy of life. It took a lot of courage for her and Alana to search for the horse barn. He led her to a log and sat down, slowly sliding his arm around her, unsure whether he was too forward. She settled herself, leaning back comfortably, humming a tune.

"Your voice is beautiful. Do you sing much?"

"I sing at all our ceremonies. I'm called the Caller because my songs call for the blessings of Mother Earth."

Against his cheek, her hair was silky and smelled of flowers. Jared hadn't known what to expect with an Earth woman. Maya was glad that Jared was so nice; she'd always thought that if he had been in charge, Alana wouldn't have had to argue so hard for the rescue. It was special that he cared for the animals.

"I'm glad that we can be friends now," she whispered in his ear, and his ear tingled at her breath. "When we came to the barn that day, and you were so mad, I didn't think you liked me much," she pouted.

Jared thought, you didn't notice how I couldn't keep my eyes off of you? "Well, we were under orders. I didn't have a choice," he said, distracted by the beauty of her eyes. "Let's not talk about that," he murmured, relieved he no longer had to push her away. "Although I've always wondered, how did you get there?"

"Ah," she sighed, and told him about the Lady of the Glen. "Alana had seen a ship disappear behind the waterfall, so she knew you had to be there."

"She did?" he asked, scratching his head. They would need to change their entry procedures.

"I thought I heard horses, but we were *so* frustrated that we couldn't find a way in that Alana started throwing rocks at the mountain, and they disappeared. So, since we had seen your ships disappear when they were really there, we thought maybe the scary crevice that kept us away from the wall under the vines wasn't really there." Jared raised his eyebrows, impressed by Maya's intelligence.

Squeezing his hand, she chirped, "I'm *very* glad things are different now...." She stroked his arm. "I liked you from the moment I saw you, and it's much nicer now that I can see your eyes, brown like mine. You have *such* a kind and intelligent face," she said, touching his face, which felt smooth. He tingled at her touch. "And...you're *so* much cleaner than the smelly men around here." She giggled. "I love the way you smell." She snuggled close, and Jared sighed contentedly.

* * *

Morgana circled the hearth fire, uncomfortably watching the others. Not being a villager, she didn't have old female friendships upon which to resort when the conversation lulled. But that didn't truly matter; she was interested in the new men.

For the first time in her life, she didn't tower awkwardly above everyone. And these men seemed cultured like the Atlanteans. But how would she find a good partner? Someone who would accept her child? Most looked nearly alike, as if produced en masse by a giant mold. She had chatted for a while with various men, including a man named Rameel, but he had grown uncomfortable with her intensity. After she had slid in and out of the coalescing groups around the cooking pit and the cave fire, one man stood out. Watching him from afar, she found that he had an air of dignity and self-confidence. He lacked Jared's elegance and didn't seem as talkative as others. He wore a plush black shirt, high necked with white lace at the edges. The belt cinching his waist accentuated the strength of his massive chest. His manner seemed a little gruff, but when he spoke, others deferred to him. As she shyly approached his group, grandmother Marita extended an arm with a warm smile to welcome her, saying kindly, "This wonderful lady is Morgana. She is new to us. Your people rescued her from the Danes. We're fortunate that you did, she's been an immense help."

"Yes, I'm so grateful," Morgana gushed with a shiver. "The Danes are monsters!" Old memories came rushing back. She shoved them away and tugged at the fur around her shoulders to dispel the demons.

"My name is Azazel. I'm glad that you joined us. Where are you from?" He noticed that she was much taller than all the women other than Alana. Like her, she had a light complexion. She had pulled the sides of her blonde hair away from her face and tied them back with an intricate feather-and-bead arrangement. Her new hide clothing, which cleverly used the linen fabric they had brought, was decorated with little fish bones and was more skillfully made than the others' clothing. She had applied something to accent her blue eyes, and her mouth had the reddened look of crushed berries. She stood straight, almost regally, yet Azazel thought that she had a sadness about her, perhaps lingering from her lengthy captivity. She must have had a strong will to survive.

"I was born on an island that no longer exists, called Atlantis," she said, looking without hesitation into his large brown eyes. "It was destroyed when I was a girl."

"You've certainly had more than your share of tragedy," he remarked, unwilling to detach from her intense gaze. "Although I've observed many tribes that prey on those who live peaceful lives. One must always be wary."

"Yes, but I hope it's all behind me now," she said firmly, glancing away. "I prefer to look forward."

Azazel poured a drink, offered it to her, and poured one for himself. After a sip, he casually asked, "Do you remember much of Atlantis?"

"Oh yes," she said longingly, fiercely proud of her Atlantean heritage. "I remember going to school and to the temples and to the markets. Atlantis was a magnificent place, as I imagine your home must be."

"That's interesting," said Azazel, intrigued, as his companions drifted away. "Your volcanoes erupted, didn't they? The island broke apart and sank into the ocean, as I recall."

"Yes, it was horrible. Not as bad as being kidnapped by the Danes, but it was awful," she said, shaking her head. Again peering intensely, she asked, "How did you know about my island?"

"Actually," Azazel paused, sipping his wine, "I was flying overhead when it happened." He hoped his revelation wouldn't frighten her. He had observed many Earth people who seemed too primitive for conversation; they might have died from fright if he had uncloaked and spoken to them. Since she was born on Atlantis, he assumed Morgana was more sophisticated. If he were to choose a wife, he'd need a smart, independent woman.

"You saw our volcanoes erupt?" Morgana asked with wide-eyed amazement, too stunned to ask more. It had never occurred to her that unseen spirits had actually been floating above her.

Azazel cleared his throat. "Yes. I remember the crowds at the harbor trying to board the last ships before the black smoke overtook them. Unfortunately, there was little I could do, other than to blow exhaust from my ship. I think I succeeded in diverting ash clouds away from some ships so they could escape." He hadn't reported to the captain that he'd breached the directive.

Morgana gasped, her lower lip quivering; she laid her hand to her chest. "Blessed Poseidon! I was on one of those ships! We were saved by you? Sir, I owe you my life. After the clouds parted, my father and the entire crew knelt and thanked the gods for saving us." Her eyes glistened as she studied his face, overwhelmed at meeting her unseen savior. This night was more momentous than she had ever dreamed.

"Oh, I'm no god," Azazel stammered, looking down uncomfortably. That was why they had had the directive, was it not, so that the primitive people wouldn't interpret their technology as the actions of a god? Still, at the moment he was certainly glad that he'd violated it.

Morgana reached out and squeezed his hand, feeling a large, sculpted ring. "Then, I thank whatever god caused you to be there to help us." This Azazel has a good heart, she thought, he'll protect me; will he accept Tara? She stayed by his side the rest of the evening. Although at first she had thought Azazel was gruffer than other men, during the evening she discovered that, in his own way, he was endearing. Azazel was amazed that the woman he regarded as his favorite had sought him out; he hadn't believed in destiny, but maybe there was something to it.

*　*　*

Rameel drifted around the cooking pit. Although he'd voted to do this, he hadn't accepted the idea of mating with an Earth woman, and so he hadn't converted his silver uniform into something more presentable. On Alterra, he'd been an executive in the Ministry of Central Planning, where most women were single and vying for his attention; he'd never needed the crassness of putting himself on the Net. He was accustomed to sophisticated women, and he was a man who appreciated culture. Believing it impossible to find a suitable mate among these primitive women, he'd decided instead to enjoy Yamin's music. Yamin played a flute, accompanied by child musicians. Smiling, Yamin recognized talent in one remarkable youth.

"Yamin, you're amazing," applauded Rameel when he finished a melodic tune.

"I thank you," said Yamin, bowing low with a broad smile. "What's astonishing is the sound you get from something you'd think crudely made. These flutes are sophisticated, with a range varying with the bone type." He pointed out the artfully chiseled air nodules.

Yanni's son drew near. "Hello, Tomin," said Yamin. "I enjoyed playing with you. You're a natural musician." He gently slapped him on the back.

Tomin, a skinny, black-haired boy of about ten, smiled happily at being complimented by a master musician. His mother overheard Yamin, and she put her hands on Tomin's shoulders, saying, "Thank you for taking him under your wing tonight. Tomin's had a tough time. We were captives." Yanni was surprised; it was the first time she could say that without erupting into tears.

"Oh, my pleasure," said Yamin. "I'd be happy to come back and teach him more tunes. There's nothing I enjoy more than playing music."

"That would be wonderful," said Yanni. "I love music. Tomin has far surpassed what I can teach him."

Rameel raised his eyebrows. "Oh? Do you play?"

"Yes, but—" Yanni started to say that she hadn't played since she was captured.

"Why don't you play with me?" said Rameel. Without waiting for an answer, he picked up two flutes and handed her one. Rameel's melody was quick and lively, and Yanni joined with harmony, while Yamin tapped on a drum. Soon, a crowd gathered before them, dancing to the rhythms. When they finished, the audience cheered and Rameel grabbed Yanni's hand for a deep bow.

"You're an excellent musician yourself," she said, handing the flute back to her son, who began to play again with Yamin.

"I don't suppose many here enjoy good music," said Rameel, folding his arms.

"Enjoy? Probably most of them enjoy it," said Yanni. "But I think I'm the only woman who can play. It goes well with stories."

"What kinds of stories?" asked Rameel. He was an avid reader, and he had helped Azazel stage theater pieces at Hawan. The new Alterran literature, with its emphasis on social improvement, was dry in his opinion, and like Azazel, he preferred the excitement of ancient epics.

"Well, we typically eat our evening meal around the hearth, and then someone tells a story, or two, or three." She almost laughed. "Sometimes even you might find them to be entertaining, especially when we have a professional storyteller."

"Really?" he asked, his face showing his surprise. "Someone here can actually make a living being a storyteller?"

"A great living, from all appearances. I think you'd like him. Koko acts out the story with his own musician. He's also a trader, and he delivers news throughout the land," she said. She whispered, drawing her head to his ear, "We're not as primitive as you might think. Things are always changing."

"I bet they are," he replied.

* * *

"I have something for you," Lil had said earlier in the evening. "It will look nice with your headband and your fur. Right here is just the spot." He touched her below her unblemished white neck. Alana had let her fur slip lower than she'd worn it before; she'd planned to create a necklace from animal teeth, but with her never-ending duties, she hadn't had time. She cried when he hung around her neck a large teardrop ruby on a silver chain because she didn't have a proper gift for him. "You're gift enough," he whispered, his eyes and lips as warm as she'd hoped they could be. She touched the ruby, thinking that it was larger and more exquisite than all the jewels that Priestess Petrina had worn.

Later, Lil and Alana sat holding hands apart from the others, cautiously optimistic about their experiment's success. Everyone had drifted into the cave when the cooking fire cooled. Alana looked beautiful in the flickering firelight, he thought. The silver headband with little carved trinkets teasingly tinkled when she moved her head, and the ruby glittered enticingly on her unblemished chest above her cleavage. To his relief, the stress had disappeared from her face. Alana was overjoyed that, in the dim light, she was able to gaze into Lil's lovely, deep blue eyes and that, when he wasn't acting as the commander, he was kind and affectionate. With nothing demanding their attention, Alana slid close, resting her head on Lil's chest.

She enjoyed the music and especially the laughter. "Oh, Lil, some of these women haven't smiled since they were captured. I'm *so* happy for them. Thank you for arranging this." She pulled his arms closer around her, feeling his strength.

"My men look happy as well." He breathed deeply, smelling the floral scent of her soft hair. "Come with me." Alone outside the cave, he expanded his tunic and, enveloping her with his arms, kept her warm. Lil had a solution for everything, she sighed contentedly. Snuggling, he kissed her. "Alana, somehow this seems to be working. I never would have believed it," he said, holding her tight, swaying to Yamin's music. Nevertheless, he had a vision of his grandfather Ama, even Zeya, berating him for tonight's actions. He dispelled the image from his mind—*Grandfathers, I never expect to see any of you again. This is my life now. I'm doing what I must.*

Alana noticed his faraway look and gently stroked the side of his smooth face. "Hey, where are you?" she said softly. When Ewan had been distant like that, she knew that he'd been remembering his precious Atlantis. "Do you miss your home?" Getting lost in her green eyes and feeling her soft mouth, he couldn't bring himself to feel this was wrong. "This is home now," he said, smiling, and kissed her again.

* * *

When it grew late and Lil insisted that the men return to the hovercrafts, both sexes resisted. Invoking his rank, he prevailed. He meant to keep his promise.

"Azazel, you included," Lil said jokingly, seeing Azazel, who was piloting the second craft, linger with a tall, blonde-haired woman.

"May I call on you again?" Azazel asked. He kissed Morgana's hand as he imagined the chivalrous knights of old Alterra had done. Morgana's eyes lit up happily, and she answered elegantly, "I look forward to it, kind sir," feeling there was something mystical about Azazel.

* * *

On the way back, Lil sat in the cockpit with Jared. Although the men sitting in the dimly lit rear chamber spoke in low tones, Lil, his hearing more sensitive, could hear them.

Erjat poked Mika. "Well, it's back to the mines tomorrow. The Dalits are probably running wild down there."

"Hmmph," Mika murmured, lost in thought. He was glad that, for once, he'd met a woman shorter than he was.

Rameel whispered, "You know what I found most surprising? I can't get over how much more intelligent they were than I'd thought. I used to think they were all so primitive. With this universal translator, I actually carried on a decent conversation. It was pretty interesting."

"Yeah, and they're resourceful," said Kamean. "They pretty much create for themselves from animal parts things that we replicate."

"I wouldn't have thought that living in a cave would be cozy, but with the fire going, it was warm and comfortable," said Tamiel.

Mika nodded. "I sure could get used to their cooking. If I never had another one of those stupid bars again, that'd be all right with me."

"Yeah, that meal was delicious. I ate way too much," said Kamean, not wanting to admit that his intestines felt a little funny.

"Well, Rameel," said Tamiel, "can you see a cultured man like yourself actually living in the wilderness? Living in a cave or one of those little huts you've seen?"

"If you'd asked me that a couple of months ago, I'd have said you were insane. But now? I don't know, maybe." Unlike a few, Rameel hadn't paired off with anyone, but there was one whom he'd found interesting.

"Let's not get too carried away, though," cautioned Tamiel. "It'd be a hard life. We'd have to work with our hands. We'd have to make everything—grow our own food or hunt for it, and we wouldn't have medical facilities. It'd be a risky life, that's for sure."

"You know, I don't think that would be so bad," said Mika. "There wouldn't be any bosses. We could run things ourselves, take control of our lives. There's a lot to be said for that." Mika's destiny certificate had assigned him to work in mines, even on Alterra. No matter how many protests he'd made, he'd always been told not to question divine destiny.

"I kind of like working with my hands, tinkering with things," said Erjat. On Alterra, after the Ministry closed his copper mine, his destiny had been redetermined to be in a crew that maintained the city infrastructure. If destiny could be redetermined, he'd argued to no avail, why couldn't he be a supervisor?

"I think I'd rather live in a hut than a cave," reflected Rameel. "I probably still won't be able to choose the color of my walls," he laughed, "only available in tree trunk, with a splash of green moss." Each guardsman's living cubicle on Hawan was beige when the panels weren't lit with the holograms of his choosing. But the cubicles were larger than those in the Alterran dormitories, giant skyscrapers in which every floor plan and wall color was the same, for the sake of equality.

"Yeah, maybe find a nice little stream with a great view of the mountains," Tamiel joked. "In the future, I bet somebody might give us a good fight over that land!" Since, in the Great Awakening, the Alterrans had abandoned the concepts of private property and money, it never occurred to them that any individual might own the land.

"You can have the land," said Kamean, stretching his legs, "if I could have meals like that all the time and that little sweetie I talked to tonight. Yeah, maybe this life would work. I'd have to think about it some more, but it might work."

"We might not have a choice," cautioned Tamiel. "We might be forced into this." They were silent for a while.

"I liked going hunting. I'd do that again anytime," said Kamean with a yawn.

"Hey, Erjat, what would you have been if you had had a choice?" Rameel asked.

"What kind of a question is that? Since when does harmony and stability permit us to choose anything?" Erjat snorted. "It never occurred to me that I might choose my life. If I had, I think I would have been a magistrate and ordered people around." He walked the aisle parodying a magistrate, and they all laughed.

"But here, we're starting over. Can't we choose whatever we want?" asked Mika. "Won't we finally be in control of our lives?"

"I don't see why not," said Erjat. "I don't know who appointed the House of En to run everything. It'd be nice to have a say."

"Yeah. It was a giant step forward that we voted to see the women," said Tamiel. "Maybe we should vote on other important things."

"You're right. The captain did a good thing," agreed Erjat.

"Yeah, he's the only one of the ruling class who seems to understand," added Mika.

"I never gave much thought about this before, since it's always and forever been the way things are, but who appointed them as the rulers?" asked Erjat. "That divine destiny stuff sounds made up to me. Just a way to justify their control over us."

"Shh," cautioned Tamiel, pointing toward Lil's back.

"It sure would be great to have more control over my life," said Mika. "I sometimes feel like a hologram, or even worse, a Dalit."

Rameel mused, "Everything has its own constraints. Here, life will impose them rather than the House of En. But, they're constraints nonetheless."

"Now that we've started thinking about leaving, I'm seeing things a lot more clearly," said Erjat. "I think that having control over my life is as important to me as having children, even more important. Maybe those scribes are right about destiny. Our destiny is to break free of these controls and start a new life of freedom."

"Now that's a heavy thought," said Rameel, and they were silent the remainder of the trip.

The men had never thought much about their lives before. The recent upheaval had cast a new light on the sacrifices everyone made to achieve harmony and stability. As the plan to leave Hawan blossomed toward fruition, they more clearly yearned to break free of Alterra's chains. They knew that Lil had overheard their conversation, but they trusted that his participation in their conspiracy thus far meant that he wouldn't betray them. Jared examined Lil's face for any trace that he would resurrect his elitist family status. Lil returned Jared's gaze and asked what new symbol they should prepare for their tunics when they removed the Alterran sacred triangle. Lil understood that the die had been irrevocably cast.

CHAPTER 27
AZAZEL AND MORGANA

"Everyone, come look," shouted Vesta, giggling, as she peeked through foliage that, together with the rock illusion created by Lil, concealed the cave entrance. "What is it?" asked Alana, moving branches to peer out through the haziness created by the illusion. "Oh! I think Morgana needs to see this," she laughed. She was surprised, though, because Lil hadn't told her about Azazel's visit, and he'd been very specific about when he'd permit the men to come and what they could do. Maya called Morgana, who was busily sewing the latest hides into clothing by light of a glow-globe the men had given them. "Morgana, come quickly."

Morgana threw down her hides and ran. "Oh, no, what's wrong now?" she asked worriedly. The women drew back to let her pass, barely holding back their grins. Unable to suppress her giggles, Maya hid her face behind Vesta's back. Baffled by the laughter, Morgana whirled, mad that they mocked her. "What is it, tell me! Has something happened to Tara?"

Smiling, Vesta shook her head, feeling Maya behind her back trembling with laughter. "Don't worry, it's nothing bad.

Come look." She invitingly held the branches apart as Morgana peered out.

Against the background of the ever-overcast skies, she saw a large figure dressed in a black, high-necked shirt, with white lace at his neck, wearing a scabbard across his back. He sat astride a black stallion, accompanied by a saddled, but riderless, spotted mare. "Morgana," he called in his baritone voice.

"Oh, my!" gushed Morgana, blushing until her face turned as red as Maya's apples. She nervously ran her hands through her disheveled hair.

As the women chattered advice all at the same time, Alana called out to him, "Azazel, give her a minute." Maya produced water for her face and a reed comb for her curly hair. Alana gave her a mint herb to freshen her breath, and Marita put a fur around her shoulders. Morgana was glad that she'd bathed the night before. It wasn't easy carrying the water from the icy stream and heating it, but she liked feeling clean. Maya smoothed her hair and clothing, giggling. "You look as beautiful as ever, Morgana. Go and have fun." She playfully pushed her toward the entrance, wishing that Jared would come for her.

A toddler girl of two came running from the passage from the large cavern, calling, "Mommy, mommy, I go?"

Looking torn, Morgana picked her up and pressed her lips. After her birth during her captivity, Tara had been the sole reason that she'd persevered. "Maybe next time, my sweet." How would Azazel react if he knew she'd given birth to a daughter in captivity? That the evil Shylfing was her father? A fact that she couldn't even divulge to her new friends. Yanni, smiling gently, extended her arms, inviting Morgana to trust Tara to her safekeeping. Kissing Tara on the cheek, she received the last advice from the giggling women and pulled back the foliage. Putting her hand out, she went through the illusion, frowning at the ticklish feeling that she couldn't get used to.

"I hope that frown isn't for me," Azazel said, struck at once by how lovely she was. The perfect maiden of his dreams.

Her eyes widened, concerned that she'd offended him. She was impressed that her champion had come for her. "Oh, no, *of course* not! I can't get used to the illusion, that's all."

"No problem." Azazel smiled, dismounted, and gave her a slight bow as he elegantly reached for her hand, which he kissed. "I thought you might like to take a ride this afternoon. The weather's passable today."

"I've never ridden before," she said, distressed that he might leave.

"That's no problem. This horse is under my control, and I had a special saddle created. Come, give it a try," he said softly. "I think you'll enjoy it."

"All right," she said gamely. "But how do I get up there?" No sooner had she uttered the words than Azazel whisked her up to the saddle.

"You're light as a feather," he said, laughing, hearing the twittering voices coming from the cave. He mounted and walked the horses slowly, giving Morgana time to adjust to the mare's rhythm.

"I love riding," said Azazel. "Things are tame on my homeworld, and riding wouldn't be permitted there."

Homeworld? Although she'd wondered how he could have had a flying ship, it hadn't occurred to her that he was from an entirely different world. All the others must know. Why hadn't they told her? Still, she was fascinated, and he'd been *so* thoughtful. She gulped and asked, "Why not?"

"Over time, a civilization develops many minute laws in response to unusual circumstances. Someone, with good intentions, of course, is always trying to prevent the next freak accident. Pretty soon, these rules eliminate anything that's actually fun. But we do prevent injuries." One would think that with the medical treatment chambers, it wouldn't have been such an issue for them. But for reasons he couldn't fathom, the Ministry of Central Planning preferred to ration their usage. When he had obtained special permission to absorb the programs on ancient athletic contests, he'd learned that in more recent

306 | Colony Earth

times, there had been athletic games played in huge stadiums. The information on that time had been very limited, though, as if he'd found only a fragment of what had otherwise been deleted. Although the games had been hugely popular, they'd been banned, even long before the Great Awakening, because of occasional, yet severe, injuries. He was quiet for a while; in the House of En's view of extreme safety, all fun had been taken from Alterran life. Shouldn't these risks be left to the participants' judgment?

"What are you thinking?" she asked tentatively, hoping he wouldn't find her question intrusive. Alana had mentioned that when Lil grew distant at times, she had to draw him back.

He laughed, catching himself for being deep in his own thoughts. "You'll think me strange."

"How could I possibly think that?" she replied, holding her tongue. She was riding a horse with a stranger from a distant place, using magic devices; everything was strange, how could she distinguish?

"I love stories from long, long ago when life at my home was completely different. Our home is similar to yours, just greatly advanced with technology. There was a time when people traveled by horseback in their daily way of life, and they made metal weapons like the one on my back."

"You don't use them now?" she asked, wondering why someone with flying ships would carry a simple sword.

"I had this made for a theater piece," he explained, as if reading her mind. "But I love the feel of it, so I brought it along with me. I feel like a warrior who had a code of honor and lived to protect those in his care." To himself, he muttered, "Not constrained by myriad pointless edicts issued by dictators."

"Sounds exciting," she said, patting her horse's neck. She grew less tense as she became accustomed to its rhythm. "I always enjoyed reading and going to the theater on Atlantis. It's something that I miss," she sighed.

"What kinds of stories do you like?"

"Being a child, there were magical talking animals and fairies, sometimes an evil ruler who met his doom. I once went to see trained animals perform. Ah, it was wonderful." It was sad that Tara wouldn't know these things. "At night here, the women try to remember old stories from their village, usually hunting stories. Though there was one about a hidden treasure and a magical mirror that Yanni told the other night that was different, more like the stories I remembered from Atlantis." They rode in silence for a while, Morgana sensing that Azazel was not one for small talk.

As the blustery wind swirled the dry leaves around them, they began the gradual descent from the rocky highlands, where the trees grew more densely. "I rode through here on the way to get you, and I thought I saw shadows following me. If you see anything, let me know." He winked at her. "I'll protect you, don't worry." She smiled, content to be safe for once.

"We'll stop up ahead," he said, pointing to a thicket. "Do you know the area?"

"No. I haven't ventured far from the cave, only to the stream for water and to check the traps close by." A little farther, he led her off the main path. He gently lifted her down from the horse and carried her in his massive arms over a rocky ledge. On the other side was an idyllic, crystal-clear pool beneath a small, tinkling waterfall. Defying the cold, songbirds chirped in the trees. As he set her down, she gushed, "Oh, Azazel, this is *such* a darling little spot. You are a romantic." Who ever would have thought?

"I saw it from my ship and thought you might like it," he said, pleased by her reaction. Leading her to a grassy area, he spread out a cloth, and they sat watching the waterfall playfully dance off the rocks. He offered her an apple. Hawan had little food to spare, and he certainly would not offer a nourishment bar.

"What's that?" she asked, pointing to a rectangular object hanging from a clasp near his waist.

He detached it and let her feel its smoothness. She touched something, and it lit up with little colored symbols.

"Oh!" she jerked back, with surprise turning to worry. "I'm sorry, did I break it?"

"No, no, it's fine," he laughed, his huge smile showing his perfect teeth. "You simply made it start, so that it can be used."

When he smiles like that, she thought, he doesn't look like a warrior, but a big, cuddly bear. "What are those little pictures?"

"I touch them to begin what I want to do," he said, not knowing how to explain. "You see, this device permits me to do many things. When I'm traveling, for example, I record notes about what I see and hear. I can even let others see what I'm seeing." He paused. She seemed to comprehend more than he'd thought possible, so he continued. "Let me show you." He touched a colored picture, and a hologram extended from his device, showing a grazing herd of reindeer.

"Those are your memories?"

"Yes. I can save these so I don't forget them," Azazel said. "I can also read stories that my people have written."

"Like your old legends?"

"Exactly. Here's one I love. He pressed a picture, and writing appeared. Scrolling through the screen, he found the picture he wanted. "This structure is called a castle. It's where people who rode horses and used swords like mine used to live and have their adventures. I can read the story, but if I want, I can live the story." He moved to open space, touched the screen, and a picture-size hologram of the castle appeared. "I can make it as large as I want." As he held his thumb on the castle picture, it grew larger until a three-dimensional image about the size of the mountain housing her cave appeared on the ground before her.

Morgana stood up and studied it, putting out her hand, but she abruptly drew it back. "It looks solid, but it's not really, is it?"

"It's solid. Go ahead, touch it. You can even go inside and walk around. I could make it as large as a true castle, but I'd need more space."

She felt the smoothness of the castle wall. Azazel opened a door and invited her inside. She entered a great hall, with stones for walls and a floor, and with clothing made of hard, shiny material hanging from the walls. Azazel led her to a box whose top layer was a transparent material. Inside lay a sword like the one he carried. "This is the sword I copied for myself. In its time, it was owned by a legendary hero and possessed magical properties." He led her through more rooms. "Up those stairs are the rooms of the castle lord; perhaps we'll visit there another time."

"I've never seen such wondrous things," she said when he led her back outside. The castle disappeared when he turned off his recorder. "We didn't have this much magic on Atlantis," she exclaimed, returning to sit down on the cloth.

"Enough about me." Leaning back on one elbow, he said, "You've had a difficult life. Do you feel like telling me about it?"

Looking away, she said softly, "Some of it's hard for me to tell."

"There's no pressure." He pressed her hand. "Only what you're comfortable with."

Morgana told about her escape from Atlantis, her days with her adoptive family, and her capture by the Danes.

"Did they treat you badly?" he asked, stroking her back.

"I don't usually tell people about this," she admitted, gazing from him up to the sky. She shivered, and Azazel used his recorder as a laser, warming nearby stones. "When they dragged me off the boat, they lined up the women, and Shylfing strode before us. As I learned later, he always got the first pick. Well," she paused and then rushed out the words, "he picked me." Feeling the heat of her blushing cheeks, she nervously tossed her head and moved her hands, trying not to cry. "His men pushed me forward, and some filthy, raggedy women grabbed my arms and took me to a room in the Great House. They bathed and oiled me, gave me a lovely sleeping gown to wear, although it was too short, and left me in a room with a large bed. That night and many after that, Shylfing came to my bed and raped me," she said evenly, as if it had happened to a stranger. "Shylfing wasn't a beast. Although I disliked being touched, and as a prisoner I wasn't allowed out of the room, my people were tortured and many were thrown into the wolf pit. Women were repeatedly taken by different men. So, in some ways, I guess, I was the lucky one," she said slowly, gazing downward in a low tone, feeling survivor's guilt. She plucked blades of grass, needing something monotonous to do while gathering her thoughts. She felt a gentle breeze. Could it carry away her sorrow? After a while, Azazel took her hand and kissed it.

She took a deep breath. "When I became large with child, Shylfing quit coming. He allowed me to stay until I gave birth. When the baby was a girl, he didn't want us. I was moved in with his other concubines, who played mean tricks on me. One day, his new favorite was jealous, and she persuaded him to get rid of us. We were moved to the stockade to work the fields, where the other women gave up hope and didn't survive long. I claimed the small shelter under the lean-to. This happened not long before Alana's villagers were captured. I tried to care for my baby in that rodent-infested place, using the little shelter that was available. I barely had enough milk to feed her. My daughter and I wouldn't have lived much longer if we hadn't been rescued." Morgana was dry eyed but sad.

"Where's your daughter now?" asked Azazel, rolling onto his stomach.

"Yanni is taking care of her," she said, her stomach in knots awaiting Azazel's reaction. If he shunned her, she'd do her best to graciously understand. Alana had told of living with the Earthkeepers in the south, and she'd go with her.

"I'd like to meet her. We should bring her with us the next time," he said casually and got up, carrying a filtered cup to draw water. With a surge of joy, Morgana choked back relieved tears and pressed her hands to her legs to absorb her emotion. In her mainland village, women who'd been stolen were never welcomed back. They were damaged, and they might as well have been killed; it was sometimes more merciful than dying from exposure. The children of captives were outcasts, as well. Azazel returned with the cold, clear, filtered water and handed it to her, oblivious to her turmoil. After taking a sip, she dared to look up into his face. He thought she seemed less tense, more serene, and her eyes glistened. She noticed how his features were more sharply chiseled than some of the other guardsmen's, giving him a noble and dignified expression. He smiled at her and stroked her hair, which blew in the wind. Morgana couldn't believe her good fortune.

"Did you hear that?" he cocked his head and bolted up.

Morgana shook her head. His hearing must be much better than mine.

"I heard leaves rustling. I don't think it was the wind. I don't like this." He held out his hand to help her up. "Anyway, we should start back. I'd like to make it to Hawan before dark. There are many wolves around here." Azazel hadn't had Lil's permission to come; Rameel had reluctantly agreed to cover for him, and he didn't want Rameel to suffer punishment.

He helped her mount the horse and then suddenly turned, taking his sword from his scabbard. Using it to probe the bushes, he found nothing. Behind it, he found the ground to be too even, as if the sandy soil had been brushed smooth. To remove footprints, he wondered? Who could be following him?

"Are you able to ride a bit faster?" he asked, unsure who was stalking him and not wanting to give them time to keep up and find the cave.

"I think I can handle it," she lied, hanging on uncertainly with both hands to the horse's mane. Azazel returned to the main path and set off at a canter, carefully watching that she was all right. Not seeing the shadows again, he traveled a different, less direct, path back to the cave. In his diligence, he rode silently and highly alert.

Arriving safely, he smiled warmly, lifted her from the mare, and kissed her. "Do you have time for me to bring out Tara?" she asked shyly.

"Sure," said Azazel, letting her arm slip through his fingers and squeezing her fingertips, reluctant to let go. Morgana was gone just a moment. She returned carrying her toddler, who shared her curly, blonde hair.

"Tara, this is Mommy's friend, Azazel," she said, walking toward him.

"I'm pleased to meet you," said Azazel, holding out a finger to her, which Tara grabbed. "Oh, she has a strong grip," he laughed.

"She's usually afraid of strangers, but she obviously likes you," said Morgana as the child smiled up at him, shaking his huge hand as if it were a rag.

"I'm sorry that I must leave, but bring her with us the next time. She's charming," he said with a grin. "Can I have my finger back now?" He patted Tara's head when the child reluctantly released him. "Will you take special care of Mommy for me?" Tara nodded her head yes. Azazel gave Morgana one last kiss, and heard the twittering in the cave increase.

"Good-bye, my precious, I'll see you both soon." Azazel led them to the entrance, looking around for the shadows. "Now, go back inside. I want to see that you're safe before I leave." He pulled the branches across the cave entrance, had Morgana reactivate the illusion, and arranged the branches to be sure that the entrance was hidden and that their footprints were brushed away, before mounting Lil's horse and riding away. He would be glad when they all lived together so that he could better protect them.

CHAPTER 28
THE DEPARTURE

Morgana had only to put a finger into the deep, frigid snow outside the cave entrance to be thankful that Azazel and the other small groups of men who visited kept them well supplied. She wore soft brown boots that Azazel had brought her, together with a heavy shawl. Although Maya and Vesta wore necklaces given them by Jared and Kamean, they still complained about being stuck in the drab cavern and being reduced to spending their time drawing pictures on the walls with the red ochre that Kamean had brought them. As much as the women complained, Rameel and the other men grew even more discontent. The mood at Hawan was bleak. With the medical staff unable to treat its patients, feverish colonists, some of them guardsmen, died after prolonged bouts of coughing blood. With Ki unable to restore power to all buildings, colonists were moved into the usable buildings; many now slept and worked at their cramped Ministry worksta-tions. Squeezed into a former closet on the Ministry's science floor, Rameel was awakened by a heated argument among the normally placid scientists. He'd worked for two days straight futilely trying to repair a section of the power grid, and he snapped at being disturbed. Dressed in a sleeping shirt with his gleaming insignia, not caring that his legs were uncovered, he confronted the group arguing before a monitor. "What's the matter?" Startled at the sight of a furious guardsman, who was vested with the authority to inflict punishment for disharmony, the scientists ceased their argument, lowered their heads, and scurried away before he could question anyone. Curious and now fully awake, Rameel transformed into a silver uniform and searched the scrolling monitor for reasons for the argument.

While pushing down the hall a cart full of experimental, wiggling rodents, Mikhale casually whispered into Rameel's ear, "Anu has ordered us to devote *all* our efforts to reestablishing contact with Alterra. We're to cease work on *everything* else."

Rameel's stomach growled from having been given only a quarter of his food ration. His hair was grimy from crawling through ducts, and he hadn't had time for the lineup at the few hastily improvised grooming stations. "It seems to me that we should be more concerned with sustaining essential power and living facilities," he complained in a lowered voice. He suspected that Mikhale knew of their departure plans, but all guardsmen remained cautious. Lil had permitted only small groups to periodically help the women, but one could never tell what had been seen. Lil's Dalit had told him that rumors were racing among the Dalits, and they were near panic at being left behind.

"It's a gamble," agreed Mikhale, shrugging his shoulders. Ki hadn't given up on Hawan, and he relied on Mikhale and Laurina to stick with him in his desperate drive to solve their problems. "If people at home have recovered, then theoretically they might be able to reactivate the portal. If this were a realistic possibility, everyone would agree with Anu. Based on our last communications, I'd say that there's no chance of that happening. Ki's desperately searching for a new power source. Even if he succeeds, it doesn't make sense to go back to a dying planet. So I agree with you, we should be spending our time focusing on survival here."

"What's Anu thinking?"

Scientists scurried by with equipment. "To follow Anu's order, it looks as if they're ripping out equipment that you've wasted your time trying to fix," Mikhale surmised, pretending to pacify his laboratory rats. "What's he thinking? We never get an explanation. The scribes tell me that the star reports they give him don't predict disaster, just a return to harmony. Nothing specific, though. It's the same ambiguous reports they've rendered for centuries."

"So Anu's convinced that these reports mean that our home world will make a full recovery and they'll get us home?" asked Rameel, too tired to mask the incredulity in his voice.

"Keep it down," Mikhale cautioned, poking a rat to make him continue to fuss. "That's our guess. Ki won't criticize his father, at least not openly. He still has dreams of being the supreme leader himself." Particularly if Lil's out of the way or discredited, he thought. He'd performed sufficient unorthodox tasks at Ki's request to guess his true motives.

"Anu's is a fool's hope, I'd say," Rameel whispered, changing the monitor screen to review Lil's daily briefing. At the Ministry of Central Planning, they'd always relied upon hard data to govern the economy, not astrological interpretations. The more he learned about how they were governed, the more disgusted he grew. He'd confided his disgust only in Azazel, who he knew was so eager to leave that he'd been sneaking out of Hawan to visit his lady friend even without Lil's permission.

Mikhale whispered, "A few ideologues support Anu, but most consider his directive to be suicidal, even though they're still too docile to speak up." Pointing to the cage, he said, "These rats have more backbone than most here. Well, our rodent friends are needed for experiments on the virus treatment, so I need to go. Give me a sign if we need to speak again."

Rameel alerted Lil about the peoples' fear of Anu's directive, ignoring that Lil was Anu's son. "Shouldn't we let all those who wish come with us? Anu would have to see reason then."

Lil tensed, livid at hearing his father criticized, even if he agreed. "They're not in immediate danger, and Anu's orders should be obeyed absolutely," he said curtly.

"If his plan doesn't work, what then? Will they be left to starve and freeze?" Rameel persisted. Maybe Azazel was right—Lil will quit his plan and turn them in.

"We won't let anything happen to Anu, my mother, or *any* of them, I promise you," Lil said tersely. His jaw tightened and he clenched his fist. His stomach was knotted again, feeling disgust with himself for leaving his people at risk. "In case they need to escape, we'll leave them the ships, as well as the lasers. Without energy for the fuel cells, those things are of no use to us. After we get settled, if Hawan must be evacuated, the rest will be welcome. Unless Ki devises a better plan for all of us."

Disgusted, Rameel tried going to Guard Hall to sleep in a hologram room. If he were in Lil's shoes, he'd confront Anu so that they wouldn't need to foolishly run away from their problems. They'd have a far greater chance of success if they kept using their equipment until a new city was built. Why did he care so much? He should think of himself. The only thing that made sense to Rameel was leaving with as much equipment as he could carry and then playing flutes with Yanni and Tomin. That and the natural grains and vegetables he planned to grow; Lil had persuaded his father to let Rameel absorb the Teacher's agricultural programs. Ki had cultivated special seeds and grapevines that would grow despite the increasing cold and diminished sunlight. Searching through his old legends, Rameel even devised a way to make fertilizer by building a clay enclosure for keeping some of the hordes of pigeons that blanketed the skies.

Internally torn apart by his conversation with Rameel, Lil strode back to his suite and plopped down on his bed with agitation. After tossing and turning, unable to rest, he began pacing, noticing the prized possessions that he'd leave behind—his commendation from Ama, as well as the truly prized one from Zeya, or his picture with Jahkbar—with it were recordings of Jahkbar's endless lectures on decorum, family history, self-defense, and a myriad other topics. There was, of course, the miniature family picture that, when full size, consumed the entire wall, with all his ancestors chattering advice whether he needed it or not. And, there was the small, intimate picture of Anu and Uras laughing with their three smiling little children, posing happily before an illuminated unicorn, taken during a Darian Festival of Lights. Was he insane in abandoning Anu when he was needed most? Could his mother cope? He didn't want to be blinded by attraction to Alana; he could replace Nersis with Alana's hologram if he had to. His duty lay here. Why had his father not consulted him before diverting resources from vital projects? Lil alone could persuade him. He had to try. He'd rein in the guardsmen again. Going to his father's suite, he announced his name, but the door didn't open. Perplexed, he called his mother. "Mother, I can't enter father's suite. What's going on?"

"He's meditating to restore harmony." She sounded sad and depressed. Too many colonists had died, and the responsibility fell on her shoulders. Lil could envision the dark circles under her eyes from lack of sleep. She needed him.

"I need to speak to him. Can you let me in?"

"He canceled all permissions, so I can't help you. He doesn't want to be disturbed by anyone, even you or me," she said glumly. "I've been sleeping here. If I sleep."

"Can't you try?"

"Lil, I can't help you," she snapped. Her voice sounded thin and brittle from the strain of confronting not just injuries, but a mysterious virus that had arisen soon after the catastrophe. "Three more patients are near death. Ki has a new theory about the virus, but we might not have a solution in time. It's not wise that everyone has moved closer together. Sorry, I've got an emergency."

Unable to tear himself away from Anu's locked door, Lil sought out Ki.

"Lil, don't feel guilty," Ki assured him. "Father won't speak to me either. Planning a new settlement and growing food is the only way to preserve our options. As long as I can, I'll remain to search for solutions. Who knows, maybe we'll turn this around, or it will get so bad that the alarms will sound in stasis and the Council members will wake up and overrule him. You can always come back if we do. Father will eventually come to his senses."

Usually suspicious of Ki's advice, Lil thought he made sense. They were working together to preserve options. He envisioned a new relationship forged with Ki—together they'd build their dominion on Earth. So he needed to begin work in earnest for the guardsmen to leave; with the injuries and sickness, only 120 now remained. After dispatching Jared to survey for the site of a new city, Lil chose a wooded site in the southern peninsula near the lowlands between a tributary river and a steeply rising hill, high enough to provide protection. The land was fertile and was close to hunting grounds. To ensure safe drinking water, he had a team drill to an aquifer. Jared, finally putting his architect skills to good use, solved the challenge of having limited resources by designing dwellings of hewn logs, reinforced with dried mud, which would be built over their insulated emergency shelters and strengthened by stonework brought to the site by hovercraft. Although the harsh weather wouldn't permit them to build until late spring, Lil had men fell trees with their laser guns and transport the logs. He had a Great House built in the city center so that the women would have a place to stay when they arrived, until all the huts were built.

At the cave, the women stayed comfortable with the fires built in the great cavern. The men had bored a hole through the rock above them to permit ventilation for their fires, for which they supplied ample firewood. Alana followed her usual practice of tracking days by using her sharpened flint blade to carve a notch into a mastodon bone. She grouped her notches from full moon to full moon, beginning after the Rite of Summer. From this, the villagers knew when to search for berries, tap the sap of the trees, gather the honey, and when to travel south to the next Summer Meeting. After an endless winter, Alana announced that the time had come; either the women would disperse to the southern villages or Lil's men would make progress on a new village and attend the Summer Meeting. She sent a message to Lil through one of the small groups that he sent to help them, since he didn't have time now to visit her. Morgana saw far more of Azazel.

Lil had the Dalits prepare long robes with overhanging hoods that would hide their eyewear, elongated foreheads, and skin. Because concealing their height was hopeless, Alana would simply say that they'd traveled from a distant land, hoping people would infer they were from an island similar to Atlantis. As a precaution, Lil would be introduced under the Atlantean name Semjaza. The men reprogrammed their tunics to appear as boiled wool shirts and hide breeches. Since the power charge wouldn't last more than a few weeks, the women began making them similar clothing from sheep's wool and actual hide.

Except for Lil, no guardsman had family at Hawan. Lil agonized about leaving his over-burdened mother without saying good-bye, but he didn't want to compromise her. Believing it unwise to compose a message in his recorder, which Anu might monitor, he wrote to his mother on a clay tablet, which he left with his Dalit. He said he was sorry for leaving, but his destiny lay elsewhere. He was preserving options for their civilization, and he hoped his absence was only temporary. He loved her and hoped she'd understand.

Having stored supplies in the barn, as the departure hour neared, they packed their last personal items. Yamin packed his portable musical instruments, and Rameel brought his flutes and took down from his wall his Awards of Merit given him by the Ministry of Central Planning. Azazel, having already built up a supply of swords and knives that he'd left with Morgana, saved the Guard service commendations that had been awarded to his grandfather, his father, and himself.

Ki and Laurina gave each guardsman a shot. The men didn't ask for an explanation, but Lil had requested a formula to counteract the contraceptive effects of the nourishment bars. The men drained each craft's fuel cells to ensure no pursuit during the several days that it would take to recharge them. Since only guardsmen cared for the horses, wolves, and hawks, Lil felt free to take them. For weapons, Lil chose the swords, knives, breastplates, and shields developed by Azazel. Over the men's protest, Lil forbade taking lasers or soundguns since the survivors at Hawan might need them; the fuel cells would soon be spent, anyway. Lil permitted them to take recorders with additional fuel cells so that they could record their experience for posterity.

Having horses for only half the men, Lil divided them into two groups. Early in the evening of the appointed day, after logging an emergency mission, Azazel and Jared transported half the men to the new site, where they erected emergency shelters. The two men then brought the women. After Ki's scribes ended their nightly duties, the remaining group met at the horse stables, masking their departure by inserting false images in the monitoring system. Jared released the wolves and hawks from their pens, controlling them through *mencomm*. With the horses saddled, each man set out in the darkness toward his new life.

Since the scientists and scribes had never been permitted to leave Hawan, being too pacified to protest, they didn't know what lay beyond its walls. Anu would be too busy meditating, and it wouldn't occur to him that they'd have the ambition to leave. Thus, Lil counted on harmony and stability.

CHAPTER 29
THE SUMMER MEETING

The deep snows of the endless, bone-chilling winter relented a bit, though the southerly wind did not bring the sweet hint of warmth until nearly the summer solstice. Disappointed at how few songbirds greeted her in the quiet, misty morning, Alana openly fretted when familiar flowers didn't blossom; she desperately needed to replenish her medicinal supplies. Lil explained during their hearth stories how the Earth had cooled so abruptly because of the dragon and the heavy clouds. Departing the Great House, they all traveled west to the Meeting Place, going by horseback and by foot, carrying their supplies as others on the peninsula did, suspended from poles or letting a horse drag a travois. Tired of the great stretches of muddy ground left by the still-melting snow, Maya pouted and bitterly complained to Jared that he'd abandoned their flying ships. Alana and Morgana chastised her—the men had chosen the women over their flying ships. Didn't that prove their sincerity? They made all the women promise not to mention them again.

The Albion people met on the open plain in the south. The earliest arriving clans had staked their claim to the small huts built by their ancestors, bringing the aromas of stews and roasting meat from their cook fires. Dirty, black-haired children, their hair matted and their bodies dirty, noisily chased one another through the campsites. When Alana and her group walked down the center lane to an open location, the people stopped their chattering to silently gape at the well-dressed women accompanied by tall, robed men and tame horses.

After supervising the creation of their large camp, Alana wove her way through the helter-skelter campsites to make the customary greetings to the Earthkeepers. Despite knowing about the flooding, she was shocked at how many familiar faces were missing. Entire campsites were empty. Reaching the largest hut, she removed her muddy boots and walked on the reed mats that lined the floor. "Zedah! Yoachim!" she exclaimed, rushing to hug them. The tip of Yoachim's head was at her eye level, but she had to bend double to reach Zedah, feeling her frailness. "I'm *so* glad that you're both alive." Zedah's joints were so painful now that she could barely hobble back to her mat, and she was helped to sit by two young girls. "Come, sit near me." Elder Zedah was the true Earthkeeper, but because of her growing frailty, Shaman Yoachim now performed the public ceremonies, although he didn't share her talents. Elder Zedah's mind remained alert, and her penetrating eyes danced with an inner light. She could see things in the spirit world that no other could, even without drinking the mushroom and herb mixture.

"We're *so* relieved to see you, Alana." Elder Zedah, her ancient bronzed face deeply lined, stroked Alana's arm with affection. Alana had been her most promising acolyte, and she hoped that she'd take her place. "We don't know who survived until we see their faces." A young girl, her hair neatly washed, brought her hot tea. Alana smiled warmly at her; she was no doubt an acolyte, as Alana had been. "Many people, even entire villages, went to live with the spirits this past year. After the dragon appeared, there were strange lights in the sky. An odor of burning. The coast flooded. Entire villages lost."

Unwilling to explain how she knew, Alana simply shook her head with sorrow. "It's all so terrible. My heart has no words for the loss of so many."

"Since some villages have no one left to remember them in the Walk of the Ancestors, we're arranging a special tribute." Smoothing Alana's golden hair, Elder Zedah gazed into her green eyes, a maternal gaze that Alana felt deep inside. "You've shouldered many burdens. Is there anything you'd like to share with us, Alana, dear?"

With intermittent tears, Alana told them, "After the Danes burned our village, Ewan was so worried that we couldn't survive without sleeping furs that he left to kill a cave bear. He never returned." She lowered her head, and Zedah reached out her bird-like arms to hold her against her thin chest, while Alana sobbed inconsolably, finally able to release her emotions. As she cried, Zedah put her hand over her forehead. Zedah closed her eyes, envisioning Ewan being overcome by the bear's strength and feeling how brave Alana had been in rescuing her people.

"These are trying times for everyone, dear." Zedah stroked her hair. "Take comfort that among all this death, you wisely guided your people. I understand you brought many with you. That's a *remarkable* accomplishment." In her visions, Zedah had watched Alana and the strangers, but it was not her practice to reveal what she knew. "We'd like to hear your story," she said softly.

When Alana could speak, she told of the destruction, the kidnapping, the men's rescue attempt, and their deaths. The strangers had helped with the women's rescue, although she skipped the details, hoping that they wouldn't press her into a lie.

Hazily envisioning the rescue, Zedah probed to understand the shadowy images of flying that she couldn't explain. She tilted her head and examined Alana with an intensity of a mother bear protecting her cub. Was Alana so committed to these strangers that she'd lie even to her? "Please, tell us about these strangers."

"The strangers came from across the ocean," she explained levelly, diverting her gaze and not noticing the thin line of Zedah's mouth grow tighter. "In a storm, their boat smashed against the rocks, stranding them. My village women were lucky that they helped us. We would have died without them. The men respected our customs by waiting until the Rite of Summer. They have proved their honor. We've grown fond of them and wish to choose them as mates."

"There are more men than you have women," observed Zedah.

"Yes," she replied with a nod. "We hope women from other villages will choose some of them. They would be wise to do so."

Zedah cocked her head, thoughtfully considering how protective Alana had become. "I'm sure that when your story is told, Alana, many women will be interested. We have many widows this year since other brave men tried to save their families."

"Zedah, I hope the elders will open their hearts to the strangers," Alana pleaded.

Recognizing that Alana was lost as Zedah's replacement, at least the life she had led, Zedah assured her, "My dear, men who have been so kind will, of course, be welcomed. Who will you choose?"

Alana proudly said, "I will choose the leader, Semjaza. I will be the Earthkeeper of our new village."

"I'm glad, child, that you've found a mate," Zedah said, her wrinkled face becoming one big smile. The life of an Earthkeeper was a solitary commitment, and she didn't begrudge that Alana had a new path. "In the spirit world, Ewan is ecstatic. I look forward to meeting Semjaza."

As Alana stood to leave, she casually added, "In their land, Semjaza's people grow tall, and because the trees thickly cover the sky, they create a blanket dimming the light. Since their eyes are sensitive, they wear a covering. Don't be concerned."

"With your guidance, child, I'm sure they won't," said Zedah kindly, yet she was disappointed that Alana hadn't thought to withdraw as her acolyte. Zedah decided not to press her; things frequently change. She would secretly give Alana the remaining initiation, to preserve her options.

Relieved that her story was going well, Alana asked to be excused. She hoped that old friends still lived. Appearing wealthy and striking in her new fur clothing and hide leggings, Alana visited campsites where prospective suitors sought her eye. Noticing more than ever that many were filthy, with matted hair and beards, she thought that their elders had died before teaching them how to make soap, combs, needles, and thread. In the days leading up to the Rite of Summer, the elders of other villages would teach the young ones basic skills. Women would gather to compare cooking methods and garment-making skills. Alana's attention was drawn to a woman with little blue beads laced through her leggings, which she'd discovered when the floodwaters receded. Alana promised to return with an extra rabbit skin to trade.

During the day, men gathered to compare hunting and fishing techniques, and a huge crowd gathered noisily to watch a slingshot competition. Gray-haired and scarred Brewk, an accomplished hunter, demonstrated throwing with his slingshot not the usual sharp-pointed stones but a mastodon bone that he'd chiseled into a point sharper than an eagle's beak. He claimed that he'd killed a mastodon with one shot into the heart. Elsewhere, people traded extra furs and hides for new knives and fishing hooks carved from bones. In prior years, ships had come up the river, having crossed the sea from the mainland port cities, bearing pottery and weapons for trade. This year, only local items were available.

The guardsmen disdained the noisy gatherings, preferring to stroll along the perimeter or to care for the horses. All except Azazel. Startling the crowd, he rode his gray dappled mare into the midst of a knife competition, hurling a shiny metal knife from his cloak's sleeve at the wooden target, destroying it. He quickly retrieved it before the gawkers could see that it wasn't a simple stone knife like theirs. Later, Azazel challenged the reigning champion in a combat game using a staff, so easily overpowering the much shorter man that his hooded face remained concealed. Yanni's son, Tomin, proudly recognized him, calling out loudly, "That's Azazel!" The tale quickly spread of the giant Azazel's unequaled strength. The storyteller Koko witnessed the competitions and was mightily impressed by Azazel, as well as his unique, gleaming knife. Afterward, Koko congratulated him, asking to touch the knife. Receiving no answer, Koko stretched to grab it. When Azazel growled and secured it in its sheath, Koko peered into his hood, studying his face, intrigued by his eyewear.

At night, the tribes shared their stories around the small campfires dotting the gently rolling hills. Koko, wearing fine woven clothing purchased in the southern mainland, roamed from camp to camp, telling tales of heroism during the great flood. To Alana's surprise, Koko told intricate details of her village's attack by the Danes. How did he know? Spying her alone for once, he prowled into her campsite. Yoachim had conscripted her people to fix posts at the place where they'd welcome the sun, and Lil, finding the nearby campsites too noisy, had gone to the woods to think. "Alana, my dove, tell me exactly how the rescue was made." He helped himself to a generous portion of stew from her simmering pot.

"Why?" she asked, busily preparing remembrances for the Walk of Ancestors. Each woman had brought trinkets used by her loved ones. Yanni had brought teeth from Maliki's prized necklace. Alana had brought the little Atlantean knife that Ewan had used to trim his beard. Following tradition, they would slide them into the River of Remembrance, taking their spirits to the immortal sea. So that they'd float awhile, colorful bird feathers were attached with a honey paste.

"I want to know every juicy detail," he replied, waving his hands and smacking his lips, as if performing already. "I'll compose a ballad to preserve this amazing story. It's not every day that someone escapes from the Danes, you know." He licked his lips, never averting his eyes so as to gauge her reaction. "In fact, I don't think it's *ever* been done before. Not to mention an entire village of underfed, weary women, some with small children, escaping from right under their noses—when not a single one of their big, strong male protectors made it out alive. And traveling that far in nearly the blink of an eye! However the new men did it, amazing bravery like that certainly deserves its own special song, don't you think?" He cocked his head, searching her face and waiting for her reaction. Holding him in awe, the simple people rarely held anything back from him. Alana was much more reserved than he'd known her to be.

In the past, Alana would have thought him charming; now, she recognized something sinister. How did he know so much? "We're flattered by your interest, Koko, but I'm really too busy at the moment. I *must* be prepared for the Ceremony; surely you understand. Some other time." She sorted through the Remembrances, wanting him to leave.

"Well, if you won't tell me about the rescue, how about telling me about Azazel?"

"Azazel?" she asked with alarm, dropping the trinkets she held in her hands. "Why do you ask about him? How do you know his name?"

Koko inwardly chuckled, having finally provoked a reaction. "Surely you know that he was the hero of today's games. No one else came close." He squatted down and stirred the fire, trying to be casual, all the while watching for the slightest reaction.

"No, I hadn't heard," said Alana, her voice trailing off as she wondered what this attention would mean; Koko's burning stare made her uncomfortable.

"Yes. I'm particularly interested in that knife of his," said Koko, sounding like one of his story villains, as he stood and took another bite of food. "I've never seen anything like it, even at the trading bazaars at the old port cities. Do you have more?"

"Why do you ask?" she gasped, glancing around her, nervously looking for a sign that the women cooking in the hearth only a stone's throw away had pricked their ears to listen to their secrets.

"A knife like that would be worth a fortune on the mainland, my dear," he whispered in return, fingering her hair and attempting to excite her by blowing his hot breath on her neck. "In fact, do your new friends have any other treasures?"

Shivering with revulsion, she jerked her arm away and unconsciously flicked her hair to dispel his evil touch. "Koko, I don't think they're interested in trading," she mumbled, feeling the urgent need to rid herself of him. She used to adore him; now, he was as nauseous as those smelly, matted-haired tribesmen from the deep woods who swaggered and sneered that they'd let her take them as her mate. Koko's darting eyes, as black as Lil's were deeply blue, frightened her like a malicious raven.

"Oh? Why not?" he persevered, enjoying that she felt trapped. "Have they no need for treasure?" He narrowed his dark eyes and drew closer to her. Normally at a time like this, he'd bed his prey. He wasn't accustomed to being put off. Lusting for the fortune he'd make, he caressed her arm and gazed seductively into her eyes.

"They're not interested, that's all," said Alana firmly, shaking him off and returning his glare. Why couldn't Maya or Yanni be here? Everyone's always leaving me with all the work.

Surprised by her defiance, Koko saw too much wealth to relent. He firmed his grip on her arm, letting his nails dig into her skin, just enough to hurt but not enough to draw blood. "Alana, my sweet, I've known you a long time, so we can be frank. In all my travels, I've never met any like your new friends. You must tell me. Where do they come from? What else do they have?"

Chills running down her spine, and she jerked her arm as forcefully as if protecting herself from the bite of a wild pig. His smile resembled a wolf's fangs. Surely he wouldn't harm her with all the people nearby. She furtively glanced at the nearby camps, hoping that she could catch someone's eye or that one of her men would return. Any one of them would throw this devil to the ground. Maybe she was imagining his malice. Calming herself as Ewan had taught her, she said as lightly as she could muster, "Koko, you have *so* many admirers looking for you that I shouldn't consume all your time. I must finish these things for the Ceremony tomorrow. Please excuse me." She turned her back, closing her frightened eyes, terrified that he'd touch her again; she *must* be a virgin on her mating night so that she could remain an Earthkeeper. Zedah would know.

"Of course, I'll speak to you later." Koko grimaced, sliding his hand across her bottom in chastisement. He picked up a blanket and fingered the tight weave, holding it up to the light. Impressed, he laid it down and slowly backed away, carefully noting everything he saw. Throughout his strolls among the campsites that evening, he kept an eye toward Alana's camp to study the new men, asking others what they'd observed.

Koko wasn't the only one interested in the new men. Many women were fascinated. In years past, the people had accepted the surviving Atlanteans into their villages. They'd been good, intelligent people who had brought new knowledge and skills that had benefited all. Occasionally, travelers would come to trade new hunting knives and trinkets. The people knew that Mother Earth had many places they hadn't seen. The people therefore were accepting of strangers and welcomed the new men. Women whispered how good looking they were and noticed that they outnumbered the women of Alana's village. To their amusement, guardsmen soon began to receive small gifts and invitations. Alana's women became jealous although glad that all would find mates.

* * *

At dusk the next day, a steady drumbeat summoned the nearly eight hundred who had survived nature's inexplicable fury, and they straggled to the plain at summer solstice, anxious to discover who among them still lived. They sought the solace of honoring the recent dead, properly as their parents and grandparents had taught them, and remembering their long-deceased ancestors. Memory let them live forever and lent meaning to their harsh lives. So extra sweet this year. Mothers scolded their children to stand straight and quiet when young and old descended into the field by torchlight. Village groups banded together, with many a mourner receiving consolation from family members and friends.

Shaman Yoachim stood before them, impressive in his ceremonial white robes, his long white hair carefully combed. With his deep, melodic voice, he greeted them, followed by prayers to Mother Earth and the ancestors. Adhering to custom, he called each person who had lost a loved one during the past year to pay a tribute; this year, every village had suffered many losses. This was the time for tears and praise. When the people suffered through difficulties, their one comfort was the knowledge that one day, they too would be revered. When those suffering a loss at Alana's village were called, every single woman and child slowly, tearfully stood. The story of their ordeal having been spread by Koko, people lovingly called out to them. Overcome with emotion, they wept openly as they walked, hugging one another, to stand beside Yoachim. Alana gave a tribute to Ewan, followed by Yanni, and each of the others.

When the last words of those suffering a loss were spoken, Yoachim named each destroyed village with no one present. He concluded, saying, "We do not understand why these things have happened. Mother Earth is ever changing. The people are but a part of this place, and we must be prepared for change and renewal, the same as the trees shed their leaves in the fall only to have them appear again in the spring." Yoachim paused, and his assistant opened reed cages and released white doves, which, flapping their wings, escaped over the gaping crowd.

The drummer's rising cadence stilled the night until it too ceased. Yoachim's voice rang out, "We might not be as strong as the bear or the mastodon, we don't soar high into the clouds like the hawks and the eagles, and we don't run fast like the wolves and the horses. Nevertheless, we the people rise above the forest animals because we are smart, and we *never forget.*" The people cheered, jumping with their arms raised into the air. "Our loved ones remain in our hearts, and through our remembrance, they live forever. As we will, too." Motioning toward the river, he invited them, "Come. Let us take the Walk of the Ancestors. Set sail to your memorials in the River of Remembrances. All the while, let us remember that life is for the living. There are children to be born and cared for, mates to be loved, and things to be created as only we, the people, can do. Tomorrow is an important day, a day of renewal and hope. When the morning sun shines through the portal, feel the life and the energy flowing about you, the power of Father Sun mixing with Mother Earth to produce life! Let us begin."

Yoachim walked ceremonially toward the river, followed by the white-robed acolytes. They patiently waited for the procession to form. By torchlight, the people began the Walk of the Ancestors along a path taken by many thousands over the ages. Mixed with the music of the river bullfrogs and the night insects, flutes played and people hummed. Maya sang softly until the people encouraged her to sing loudly. Along the riverbank, family groups huddled together, laughing at humorous stories or recounting acts of bravery until, wiping their eyes, they tossed carefully crafted trinkets, carvings, decorated stones, anything that reminded them of their loved ones, into the gentle swirls of the River of Remembrance. Alana stood beside Yanni and Tomin, who kissed Maliki's saber tooth memorial and remembered his exaggerated hunting stories. Brushing aside her tears, Yanni gently set it afloat in the water, watching the swirling moonlit water take his spirit away. Saying good-bye to Ewan, Alana kissed her memorial containing his little knife and set it adrift. Maya set sail to an ornament made of fish bones, singing sweetly to long-deceased parents. The stream grew plentiful with memorials floating in the eternal currents, lit by a kindly crescent moon. With the Walk taking most of the night, those at the beginning of the procession rested quietly at the trailhead, eagerly listening for the first, lone bird to begin chirping its invitation to the dawn.

As dawn approached and the full bird chorus excited them, although they were not so many as in years past, people's pace quickened. Yoachim urged the processional up the hill. At the top, the line broke as the excited people rushed for the best views. Long ago, revered ancestors had constructed a large circle of evenly spaced wooden poles, with a second staggered circle within. Smiling broadly at the breaking clouds illuminated in deep purples and reds, Yoachim took his place in its center, where he was joined by Zedah, who was carried in a litter. The soulful night's flute music was replaced by slow, steady drumbeats. The people held hands and waited expectantly.

When the pinkish fingertips of dawn lit the sky, the drum cadence quickened. Alana, Maya, and Vesta held hands, their knuckles turning white with excitement. Lil, his arms around Alana's waist, along with Jared and Kamean, stood behind. Azazel, holding Tara, and Morgana pushed close behind them. As the first rays of the rising sun erupted through the window created by the stakes, the crowd hushed; for an instant, the people captured nature's most wondrous trophy, as only they could do, proving their superiority over the awesome beasts that frequently threatened their lives. Feeling his skin prickle from an energy surge in his clothing, Lil pulled up his sleeves and slid back his hood, noticing that the others were doing the same. "An electromagnetic surge," he whispered, rubbing his arms. "We must be in a hot spot. It should subside when the sun is overhead."

The corona filled the window, and a bright beam struck the center stone table laden with baskets overflowing with summer seeds. Having been blessed by the sun after the days of endlessly oppressive clouds, the people cheered, screamed, and jumped to prove that they'd conquered nature's greatest secret. Kissing and hugging one another, they released the intense emotion of the preceding night. When the cheering slowly faded, the flutes resumed, but their soulful tunes were replaced by light and cheery ones. This was the day to celebrate life. Young girls joined hands with older women to circle dance. Throughout the day, children chased one another in the broad, open field, and teenagers and young adults engaged in races and slingshot competitions. Fermented berry drinks were plentiful. Older ones prepared the evening feast of wild boar and geese roasted over the spit.

Maidens teasingly paraded the field, flirting with their suitors. Tamiel, not having attached to a woman of Alana's village, was surrounded by black-haired young girls who pled for his attention. Erjat and Mika, also uncommitted, entertained their giggling admirers by juggling apples and performing acrobatics. Seeing all the maids and widows eying the guardsmen, Morgana put her arms around Azazel and refused to let anyone near. He laughed and repeatedly assured her that she had nothing to fear. Alana and Maya stood to the side watching none too happily as women chased Lil and Jared. Seeing them scowling, the men broke away and laughingly picked them up, twirling them around.

"Jared, put me down," Maya cried, kicking her legs and giggling uncontrollably.

Lil smiled teasingly, not releasing his grip on Alana's soft skin. "Well, Alana, I trust you're going to choose me. But it's all right if you don't. Those women over there offered me many fine things." The glint of the sun lit up Alana's green eyes, and blonde hair tumbled over her serene face. Lil felt glad that duty didn't require him to be content with her hologram. He pulled her close, rubbing his leg against hers. Feeling his hot breath tingle her neck, Alana punched his ribs and teased back, "Really? Actually, I was considering choosing Koko, since I've seen you so little. What do you have to offer me?"

Lil kissed her neck and whispered in her ear, "Just my kingdom." She squinted at him and assumed he was joking but was reminded that she still didn't know much about him. She hadn't truly believed that he'd leave his colony until she'd stepped off the flying ship into his waiting arms. He'd carried her all the way to the new Great House that he'd had his men build for them. Although men had visited throughout the winter, Azazel most of all, Lil had not. That would change, she was confident. Each day after he'd arrived, Lil had made a point of having her with him, even though they were never alone. Still, they hadn't professed love for each other, and she didn't wish to foolishly be the first.

Feeling her body responding, she shook herself away and firmly grasped Maya's arm. "Later," she said, waving and blowing a kiss, giving him a pouty smile. "We need to get ready, and so do you!"

In the late afternoon, young people drifted back to their camps to take naps, or like Alana and her friends, to wash in water warmed for them by the mated women. Alana found daisies, which she wrapped in her newly washed hair. The brides changed into knee-length, braided skirts that swayed seductively when they walked. Before returning to the main field, each bride found a soft, secluded spot among the trees to leave her sleeping furs.

When dusk approached, expectant mates and spectators loaded up on food and drink and noisily took seats around a series of flat-topped stones. To one side, Lil leaned back on an elbow, feeling relaxed with the buzz of the berry wine. Nearby, Jared had slid his hood back slightly, and Azazel had let his drop. "Jared, that's the silliest grin I've ever seen," Lil teased.

"Keeping our promise has been a tough wait." Jared grinned, glad that his robe covered his manhood. "I'm more than ready."

"So, no one wants to turn back?" Lil asked, raising his brows. His own desire for Alana had grown so consuming that he couldn't think of anything but finally taking her.

"Certainly not me," said Azazel a bit too seriously. "No one could keep me from Morgana."

Like the night before, the drum cadence reached a crescendo and then abruptly stopped. Helped by his acolytes,

Yoachim climbed onto the flat stones. To cheering and clapping, he smoothed his white robe and stroked his gray beard before announcing, "I hope everyone had a wonderful time today and that you've all had plenty to eat. We will soon begin the Rite of Summer ceremony." The crowd clapped as the drummers beat a rapid cadence. Giggling, the maidens lined up behind Shaman Yoachim, their braided skirts swaying. Morgana had attached to her skirt little seashells that tinkled when she walked. Yoachim signaled for the drums to stop. With a laugh, he said, "This is the last chance if anyone has a final proposal to make to a prospective mate."

"Alana!" a husky male voice yelled, his voice laced with menace. "You were promised to me!"

"It's Maku! Drood's son," grumbled an old man. Sighs of alarm spread through the crowd, and those closest to Maku scrambled to safety.

Rage coursing through his body, Lil searched for the menacing voice. He'd never known the urge to kill with his own hands, but he would if Drood or his nasty son came after her.

Before Lil could move, one-eyed Brewk roared at Maku, "Forget it, you smell too bad." Brewk's full-throated laughter ignited the crowd, and Yoachim shook his head, diplomatically trying to remain impartial. All Albion tribes were welcome at the Summer Meeting. Maku jutted his bearded chin and strode angrily toward Alana. Roaring, Brewk punched him in the stomach, making Maku crumple to his knees. Leering, Brewk bellowed, "The women choose. Your kind isn't welcome here. Leave!" Escaping the vicious kick of Brewk's thick, hairy leg, Maku scrambled a few paces away, holding his bruised ribs and glaring with hatred. Brewk drew back his muscled arm, a jagged stone knife clenched in his dirty fingers. "Go on. I'll have no trouble here."

"My father will get you!" Maku growled before running into the night.

"I swear, he vanished!" an old woman gasped.

Yoachim cleared his throat and ordered the drummer to beat the cadence, waiting until the people were calm. "That's better. Let us begin again." Alana's village was permitted to choose first. Earlier in the day, when she'd seen all the maids' attention being given to guardsmen, Alana had asked Yoachim for this special favor, and he'd seen the wisdom of it. Ceremoniously, Yoachim raised his hands and intoned, "First, I call Alana, daughter of Ewan, Medicine Woman of the northern village, and one of our own Earthkeeper acolytes." Smiling happily at the cheering audience, she waved and took her position beside Yoachim on the flat stones, her braided skirt seductively swaying and teasing with what lay beneath. In one hand she carried a white cloth. The crowd murmured in awe at the sight of her silver headband, which melodically tinkled as she moved, and hanging at her breast, the large ruby that caught the torchlight rays, all the more accentuated by her pale, unblemished skin.

Raising his hands to quiet the murmuring, Yoachim's mouth twisted into a droll smile. "Alana, my dear, are you prepared to choose a mate this evening?"

Grinning and bouncing on her toes, she proclaimed, "Mother Earth has truly blessed me. I've fallen in love with a wonderful man who saved my people more than once. With all my heart, I choose Semjaza!"

To frenzied drumbeats, Lil, as Semjaza, slid through the dancing crowd. With the people too filled with drink to notice his appearance, he carelessly threw back his hood. He leaped onto the flat stones, his face appearing so young and happy that Alana's heart skipped a beat. He squeezed her hand, and she felt his special energy pulsating through her body. He grinned, his cobalt blue eyes shining with desire. "You are mine," he whispered slowly with a hint of a smile, his sexy voice sending chills down Alana's spine.

Alana stared into his eyes, awed by this new Lil and overwhelmed by his salacious look. From far off, her brain foggily registered Yoachim's voice. "May the Mother bless this mating and make you fruitful." Lil grasped her waist, pulling her forward, and she tilted against him. With a finger raising her chin, he lightly kissed her. Seized by desire, he suddenly pressed her close and hungrily kissed her mouth. As their wedding kiss lingered, Yoachim chuckled and waved his hands, "Okay, you two, we believe you are in love. Now, run along. There are a great many others eager to choose mates this evening." Lil easily swept her into his arms and carried her toward the woods.

"Kiss me like that forever," she murmured, touching her throbbing lips.

"I intend to." *Nersis is a ghost compared to her. You've captivated me, Alana.*

"My sleeping furs are prepared, but Maku might find us there."

"Don't worry, I'll protect you. A privacy cocoon will surround our bedding."

She had no idea what a privacy cocoon was, but she loved his command of every situation. She snuggled her head against his chest, enjoying the rhythmic beating of his heart and drinking in his ethereal scent. *If only I could capture this moment and create my own spirit world with this lovely feeling.* Until this very moment, she hadn't let herself believe that he'd truly come to her. She'd dreamed of piercing her knife into her breast after calling out Lil's name as her mate, only to be left standing alone in humiliating, bone-chilling silence. Needing reassurance, she sniffled and squeezed his arm.

"Am I hurting you?"

"No," she said firmly, and then softened her shaky voice. "I just can't believe that you're really here." In the distance, Yoachim silenced the drum and called Maya's name. A squealing voice shouted, "I choose Jared." Giggling, Maya threw up both arms and bounced up and down. Jared bounded to the stones and twirled her around.

"I'm so happy for Maya," Alana whispered. Her voice trembled, and she wiped a tear with the cloth.

"Why the white cloth?"

"So that I can prove to Zedah that I'm a virgin," Alana said innocently with a toss over her golden hair.

Lil remembered how adamant she'd been during his proposal; for Alterrans leading many lives through rejuvenation, virginity was a forgotten concept. *He'd kept his promise.* "You complained that I didn't visit you over the winter. If I had, you wouldn't still be a virgin."

She wiped the last tears away and admired her mate's handsome face. He wasn't joking. *It doesn't matter now. He really is here—my mate.* Giving him a mischievous smile, she planted soft kisses along his neck, tickling his neck with her tongue. He exhaled sharply and pulled back, smirking. He growled softly, "If you keep kissing me like that, we won't make it to your furs. I want tonight to be perfect, so we'll wait." He reminded himself to take it slow in the beginning; she wasn't Nersis. He wouldn't forgive himself if he hurt this innocent girl who gazed at him so adoringly with blind trust. With his sense of destiny, he fantasized that tonight was the commencement of a grand plan, enveloping both their worlds, and it needed a ceremonious, reverent beginning. He hadn't anticipated the mind-numbing passion that subverted his plans.

Inflamed by his carnal tone, she peered into his dazzling blue eyes that had become so serious and dark. His glance sent erotic desire shivering through her body from head to toe.

"What's wrong? Are you cold?" he worried. He clutched her protectively to his chest, opening his cloak to give her warmth.

"Ah," she moaned, her mind reeling. "Your gaze and scent overwhelm me. I feel you possessing my mind like the tentacles of night ensnaring the Earth."

He reveled in his unintended effect on her and cherished his own arousal.

"The more I think of you, the more lost I am," she murmured dreamily.

"We're nearly there," he sighed. *I feel it, too. If only I could tell you.* He couldn't, being paralyzed by the irreconcilable conflict presented by an Alterran leader taking an Earth woman. As if viewing someone else, his hungry body plunged forward to his mating bed. *Am I doing this for Alterra? Or only for me?* For both, he resolved, flicking away the hint of disapproving voices demanding entrance to his thoughts. *I am Alterra.*

Reaching the path, he gently put her down. He kissed her softly on the lips and stroked her golden hair. "You looked so incredibly beautiful standing on stage. This skirt mesmerized me. I nearly took you right there." He smirked, pushing his hips against her.

Alana giggled and tugged greedily at his cloak. "Take that thing off."

With a blink of his eyes, he made it invisible. "Better?" His pale skin cast a soft light in the darkness. Alana's eager fingers stretched for his chest. With a hiss, Lil clutched her wrist. "Wait, my precious!"

They faintly heard Morgana choose Azazel.

"Azazel's a good man. I'm glad for him," said Lil, distractedly. He slid his hand through the swaying cords of her skirt and felt her tingling skin. He hissed, "Uh, let's go. *Now!*"

"It's not far," she murmured, taking his moist hand, mystified how her body had been ignited by this intense, beautiful man whom she barely knew.

* * *

"Your bruised ego doesn't concern me, Maku," admonished Drood, his voice gravelly. His cold eyes gazed into the bonfire, where the red-and-yellow leaping flames formed dancing images. Seeing the bodies of Alana and her new mate consumed with passion, he scowled, knowing that Maku would be incensed.

Maku stormed with hatred around the fire. Pointing with clenched fist at the lovemaking, he spat, "Let me go back so that I can kill this white demon with my bare hands! She's mine to tame. You promised."

"Sit down," Drood ordered calmly, not diverting his eyes from the images. "The starmen destroyed the dragon, and I'm not attacking, nor are you, until I know what other powers they possess. Content yourself with some other woman."

"No one is more powerful than you! Why are you afraid?"

Drood slowly turned his head. His chilling smile didn't extend to his icy stare. Maku had seen that stare before, usually before the victim lost a head. He trembled and drew back, stumbling on a tree root. Glancing back in fright, he picked himself up and ran out of sight.

With a tip of his hand, Drood caused the faraway images to flit about until they became Azazel making love with Morgana. He chuckled and circled the fire to examine the image. "Only the dragon slayer interests me now."

Alterran Legacy Series, Book 2: Khamlok

ACKNOWLEDGMENTS

I wish to thank those who provided invaluable help in commenting on my manuscript—Thomas Joseph, Chris Joseph, Jennifer DeCamp, Bonnie Jo Bankinship, Mitchell Howard, Nancy Burke, Sandy Burke, Jim Larson, and Barbara Ardinger. Thanks also to Chris Joseph for his emotional support.

.

Made in the USA
Lexington, KY
30 November 2012